A Perfect Victim

Patricia Dusenbury

ISBN-13: 978-0692468555
ISBN-10: 0692469552

Cover Design: Saille Graphic Design for Books / www.sailletales.com
Photography: © Paulus Rusyanto / Dreamstime.com

A Perfect Victim was initially e-published with a different cover by Uncial Press
www.uncialpress.com
ISBN-13: 978-1-60174-164-6

DEDICATION

To New Orleans, where I've spent many happy hours, and particularly to the Jazz and Heritage Foundation, which every spring delights the world with Jazz Fest then uses the profits to keep the music alive. A portion of the proceeds from the sale of this book goes to support their good work in education, economic development, and cultural enrichment.

ALSO BY PATRICIA DUSENBURY

Secrets, Lies & Homicide

A House of Her Own

ACKNOWLEDGMENTS

I am grateful to George for his encouragement, to Alicia for her constructive criticism, and to the many other people, too numerous to name, who helped me along the way.

1

Wednesday, October 12, 1993

Daniel Doucet motored away from Ray's Dock, feeling pretty good about himself. The morning breeze kicked up a light chop that sent brackish spray across the prow deck, adding substance to the hovering fog. His Saint Andrew medal bounced against his chest, and he rubbed it for luck. The gold was silky smooth; the back worn concave by calloused thumbs belonging to generations of Doucet watermen. Daniel gave thanks for the poor visibility, which meant he didn't have to keep an eye out for snoops from Wildlife and Fisheries.

By midday, the fog had lifted and Daniel's mood had soured. The too heavy shells in his tongs said his luck hadn't changed, but he checked anyway. A push and a twist of his knife popped a shell open, revealing a stinking glob of black muck. He threw it back and opened another. More of the same. Last year, this bed had been healthy. He cursed the dredging and canals that were letting the Gulf's salt water ever deeper into the marshes.

Daniel loved the bayou country with its wide lakes and black-water swamps, its grass marshes and sheltering trees. He took oysters with tongs as his grandfather had done. He'd never use one of those goddamn mechanical harvesters that tear up everything in their path. He'd never go out in the Gulf on a shrimp boat with nets so big they had to be pulled in with motors operated by men like his father and older brothers, and the fish you didn't want died before you could throw them back.

He swept his tongs across the deck, returning the dead shells to the water, and motored to another spot. Pickings were better but still lousy. Half the shells he pulled up were dead and the live ones, too puny to bother with. He needed to stop wasting time and head over to Bayou Perdu. He thought about why he hadn't started there, and his scowl deepened.

Weekend before last he'd had a run-in with a cabin owner. This big shot from New Orleans, who ran his big boat with its big motors too fast through the marshland, had spotted him taking oysters from posted water. The asshole shook his fist and hollered that he was going to call Wildlife and Fisheries. Like it was any of his business.

Daniel had gotten out of there fast and not gone back. Not yet, but he was thinking about it. There were no other cabins up there. The odds of anyone being around on a Wednesday afternoon were slim, and finding live oysters was a sure thing. He'd be more careful today.

He restarted his motor and headed for Bayou Perdu, past the big yellow signs warning that he was entering a posted area. Shellfish taken from these waters could cause serious illness and possibly death. Anyone caught harvesting oysters risked a $1000 fine. Big deal. He didn't plan to get caught, the oysters were probably fine, and he'd never heard of anyone dying from a bad oyster. Sick yes, dying no.

Truth was, Daniel didn't care about the rich people and tourists who'd be eating his oysters. They and people like them were responsible for the slow destruction of the swamplands. *Reap what you sow, fuckers.*

He was about to cross the channel that led to the asshole's dock when he heard the drone of another motor. Or was it a car engine? He couldn't tell. He turned his off and listened, but the noise was gone. He poled into a small cut and waited in the shelter of the tall grass, every sense on high alert, but the sound didn't recur.

Down the channel, the asshole's big boat floated alongside the dock, tied up and deserted looking. A big gator swam lazily down the channel, and a few minutes later a school of minnows cut a wider vee on their way out. A pelican eyed the little fish from his perch atop a piling but didn't bother. Reassured that whoever he'd heard had moved on, Daniel continued to his destination and dropped anchor.

A hundred years ago, Bayou Perdu was a creek running between tree-shaded banks. When rising waters transformed the land, the creek became a current running through a swamp, and the trees died. Their underwater skeletons became home to oysters instead of birds—and the sweet spot only he knew about.

He grasped his tongs in both hands, raised his arms toward heaven, and thrust deep, pushing down until he felt the steel tines scraping against shell. He let the handles spread apart and then pulled them together sharply. Open, close, open, close.

Daniel wasn't a big man, five-nine and a hundred fifty pounds, but he was strong. The muscles in his arms and shoulders tensed and released in tempo as he ripped the oysters from their purchase on the old wood. When he felt their weight fall into the basket, he pulled the handles together and, sliding one hand then the other down their length, hoisted his catch out of the water. He released the shells onto the prow deck and sorted them by size.

His movements were quick but careful. An oyster shell will slice a man's hand so neatly he'll see the blood before he feels the pain.

Daniel popped open a big one and smiled at the oyster lying fat and juicy on the shimmering shell. He tossed it back into the water, picked up his tongs, and eased into the rhythm. Soon, he was a man at peace, sweating the healthy sweat of hard work, his scent blending into that of the swampland.

Tomorrow, buyers from New Orleans restaurants would be at the docks looking to stock up for the weekend, and he'd be ready. The burlap bags stacked under the prow would be bulging with oysters, big ones that commanded top dollar. He might be a twenty-two-year-old high school dropout, but he made a good living.

He was bringing up another full basket when something behind him exploded. Before he could turn around, there was a second, bigger, explosion. A blast of hot air sent him tumbling forward. *What the hell?* He knelt on the bottom of his boat and peered over the gunnels.

The asshole's cabin was on fire. Big time. Raging yellow flames poked through the roof, and more shot out the windows. The cabin sat a good hundred feet away, but the heat was so intense it prickled his bare skin.

An engine turned over, and firelight glinted off the windshield of a vehicle moving away from the cabin. Then blinding smoke closed in. Daniel heard but couldn't see the vehicle speed up the dirt track to the top of the old levee. It must have been parked behind the cabin. That was what he'd heard, them driving in.

Shit. He retrieved his tongs, started the motor, and got the hell out of there.

Hungry flames devoured the wooden building. They ate away walls and gnawed holes in the roof. A chunk of rafter crashed down, sending new licks of orange and yellow into the sky and fresh waves of heat rolling across the water.

Inside the cabin, burning shingles rode currents of scorched air, spiraling downward like spent roman candles and igniting everything they touched. Sparks landed on the linoleum floor and the old Formica table in the kitchen, on the overstuffed sofa in the front room, and on the man who lay on the sofa. Embers burned holes through his clothing and into his flesh. They bored tunnels in the upholstery, and the sofa erupted into a blazing funeral pyre.

Like a foolish parasite, the fire consumed its host and then starved to death. Gray-layered clouds absorbed the smoke, and the breeze carried it away. In the swamp, insects resumed their droning chorus and animals their eternal hunt. Unimpressed by man's handiwork, the bayou continued its slow passage to the Gulf.

2

A day later and a thousand miles away, Claire Marshall shook a pill from the vial she kept in her purse. She swallowed it dry and sat in the car, listening to the radio, until the drug kicked in. Then she walked up the hill. Coming to the cemetery had taken courage. No sane person tries to have a panic attack, but Claire was determined to learn what triggered hers. She couldn't take pills forever.

Thomas Wright Marshall beloved husband of Claire. The inscription said he'd been hers, yet when she closed her eyes she couldn't picture his face. She couldn't remember the warmth of his body, his smell the taste of his kisses. Tom was lost to her more thoroughly than she would have thought possible. She traced the curving letters with a fingertip and felt only emptiness.

The ground had subsided over his grave, leaving a coffin-shaped depression that reinforced the futility of her visit. She slipped the pebble from her pocket, a flattened translucent sphere she'd found on the beach—children call them angels' tears—and left it beside his headstone. The Xanax hadn't been necessary.

Fallen leaves crackled underfoot as she walked back to the parking lot. Faint honking drifted down from geese flying south in an impossibly blue sky. A murmuring wedge of dark-clad mourners approached, and she stepped aside so they could pass without breaking formation. Fifteen months ago, she'd been the center of a similar group.

"I'm sorry, I'm so sorry," she whispered, despite knowing the new widow couldn't hear and that it wouldn't help if she did.

Rather than drive straight back to her mother's house, Claire detoured past Mecosta County High School. The old brick building with its white columns and tall multi-paned windows looked just as it had twenty years ago when she and Tom sat next to each other in ninth-grade homeroom. Inside, the air would still smell of chalk and teenagers, wool sweaters and canvas sneakers. And dreams. Even then, Tom had known he wanted to be a pediatrician. Saving the world one child at a time, he'd joked, but he'd meant it, and she had vowed to help him.

The same shops lined Main Street. Too far from Grand Rapids to be a suburb and too far off Lake Michigan to be a resort, Centreville seemed to exist outside time. They and all their high school friends had left for college. Several moved back to raise families, but she and Tom had wanted a larger world.

After Ann Arbor, they'd moved to Baltimore for his med school and then New Orleans for his residency. He would have begun practice in New York City. They'd laughed about starting their family in Manhattan of all places. She'd buried him in Mecosta County where his family, and hers, still lived. He'd died before they had time to put down roots of their own.

She parked her rental car in front of the white clapboard colonial her parents bought when she was in third grade. The house hadn't changed, but time's passage showed in the yard. The maple tree she'd helped Dad plant stood forty feet tall. The shrubbery around the front porch had grown, maybe a little too much. She made a mental note to ask her mother if she wanted it trimmed and climbed familiar steps to the front porch.

A note on the hall table said, "Gone shopping, back soon, call Jack at your office." Claire hurried to her room and dialed the number. Her partner wouldn't have interrupted her vacation unless there was a serious problem. He picked up on the first ring.

"Hey, it's me," she said. "What's happening?"

"The bank returned Frank Palmer's check. Forty thousand dollars we thought we had in the bank isn't there."

"There must be a mistake." This couldn't be happening. She'd written checks against that deposit and mailed them before leaving town. A bunch of bad checks would destroy the financial credibility she'd worked so hard to build. Subs and suppliers would start demanding payment in advance. Without credit, Authentic Restorations would be back on the ropes. "It has to be a mistake. Frank's a wealthy man."

"The bank says no mistake. I can call Palmer, but I wanted to talk to you first." He cleared his throat. "I'm thinking he stopped payment."

"Why would he do that? He's been happy with our work."

"Last time I saw him, he didn't look happy."

Jack was right; Frank had been livid. He'd stopped by the office to suggest she visit his fish camp down in the bayou country. It wasn't the first time he'd mentioned rebuilding the cabin, fixing it up without telling anyone, and then surprising his fishing buddies. She'd been noncommittal about a small job that far from town, but Frank had persisted. He wanted her to see exactly what he had in mind, a major renovation that would, he promised, be worth her while. And he was anxious to get started.

She'd explained that she'd be out of town all week and suggested Jack go. They'd already talked about it. The words were barely out of her mouth before Frank exploded. He went white-lipped with fury because she'd told Jack about his secret project. For a moment, she'd thought he might actually hit her.

Jack's arrival had defused the situation, and the next day, Frank apologized for being unreasonable. Of course, she had to discuss potential projects with her business partner. He'd been caught off guard because she hadn't seemed interested in the job. He'd been distracted and upset about something else and had taken it out on her. None of his excuses made any sense to her, but she'd accepted his apology, and they'd both moved on.

"The check was for work on his cottage in town," she said. "The fuss was about the cabin at his fish camp, and it's all blown over. I'm meeting him down there next Wednesday."

"So, do you want me to call him?"

"No. I'll do it." She told Jack not to worry, although she knew he would.

Any hint of money problems sent her partner into a tailspin. He had a family to support and a mortgage to pay. Before she came on board, he'd had a close brush with financial disaster. Now, finances were her responsibility, and she'd better do something fast. She called Frank's direct line. His secretary answered, a bad sign.

"Good morning, Jeanette. It's Claire Marshall. Is Frank available?"

"He's gone fishing. Do you want him to call you when he gets back?"

"Sooner if possible, please. I'm in Michigan. Let me give—"

"I know where you are," Jeanette interrupted. "Frank wanted you to go down to his fish camp with him, but you couldn't because it's your mother's birthday."

"He told you?" Frank, who threw a fit because she discussed his cabin with her partner, had told his secretary?

"Of course. I keep his calendar. You've never been down there, have you?"

"No, but—"

"I hate the bayou country. I don't even like driving through. I mean, what happens if you're in an accident or your tire blows out or something and you end up in that nasty black water? It's full of horrible things. Half the time what looks like an old log is really an alligator. Snakes are the worst; a moccasin will attack a full-grown man."

Jeanette paused for breath, and Claire grabbed the opportunity to leave the swamps behind. "Do you have a number where I can reach him?"

"Uh-uh. It's the middle of nowhere. There's no telephone, and his mobile phone doesn't work down there."

"When he checks in, please ask him to call me. It's important."

"If he checks in," Jeanette said. "When you couldn't go, he decided to take Hatch fishing. The two of them go way out in the Gulf, lots of times overnight. Now I like the Gulf—"

"There must be a way to contact him." The CEO of a major commercial construction company would have to stay in touch or, at least, be reachable.

"He'll be back tomorrow. You don't know? I can't believe he didn't tell you. Frank is the Crescent City Club's Citizen of the Year. You know, for his work with The Children's Home. The ceremony is tomorrow night. It's a real honor."

"I'm sure it's well deserved." Claire rested her forehead against the windowpane. Outside, a red leaf circled slowly downward, fluttering in the breeze, while Frank's secretary babbled about his volunteer work. The leaf reached the ground.

"Let me give you my mother's number. Frank has it but maybe not with him."

"He's not going to lose your number." Jeanette's tone became girlish. "You don't need to pretend with me, Claire Marshall. You're unhappy because you can't talk to Frank, but he'll be back." She giggled. "Absence makes the heart grow fonder."

"Excuse me?"

"I know it's a secret, but he had to tell me." Another giggle. "I'm making your honeymoon reservations."

"What?" Claire gasped.

"The only other person who knows is Sherry, in bookkeeping. She's my best friend. I had to tell her, but it's okay. She won't tell anyone."

"Frank and I have a business relationship. Business, that's all. I don't know where—"

"He was so broken up after Annie Lewis died. I never thought he'd get married again. Neither did Sherry." Jeanette rattled on as if Claire hadn't spoken. "And you're so young, I never would have guessed you're a widow, but he told me all about it." A loud sigh. "Both of you lost the person you loved, but now you've found each other."

"No one's found anyone. Frank and I are not in love. We are not getting married. We're not even dating. My company is restoring a property that Frank owns."

"I know. It's a secret romance."

"There's no romance, secret or otherwise. There is a problem with a check." Claire spoke through clenched teeth. "Can someone else help me?"

"Sherry writes all the checks, but Frank gave her the week off, you know, because he wasn't going to be around."

"Please have him call me as soon as possible."

She returned the receiver to its cradle, gently, not the slam that would have been more satisfying. *Honeymoon reservations? Where did that come from? If Jeanette stopped talking long enough to listen, she might get her stories straight.* She cursed Frank's long-winded secretary and dialed her office. Jack would have bitten his fingernails to the quick by now.

"Hi. It's me again."

"What did Palmer say?"

"I couldn't reach him," she admitted. "Who'd you talk to at the bank?"

"I worked my way up to the branch manager, who wasn't giving an inch."

"I can go higher. Frank introduced me to Bobby Austin a couple weeks ago. Hold on while I look for his card."

"Bobby Austin who runs the bank?"

"Uh huh." Frank had said Bobby was both his banker and his best friend. Asking Bobby for help might be seen as an imposition, but she was desperate. She wedged the phone against her shoulder and rummaged through her pocketbook. "Here it is. Let's hope he remembers me."

The woman who answered the phone sounded doubtful, but moments later Bobby came on the line. "Claire, to what do I owe this unexpected pleasure?"

She described the situation, hoping he couldn't hear her desperation. As every banker knew, the construction industry was littered with the corpses of small firms gone belly up due to cash flow problems. And without Frank's check, Authentic Restorations had more flow than cash.

"There's no reaching Frank when he's gone fishing." Bobby repeated what Jeanette had said. "But don't worry, we'll cover his check. Tell your partner to bring it to any branch and have the teller call my office. We're open until four this afternoon."

"Thank you, Bobby." Claire's shoulders relaxed, and she realized they'd been hunched up around her ears. She had more than money invested in Authentic Restorations. "Jack Giordano will be at your Saint Charles branch within the hour."

"Frank can be careless about details, but he's a good man."

"I appreciate your taking time to help me." Maybe Frank was a good man, maybe not, but Bobby had earned a gold star in her book. "I know you're busy."

"My pleasure. And Claire, Frank told me about your plans."

"What plans?" Had Frank told Bobby about fixing up the cabin?

"Have it your way." He chuckled. "Your secret's safe with me. And I'm very happy for both of you."

"But we're not… There's no…" Claire realized Bobby had hung up; she was protesting to a dial tone. She stared, befuddled, at the receiver in her hand. Could Frank be telling his friends that they planned to marry? Why on earth would he do that? They hardly knew each other. She searched her memory for anything that indicated romantic interest on Frank's part and found nothing except, perhaps, the watch…

Frank had insisted on driving her to the airport. Part of his penance for being unreasonable, he'd said. He'd pulled up in front of the terminal and walked around to get her suitcase out of the backseat while she waited on the sidewalk. Then, instead of handing it over and driving away, he put his hand on her arm. He apologized again for losing his temper and said he was very pleased with the work her firm was doing.

"I don't want you deciding I'm more trouble than I'm worth." He slipped an oblong box into her jacket pocket. "Open it after I leave."

Inside the terminal, she'd opened the box, expecting a nice pen, and been surprised by a sparkly watch. Costume jewelry was an odd present for a business acquaintance. She'd told herself that Frank meant well. He just wasn't accustomed to female colleagues—or to apologizing. She'd tucked it into her suitcase, planning to write a thank you note when she returned to New Orleans, and boarded her plane.

Maybe she ought to take another look.

She pulled her suitcase out from under the bed and retrieved the box. The watch really was pretty, an art deco design in white metal embellished with a dozen of glittering stones. She took it out of the box and turned it over. Elegant letters engraved on the back spelled *Piaget* and, beneath that, *18K*. Piaget didn't make costume jewelry. The metal was white gold, and those stones were diamonds.

"Did you see my note?" Her mother stood in the doorway.

"I did, thank you." Her hand closed around the watch. If her mother saw this extravagant gift, she'd jump to the wrong conclusion about her relationship with Frank. Anyone would.

"What have you got there?"

"A rhinestone bracelet," Claire lied. "I bought it this morning. Jack's wife has a birthday next week, and she likes sparkly things." She returned the watch to its box and closed the lid.

"Are you hungry? I picked up deli sandwiches for lunch. Hot pastrami."

"My favorite, thank you." She found a smile. "I have one more quick call. I'll be through by the time you unwrap them."

Her mother went downstairs, and she called Jack to give him the good news.

"I'll be at the bank in ten minutes," he said, "unless I have a heart attack on the way."

"Bobby Austin, himself, told me not to worry. I'm passing it on."

She'd mailed the checks Monday afternoon before leaving for the airport, too late for a Tuesday delivery. People would have gotten them yesterday at the earliest, more likely today. Maybe everything was going to be okay. She hoped the knot in her stomach left room for a pastrami sandwich.

Jack didn't call back, which meant the bank must have honored Frank's check, but the more Claire thought about the situation the less comfortable she felt. She dialed her office number. Jack was there and happy to reassure her.

"The minute I walked in, the manager hurried over with his hand out and a big smile on his face. No kidding." He laughed. "I looked to see who was standing behind me."

"Did you tell him I've already written checks against the deposit?"

"If any checks bounced, the bank will take full responsibility, say it was their mistake. I don't know what you told Austin, but it worked like magic."

Jack's story heightened Claire's unease. Bobby must have called the branch manager, and he wouldn't have done that unless he thought she and Frank "had plans" as he put it. Jeanette was an airhead, but being asked to make honeymoon reservations would be hard to misinterpret.

"Has Frank called the office?"

"Nope."

"Don't do any more work on his cottage until I talk to him. Shift the crew over to the Esplanade project."

"You said there wasn't any problem."

"I want to be sure there isn't. Better safe than sorry. Right?" Claire ended the call on a light note she didn't feel.

If Frank was telling people they planned to marry, there was a big problem. As bizarre as that was, she could think of no other explanation, and she couldn't bear to have people thinking she was involved with him, much less engaged.

She called the airline and switched her return flight from Sunday evening to tomorrow morning. Then she called Frank's office and told Jeanette she'd be flying back to New Orleans tomorrow and would like to schedule an appointment with Frank any time after two.

"Schedule an appointment?" Jeanette echoed. "Don't be silly, Claire. If he's back in time, he'll want to meet your plane. After all." She giggled.

"Delta 1320, due in at twelve forty-seven." She wasn't going to waste any more energy arguing with Jeanette, and it was fine with her if Frank came to the airport. The sooner she talked to him, the better. "If he's not there, I'll call you." She hung up and went downstairs to tell her mother, who was not going to be happy about the change in plans.

"But you just got here."

"I don't want to go, but I have to." She gave her mother a one-armed hug. "It's been a wonderful visit, and it's not over yet. We have your birthday party tonight."

"Can't Jack handle a problem with a subcontractor?"

"Jack is a wonderful person and an incredible craftsman, but he's a lousy businessman." She'd explained it all before. Jack had started his construction company without enough capital and compounded the problem by trying to please everyone, pricing projects too low and paying subcontractors too much. He'd quickly found himself in financial hot water. She'd brought in enough money to stave off bankruptcy and the business skills to get the company on track. "That's why we're partners, and the business end is my job."

"Can't you take care of it over the phone?"

Claire shook her head. "I'm sorry, Mom. Some things have to be worked out face to face, and I have to do it. That's a problem with a small company. No back-up."

She hated lying to her mother, and she'd done it twice today, but the truth was too weird. And too disturbing. She had to straighten things out with Frank before he went to his banquet tomorrow night and told more people.

Tom had been dead only fifteen months, and some days the loss felt as fresh as yesterday. She wasn't interested in any other man—not yet and maybe never. Certainly never Frank Palmer.

How dare you, Frank?

3

Attorney-at-law Paul Gilbert pulled under the porte cochere of The Pontchartrain Hotel and took a moment to admire the familiar facade. One of the big new downtown hotels had offered free meeting space, but after he and several other long-time members objected to any move, the offer was politely refused. The Crescent City Club had always held its awards ceremony on the second Friday in October at The Pontchartrain and would continue to do so.

Paul valued tradition. His family had been prominent in New Orleans since before the Louisiana Purchase. Local historians said his ancestors had opposed it. Paul had no idea if that was true or not, but the story amused him, and he enjoyed his position as a member of the elite. He also prided himself on good manners, which included promptness. He tipped the valet and hurried into the hotel, at home in his formal attire and confident of his welcome.

Andrew Walsh intercepted him in the lobby. "Have you seen Frank Palmer?"

"Hello, Andrew. Good to see you. Will you be introducing Frank tonight?" Although not a member of the Club, Andrew was director of The Children's Home, a position that made him the logical choice.

"Yes and he was supposed to meet me here at six thirty. I've been here since six." Andrew wiped his brow, leaving a damp streak on the sleeve of his dinner jacket.

"Perhaps Frank used a different entrance. Let's look in the ballroom."

Paul had little use for Andrew, whose usual attitude toward those above him on the social ladder was a smarmy combination of obsequious and self-righteous. Tonight, however, tension made Andrew abrupt, and his apparent stage fright was almost touching.

They joined a group of men occupying a strategic spot between the main bar and a buffet table laden with silver platters of oysters, shrimp, and crawfish. These were Frank's friends, but questions about his whereabouts elicited only shrugs and surmises that he was in some corner, working on his latest deal. Still sweating, Andrew charged off to look elsewhere.

Paul wished him luck. Spotting one man among two hundred middle-aged men wearing essentially the same suit wouldn't be easy. He accepted a glass of wine from a passing waiter and joined a conversation that ranged from the weather—heavy thunderstorms were predicted—to politics to sports.

Tulane and LSU graduates traded amiable insults about whose football team was worse. Neither was having a good year. Paul, who'd left Louisiana for college, listened with only half an ear as he scanned the room for Frank. He was looking forward to the reactions when Frank announced his impending marriage to Claire Marshall. He was also hoping someone else would suggest caution. Frank had pooh-poohed all his warnings about young women and wealthy older men, insisting that Claire was different. Paul had heard that before, usually from an older man about to become poorer but wiser.

A chime signaled dinner, the group migrated to a table near the front, and Paul forgot about Frank until the awards ceremony began. After presentation of the lesser awards, Andrew Walsh was introduced. He carried an ominously thick stack of note cards up to the podium. Frank's work with The Children's Home went back at least a decade, and it looked as if Andrew planned to describe every moment.

Paul ordered two snifters of Armagnac from a passing waiter. When the brandy arrived, he slid one over to Bobby, who was also eyeing that stack of notes. Bobby had managed the LSU football team that Frank captained, and he'd been best man when Frank married Annie Lewis. His bank had supported Frank through the early lean years and, no doubt, still carried a fat portfolio of loans to FP Development Company. Andrew could say nothing that Bobby hadn't heard many times before.

Their glasses were long empty by the time Andrew turned over his last note card. "I'd like to present your Citizen of the Year," he said. "Franklin W. Palmer II, chairman of The Children's Home Board of Directors."

The applause began with great enthusiasm but died when Frank didn't appear. Heads swiveled as people searched the room, but the banquet was open seating, and no telltale chair sat empty at a designated place.

"My friend, Frank Palmer." Andrew's voice quavered.

After another long silence, Bobby stood. "I'd like to accept the award on Frank's behalf." A clap of thunder followed by the *rat-tat-tat* of heavy rain added to the strangeness of the moment. The expected storms had arrived.

Paul marveled at the persistence of character. If half the stories he'd heard were true, Bobby had been covering for Frank since they were undergraduates.

The awards ceremony ended with Bobby's brief acceptance speech, but people lingered, speculating about possible reasons for Frank's astonishing absence. Andrew darted from table to table, asking everyone when they'd last seen Frank and generally making a nuisance of himself.

Bobby returned to the microphone and advised everyone to go home. The hour was getting late. With this heavy rain and more coming, driving conditions would only worsen. He pointed toward the waiters, standing by the kitchen door.

"These hardworking men can't clear the room until we leave."

Paul asked one of the hotel staff to let him use an empty office and began making phone calls. Several minutes later, Bobby joined him.

"Have you learned anything?"

"Nothing useful. Jeanette hasn't seen Frank since Tuesday. He left the office early, she thinks, to go fishing with Hatch. She had more to say, as you can imagine, but the bottom line is she doesn't know where he is. The police are checking his house, discreetly, of course. I've been unable to reach Melissa."

"Melissa?" Bobby raised his eyebrows. "Hasn't Frank told you about Claire Marshall?"

Paul nodded. Frank had told him, and Jeanette certainly knew. She'd gone on and on about Claire's devotion, how she had cut short her vacation because she couldn't stand being apart from Frank, how she'd called the office several times today, increasingly frantic about not being able to reach him.

"Frank wants to shout it from the rooftops," Bobby said, "but Claire doesn't want any big announcement. You know she was widowed just last year. He told me a few days ago, and I couldn't resist wishing her well when she called the bank about Frank's account."

"Already?" Paul's eyebrows rose. *Had she tried to investigate his financial situation?*

"No, no, no." Bobby answered the unspoken question. "Nothing like that. Her company's doing some work for him, and they had a problem with one of his checks. I was happy to help. Have you met her?"

"Only briefly. But I'm aware of their plans to marry, and you're right. We should call. Do you have her number?"

"No, and when we spoke, she was in Michigan."

"Jeanette said she returned today."

"Really? I had the impression she was staying through the weekend." Bobby picked up the phone book. "I like Claire, and she strikes me as a woman who'd have a listed number. Aha, here she is." He dialed but hung up without speaking. "Her machine picked up, and I couldn't think of a tactful message."

The police called back to report that no one was home at the Palmer residence. A note on the front door, dated Friday 3:30 pm, asked Frank to contact Claire. Paul relayed that information along with a summary of Jeanette's romantic blather.

"She thinks he's with Claire. If I hadn't cut her short, she'd still be mooing about their glorious romance. I don't understand how Frank puts up with that woman, much less why he employs her." Actually, he did. Frank valued loyalty above all other virtues, and if Frank asked Jeanette to jump off a bridge, she'd ask which one.

"This time, Jeanette might have a point," Bobby said.

"Why do you say that?"

"Claire planned to spend the weekend in Michigan, but she didn't. Frank planned to be here, but he isn't. It's almost midnight, and we can't locate either of them. I'll bet they're together." Bobby smiled. "I wouldn't be surprised if they've eloped."

Paul walked over to the window and watched the rain pelting down while he considered Bobby's words. He would never describe Frank as a romantic, nor could he imagine him skipping this award, which was a triumph for an ambitious man from humble beginnings.

Frank Palmer cared deeply about his reputation, almost to the point of obsession, and he'd worked hard to attain both social and financial success. Being named Citizen of the Year validated that success. He shook his head.

"I don't see it."

"You know Frank. Once he's made up his mind to do something, he does it, and Claire doesn't want a lot of fuss."

"Perhaps you're right." He hoped not. Frank's will had been changed, but the prenuptial agreement hadn't been finalized. Frank would be a fool to marry this impecunious young widow without it. Nor was Paul reassured by Bobby's good opinion of Claire. Yes, she seemed like a pleasant person, but neither one of them knew much about her, and Bobby trusted too readily. He was president of the bank only because he inherited the position. He was far too easy-going to have scratched his way to the top.

"Don't look so gloomy," Bobby said. "The more I think about it, the more I think they're together."

"We've done what we can." Paul shrugged. "I'm ready to go home. I'll call if I hear anything. You do the same."

Paul was halfway home before he saw the implication of his calling Melissa first, although he knew Frank intended to marry Claire. He chuckled and admitted to himself that he might just be the most cynical man in New Orleans.

4

Dawn had given way to morning, but the Garden District remained silent, so still it could have been preserved in amber. Claire turned the key in the ignition and, when her engine caught, felt as if she should apologize for the disturbance. The gravel driveway crunched under her tires, compounding the offense. Across the street a man walking a small white dog looked up as if surprised to see another human being. New Orleans is not an early-to-rise city, least of all on Saturday.

Her car, a bright blue Miata, was Claire's only extravagance. She'd named the car Felicia because just sitting behind the wheel of the spiffy little roadster made her smile. Once she'd taken care of the difficult business with Frank, this would be a nice day for a trip to the beach. If Frank weren't at his cabin, it would still be a nice day for the beach.

She drove slowly, admiring the lovely old houses. Midday's harsh sun might reveal peeling paint, crumbling fascia, and rotted soffit, but the early morning rays landed gently and blurred flaws. She slowed by one of her favorites, an Italianate mansion that while far from the biggest house in the Garden District, was arguably the most graceful. She imagined a family safely asleep inside, sheltered behind the tall windows made golden by the sun.

Even St. Charles Avenue was tranquil. No cluster of tourists waited in the median for a streetcar. No herd of vehicles charged from stoplight to stoplight. A left under the overpass took Claire onto the ramp that led to the elevated highway. Despite rumble strips on the shoulders, the heavy guardrails bore multiple scars from encounters with vehicles steered by the overtired, the reckless, and the inebriated.

Outside New Orleans, the road narrowed to four lanes, a cement ribbon cutting through swamp forests interspersed with open water. Claire drove on automatic pilot, distracted by the challenge of refusing a proposal that had never been made. With every mile traveled, the situation felt more ridiculous. Why tell Frank she wouldn't marry him when he'd never mentioned the possibility? Not to her, but he'd told his secretary and he'd told his best friend. Or had he?

What if he was involved with someone else named Claire and everyone just assumed she was that someone? But what explained a diamond watch worth thousands of dollars? The watch was far too expensive a gift to accept from a client, no matter how wealthy or how apologetic. Frank would know that. She took a deep breath and let it out slowly.

Directions to Frank's fish camp lay on the passenger's seat. The watch sat in her glove compartment. She had rehearsed what to say. She was nervous, but she'd taken her morning meds, and the vial in her pants pocket held more if she needed it, which wasn't likely. She hadn't suffered a full-fledged panic attack in months. Worst case, Frank wouldn't be there. No. Worse case, he'd laugh in her face.

Six miles late she reached her exit.

Off the highway, each turn led deeper into the country. Across cleared fields, barns and houses seemed to hover in the mist. Then fields gave way to forested wetlands, and the structures disappeared. The pavement ended, reminding her that Frank had suggested she drive her company truck. He always took his Jeep. She downshifted into second and drove slowly to avoid kicking up gravel or scraping Felicia's low-slung underside.

The last road, its dirt surface as bumpy as an old-fashioned washboard, ran along an obsolete levee, a barrier left behind when the river moved or was moved. On either side, the land dropped away and ground fog turned treetops into leafy islands. Two hawks soared overhead. One dove into the fog and emerged seconds later, a small bird dangling from its talons. Claire winced, wishing she hadn't seen.

Up on the left, tree trunks painted with Frank's initials in bright orange marked the turn to his fish camp. Claire steered between them onto a narrow and rutted dirt track that snaked down the side of the levee. She descended, and the fog closed in. The sun disappeared, and the temperature dropped. She crept along in second gear, leaning forward to peer through the windshield, but still unable to see more than a few feet ahead.

Smoke mixed with the moldy forest smell and thickened the fog.

Frank must have built a fire to ward off the morning chill. The smell of smoke intensified, and trees gave way to a clearing.

A dark silhouette emerged from the fog. The burned remains of a small building sat atop blackened pilings. Charred rubble covered the ground beneath and around it. Fog swirled through the wreckage and stretched long fingers toward her.

Claire slammed on the brakes and gaped at what had been a cabin. Skeletons of walls rose stark and irrelevant, supporting nothing. The roof had fallen in. A scorched metal stovepipe disappeared into the fog.

She scrambled out of her car and ran across the clearing, leaping blackened spars and chunks of roof, heedless of possible danger from smoldering embers. A bit of stairway dangled from what must have been the front deck. She tried to reach the lowest step, but it was too high up. She couldn't get inside, but it didn't matter. No one survived inside this ruin.

A silver Jaguar, coated with ash and barely visible in the fog, sat at the far edge of the clearing. Claire walked over and brushed the ashes from the license plate. *Palmer 1*. Frank had told her he never took the Jaguar down here, but this was his car. The driver's door was unlocked. Keys lay in the console as if the driver planned to return any moment.

Claire told herself not to jump to conclusions. Jeanette had said Frank and Hatch planned to go fishing in the Gulf, and they often stayed out overnight. They were probably out in his boat and didn't even know there'd been a fire.

Go check the dock. You'll see. The boat will be gone.

The dirt track continued down toward the water. She followed it, walking faster, then half running despite the thick fog and muddy ground. A protruding root sent her sprawling. She struggled back to her feet, saw that she'd ripped her slacks, and proceeded more carefully.

The track ended at a bulkhead and a wooden dock. A white cabin cruiser, moored at the end of the dock, floated in the mist like a ghost ship.

"Hello? Hello, anyone there?"

A seagull squawked the only response. It hovered overhead, scolding as she ran the length of the dock and jumped on board.

The cabin, like the car, was unlocked. Claire studied the elaborate control panel and pushed the power button for what looked like a ship-to-shore radio. Nothing happened. She held the button down—still nothing. She checked under the console. No switch, and all the wires appeared to be attached. The dials and gauges told her nothing. She tried other buttons, but nothing responded. Maybe the boat engine had to be on. But she didn't have the key.

She trudged back up the path, back to the fog-shrouded clearing and the burned ruin that had been Frank's cabin. The pervasive smoke stung her throat. It made her stomach churn and her eyes fill with tears. Or was she crying?

It was the smoke.

That's what they'd told her when she went to the morgue to identify Tom's body. There were no visible burns. The damage was all on the inside. Hot smoke had seared his lungs and stolen his breath. Claire felt the pain in her lungs. Her unease intensified into apprehension and then dread, the sense of impending doom that signaled the beginning of a panic attack.

Her therapist had told her that most people's panic attacks were metallic—the taste in their mouths, the chains around their chest, the weights on their arms and legs. Hers were scorched plastic, a foul-smelling gray bubble that cut her off from the rest of the world.

She pulled the vial from her pocket and wrenched it open. The smooth container slipped through her trembling fingers, spilling her pills. She dropped to her knees and sifted through the ashes until she felt a small hard oval. Gratefully, she swallowed it. Ash coated her lips and gritted on her teeth, but she didn't care. She found two more pills, swallowed one, and put the other back.

The bubble's not real. Inhale two three; exhale two three. It's not real. Hold on until the pills kick in.

Claire had learned to manage her panic by visualizing gentle surf. If she could see waves breaking on a beach—one after the other, slow and steady—their rhythm would guide her breath and help her regain control. She'd practiced until she could imagine waves in a store, in a meeting or walking down the street, but now she could see only ashes. They surrounded her, gray like the bubble, forming a bubble.

The bubble began to contract, closing in until thick plastic restrained her arms and legs. It compressed her chest, covered her face and sealed her eyes. The stench of burned plastic filled her nose and mouth. Fear of a panic attack merged with the attack itself. Her heart pounded against her ribs. Each beat sent sharp pains across her chest, down her arms, and her legs. She couldn't see. She couldn't breathe. She was dying.

The world turned black.

Some unmeasured time later, Claire drifted back to consciousness in the lethargy that follows a panic attack. Gradually, she became aware of the ash-covered ground on which she lay, of the cold, the damp, and the smoke. She turned her head and saw her car. She remembered looking for Frank and finding the burned cabin. There it was, behind her.

I have to get away from here.

She pulled herself to her hands and knees, paused to gather her strength, and then stood. She found her balance and staggered to her car. Driving as fast as she dared, she retraced her route up the bumpy track, desperate to escape the eerie clearing with its fog and smoke, its ashes and the memories it evoked.

The sun shone on top of the levee; she'd left the horror behind. Claire told herself that she'd over-reacted because of what happened to Tom. Frank and Hatch weren't children. If they'd been in the cabin, they would have escaped.

Frank said he always drove his Jeep, but it wasn't there. They could have gone somewhere in the Jeep and left the Jag behind. Or they were out on the Gulf fishing with some of Frank's friends on another boat. They were probably okay, but she should report the fire. She'd stop in the nearest town and find a phone.

The extra meds kicked in shortly after she reached a paved road. Groggy and disoriented, she wandered for what seemed like hours before finding the highway, which was now full of cars heading toward the Gulf. She squeezed in behind a minivan with surf mats tied onto the roof and followed it to a parking lot across from the beach.

"Are you okay, ma'am?"

Claire lifted her head from the steering wheel. A man stood beside her car. He looked concerned.

"I'm fine. Just tired."

Her tongue was thick in her mouth, and she slurred her words. Her body felt heavy and unresponsive. He watched, frowning now, as she swung her legs out of the car and pulled herself upright. She'd taken too many pills. He probably thought she was drunk.

Across the street, wooden stairs led down to the beach. She held on to the railing, and took the steps one at a time like a toddler just learning to walk. Down on the sand, she threaded her way through the towels and blankets, sand sculptures and volleyball games, apologizing when she bumped someone, meeting no one's eyes.

She followed the water line to a quiet spot at the far end of the beach, sat, and looked out at the Gulf. The steady rhythm of the waves comforted her. One, two, three… She counted up to seven and then backwards from seven to zero. Up to seven and back down again, over and over. She counted waves, dozed off, half woke to count some more, and dozed off again.

Water splashing her legs startled her awake. The tide was coming in. She moved back up the beach and thought about this morning, her first panic attack in months.

Doctor Bennett had warned that drugs and visualization could help manage her attacks, but the only cure was to address the underlying cause. Something had frightened her so badly that she'd suppressed it and, when reminded of it, panicked rather than face it.

The attacks began after Tom died and had to be related to his death, but even with therapy, she hadn't been able to discover how. What was left to fear? The worst had already happened. And there was nothing suppressed about her sorrow. She mourned Tom every day.

Smoke had contributed to this morning's panic attack—she was sure of that—and it had followed her here. Hours later and miles away she could still smell it. She sniffed the sleeve of her blouse. The scent was in her clothes, which were also mud-stained and wet. She was a mess. She was also dehydrated. Her lips stuck to her teeth, and her eyes scratched as if she had sand under her lids. How many pills had she taken?

I need clean clothes and something to drink.

There were stores up on the street. Someone would be selling soda; someone would know who to call about the fire. There'd be a phone she could use. She stopped by the public rest room to tidy up and gazed in dismay at the creature in the mirror, at her tangled hair, tear-striped face and bloodshot eyes. No wonder people had stared.

The sky was dark by the time Claire returned to her carriage house. Dorian, who'd been waiting on the porch, meowed and rubbed figure eights around her legs as she unlocked the front door. She picked him up and carried him inside.

The red light on her answering machine was blinking. Frank? The Lafourche Parish Sheriff's Department? She'd reported the burned cabin to them and left her number. Although once the operator learned the fire was out, she hadn't seemed very interested.

The message was from Bobby Austin.

"I don't want to worry you, Claire. We both know Frank likes to get off on his own, but I'd appreciate a call if you know how to reach him." He recited a phone number and after a pause, added, "Marie joins me in wishing you and Frank the very best, a lifetime of happiness together."

"Frank and I are *not* getting married." Claire shook her head, and pain zigzagged across her forehead.

No one answered the phone at Frank's house. She called Bobby back and spoke to the maid, who said the Austins were at the theater and not expected back until late. She tried in vain to think of someone else to call. She didn't know Jeanette's last name, much less her phone number.

Claire gave up. She opened a can of tuna for Dorian, an apology for the late supper, took a long hot shower, and then killed time picking dead leaves off houseplants while she waited for ten o'clock and the local news. It anything had happened to Frank Palmer, it would be news.

The opening promo promised an update on the tragic story from Lafourche Parish. Claire sat through an endless series of commercials, chewing on her lip, afraid of what she was going to hear. Finally, the news team reappeared.

"James Oreille, the seventeen-year old Raceland resident who was injured in a vehicle explosion Wednesday afternoon, has died of his injuries. Dirk Stone brings us an update live from the scene. Over to you, Dirk."

A dark-skinned man stared into the camera. Behind him spotlights cast bright circles onto a parking lot. Their beams bounced off ribbons of yellow crime tape and disappeared into a large hole burnt into the asphalt. In the background, neon signs advertised beer and snack foods. The man raised a handheld microphone to his mouth.

"Wednesday afternoon, this convenience store parking lot was the scene of a powerful explosion. It created the crater behind me and took the life of a young man. Doctors did all they could, but this afternoon, James Oreille lost his battle for life. His family is too distraught to appear on camera." He drew an audible breath. "The Lafourche Parish Sheriff's Office tells us the vehicle, an army-type Jeep, was driven here by a white male who was inside the store at the time of the explosion."

The camera panned to the storefront and then returned to the reporter, now holding up a large piece of paper.

"A police artist developed this sketch of the driver, who disappeared shortly after the explosion. A white man approximately six feet tall and 160 pounds, he was last seen wearing dark blue or black jeans and a black tee shirt."

The camera closed in, and Claire stared, dumbfounded, at the screen. The drawing looked like Hatch. Jeanette had said Frank was fishing with Hatch. Hatch was Frank's driver. Frank owned an old Jeep. He'd told her he always took the Jeep down to his cabin, but the Jag was there.

Was that really Hatch? And Frank's Jeep? Where was Frank? Who was James Oreille?

The scene switched back to the studio. "Law enforcement officials describe this series of events as both tragic and puzzling. Anyone with any information about either the vehicle or the individual allegedly seen driving it is asked to call the Deputy Jason Corlette at the Lafourche Sheriff's office." A telephone number scrolled across the bottom of the screen.

Claire wrote the number down but didn't pick up the phone. She was exhausted, and she'd already reported the cabin fire. The Sheriff's Department had her phone number, but they hadn't called her. If that really was Hatch, Frank's friends would recognize him and they'd call.

5

Captain Mike Robinson, the new head of the New Orleans Police Department's Homicide Division, watched tourists jaywalk across Canal Street and clamber onto a waiting streetcar. If anyone noticed the light had turned red, they didn't care. A harassed traffic cop blew his whistle at a car taking advantage of the blockage to turn left under the No Left Turn sign. Chaos, but everyone seemed in a good mood.

"You ever direct traffic?" Lieutenant Al Breton, who was driving, said.

"Yes." Mike didn't elaborate. "Why the scenic route?"

"I thought we'd go by way of Bourbon Street." A sour chuckle. "They'll think we're vice."

"Long as we end up at Palmer's house." Mike didn't see the point, but if annoying petty criminals made Breton feel better about working on a Sunday morning, he could have at it.

They turned onto a street littered with the debris of Saturday night. Half empty, or was it half full, plastic drink cups sat along the gutters and leaned against buildings. The heat—temperature and humidity were both pushing ninety—intensified the odors of alcohol, urine, and vomit that lingered over the street. Mike switched the air conditioning to recirculate.

Their unadorned Crown Vic proceeded slowly, its windows up, its occupants impervious to the baleful stares that marked their passage. The local riffraff recognized an unmarked police car and, as Breton had expected, resented the intrusion. A crunch told everyone that the cops had run over a glass bottle, a dead soldier not yet kicked to the gutter. A man in a shiny blue dress looked hopefully at their left rear tire.

27

"That's more like it," Breton said. "Folks ought to be praying on a Sunday morning."

"Praying?" Mike played the straight man.

"Him and his buddies are praying we get a flat. They want to watch us sweat while we change it." The Lieutenant chuckled at his own dark humor. "It won't do them any good. Our Firestones are stronger than their prayers."

A painfully thin girl wearing fishnet stockings and what looked like black vinyl underwear tottered along on stiletto heels. When she turned to watch them pass, a credit card imprint machine swung from her waist.

Breton pointed with his chin. "That sweet young thing is on her way to church. She's singing in the choir today."

This time Mike didn't smile. The girl looked about fourteen. Cleaned up, she might be pretty, but she'd be haggard by thirty, if she lived that long. There was not one damn thing funny about her.

Breton caught his mood. "Might as well laugh. Pick her up and her pimp has her out in ten minutes. Whatever it costs him, she pays back the hard way."

Mike's nod acknowledged the truth of that statement, but he still didn't smile. After twenty years in the army, beginning as an M.P. and ending in the Judge Advocate Group, he'd picked New Orleans and police work for his re-entry to civilian life. They'd picked him to be fresh blood in a department that needed it. Two and a half months in, he wasn't sure either had made a good choice, but he was giving it a year.

He liked a lot about this city, its easy-going generosity, the appreciation of life's simple pleasures, the food, and the music. He'd not foreseen the pervasive corruption that was the dark underside of *Laissez les bon temps rouler*. Thank God he worked homicide and not vice.

"Vernon said you'd fill me in." Breton pulled up next to a No Parking sign in front of a café. "Long as we're here, what if we stop for beignets? Talk while we eat. Twenty minutes from now, Palmer will still be dead."

Mike had planned to brief him in during the drive to Lafourche Parish, but Breton was antsy, and now was as good a time as any. He waited on the sidewalk while the Lieutenant eased his girth from behind the steering wheel. Both patio and indoors were crowded. Tourists lined up outside the door, laughing and talking as they waited for another famous taste of New Orleans, not noticing the locals who slipped in and out on a faster track.

"You order," he said. "I'll grab a table."

"How many do you want?"

"Coffee will do me." He caught a busboy's eye, flashed his badge, and was given the next open table.

Breton returned with two coffees and a bag of beignets. He helped himself to one then asked, "Why do we care about a fire-related death in Lafourche Parish?"

"Someone called Superintendent Vernon Friday night when Palmer missed an important engagement. Said Palmer had gone fishing in the Gulf with an employee earlier in the week and hadn't been seen since."

"Someone had Vernon's home number?" Breton was surprised enough to talk with his mouth full. "That's a well-connected someone. I assume we rose to the occasion."

"A patrol officer stopped by the house, found no one home and a note from Palmer's fiancée taped to the front door. She's looking for him, too. That was it until yesterday afternoon when Lafourche Parish called. They're looking for Palmer because his cabin burned and his Jeep exploded, killing a kid who was trying to steal it."

"Jeez." Breton stuffed another beignet in his mouth.

"The Jeep blew last Wednesday. The cabin fire, they don't know yet. Someone passed the call to Vernon, who got back to the well-connected friend, who leaned on the Sheriff's Office. Deputies searched the cabin and found the body."

"The Jeep blows up Wednesday and Lafourche Parish calls us Saturday?"

"They found the VIN late Friday. The Jeep belonged to Palmer's company, which was closed for the weekend. They planned to call Monday morning. Follow-up became more urgent when someone reported the cabin fire, and the kid died."

"Does Palmer's well-connected friend have a name?"

"Not yet." He'd asked for a name but Vernon said, later, if they needed to talk to him. It was a bullshit answer, the implied lack of trust noted and not appreciated. He took a swallow of the heavily milked coffee.

"Vernon's a jackass, and Palmer's friend, whoever he is, doesn't know shit. Lafourche Parish can handle a cabin fire or a homicide without our help." Breton took the last beignet. "But that's politics, and this city is full of it."

"Politics happen everywhere." There had been plenty of politics in the military. There had also been honor and a shared sense of purpose, the belief they were working together for a greater good.

"If something goes right, Vernon grabs the credit. If something goes wrong, it's your ass in a sling." Rising color in Breton's face suggested both anger and high blood pressure. "The Vermin, that's what they call him. Palmer's a big deal. There's going to be a lot of heat. The Vermin wants me on the case because I'm two months away from retirement. If someone has to be thrown to the wolves, I'm expendable."

Mike held up a calming hand. "A. I assigned you to the case. B. We don't know yet if Palmer's death was homicide. No need to go off the deep end."

But Breton was already there. "What about the employee? Anybody ask what happened to him? And the fiancée, anyone talk to her?" When Mike raised an eyebrow he added, "Sir."

"We've tried, so far without success, to locate both Ronald Hatch, the employee, and Claire Marshall, the fiancée. We'll encourage Lafourche Parish to have an arson team go over the cabin. There'll be an autopsy on Palmer's body. If they don't want to do it, we will. Vernon wants all possibilities covered."

"Vernon wants to cover his own his high-ranking ass. Everything else comes second."

"Let's go." Mike had heard enough. "We can talk about details later, on the way to Thibodaux. Palmer had a fiancée, but he lived alone. His housekeeper is waiting for us."

Frank Palmer had lived in a neighborhood of quaint, well-maintained homes. Fresh paint and window boxes overflowing with colorful flowers created a festive air. The heavy wrought iron that guarded every exposed window or driveway told another story. Graceful curlicues interspersed with sharp spikes performed the same function as razor wire did in less affluent locations. Number 43 was the largest house on the block and the only one with a real front yard.

Breton pulled up to the curb. "Look at that place," he said. "It's a goddamned fortress. Palmer should've stayed home where he'd be nice and safe. Hell, I should stay home where I'm nice and safe. Being a short-termer makes me nervous. You know what I mean."

"The housekeeper's name is Rosa Taylor." Mike climbed out of the car and walked up to the front door.

A dark wraith in a maid's uniform answered the bell. She looked to be a hundred years old and thin enough to slip through the spaces in the ironwork.

"Mrs. Taylor?" He showed his badge. "We're from the police department."

She eyed them suspiciously. "They told me you were coming, but like I told them, Mr. Palmer's not home."

"We have some bad news, and we're hoping you can help us. May we come in?"

She pulled a ribbon necklace from under her dress. Two of the several keys threaded onto it unlocked the deadbolts on the security door. She stepped back to let them enter and waited. Her expression gave nothing away.

"We're here with bad news." He said it again to give her a chance to prepare herself. "Would you like to sit down?"

"I'll stay standing."

"Mr. Palmer has passed away."

Her expression didn't change, but she swayed on her feet. He put a supporting hand under her elbow, a bone so delicate it felt like holding a bird.

He helped her to a chair. "Can I get you a drink of water?"

"I don't want nothing. What do you want from me?"

"We're hoping you can help us locate Mr. Palmer's next of kin." The mysterious well-connected friend might have informed them already, but Vernon wanted to make sure the Department did its part.

"There's none that claims him." It was a flat statement, but when he didn't respond, she expanded upon it. "Miz Annie Lewis passed five years ago, his mother and father before then, and he didn't have brothers nor sisters. The only ones still on this earth are Miz Fulton, Annie Lewis's mother. She's got no use for Mr. Frank." She paused for two breaths that ended with a long sigh. "And Annalisa, who don't want nothing to do with no one."

"What about Claire Marshall, Mr. Palmer's fiancée?"

"Never heard of her." A flip of her hand dismissed Claire Marshall.

"Do you know where we could find contact information for Mrs. Fulton and Annalisa?"

"His phone numbers are in a box on top of his desk, but I expect you want to talk to Mr. Gilbert."

"Would that be Paul Gilbert the attorney?" Breton joined the conversation, his short-timer disease temporarily cured by curiosity.

Rosa nodded assent. "Mr. Frank always said the first thing to do when trouble strikes is call Mr. Gilbert."

"When was the last time you saw Mr. Palmer?" Mike said.

"Tuesday morning at breakfast. I left him dinner in the icebox, but he didn't eat it."

"Did he sleep in his bed Tuesday night?"

"Not that I could tell. You want those phone numbers?"

She led them to a room at the back of the house. Heavy shutters closed against the heat of the day kept the room near total darkness. Rosa flicked a switch by the door, and several lamps came on, revealing walls covered with hunting trophies and furnishings that looked as if they'd come from a nineteenth century barrister's office.

"In there." She nodded toward a large Rolodex beside the phone, and then pointed to a brass circle embedded in the floor. "Mash that when you're ready to leave, I'll come show you out."

"We'll just be a minute," Mike said. "Why don't you wait here?" If Palmer's death was a homicide, they'd come back with a warrant, and he didn't want any questions about what he and Breton had done today.

"I'll wait in the hall."

"Bet she doesn't like all the dead animals." Breton nudged a footstool made from an elephant's foot. "Is this thing real?" He started to turn it over.

"Don't poke around," Mike said. "We're looking for phone numbers, period."

"Rosa talking about Annie Lewis rang a bell, but I'm not coming up with anything."

"Palmer's late wife. She died five years ago. Annalisa, their only child, was fourteen at the time."

Breton did the math. "Which would make her nineteen."

"She ran away the day after her mother's funeral. Vernon said rumor is Palmer found her. She didn't want to come home. She was safe, so he agreed to let her stay gone. See if you can find her contact information. Estranged or not, someone has to notify her of her father's death. While you're at it, see what you can find for Mrs. Fulton and Gilbert."

Breton's search of the Rolodex produced numbers for Annette Fulton and Paul Gilbert but nothing for Annalisa. "Two out of three ain't bad." He said.

"We'll call Gilbert first. He might have contact information for Annalisa. If we're lucky, he'll want to notify the family." Mike wouldn't mind handing that dirty job over to the family lawyer. Informing a person that someone they loved had died, not of old age or in their sleep but suddenly and violently, was difficult no matter how many times you'd done it.

"Gilbert is Mister fix-it."

"Do you know him?"

"Only by reputation. They say Paul Gilbert knows where every skeleton in New Orleans is buried and how many teeth it has." Breton's tone conveyed disgust and a grudging respect. "Word is, he helped bury most of them."

6

Claire slept late and would have slept later if Dorian hadn't run out of patience. He positioned himself on the floor, just out of reach, and meowed until she gave up.

"Okay, okay, I'm hungry, too." She crawled out of bed and followed the cat into the kitchen.

The number scrawled on the pad beside the phone brought her fully awake. She fed Dorian and went outside to check on her car.

The trip to Frank's cabin hadn't resulted in any dents or scrapes, but Felicia's dirt-encrusted grill and mud-splattered sides called for more than a hosing off. After a quick breakfast of tea and peanut butter toast, she dressed and went looking for a car wash that was open on Sunday morning.

By the time Claire returned home, it was almost noon, and there were no new messages on her answering machine. She tried without success to reach Frank, decided she didn't want to talk to Bobby, and called the Lafourche Parish Sheriff's Department. The switchboard operator put her through to Deputy Jason Corlette, who recognized her name and said he'd been planning to call her.

"You reported a cabin that had burned."

"Yes, Frank Palmer's cabin. And the man who was driving the Jeep that blew up at that convenience store? From the picture on the news, it could be Frank Palmer's driver."

"Is Frank Palmer a friend of yours?"

"He's a client."

Two hours later, Claire was sitting in Jason Corlette's office, across from his desk. The deputy looked young and very Cajun, with dark hair and sharp features. His voice had sounded harsh on the phone, but in person, it was deep and twangy, like a country singer's.

"Thank you for coming in, Miss Marshall. Or is it Mrs.?"

His eyes slid down to her left hand, and she tucked it under her arm, hiding the band of pale flesh that was the ghost of her wedding ring. "Claire is fine."

Although she'd agreed to let him tape the interview, he also took notes. She told him about recognizing Hatch, adding the caveat that she wasn't absolutely certain because she'd only spoken to him once.

"I don't really know him." Nor did she want to.

She'd seen Hatch sitting behind the wheel while he waited for Frank, but they hadn't spoken until the first time she and Frank went out to dinner. Frank had suggested they take his car and introduced his driver. Hatch, who responded to Frank's orders with squared shoulders and immediate obedience, had flicked a dismissive glance in her direction and grunted a hello. He'd pulled away from the curb while she was reaching forward to shake hands.

At dinner, her inhibitions loosened by two glasses of wine, she'd asked Frank why he employed such an ill-mannered chauffeur. He laughed it off, but that was the last time she saw Hatch. From then on, when they met at his cottage, Frank drove himself.

"Your identification is consistent with what we've learned so far," Deputy Corlette said. "What else can you tell us about Mr. Hatch?"

"He works for Frank Palmer, drives him around and runs errands. That's all I know."

"All you know about Hatch," he qualified her statement. "What about the cabin that burned? What were you doing there?"

"I wanted to talk to Frank—Mr. Palmer. As I told you on the phone, my company works for him. We're renovating a cottage he owns in New Orleans, and he's been asking me to look at his cabin, the one that burned. He wanted to fix it up. Yesterday was a nice day for a drive." She shrugged. "I had some free time."

Each statement was true, but together they obscured the truth. At least she hoped so. She wanted to avoid the complicated and ridiculous story of not being engaged to Frank Palmer, especially because she wasn't absolutely sure he was the one telling people. But if not Frank, who else?

"You called us from a restaurant in Grand Isle."

Claire nodded. The sheriff's department must have traced her call.

"You drove all the way to the beach before reporting the fire?"

His question could have been an accusation, but his sympathetic tone made it sound like an effort to understand. Would he understand if she told him that she'd suffered a panic attack and ran to the water the way a wounded animal runs to its lair? She'd have to admit that taking too much Xanax had clouded her judgment. She'd driven when she shouldn't.

"I didn't see any other cabins," she said, "and once I was on the highway, I just kept going. It wasn't far."

He tapped his pen on several papers that were lying face down on his desk. A half frown raised his eyebrows and gave him a puzzled expression. "What did you do the rest of the day?"

"I walked on the beach, went swimming. It was a spur of the moment trip. I had to buy myself a bathing suit and a beach towel." She tried a little joke. "The store was having an end of season clearance. I bought a new outfit too. Can't resist a sale."

He ignored her weak attempt at humor, and Claire put herself in his shoes. A deputy sheriff would see nothing amusing about a woman who ran away from a burned cabin and went to the beach. What would he think if he knew that at least four hours elapsed between the time she discovered the fire and the time she reported it? Did he suspect she'd delayed calling about Hatch because she hoped someone else would call first? She wasn't like Tom, who saw a house on fire and ran inside because he could help.

"Claire?"

She brought herself back to the present. "I'm sorry, what did you say?"

"What did you do with the clothes you were wearing?"

"I threw them away." When he looked surprised, she said, "They were filthy and torn. I fell in the mud on the path to the dock."

"You said this was your first visit to Mr. Palmer's cabin." When she nodded, he continued, "Your first trip, and you drove alone from New Orleans to an isolated cabin on the off chance that he'd be there?"

"It was more than an off chance. His secretary said he was there or out fishing." She raised her chin and looked him in the eye. "I drive alone to lots of places."

He made another note and asked several questions about what she'd done after finding the burned cabin. Then he just sat there, as if he had all the time in the world to listen to whatever she had to say and to wait for her to get around to whatever she wasn't saying.

Were there things he wasn't saying? Like where was Frank.

"I'm worried about Frank," she said. "I've been unable to reach him. I thought he and Hatch had gone somewhere in the Jeep, but the news said Hatch was alone. Do you know? Has something happened?"

Deputy Corlette put his pen down and picked up the top piece of paper. His eyes flicked from whatever was written on it to her face.

"What?" Claire said, alarmed by his solemn expression.

"I regret to inform you that we found a man's body in the cabin. From all indications, it is Frank Palmer." He put the paper down and placed his notepad on top of it.

"Oh, no. That's awful. I'm so sorry." Frank's body had been there the whole time. No wonder that clearing had felt haunted. She shuddered. If she'd gone inside that burned cabin, she would have found him.

"I know it's a shock. Are you all right?"

"I'd convinced myself they weren't there," she said, "that they were out in another boat or off in the Jeep. Even after I saw Hatch on TV… I don't understand what could have happened. Why didn't Frank get out?"

"We're trying to understand, too. So, can you tell us anything that might make our job easier?"

She shook her head. "No, I'm sorry. If I think of anything, I'll contact you, but…" She raised her hands in a gesture of helplessness.

After a long silence, he stood up. "So, thank you for your cooperation, Ms. Marshall. I'll walk you to your car. I'd like to stretch my legs before my next meeting."

Claire had intended to drive back to New Orleans, but once in the car, she changed her mind. She wanted to go back to the beach, to sit and watch the waves again, this time while she digested the horrible news about Frank.

At Grand Isle, she parked in the same lot. Thick clouds had replaced yesterday's sunshine, and a cool wind off the water raised goose bumps on her arms. The beach, crowded yesterday, was deserted except for a scattering of fishermen. She sat well up the beach and looked out at the water, gray now and blending into the clouds at an invisible horizon.

Twenty yards off shore, waves rose from the choppy surface, each one crested with a pale line of foam. When a wave reached the shallows, it lifted and curled inward as if it had changed its mind and wanted to return to the depths, but those behind permitted no retreat. They pushed forward until the lead wave broke on the beach and melted into the sand. In the shallows, the next one had already begun curling inward.

Lingering backwash from an exceptionally large breaker might reduce the ensuing landfall to disorganized churning, but the waves that followed always restored order. The implacable Gulf sacrificed wave after wave on the shore as it had done for thousands of years and would continue to do long after she and everyone she loved had turned to dust.

That thought, which could have been depressing, reassured her. She lay on her stomach, chin on her fists and elbows in the sand, and watched the waves. Now and again, she raised her gaze and searched for the horizon, a change of shading within a world of gray.

Happy chattering announced the arrival of two boys carrying boogie boards. They raced toward the water and stepped onto their boards, but the small dog that accompanied them hung back, barking anxiously. The boys skittered along the wash of the waves, miraculously afloat on an inch of water. The dog, an indeterminate mix, stayed as close as he could without getting his paws wet, charging and retreating as the waves ebbed and flowed.

Claire watched, amused by the dog's antics and by the boys' nonchalance. With their hard, skinny bodies and still soft faces, they looked about ten or eleven, children on the verge of adolescence. Tanned skin and sun-bleached hair testified to long hours in the sun.

A big wave broke, and the dog scampered up the beach. The smaller boy tottered precariously between the necessities of hitching up his shorts and spreading his arms for balance. Somehow, he managed to reach out and hold on at the same time. Claire clapped.

"Very good. Nice recovery."

He smiled at this praise from a stranger. The dog trotted over for a pat on the head and ventured a hopeful snuffle at her pocketbook before returning to his duties. The boys moved on, and Claire checked her watch. She remembered Frank's extravagant gift. What on earth was she going to do with it now?

The boys, now halfway down the beach, gave her an idea. She could return the watch to the store—there was a name on the box—and donate the money to the Children's Home. In Frank's memory. He was a longtime supporter and on the board. It was where they'd met.

It was the right thing to do, and with every wave that hit the beach, the Gulf agreed.

7

The desk officer at the Lafourche Parish Sheriff's Office directed Mike and Breton to Deputy Jason Corlette's office. They exchanged introductions, and the deputy got the meeting off to a fast start by announcing the fire at Palmer's cabin was arson. He pushed a folder across his desk.

"The report. It's preliminary, but there's no doubt. Gasoline was the accelerant. Early next week, the lab promises a timeframe."

Mike flipped through the document and passed it on to Breton who glanced at the cover and put it down.

"The med tech says it looked to him like Palmer was dead before the fire. An autopsy is scheduled for Monday morning, and we'll find out if he was right or not. Given the arson finding..." Corlette shrugged. He slid another folder across the desk. "Here's what we found in the cabin."

"You've accomplished a lot in under twenty four hours." Mike was relieved. The Sheriff's Department had already initiated every action he and Vernon had discussed. Lafourche Parish couldn't be thrilled about New Orleans taking an interest in their case, but this deputy had no visible chip on his shoulder.

Corlette's nod acknowledged the compliment. He picked up a stack of photographs and laid them on his desk as if he was dealing cards. "These pictures, they're from the scene." He pointed to a photograph of muddy handprints. "From Palmer's boat. They belong to a woman named Claire Marshall."

"How do you know that?" Mike said.

Breton, who'd been slumped in his chair with his eyes half shut, came to life. "*Cherchez la femme*, and we've found her."

Corlette looked from one to the other. "She's not hiding. She's stepped forward twice, yesterday to report the burned cabin and today to identify the driver of Palmer's Jeep."

"What's she look like?" Breton said.

"Nice face. A little on the skinny side. Five-seven, five-eight, maybe one twenty-five. Red hair, dark not orange. She was cooperative, drove right down to talk to me. Still, her story is strange."

"We'd like to hear it," Mike said.

"I taped the interview, and we're making you a copy, but I can give you a quick recap." After summarizing the interview, he said, "One thing isn't on the tape. When we finished, I walked her out to her car. She has a bright blue Miata, sits about six inches off the ground. I said it was a good thing she hadn't tried to drive it down to the cabin. She said she had. It was clean because she'd just run it through a car wash."

Breton leaned forward, forearms on Corlette's desk. "Strange? She drives all the way down here looking for Palmer, finds his cabin burned to a cinder, and goes to the beach. She disposes of the clothes she was wearing and runs her vehicle through a car wash. You call it strange. I call it destroying the evidence. And you just let her walk out of here?"

"I had no reason to detain her."

"You have an attractive young woman and a rich older man. He falls for her, and *voila*." Breton slapped the desk. "He's a rich older dead man. This is not a new story. Five will get you ten she's in his will."

Breton's expression said they'd finished their investigation. It was time to go home. Corlette was frowning.

"Nor is it the only possible story." Mike gave Breton a hard look. He could be right on target, but that wasn't the issue. They were on Corlette's turf, asking for and receiving full cooperation. There was no indication that Claire Marshall was avoiding law enforcement. Just the opposite. They'd catch up with her later.

He moved on to the next topic. "Do you know where Palmer's Jeep fits in?"

"It's a second suspicious and fatal fire. Witnesses told us both the Jeep and the driver smelled strongly of gasoline. Here are their statements." He added paper to the growing stack on their side of the desk. "The driver parked and went inside, leaving the windows wide open. A group of kids was hanging around, and one decided to take the Jeep for a ride. Moments after he entered the vehicle, it exploded.

Yesterday he died. So, there's one less juvenile delinquent in Lafourche Parish."

Corlette's words were flippant, but a tightness around his mouth revealed anger. He could have known the victim, known his family. This was personal, and no kid should get the death penalty for a joyride. Mike agreed. He signaled Breton to sit back and shut up, let Corlette tell the story at his own pace.

"The driver was in the restroom when the explosions occurred. He ran out, saw his vehicle on fire, and made a call from the outside pay phone. He was gone when the fire trucks arrived, no one noticed his departure, and he hasn't been seen since." Corlette slid one last piece of paper across the desk. "We asked TV news to show this sketch of the driver. Claire responded. She said it looked like a man named Hatch, who is Frank Palmer's driver. She couldn't tell me anything else about him. I'm hoping you can."

"His full name is Ronald Hatch," Mike said. "We were under the impression he'd driven Palmer to the cabin early last week and that they planned to go fishing together. After you called this morning, we sent a patrol car to his apartment. He wasn't home."

"Lafourche Parish would like to talk to Mr. Hatch about both fires."

"It's possible he's a link." Breton conceded.

"The vehicle he's driving blows up, and he disappears," Corlette said. "He's guilty or he's scared. Either way, he's a link."

Mike began laying the groundwork for a cooperative effort. "Have you considered the possibility that Palmer died in New Orleans and the body was transported to Lafourche Parish?"

"The sheriff's department agrees the motive is most likely to be found in New Orleans."

The door opened, and a pretty young woman walked in. She placed another manila folder and two tape cassettes on the desk. "Two of each. As fast as we could, Jason."

"Thank you, darlin'." The deputy returned her smile and slid one of the tapes across the desk. "Claire Marshall's interview. I didn't probe her relationship with the deceased," he admitted. "She said he was a client, and I left it at that. But listen to the tape. She was rocked when I told her Palmer was dead."

He opened the folder. "The tire track analysis—I haven't seen it yet." He passed one copy across the desk and scanned the other. "No surprises. We've identified three of the four sets found at the scene:

Claire's Miata, Austin's Suburban and Palmer's Jaguar. Recovered pieces of the Jeep tires are being analyzed to see if it was vehicle number four."

"Who's Austin?" Mike said. Was he Palmer's well-connected friend?

"Bobby Austin. He and Paul Gilbert contacted us about the cabin fire several hours after Claire did." The deputy gave him a quizzical look. "They said your department told them the cabin had burned."

"We told Gilbert. Did you talk to them?" Mike wondered why Palmer's lawyer hadn't mentioned this when they discussed notifying next of kin.

"They met us at the cabin. Preliminary identification of the body was based on the circumstances and the general description they provided. It's in the reports." Corlette nodded toward the stack of papers. "Can you get us the victim's dental records? We want to be certain."

"Palmer's cabin, his car, a body that matches his description, and the guy's missing." Breton's elbows were all over Corlette's desk again.

"Lieutenant Breton will contact Palmer's dentist first thing tomorrow." Mike said. "We'll step up the search for Hatch. We'll ask Palmer's friends about the man and what he was doing in the days before his death. Is there anything else we should be covering on our end?"

"The phone company has promised a list of numbers called from the payphone Hatch used. If any are in New Orleans, we'll pass them on. Who do I call?"

"Me." Mike had intended to assign Breton lead responsibility, but his role was in doubt after this afternoon's performance.

"I'm the contact here," Corlette said. "My first priority is looking for a witness. The cabin was isolated, and anyone out there was probably up to no good. So we'll check with the usual suspects: small time smugglers, poachers, burglars." He grinned and added, "Lovers."

"Do you think it's possible Palmer was just in the wrong place at the wrong time?"

"I don't think so. Smugglers would have taken the boat, at least the electronics. Thieves would have taken the car. Poachers and lovers just want to be left alone."

"And none of those explain the Jeep," Mike said. "When will you know more about that?"

"We've called in the state crime lab, but they're backed up as usual."

"We can encourage them to make this a priority." He'd ask Vernon to make the call. "Mr. Palmer was a prominent citizen. Our department is under pressure to get this cleared up quickly."

"Lafourche Parish is treating both deaths as potential homicides. We consider every homicide high priority."

"Has it occurred to you that Palmer might have committed suicide?" Breton said.

"If you believe that a corpse can start a fire." Corlette leaned back and crossed his arms over his chest.

The meeting ended soon afterwards. Until they knew otherwise, both departments would proceed as if they were dealing with a homicide.

Breton started bitching before they left the parking lot. "Say Palmer wanted to kill himself and make it look like an accident. There's no reason he couldn't pour gasoline on the floor and run a wick, wash a handful of pills down with a big glass of vodka and strike a match. Shit, he could use a candle. We're not talking rocket science."

"We'll see what the autopsy says, but if he was dead before the fire, your scenario doesn't work. He'd be unconscious, not dead. And there's a bigger problem. Suicides don't make plans for the future. Palmer was about to get married."

"To Claire Marshall. Did you notice Corlette talked about her like they were old friends? One interview and she's got him wrapped him around her little finger." A snort of disgust. "And okay, maybe it wasn't suicide, but don't tell me Boy Wonder isn't enjoying his fifteen minutes of fame. I've been a cop for thirty years, and I don't need a wet rookie explaining the facts of life."

The old cop approaching retirement resented the young cop making his first big case, and Corlette's breezy manner could be perceived as cocky. Mike understood, but he wasn't going to tolerate unprofessional behavior.

"You did us no favors in there. Corlette is doing a solid job, and he went the extra mile. If you can't work with him, let me know. I'll assign someone else. If you want to retire tomorrow and not in two months, let me know, and I'll see it happens." He didn't mention the third option, two months walking a beat. They both knew it was on the table.

Breton got the message. "I need two more months for full pension," he said, "and I intend to give the Department two months of my best work. What would you like me to do, sir?"

"Get Palmer's dental records to Corlette ASAP. Find out if the Jeep was kept at the cabin or elsewhere. See if anyone knows when Palmer and Hatch drove down there and if they went in separate vehicles or together. Schedule interviews with Austin, Gilbert, and Claire Marshall for tomorrow."

"Yes, sir."

"We can meet at their offices or ours. Allow an hour for each. If possible, start with Gilbert."

"Yes, sir."

"We'll do these first three as a team." He didn't trust Breton with anything sensitive, and Vernon had ordered him to stay on top of this investigation. "Next, I want you to talk to Rose Taylor and to Palmer's secretary. Ask who else was close to the victim and set up interviews with those people, again ASAP. Palmer's death will be news. I want to question his friends before they start confusing what they've read in the paper with what they already know."

"Yes, sir."

"Vernon wants Palmer's associates treated with kid gloves. I'm passing that on, but don't let anyone push you around."

"Yes, sir."

Mike ignored the sarcasm behind Breton's stream of sirs. He'd been brought in from the outside, part of the recent reform effort, and he expected resentment. Others had wanted the job, but Breton, nearing retirement, wasn't one of them. Working with him had seemed a good way to tap into the older man's institutional memory. It wasn't happening because Breton's eyes were fixed too firmly on the door. He might have been a good cop once, but he'd become a lazy one.

"Anything else, sir?"

"Drop me at headquarters. I'll put out an APB for Hatch and initiate the warrant to search his apartment." And after he'd taken care of that, he'd ask Vernon why he had to go to Lafourche Parish to learn the names of Palmer's friends and to find out that Palmer's personal driver was involved in the Jeep explosion.

8

Claire threw on her housecoat and went to see who was ringing her doorbell at eight o'clock on a Monday morning. A sandy-haired man stood on her porch. He looked vaguely familiar, but she couldn't place him. Keeping the chain on, she opened the door a crack and asked what he wanted.

"I'd like to offer condolences on the tragic death of your fiancé." He identified himself as a reporter from one of the local television stations and held out her morning paper. The headline read *Local Business Leader Dies in Cabin Fire.*

She should have known. When someone dies in a fire, it's news. Tom had been on the front page, too. *Young doctor dies saving children.* The children's mother said she'd be eternally grateful. A four-year-old boy and an eighteen-month-old girl, they'd be going on six and three now. Would their mother see today's paper and think of Tom?

"There's been a misunderstanding," she said.

"I can have a crew here in twenty minutes. Your interview will lead off tonight's news."

"How'd you get in?" A tall fence surrounded the property, and the driveway gates operated by remote control. Her landlord and his family were still in Europe. Who had let this reporter onto the property?

"The small gate next to the driveway was open." He smirked.

"For deliveries, not for you. Please leave, or I'll call the police." She tried to close the door, but he'd jammed his foot into the crack. "Move your foot." When he did, she shut the door and set the dead bolt.

Instead of leaving, the man sat on her porch swing and pulled out a mobile phone, so she called 911. The operator didn't sound impressed with the problem until Claire asked if she'd be justified shooting the man if he banged on her door again. That question elicited a promise that a car would be dispatched as soon as one became available and a warning not to point the gun at a policeman.

Claire, who didn't own a gun, pressed the button to open the driveway gate so the police car could get in and retreated to her bedroom, where the reporter couldn't see her. She'd just finished dressing when the phone rang.

"This is Lieutenant Al Breton from the New Orleans Police Department."

"That man is still on my porch," she said. "I told him to leave, but he won't go. He says he's a reporter, but I don't know if that's true. When is someone going to get here?"

"Pardon?"

She repeated her complaint, and he promised to send a patrolman immediately. He'd be a few minutes behind him.

Lieutenant Breton was a man of his word. Twenty minutes later, Claire stood next to him on the porch and watched a uniformed officer escort the intruder, who really was a TV reporter, up the driveway.

"You're sure you don't want to press charges?" he said. "That jerk's a free man when he hits the street."

"No, thank you. I just want him to leave me alone. If he comes back, I'll press charges."

"Can we go inside and talk?" He took a step toward the door.

"Of course. Do I need to sign something?" She showed him into the living room.

"We had ourselves a little coincidence this morning. You called for help getting rid of that reporter, and I called to set up an appointment." He sat down without being invited. "We want to talk to you about Frank Palmer."

"I met with Deputy Corlette at the Lafourche Parish Sheriff's Department yesterday. I told him everything I know, and he recorded our conversation."

"Corlette gave us a copy of the tape. But we want to talk to you ourselves."

"I'd rather not." She was sorry that Frank had died, but she really didn't have anything to tell the police, and she didn't want to relive the weekend ordeal. Taking to Deputy Corlette had been difficult. Repeating everything, knowing that Frank's body had been in the cabin, would be much harder.

"You don't have a lot of choice."

"I don't? Really? I thought I lived in a country where citizens have certain rights."

"You also have certain obligations, and one is to cooperate with law enforcement agencies. We just want to talk to you. You can make a big deal of it, get a lawyer involved, and plead the fifth if you've got something to hide. Up to you."

Lieutenant Breton had entered her home under false pretenses. He was sitting in her living room as if he owned the place and lecturing her about civic responsibilities as if she were a recalcitrant child. In fact, he was sitting in Dorian's chair. Claire was pleased to see fluffy orange and white cat hair clinging to his trousers.

"Excuse me, please. I'll be right back." She went into the bedroom to look up Paul Gilbert's number. The only other lawyers she knew were real estate attorneys.

The receptionist put her right through, and Paul began by expressing his deepest sympathy. With a jolt, Claire realized that he, too, thought she and Frank planned to marry.

"I really didn't know Frank very well," she said, "but of course, I'm saddened by his passing." There was a long silence from the other end, so she added, "My condolences go to you. Frank said you'd been friends for decades."

After another noticeable pause, Paul thanked her.

"I'm sorry to bother you at a time like this, but I don't know where else to turn." She explained the situation with the police. "Do I really have to talk to them again?"

Paul's response made Claire very glad she'd called for advice. She returned to the living room where Lieutenant Breton was leafing through the magazines on her coffee table.

"This is the morning for coincidences," she said. "I just spoke to Paul Gilbert. You're meeting in his office at one this afternoon. He suggested I meet you there at two." That Frank's lawyer would sit in went without saying. "Thank you for getting rid of that obnoxious reporter. I'll see you this afternoon."

She walked to the front door, and held it open, a not very subtle invitation for him to leave. As soon as he was gone, she'd fix herself a cup of coffee and start Monday all over again.

Paul Gilbert contemplated his morning coffee. He paused to savor the exquisite aroma before taking a sip. The coffee was Hawaiian Kona, considered by many to be the world's finest. The cup was Limoges, and the hands that held it, large but delicate with long fingers more appropriate to the piano player he'd once considered becoming than to the lawyer he was.

Paul rarely mourned the road not taken. Piano players can't afford the daily luxuries that gave him pleasure, and the Gilberts, while an old family, weren't nearly as wealthy as most assumed. Paul's practice earned a generous income, and sprinkled among the mundane wills and divorces were enough sins and misdemeanors to keep him amused. He was happily immune to the heedless passions that led others into compromising situations. Nevertheless, he enjoyed the melodrama of his clients' illicit love affairs, inconvenient pregnancies and badly behaved offspring. And this morning…

He rubbed the smooth porcelain against his lower lip and considered the curious conversation with Claire Marshall, a woman who responded to the death of her fiancé by denying the relationship. Small wonder the police wanted to talk to her again. If their interest continued, he'd refer her to a criminal defense lawyer. He took another sip.

Why would Frank lie about how long they'd been friends? He'd met Frank years ago through Bobby Austin, he'd done some sensitive legal work for Frank, but Frank and Annie Lewis Palmer had not been part of his circle. After Annie Lewis's fatal accident and a suitable period of mourning, Frank joined the thinning ranks of socially acceptable single men. Their paths crossed with increasing frequency, and a friendship developed, but only within the last few years. Hardly decades. Perhaps Claire had misunderstood something Frank said.

Paul couldn't get a bead on Claire Marshall. He knew better than most that love is ephemeral. Still, her response to Frank's death had shocked him. He'd review Frank's new will before this afternoon's meeting. If memory served, she would receive a generous bequest, contingent upon their engagement and more upon their marriage. Where that stood now was an interesting question. The money could change her mind about not being engaged to Frank.

Claire may or may not have seen the prenuptial agreement—not that it mattered now. To think that Friday night, when neither she nor Frank could be found, his greatest fear had been that his friend and client would marry without a pre-nup.

The chime of his intercom interrupted his musing. "Yes, Suzanne?"

"Melissa Yates is on line one. I told her you were in conference, but she insists upon talking to you." His normally placid receptionist, sounded aggrieved, and Paul suspected she had good cause.

"I'll take the call. But first, let me apologize for Miss Yates. She's received some very bad news." He activated the speakerphone and addressed the trollop who had been Frank Palmer's mistress for longer than anyone cared to admit.

"Melissa, my dear, please accept my deepest condolences."

"What the hell's going on? The paper says Frank's dead. The propane stove at his fish camp exploded. I don't believe it. Frank's careful with stuff like that." She took a ragged breath. "Why are the cops looking for Hatch? Who's Claire Marshall? The paper Frank was going to marry her. That's bullshit. What's going on? I have a right to know."

Paul didn't share Melissa's perspective on a mistress's right to anything, but he noted that nowhere in her tirade did she mention money, her usual concern. Moreover, unlike Claire Marshall, she appeared genuinely distressed at Frank's passing. He probably should have called her. Captain Robinson had asked his assistance in notifying family and friends. Then again, he'd left a message Friday night, asking her to call him, and she'd ignored it.

He settled on a semi-apology. "I was waiting until a decent hour to contact you, dear."

"Frank's really dead?"

"It's hard to believe, but I'm afraid it's true."

"What happens now? Is there going to be a funeral?"

"Arrangements are incomplete. However, unless something changes, the service will be three o'clock Wednesday afternoon at Saint Phillip's." It was a statement, not an invitation, but Melissa would miss the subtlety.

Frank's mistress lacked any sense of propriety, an unfortunate characteristic that had amused Frank. For a man who cared so deeply about his own good name, he'd had a surprising tolerance for Melissa's bad behavior. Paul made a mental note to enlist Bobby Austin's assistance in keeping Melissa and Claire away from each other at the funeral.

"Last Monday morning—God, was it just last Monday?" Melissa's words tumbled over each other. "Right before he drove me to the airport, Frank bought a watch, a present for a woman named Claire who was fixing up some cottage for him. He said she was doing a good job, and he wanted to give her something extra. That's her isn't it?"

"I believe Ms. Marshall is in the renovation business."

"The paper says they were going to get married." The word married dissolved in sobs.

Paul tried to erase a ghastly vision of Melissa with mascara-laden tears streaming down her cheeks. Still, he felt a twinge of sympathy; Frank should have told her.

"I've been with Frank for ten years. I'd know if there was someone else."

He let his silence say they both knew that wasn't true. Frank had enjoyed numerous liaisons over the years.

She took a tremulous breath. "Do you know her? What's she like?"

Relieved by a question that wasn't fraught, Paul answered honestly. "I met her once. She seemed pleasant, but I really had no other impression." He'd thought her attractive in an all-American, red hair and freckles way—striking green eyes—but hardly a woman he'd have chosen for Frank. She'd been polite but reserved and had contributed little to the conversation until they discussed her work. Apparently restoring old houses was her passion as well as her occupation.

"Was he really going to marry her?"

"I don't know what would have happened if Frank hadn't died." Another honest answer. Although Frank most assuredly had intended to marry Claire, her reaction to his death raised questions. If she persisted in denying a relationship, it would certainly raise eyebrows.

"What about Hatch?" Melissa said. "Where's he?"

"The police posed that very question earlier this morning. As I told them, I barely know the man and have absolutely no idea where he is. Isn't he a friend of yours?"

"Why are they looking for him?"

"Because they don't know where he is. The police have this thing about loose ends."

"I can't imagine life without Frank." She sounded as plaintive as a lost child.

"You're an attractive young woman with your life ahead of you." Paul winced at the cliché. Eloquence had deserted him in the face of a grieving Melissa Yates. Could this tramp have cared more for Frank than for his money? Or was that what she couldn't imagine living without? "I assure you, Melissa, you're provided for."

"What do you mean?"

"You should have no financial problems."

"I don't. The boutique makes money."

"So I've heard." That profitable status might or might not continue without Frank standing behind her. It didn't really matter. Whatever happened to the shop, she'd still own the building. Frank had recently deeded it to her, and properties in the Quarter were appreciating nicely. Over the years, Frank Palmer had spent thousands upon thousands of dollars keeping Melissa happy—every penny against his lawyer's advice—and the subsidy would survive his death.

The conversation had become tiresome, so Paul extricated himself. "There are a few matters for us to discuss, papers for you to sign, but nothing you should worry about. I'd like to meet with you sometime next week, once things have calmed down." He transferred the call back to Suzanne and asked her to set an appointment. Half an hour would be sufficient.

Paul freshened his coffee and considered the issue of Melissa's existence. Eventually Captain Robinson or someone working for him would learn about her. He was weighing the pros and cons of being the one to inform them when Robinson called to say dental X-rays confirmed that the body found in the cabin was Frank Palmer.

"I didn't realize there was any question."

"The preliminary identification was circumstantial, as you're aware."

A slight emphasis on that last phrase made Paul wish he'd mentioned his role in the search of Frank's cabin the first time they spoke. His personal concerns about Frank's welfare had thrown him off his game, and he'd reacted reflexively. Discretion was an ingrained habit, but in this matter, it had been a poor choice.

"I just spoke to Claire Marshall," he said. "She's meeting your colleague in my office at two. Will you be joining us?"

"Both Lieutenant Breton and I will be there."

"I look forward to meeting you in person. Your excellent reputation precedes you."

Saturday evening, he'd called Assistant Police Superintendent Henry Vernon to tell him Frank's body had been found under circumstances that should be considered suspicious. He'd asked for assurances that the investigation would be competent and discreet. "The Lafourche Parish deputies appear capable, but..."

Vernon said he'd assign the new head of the homicide division to the case. If there had been foul play, they'd be one step ahead. If not, no harm done.

"Robinson came to us from the Army. He was an outstanding officer and an excellent investigator." Vernon's review of Robinson's exemplary career—military police, college and law school at the government's expense, the Judge Advocates General Corps—came with a subtle warning. *You won't be the only smart lawyer in the room.*

Paul had assured Henry that he would welcome working with someone who knew the law. He wondered what had brought this paragon of virtue to New Orleans and how long it would take him to succumb to the local culture.

9

Daniel Doucet saw the Sheriff Department's launch, but not soon enough. They signaled for him to come alongside. Bill Reese, one of the deputies, leaned over the rail and tossed him a line.

"Morning, Daniel. You're getting a late start this morning."

"Life of leisure, that's me."

"Life of poaching is more like it."

"You come all the way out here to waste the taxpayer's money, hassling me when I ain't done nothing wrong, or are you actually working?"

"A cabin burned last week, over on Bayou Perdu. We're looking for a witness."

"Can't help you," Daniel said. "This is the first I've heard about it."

"Well, you hear anything, contact the Sheriff's Department."

"How come the sheriff cares about a cabin fire?" Daniel considered it a good riddance. If he'd thought of it, he'd have blown the asshole's place up himself.

"Owner was inside," Bill said, "a guy named Frank Palmer. He's dead."

Daniel crossed himself. It never occurred to him there'd been anyone in the cabin. If he'd known, he would've tried to help. Then he remembered the loud *whoosh*, the flames shooting into the sky and the heat on his skin. That cabin and anyone in it were history the minute it blew. He would have gotten himself killed if he'd tried to be a hero.

"You're not looking too good. Was Palmer a friend of yours?"

He shook his head. "I don't like to think of bad stuff happening around here."

"Weren't for bad stuff, I'd have to get a real job." Bill pulled his line back. "See you 'round."

Daniel watched the launch move away. If deputies were out looking for witnesses, he'd best keep to legal water. Regardless, he'd be staying away from that end of Bayou Perdu. A violent death meant the asshole's spirit might linger looking for vengeance. Palmer's spirit, he corrected himself. He rubbed his Saint Andrew medal and asked forgiveness for thinking ill of the dead.

He motored over to the closest legal bed, dropped anchor and picked up his oyster tongs, but his mind was elsewhere. Whoever torched the cabin must have killed Palmer. He mulled that over for a moment. He, Daniel Doucet, a man who believed in minding his own business, had witnessed a murder. Not that he actually saw the killer. Hadn't even gotten a good look at his vehicle. He'd picked himself up off the bottom of his boat, with no thought to anything but getting out of there.

But the killer might have seen me.

With sickening certainty, Daniel realized there was no might about it. He'd sped right up the middle of the bayou. A blind man could have seen him. A deaf man could have heard him. The killer who was most likely up top of the levee by then would have seen and heard. Fear quickened his pulse. No killer wants a witness.

His first thought was to hole up in the swamps until things blew over. He knew his way around these bayous better than anybody. A second thought said that was a lousy idea. This time of year, the mosquitoes were a plague. He'd have to run into town for supplies, which meant people would know he was around.

Hiding wasn't the answer. He needed to put distance between himself and the burned cabin. A quick review of acquaintances who had moved away produced no one who'd be happy to put him up for a couple weeks, and he couldn't afford more than a couple nights in a motel.

A solution stared him in the face. He just didn't want to see it. The family shrimp boat was going back out first thing tomorrow. No killer could track him down on the boat. The old man didn't know where they'd be one day to the next. It depended on the catch and the weather. He'd be safe, but sanctuary came at a high price, two or three weeks stuck on a thirty-foot boat with his father and three older brothers giving him orders like he was a little kid. He spat into the water.

Daniel motored back to Ray's, keeping an eye out for unfamiliar craft. He winched his boat out of the water, unscrewed the plugs to let her drain and carefully hosed off the salt.

His boat was top of the line. A sixteen-foot fiberglass bateau, it could float in eight inches of water yet had enough freeboard to handle the open Gulf on calm days. The motor was one of the new four-stroke Hondas. It cost more but ran quieter and used less fuel than any two-stroke. He'd worked hard to pay for that boat, and he took good care of it.

He finished putting up the boat and walked over to the café. At midmorning, the front room was empty, but pots bubbling on the stove said Ray hadn't gone far. Daniel checked the back room and saw Ray's fat ass hanging out of a booth in the far corner. Daniel couldn't see who else was there or hear what they were talking about, and he had other things on his mind.

He pushed open the bathroom door. The sign said unisex, but that was a joke. Obscene suggestions and centerfolds torn from girlie magazines covered all four walls, and some athlete had drawn a naked woman on the ceiling. If any female had ever walked into this dump, forget used the bathroom, it was news to Daniel.

The sports page sitting on top of the tank reminded him that the rest of the paper should be out front. He hadn't wanted to seem too interested when he was talking to Bill Reese, but he better learn more about that fire. Like, did the sheriff's department suspect it was no accident? He finished his business and returned to the front room. The newspaper wasn't on the counter.

"Hey Ray," he hollered. "Where's the paper?"

His cousin lumbered out of the back room, carrying his morning beer in one hand and the newspaper in the other. "You want the sports page?" He flipped through. "It ain't here."

"It's in the can. I was looking for the rest."

Ray put his beer down, leaned on the counter until his nose was inches away from Daniel's, and stared with this bug-eyed look on his face. Then he started moving his eyes from one side to the other, shifty like.

Daniel drew back. "What's with you? How about getting me a cup of coffee. You got a fresh pot?" He picked up the front section.

"Just coffee? Sure you don't want a bowl of gumbo?" Ray lifted the lid off a big pot. He held the lid in one hand and twitched the thumb of his other hand toward the back room.

"No thanks." The gumbo smelled good, but he was too worried to be hungry, and Ray's weird behavior wasn't helping.

Before he could ask what the hell was going on, Ray got back in his face. "Jason Corlette," he whispered.

Daniel caught on. Jason was here, in the back room. He nodded to show he got the message. Jason wasn't a bad guy, but everyone knew he was the sharpest deputy in the department, which made him the last lawman he wanted to see this morning.

"Did you hear about the cabin that burned over on Bayou Perdu?" Ray poured a cup of coffee. "The paper says the propane blew. The owner was inside. A guy named Frank Palmer. You know who I'm talking about? He'd stop in sometimes, pick up some gumbo to go."

"I might know him if I saw him."

"It was one of them tragic things," Ray continued. "Palmer was getting married next weekend. This woman he was going to marry, she's already a widow. And now her fiancé, he's gone too. Man, you got to feel for her." Ray wiped the counter with a corner of his dirty apron and put the coffee down. "You didn't hear nothing about this?"

"Yeah, I did. I ran into Bill Reese and he asked me about it but I couldn't help him." Daniel spoke loud and clear so that Jason could hear every word. "I never go over there. That water's posted, and I got nothing to do with oysters these days. I'm working on the old man's boat." The coffee tasted as if it had been sitting on the burner for a week. He pushed the cup away. "This stuff sucks."

"Hey, there's nothing wrong with my coffee."

"Sorry. I didn't mean no harm. I've been sick to my stomach. You know how you get sick and everything tastes off."

Out of the corner of his eye, Daniel saw Jason Corlette duck to avoid hitting his head on the low doorframe. He stared into his coffee cup and wished he'd left when he had the chance.

"Maybe you got a bad oyster?" Jason took a stool a couple down and spun around to face him, like they were buddies hanging out together.

"Hey man, how're you doing?" Daniel played along. "How's the deputy business?"

"Keeps me busy. Hey, I'm sorry about Jimmy Orielle. He was kin to your mother wasn't he?"

"She's related to half the parish, but thanks." Jimmy had died Saturday morning. The doctors said the third day was crucial for burn victims, and he hadn't made it. The fact that he got burned trying to hotwire someone's Jeep made it worse. Jimmy was a little wild sometimes, but not a bad kid. He would have outgrown it if he'd lived a little longer.

"I heard Ray telling you about the cabin fire." Jason said. "I'm here looking for someone who might have seen what happened."

"I already told Bill Reese, you're not looking for me. I never go over there. And last couple of days, I've been sick, not going anywhere." He was pretty sure Jason hadn't noticed anything funny about his reaction, but he needed to be real careful and keep acting natural.

"We had some weather last week," he said. "Did the cabin get hit by lightning?"

"The fire was arson."

"Goddamn, that's terrible." They knew. He didn't have to feel bad about not saying anything.

"So, you remember Lucille? Little brunette, nice legs, she answers the phone at headquarters."

"Maybe," Daniel said, puzzled by the change in topic.

"She thought Palmer's name sounded familiar, so she checked her notes. Sure enough, he called about you, not even two weeks ago."

"Me? No way."

"He said you were taking oysters from posted water up by his cabin."

"It wasn't me." Daniel really felt sick now. "I didn't know the guy, and he didn't know me. This morning is the first I've heard his name, and that's 'cause his cabin blew up."

"So how do you know it blew up?"

"Ray just told me it was the propane. You must of heard him. What the hell is this?" He acted indignant, an innocent man wrongly accused.

"I'm looking for a witness," Jason said. "I don't care where you get oysters."

"Hey man, I told you, no oysters, and I don't know nothing about the fire."

"So, when I arrived, your truck was outside, but you weren't around, and your boat was gone. I hear a boat come in, and a few minutes later, you walk in. Don't bullshit me Daniel."

"What you heard was me motoring over to the winch. What I been doing is putting my boat up. I ain't going to be using it for a while, because I'm going out with the old man."

Jason leaned back and stretched his legs out, settling in. "It's not just the sheriff," he said. "The New Orleans cops, they're interested, too. They're helping us with the investigation."

"So what?"

"So, when we tell them about Palmer's phone call, they're going to think you torched the cabin in some kind of retaliation. Me?" Jason pointed to his own chest. "I don't see it that way."

"I didn't torch nothing. Who the hell are you, accusing me of that kind of shit?" This time, Daniel's indignation was genuine.

"No accusation, I'm just warning you how it looks bad. Palmer reports you poaching near his cabin. Two weeks go by, his cabin burns down, and he's dead inside."

Daniel kept quiet, trying to figure out how much Jason knew and how much he was guessing. No way Palmer gave them his name, but he could have caught the name of his boat.

"I know you, and I know you take oysters from posted water. That's between you and the boys from Wildlife and Fisheries." Jason waved his hand like he was brushing away a pesky fly. "I don't see you torching any cabins. The New Orleans cops, they don't know you. They won't understand the way you look at things. So, you have a choice. You can talk to me, or you can talk to them."

"I don't have to talk to no one. Last I heard this was still a free country." Daniel threw a buck on the counter. "For the coffee," he told Ray, who was standing there looking stupid.

He slid off the stool and stomped out the door, praying that he'd make it to his truck without feeling Jason's big hand on his shoulder. He pulled out of the parking lot, safe for now, but he'd better catch up with the old man. He'd be in deep shit if Jason got there first and found out that no one knew anything about him joining the crew.

10

Claire pushed through a heavy revolving door into a stunning lobby. Light streamed through stained glass windows high on the back wall, marble tiled the floors, and elaborate brass geometry framed the elevators. She told the man at the information desk that she had an appointment with Paul Gilbert and, after signing in, asked if Frank Lloyd Wright had been involved in the design of the building.

"The architect was one of Wright's disciples." He gave her a quick history of the building, speaking with the zeal of a man who is delighted to have found a fellow enthusiast. "The local preservation society begins one of its tours with this building. The next one starts at two-thirty."

"I don't think I'll be finished in time." Paul had told her to schedule an hour. "But I'd rather be going on the tour." She'd rather be changing Dorian's litter box. Waiting upstairs were two policemen and a lawyer, all of whom probably thought she'd been engaged to Frank Palmer.

Despite the extra half pill she'd taken, apprehension made her hands clammy. The bubble waited, threatening to close in if they started talking about... What? She couldn't predict her panic attacks. Finding the burned cabin had triggered one, but learning Frank's body was inside had not. Months of counseling hadn't helped her find the cause. She dreaded this meeting; maybe she should take the other half.

Paul's offices were on the fifth floor. The elevator opened into a reception area, less dramatic but equally as elegant as the downstairs lobby. An attractive, middle-aged woman looked up from her computer monitor and smiled a welcome. "You must be Claire. I'm Suzanne. Let me show you to the small conference room. They're waiting."

"Nice to meet you, Suzanne." She forced a return smile. "Is there a ladies' room?"

"Down that hall, second door on the right. I'll tell them you're here."

Claire locked the bathroom door and leaned against it, taking slow deep breaths, telling herself there was nothing to fear. She swallowed the other half pill, replaced the lipstick she'd chewed off, and walked back to the reception desk.

"I'm ready now."

Paul Gilbert, Lieutenant Breton, and a nice-looking dark-haired man she'd never seen before sat at a small conference table. They stood when she walked in, Lieutenant Breton the last on his feet. The stranger introduced himself as Mike Robinson. Paul pulled out the empty chair next to his. The two policemen sat across the table. Behind them a window showed blue sky.

"Captain Robinson heads the police department's homicide division," Paul murmured as he seated her.

Homicide? Had Frank been murdered? Before she could ask, Paul offered her something to drink. She requested water and took a sip to moisten her dry mouth. Everyone was watching her. She looked out the window and imagined waves rolling across the blue sky.

"Why do you want to talk to me, Captain Robinson?" She knew the answer, but she wanted more time to compose herself, more time for that last bit of Xanax to kick in.

"We're investigating the death of Frank Palmer. What can you tell us about him?"

"Frank hired my company to restore a cottage he owned. I was looking for him Saturday morning. I found the burned cabin and reported it to the local authorities. When I saw the picture of Frank's driver on the news, I called them again. Deputy Corlette asked me to come to his office and be interviewed. I understand you have the tape of our conversation." Her statement probably sounded rehearsed. It was.

"Why were you looking for Mr. Palmer?"

"There was a problem with a check. His bank covered it, but still..." Mentioning the rumor about being engaged to Frank would only lend it credence. Let someone else bring it up.

"You drove all that way about a check the bank had covered?"

"I also wanted to see the cabin. Frank was planning to fix it up. He'd asked me to prepare a cost estimate." She caught the flicker of disbelief on Paul's face and added, "He didn't want anyone else to know. It was going to be a surprise for his fishing buddies."

Captain Robinson made a note. "Mr. Palmer had his own construction company, but he hired yours?"

"His company works on large commercial projects. Authentic Restorations specializes in historic houses, small projects like the cottage we're restoring for him." She relaxed, comfortable with this topic. "Frank won the cottage in a bet, and then he learned it was dilapidated. He couldn't tear it down because it had been designated historic. The previous owner had been trying to sell it for years. Frank planned to get the last laugh by fixing it up and selling it for a good price. He hired us to do the work."

"I wondered about Frank's sudden interest in historic preservation," Paul said, "but I thought he'd bought that place."

"Our typical client is a young couple with a tight budget," Claire continued. "Frank was different. He kept close track of expenses, but he could afford to do everything right."

"You met Mr. Palmer when he hired your firm?" Captain Robinson said.

"We met at The Children's Home last spring when I spoke at a seminar on non-traditional careers for women. It was part of their program for adolescent girls, which Frank sponsors. Afterwards, he came up and introduced himself. Later—I think it was the third week in August—he called and asked me to look at this cottage. He liked my proposal and signed the contract. We began work last month."

"You must be aware that people believe you and Mr. Palmer planned to marry."

"People are mistaken." Paul was one of those people. She looked for his reaction but saw none.

"So where did everybody get this crazy idea?" Lieutenant Breton, who'd been slouched in his chair with his eyes half closed, spoke for the first time.

Before she could respond, Paul put a restraining hand on her arm. "You're asking Claire to speculate. While she isn't, strictly speaking, a client, I volunteered to sit in during this interview, and I always advise against speculation." He removed his hand. "You should do what you think best, Claire, but the wise course is usually to answer the specific question and stick to what you know is true. You'd agree with that wouldn't you, Mike?"

Captain Robinson nodded agreement, but he didn't retract his partner's question.

"I don't know," Claire said. Without Paul's intervention, she would have told them that she thought Frank was the source, and then had to explain why. And maybe she was wrong. She'd be here all afternoon, speculating. *Thank you, Paul.*

"How would you describe your relationship with Frank Palmer?" Captain Robinson said.

"Cordial. A business relationship, but cordial."

As she spoke, Claire felt everyone's eyes on her. Paul was watching her carefully, without expression. What must he be thinking? Lieutenant Breton's hound-dog face conveyed a bored contempt. Well, she didn't have much use for him either. Captain Robinson's blue gaze was thoughtful. He didn't miss a thing. If she were a criminal, she wouldn't want him investigating her.

"Did you consider him a friend?" he said.

His question caught her by surprise. She didn't, but she was reluctant to say so in front of Paul. She settled on a white lie. "If we'd had time to become better acquainted, I think we'd have become friends."

"Didn't the two of you go out socially?"

"No."

"Not even an occasional dinner date?" Captain Robinson's attention never wavered.

She glanced at Paul, who was staring down at the table. One evening when she and Frank were eating dinner at Mother's, Paul had stopped by the table to say hello and stayed to chat until their food arrived. He must have mentioned it to the police.

"Only working dinners," she said. "When you're restoring an old house, especially one that's in bad shape, you really don't know what you have until you open the walls. Friday afternoons, Frank and I would meet on site to evaluate the situation, explore alternatives, and discuss plans for the next week. If it got late, we continued our discussion over dinner."

"People who saw you together might assume your relationship went beyond business?"

Once again, Captain Robinson made the statement a question. Deputy Corlette had used the same technique. Maybe all policemen did. Claire found it annoying. And she wasn't going to speculate about what people might think. She shrugged.

"Two single adults, working closely together," he continued. "It would have been natural for a relationship to develop?"

"Our relationship was purely business."

"Your social engagements with Frank Palmer amounted to a few after-work dinners?"

"No social engagements, four working dinners since we've been working on his cottage."

"Who paid for the meals?" Lieutenant Breton said.

"Frank did. If he hadn't picked up the check, I would have billed the project. He knew that. Pay now or pay later. Those were working dinners." The police could ask their question as many different ways as they wanted. Her answer wouldn't change.

"You drove down to Mr. Palmer's cabin Saturday morning?"

"I did, and Deputy Corlette already asked about that. It's all on the tape."

"We just want to be sure you didn't forget anything."

"Why did you wash your car?" Lieutenant Breton said.

"It was covered with mud." She looked to Paul, silently asking how many more stupid questions she'd have to answer, but she didn't really care. The extra meds had kicked in and she was floating a few inches above the table.

"When was the last time you saw Frank Palmer?" Captain Robinson moved on.

"He drove me to the airport Monday afternoon."

"Do your clients usually drive you around?" Lieutenant Breton said.

"Did he drive or did Hatch?" Captain Robinson said.

"Frank drove. He wanted to talk to me, and he knew I was going to be gone for a week."

"Did he appear to be under stress?"

She remembered the scene about the fish camp, but that was several days earlier. Frank had seemed fine on the trip to the airport. "Nothing unusual. Construction is a high-stress business." She shrugged again. "I'm not sure I knew Frank well enough to judge his moods."

"I have another appointment," Paul said. "You told me to schedule an hour. We're running over." His statement brought the session to an end.

"If we have any more questions, we'll be in touch." Captain Robinson said. "Thank you for your excellent coffee, Paul."

"I hope you don't mind if I let Suzanne show you to the elevator."

"Not at all."

After the policemen left, Claire said, "Thank you for keeping my foot out of my mouth." Paul looked startled and she clarified. "By speculating. Please, let me pay you for your time."

"Absolutely not. It's all part of my job as Frank's executor, and I will bill the estate." He glanced at the clock. "There are additional considerations involving the estate that I'd like to discuss with you, but time truly is running short. Perhaps we could meet early next week."

"What considerations? Oh, the cottage. I wasn't thinking." The pills had transformed the terrifying bubble into a soft cocoon, warm and welcoming but not conducive to making business decisions. "You're right. I'd rather wait a few days."

"Whenever you're ready. May I call you a cab?"

His receptionist made the call while he walked her to the elevator.

Before she stepped in, she said, "I'm sorry. Very sorry." And she really was. She was sorry that his friend had died, sorry that she might be making him feel worse by insisting she and Frank hadn't been engaged, sorry that she'd taken up so much of his time. Paul seemed like a nice man, and she was sorry to burden him. She'd write him a thank you note the minute she returned to the office—no, not her office, home. She was tired and a little fuzzy.

The meeting hadn't been the expected ordeal. Captain Robinson was a pleasant surprise, well spoken and courteous. He'd introduced himself as Mike, but Captain fit him better. He and Paul had a lot in common. Both were tall, dark-haired, and attractive, intelligent and articulate. They were about the same age—early forties, she'd guess—but otherwise very different: the urbane lawyer versus the observant investigator. Sloppy rude Lieutenant Breton had been the odd man out.

When the taxi dropped her off at the driveway, Claire noticed that the pedestrian gate was open again. She made a mental note to speak to the Clarke's housekeeper about setting the lock and ambled down the winding drive, stopping to inhale the heady scent of a late-blooming gardenia. Living behind the Clarke mansion was like having her own private park. She'd been lucky to find such a wonderful rental.

She opened her front door, and the shrill tones of the ringing phone shattered her hazy calm. The calls had begun that morning, soon after Lieutenant Breton left. Frank's friends, people she'd never met, offered their condolences and asked if there was anything they could do for her. People she and Tom had known, doctors who'd worked with him and people she hadn't seen since his funeral, were calling too.

At first, she'd tried to explain. Of course, she was saddened by Frank's death, but there was never any romance, certainly no marriage plans. The news stories were inaccurate. He was a client, not a lover.

Reactions had ranged from embarrassed laughter to incredulity, and Claire quickly realized that her position was untenable. If Frank were alive, when time passed with no marriage, everyone would see the truth, no matter who said what. But he was dead, and she couldn't prove a negative. There was no way to win an argument with a dead man.

After several uncomfortable conversations, she'd given up and began letting the answering machine screen her calls. She waited to hear this message, expecting another stranger's voice. The call was from her mother, and she sounded upset.

Claire picked up the phone.

11

Moments after Claire finished soothing her outraged mother, the phone rang again. She ignored it. But then she recognized Captain Robinson's voice on the answering machine. She grabbed the receiver.

"What do you want?" Before he could respond, she lit into him. "I just spent half an hour on the phone with my mother, trying to reassure her that I'm not on my way to jail. Was it absolutely necessary for Lieutenant Breton to call her? And the Ryans? Why did he have to call them?"

"It wasn't our intention to upset your mother. We were verifying your statement."

"You were verifying *her* statement. When my mother said neighbors had hosted a party for her, Lieutenant Breton asked for their names and contact information. As if she was not to be trusted." Claire took a deep breath and forced herself to stop yelling. "Your partner embarrassed my mother. Lucy Ryan will probably tell all of Centreville about the call from the New Orleans police."

"It's standard–"

She cut him off. "Why did you feel it necessary to verify something as innocuous as my mother's birthday party? And why are homicide detectives investigating Frank's death?"

He ignored both questions. "I'd like to talk with you again. You and Mr. Gilbert, if that's your preference. It shouldn't take long."

"No. I've already imposed on Paul's good will today. He had other appointments."

"Tomorrow would be fine, but I thought you might want to get it over with."

"You're right; I do. And you know what? There's no reason to bother Paul." She agreed to meet him in his office at five-thirty.

Captain Robinson was on the phone when she arrived. He waved her toward a straight-backed chair facing his desk, held up one finger, and told the person on the other end that his guest had arrived.

Guest? That wasn't how she saw it. She sat down, folded her hands in her lap, and crossed her ankles like a wayward pupil called to the principal's office.

His office walls were barren of pictures and painted that unfortunate green someone in government had decided was restful. Fixed windows looked out on the brick wall of a neighboring building. An electric coffeemaker, bottled water, and a stack of Styrofoam cups that sat on the windowsill were the only signs of human occupancy. His desk was clear except for a stacked inbox-outbox, full but not overflowing, and the phone.

Claire couldn't imagine working in such a sterile environment. Her office was controlled chaos with piles of paper covering the horizontal surfaces and color-coded Post-Its stuck to the wall behind her desk. It was also light and airy, with three windows that opened and potted plants on the sills. And, despite the untidy appearance, she knew exactly where everything was.

"Thank you for coming in." He pushed a lock of hair off his forehead. "I'd like to start by clarifying the situation. You're here at my invitation, and of your own free will. You haven't been charged with a crime, but we're going to discuss events that could lead to criminal charges. Anything you say could be used against you in a court of law. You can refuse to answer any question if, in your opinion, the answer could be incriminating. If, at any point, you decide you want a lawyer present, we'll adjourn until you can arrange counsel."

Paul had warned against speculating, and now this policeman warned about incriminating herself. Criminals were warned, not witnesses. She wasn't a criminal. She squared her shoulders.

"Take notes. Tape it. I don't care."

"We're working with the Lafourche Parish Sheriff's Office."

"I've already explained. There was no way to report the fire immediately, so I called from the beach. I can't believe that's a crime, certainly not one worthy of all this attention."

He studied her for a long moment. "If the fire was out, there was no urgency. For all you knew, it had already been reported."

"Thank you for an excellent excuse. I'll use it if I ever talk to Deputy Corlette again." She tried a smile, which he didn't return.

"Deputy Corlette was under the impression that you called as soon as you reached a phone."

She started to say she'd never said anything about the timeframe but reconsidered and said nothing.

"A witness saw you exiting your driveway shortly before seven Saturday morning," he said. "You reported the fire at one forty-five, almost seven hours later. Driving time would account for no more than two or three of those hours."

"I was at the cabin for a while, looking around, trying to use the boat's radio. I got lost on the way back to the highway. I was a filthy mess. When I got to the beach, I took a shower at the public bathhouse and bought new clothes. Then I called."

His expression said he found her explanation inadequate, but she didn't expand it. She hadn't mentioned her panic attack before, and now it was too late. The truth would sound like a made-up excuse. Besides, it was none of his business. She wasn't going to tell him about her personal problems, and he couldn't prove she hadn't been lost for hours. It was a standoff.

"As I mentioned, we're working with Lafourche Parish." His tone stayed casual, but there was nothing casual about the way he watched her. "Their investigators have determined that the cabin fire was arson."

"Arson? You mean someone set the cabin on fire? On purpose?" A flutter of anxiety tightened her throat. The children Tom rescued had built a bonfire of toys and newspapers on their bedroom floor. The little boy admitted it afterwards, but he would never say why. The arson investigator said he wasn't a bad kid. Four-year-olds often play with matches.

Claire stared out the window and imagined waves washing up onto the brick wall, slow and implacable, white foam on red bricks. She slowed her breath to match their rhythm, inhaling with one wave and exhaling with the next.

"Are you all right?" His question broke the spell.

She met his gaze. "Frank is dead. The arsonist is a murderer."

He frowned, as if considering this possibility for the first time. "We don't know if that's the case or not. Mr. Palmer was dead before the fire started."

"Thank God, Frank didn't die in the fire." Claire slapped her hand across her mouth. She hadn't meant to speak aloud, but the words were out, and she couldn't take them back.

"What difference does it make if he died in the fire or before the fire?"

She could only shake her head. He handed her a Kleenex, and she realized that her cheeks were wet with tears.

"Did you set the fire, Ms. Marshall?"

"No."

"Then why are you relieved that the fire didn't kill Frank Palmer?"

"It's a terrible way to die." There would be no more tears. She was past crying. "Do you have any other questions?"

"Yes, but first would you like a cup of coffee? A glass of water?" He gestured toward the windowsill.

"No, thank you. But please go ahead."

When he stood and turned his back, her hand slid into her purse, found the vial, and removed a pill. She waited until he was pouring his coffee and popped it into her mouth—nothing extra like this afternoon, just her evening pill a little ahead of schedule.

He sat back down. "Your mother said you cut your visit short because of a problem with the work you were doing for Mr. Palmer."

"That's right." Claire thought about the excuse she'd given her mother. She wondered if the police were already looking for the non-existent problem subcontractor. Were they asking the phone company for a list of numbers called from her mother's house?

Frank's death had transformed a little white lie into a possibly criminal misstatement. She'd already told Captain Robinson about the bad check. In as few words as possible, she told him about the telephone conversations that made her decide to return early and confront Frank.

"Why didn't you mention this before?" he said.

"I wasn't sure Frank was the source of the marriage rumors. I'm still not." Her smile was rueful. "I didn't want to speculate."

She waited for him to ask, who else might it have been, a question she'd been asking herself. Instead, he asked about her activities Friday afternoon and evening after she returned to New Orleans. She answered truthfully but couldn't provide any collaborating evidence after she picked Dorian up at the kennel. She'd treated herself to dinner out because it had been such a lousy day. She'd been too immersed in her own thoughts to notice anyone, but she thought more than one person had waited on her. The restaurant didn't take credit cards. She'd paid in cash and not kept the bill. She'd gone to a movie but remembered little more than the plot and the names of the stars.

"You're just going to have to believe me. Why would I lie?"

"I don't have anymore questions, but if you think of anything else, please call me." He stood and handed her his business card.

Her fingertips slid across the raised lettering, hard and slippery on the soft paper, and a torrent of memory washed the present away. She was back in the bungalow where she and Tom had lived. The policeman who'd brought the terrible news was talking. She wanted him to leave, but he kept talking.

"We need you to come downtown and identify your husband's body," he'd said. "We know this is difficult, but it has to be done. Your husband was a hero, Mrs. Marshall. He saved the lives of two little children.

"Call when you're ready, and I'll meet you at the morgue." He handed her a business card.

She had reached out to take it, and her fingertips slid across the raised lettering...

"Ms. Marshall, are you all right?" Captain Robinson was beside her, a supporting hand on her elbow.

"I'm fine, thank you, just tired." She walked out of his office on legs that were only a little shaky.

The light on her message machine was blinking rapidly. Again. Claire checked to be sure neither her mother nor Jack had called while she was at the police station. They hadn't, but the couple who'd bought the bungalow had left their prayers that God give her strength to face this latest tragedy. They were nice people who'd written her a note after they moved in, saying how much they enjoyed the house, what a good job she'd done restoring it.

She'd talked Tom into buying that bungalow when they moved to New Orleans for his residency. The evenings and weekends when he stayed at the hospital, she worked on the house. She pulled up old linoleum and found heart pine floors, removed layers of paint and refinished the old cypress woodwork. She'd met Jack when she hired his company to help with the heavy lifting.

Selling the house was supposed to finance their move to New York City. Instead, the money went into her new business, her new life. She poured a glass of wine and carried it out onto the porch. She wasn't supposed to drink while she was on the meds, but one glass couldn't hurt.

Dorian had finished eating and sat on the top step watching swifts glide and dive, their dark swoops silhouetted against the sky and then invisible in the shadows. Above the trees, lavender clouds floated in a dark purple sky. The peaceful setting belied the ugliness of a world where people committed arson and murder.

Captain Robinson hadn't answered any of her questions, not directly, but now she understood why a homicide detective was investigating Frank's death.

Frank hadn't died in the fire. Captain Robinson had asked why that mattered, but she couldn't explain without telling him about the awful day Tom died, the lost days that followed, and the long walks that, no matter the original destination, always brought her to the burned house. She would stand on the sidewalk and imagine that things had ended differently, that Tom was still with her.

At first, he was.

Walking down the street, she would glimpse him from the corner of her eye, but when she looked again, it would be a tall, dark-haired man she didn't know. An old gray Corolla would drive around the corner, and she'd peer inside, but the driver's face was never familiar. In a crowded restaurant, she'd hear Tom's laugh and spin around, heart in her throat, to search a room full of strangers. Each disappointment brought a fresh sense of loss—and anxiety.

Eventually the sightings stopped. Claire was relieved, but then she realized that her memories had gone too. She couldn't remember Tom's face unless she looked at his picture. Her anxiety intensified, and the panic attacks began. The first time, she'd been sure she was dying. Death comes once, but panic attacks strike again and again without warning. Recovering alcoholics aren't the only people who have to live one day at a time.

Reminders of how Tom died triggered her anxiety. She still couldn't see what hidden fear lurked there—visiting his grave hadn't provided any clue—but she remained determined to figure it out. She'd been coping better until Frank's death scraped the scabs off, and she wasn't going to give up now.

Of course, how a person died mattered.

I should have asked how Frank died.

Captain Robinson probably thought she was a cold and uncaring person, indifferent to the death of this man she was supposedly marrying.

No, it's worse than that.

Someone had killed Frank and set the cabin on fire to destroy the evidence. Captain Robinson thought she was that someone. When he asked if she burned the cabin, he was really asking if she'd killed Frank. That's why he'd wanted to question her again.

As if he sensed her distress, Dorian jumped onto the swing and settled onto her lap. The purring cat was a comforting presence, warm, soft and non-judgmental. People would react differently. When those strangers who'd called with condolences learned the cabin fire was arson, their sympathy would turn to suspicion.

Part of it was her fault. She'd overreacted to everything—the rumors, the burned cabin, even Captain Robinson's business card. If only she hadn't come back early. If only she hadn't been so preoccupied Friday night. Or had just gone to a restaurant that took credit cards. If only she hadn't suffered a panic attack. If only she hadn't taken too many pills.

"If only" could be the most worthless phrase in the English language. You can't change history, she knew that. She'd gotten herself in this mess, and she'd better get herself out.

Claire closed her eyes and saw again the blackened pilings rising from the ashes. The smell of smoke and dampness of ground fog caught in her throat as if they'd followed her home. She felt the charred rubble crunching under her feet, water dripping from the trees, the cold. The clearing and everything in it had been cold. She'd walked through the ashes, rummaged around in them with her bare hands, and felt no warmth. Blackened spars lay around the clearing, none of them smoldering. The smoke had smelled old, like rotten ham.

That fire had been out for a long time, which meant the cabin had burned while she was in Michigan. If she could prove that, the police would have to acknowledge her innocence, leave her alone, and go find the real criminal.

An old wooden building would have made quite a blaze. The smoke would have been visible for miles. There were no other cabins nearby, but Frank had mentioned buying gumbo from a café across the bayou. He was going to take her there for lunch after they looked at the cabin.

She'd start with the café.

12

Daniel woke at the usual five thirty but instead of getting up, lay in bed feeling sorry for himself. His head hurt, thanks to the six-pack he'd consumed while watching the Raiders eke one out over the Broncos. He'd put twenty dollars on the Raiders, but the Broncos beat the spread. His money was gone. And today, he'd be gone, out on the family shrimp boat.

Or maybe not…

Yesterday, after talking to Corlette, he'd driven straight from Ray's down to the docks, ready to jump onboard and get the hell out of Dodge. He'd been surprised to find his father there alone.

"I decided to join the crew," he'd said. "Where's everyone? I thought you were going out this afternoon."

"One of the diesels seized up. Sammy's got it. Lucky it didn't happen offshore."

"Ain't nothing lucky about being stuck here." He'd freaked out, still thinking the killer might be looking for him. "When's it going to be fixed?"

"Sammy says tomorrow noon. If you're in such a big hurry, you can pick it up."

Picking it up meant going into town, and Daniel didn't want to do that. "Why don't you send Charlie? His truck is bigger."

"You want to join the crew, but the first thing I tell you to do, you try to weasel out." His father turned back to the rope he was coiling.

"Okay, I'll do it."

"I heard about that cabin fire where the guy died. Isn't that near where you go?"

"I don't know. I didn't see nothing." Daniel had shrugged, trying to act cool, but he could feel his eyelid twitching. *First Jason Corlette and now his father. If the killer came asking around about who might have been up there...* He'd rubbed his eye, hoping his father hadn't noticed the twitch. "Tomorrow noon, I'll pick up the diesel at Sammy's."

He'd driven home and rigged an alarm system so no one could sneak up on him. Twenty-four hours, he'd told himself, you just got to keep safe for twenty-four hours. As time passed and nothing happened, he'd calmed down and thought things over. The cabin burned last Wednesday.

If the killer was going to come after him, he'd have already come. Last night for sure, wouldn't he?

In the cold hard light of morning, Daniel saw that the bad engine had really been good luck. Otherwise he'd already be out in the Gulf and stuck on the family shrimp boat for two weeks.

He'd better pick up the diesel. Otherwise the old man would be really pissed. When he got down to the dock, he'd tell them that he'd changed his mind. Tomorrow he'd be back out on his boat, doing what he wanted to do. His positive outlook lasted until Ray called a little after ten.

"Hey Danny. You know the guy who died in the fire. His fiancée's on her way to your place."

"What the hell are you talking about?"

"She didn't say she was the one, but she introduced herself, and I recognized her name from the newspaper."

"You've been talking to the dead guy's fiancée?" Daniel struggled to get his head around what Ray was saying.

"She's looking for a witness, someone who might have seen the cabin fire."

"A witness?" His blood went cold.

"She asked about Wednesday, specifically, and I remembered you coming in Wednesday afternoon, acting kind of strange."

"Wednesday," he said. The news never said nothing about when the cabin burned, and neither did Jason. Only him and the killer knew it happened Wednesday afternoon. Only him and the killer knew there was a witness. This fiancée was the killer, and she was coming after him.

"You told her my name? Where I live?" Was his cousin really that stupid?

"She's a nice lady, but it's up to you. You don't want to help her, say you weren't there."

"When did she leave the café?"

"A couple minutes ago."

Daniel's hand closed around St. Andrew. His mother had warned him about certain women who seduced a man, took him for all he was worth, and then did away with him. Every now and then you read about one of them. The newspapers called them black widows. He used to think it was all a crock; he did not think so anymore. Thanks to Cousin Ray, Palmer's black widow girlfriend was on her way to his house. And why would she be looking for a witness except to silence him?

She could be here in fifteen minutes. He hung up and grabbed his shotgun. On the way out, he sprinkled juju dust across the threshold. Not that he really believed in that stuff, but it couldn't hurt. All she had to do was bust open his door, throw in some gasoline and light a match. His home, an almost new doublewide, would burn as fast and hot as Palmer's cabin.

Daniel made certain both barrels were loaded before he tucked his shotgun behind the passenger side seat. The black widow was not likely to find him - not when he knew she was after him, but there was nothing wrong with being careful. She probably had one of those little pearl-handled pistols tucked into her pocketbook. Any gun was dangerous, especially in the hands of a woman. You could never tell what a woman was going to do.

He killed a couple hours driving around, keeping a low profile, and at five to twelve, pulled into the parking lot behind Sammy's Engine Repair, a cinderblock building on the edge of downtown. He looked around to make sure no strange woman lurked nearby and climbed out of his truck. Sammy's new wife was minding the office.

"Where's Sammy?" he said. He knew Linda, but they weren't what you'd call friends.

"What kind of hello is that, Daniel?" she said. "You never did have any manners."

"I'm here to pick up my old man's engine. It's supposed to be ready at noon."

"Sammy didn't mention it to me, but he'll be back in a few minutes." She looked him over. "Hey, I bet you know about that cabin fire."

"What cabin fire?" He felt his eyelid twitching and turned away so she couldn't see.

"Don't pretend to be dumber than you already are. You know what I'm talking about."

"No I don't, and I ain't got all day. When's Sammy coming back?"

"I told you, in a couple minutes. Since when is your time so important? And why do you keep looking out the window? You're supposed to look at a person when you're talking to them."

He edged past her. "I'll wait in the shop." Five minutes of Linda and his headache was back worse than before.

The shop smelled like diesel fuel and hot metal. Daniel wandered around, looking at the big engines and trying not to think about the killer who was looking for him. He wished he hadn't left his shotgun in the truck. *Where the hell is Sammy? He's the one who said noon.*

"Yo, Danny, the wife said you were hiding out back here." Sammy stood in the doorway a big grin on his face. "She says you can't take a little teasing."

"I came to pick up my old man's engine." Daniel hated it when anyone outside the family called him Danny.

"Bad news, Danny. The truck came in this morning, but they didn't have the part."

"No way."

"Way." Sammy said. "Next delivery is Thursday morning. I'll call to make sure they get the part on the truck this time. Soon as it gets here, I'll start work. I'll try to have it done by noon Thursday."

"You said noon today."

"I can't fix the engine if I don't have the part. Tell the old man I'm real sorry, but there's nothing I can do about those lazy old boys back at the warehouse."

Linda came up behind Sammy. "I told you he was acting weird."

"We're leaving this afternoon." Daniel couldn't believe what was happening.

"Not without an engine you're not." Sammy put a friendly hand on his shoulder. "Come on, Danny. Two days. It's not that big a deal."

He slapped Sammy's hand away.

"Hey. Lighten up, man." Sammy gave his arm a little punch.

Linda whined some more about bad manners, and Daniel lost it. He'd taken more than enough crap from these two. He wanted out but Sammy stood between him and the door. He swung. Fist met face with a loud crack. Sammy went down, blood pouring from his nose, and sprawled on the floor, groaning.

Linda took one look and started screaming.

Ignoring them both, Daniel walked out. His hand hurt like hell, and his knuckles were already swelling. Sammy's nose might not be the only thing broken. He started the truck with his left hand and peeled out of the parking lot.

Back at the dock, Daniel shared Sammy's bad news with his father and brothers. No one was happy about two more days sitting on shore not making money, and his swollen hand, which he said he'd shut in the truck door, earned him no sympathy.

"Long as you're here, you can make yourself useful." His father pointed to a net that had gotten tangled in the winch.

Daniel started to protest that he couldn't do that with a bad hand, but stopped when he saw the look on the old man's face. He untangled the net, using his left hand. By the time he finished, his right hand was swollen up purple, and his headache had become blind agony. He said he felt sick and was going home.

He wasn't sure where he was going—he sure as hell wasn't going to hang around where the killer could find him—but he needed to get his gear first. He drove past his place, checking things out, and noticed the little blue car parked under the live oak, the woman sitting on his front steps. The killer fiancée—it had to be her—was waiting for him. He parked around the bend and reached behind the seat.

Claire had been waiting for almost two hours and was about to give up when a young man walked up the driveway, carrying a shotgun. *A hunter?* She stood up.

"Hi, I'm looking for Daniel Doucet."

"You're under arrest." He raised the gun to his shoulder. "Put your hands over your head and don't move."

Startled, she put her hands up. "The man at Ray's Café gave me directions to Daniel's house. Isn't this it?"

He waved the shotgun toward her jeans pocket. "Is that a weapon?" His voice broke and the question ended in an adolescent squeak.

"It's a mobile phone. I don't have any weapons," she added, trying to lower the tension. This strange person acted even more scared than she felt, and he was the one with a gun.

"Put it on the top step and move away."

She complied.

"Further away, next to the tree. But don't get any funny ideas. You make a wrong move, and I'll blow you away."

Keeping the gun trained on her, he walked over and picked up her phone. He held the gun against his side, still pointed in her direction, and punched in a number. He acted like his hand hurt, and it looked swollen.

"This thing don't work," he said.

"You have to dial the area code."

This time, the call went through. He demanded to speak to Jason Corlette, no one else.

"You're calling the Sheriff's Office, aren't you? Deputy Corlette can vouch for me. My name is Claire Marshall."

"Jason," he spoke into the phone, his voice urgent. "It's Daniel. I arrested her for you, the killer. Come get her."

"Ask him. He knows me."

"You shut up," he yelled. "No, not you, Jason. I was talking to her. She came after me, but I was ready. You going to come get her or not?" He lowered his voice to a conspiratorial whisper, and she caught only the occasional word, but it was enough to know they were discussing her. This had to be the man she was looking for. Why was he afraid of her?

Daniel hung up. "The law's on the way."

"The sooner the better." She hoped Deputy Corlette recognized the urgency of the situation.

Daniel grunted a reply and leaned back against his house, the gun resting against his thigh but no longer pointed at her.

Claire's arms ached from being held up. She interlocked her fingers and slowly lowered her hands until they rested on her head. When he didn't object to that, she leaned against the tree and slid down to sit on the ground.

He watched, shotgun at the ready. "Don't try nothing."

"I just want to talk to you. The man at the café thought you might have seen the cabin fire. I knew the man who was killed."

He returned the gun to his shoulder and pointed it at her. "You stay right where you are."

Time passed with excruciating slowness until a sheriff's department car pulled up beside her car. Deputy Corlette climbed out.

"I'll take over now." He put his hand on the barrel of Daniel's gun and pushed down until it was pointed at the ground. "Is this thing

78

loaded?" He took the gun, removed two shells and handed it back. "You can relax now, Ms. Marshall, but please stay where you are."

"She came after me," Daniel said, "but I got the drop on her."

"I just wanted to talk to him," Claire said.

"She was waiting in ambush."

"I was sitting on your front steps in plain view, waiting for you to come home." She turned to Deputy Corlette. "He's been holding me at gunpoint. You saw him. He's crazy."

"She was going to kill me," Daniel said.

Claire's jaw dropped. "Kill you? With what? You're the one with the gun, not me. And I want my phone back."

"One at a time," Deputy Corlette said. "Daniel first. What happened to your hand?"

"I shut it in the truck door, but I got the drop on her anyway."

Claire bit her lip to keep from protesting as Daniel expanded upon his ridiculous accusations. When he finished, Corlette, nodded to her.

"Your turn, Ms. Marshall."

She explained that she was doing nothing more sinister than looking for a witness to prove Frank Palmer's cabin burned while she was in Michigan, because the New Orleans police seemed to think she had something to do with it.

"See. She torched the cabin with the guy in it." Daniel said.

"Did you see her near the cabin?"

"I never saw no one, but you know she did it, and now she's here trying to kill me."

"You really are crazy." Claire said, but neither paid her any attention.

"How'd she try to kill you?" Deputy Corlette said. "She doesn't have a weapon."

"Yeah, well she was trespassing."

"So, did you ask her to leave your property?"

"I told her I'd blow her away if she moved," Daniel said.

"I think we need to let her go back to New Orleans."

"You're just going to let her go?"

"I have no reason to arrest her."

"Yeah, well if you find me dead, you'll know who did it." Daniel pointed at her. "You won't get away with it."

Deputy Corlette retrieved her phone and escorted her to her car. He stood at the end of Daniel's driveway, watching her drive away. Had he believed her? Claire thought she'd seen a flicker of amusement toward the end of Daniel's ranting, but he'd remained impassive while she told her side of the story.

13

Mike was working his way through case files for last year's unsolved homicides. Most had been sitting in the files for months without any resolution—or any action that he could discern. He divided them into three categories, prioritizing those most likely to be solved with a bit more effort, re-filing those that offered little or no hope of a case that could be prosecuted, and stacking those that could go either way. The phone call from Lafourche Parish brought a welcome respite.

"I don't know where to begin." Corlette chuckled. "Some days I love being a cop."

"Tell me. I could use a laugh."

"This guy Daniel Doucet is a real swamp rat. I'm pretty sure he's the poacher Palmer reported. Proving it is something else. I talked to Daniel yesterday and got nowhere. Claire Marshall tracked him down this afternoon."

"She's there?" She'd told him she never wanted to step foot in Lafourche Parish again.

"Was here. Right now she's on her way back to New Orleans. Flying low, I'll bet."

"Do you know what was she doing there?"

"Looking for a witness to prove the cabin burned while she was in Michigan. No one's told her that our arson investigators can figure it out without her assistance."

"Have they?"

"Not yet. Let me tell you what happened."

Laughter punctuated Corlette's recital, but Mike didn't see what the hell was so funny. Maybe Breton was right about this deputy. He pushed the hair off his forehead. It was longer now, although still short by civilian standards, and getting used to it was taking time.

"Do you think Doucet witnessed the fire?" he said.

"After this afternoon, I'd bet money. He's scared. When Ms. Marshall came looking for him, he got scared of her. He thinks she killed Palmer and he's next. How he got that idea, I don't know."

"Can you encourage him to talk, use the threat of an assault charge for leverage?"

"What assault? He never touched her. As for Sammy, we only heard about the fight because Sammy's wife called 911 for an ambulance he didn't need. The dust has settled, and no one has anything to say against anybody. Daniel, he shut a door on his hand. Sammy, he walked into a door." Corlette chuckled. "Doors can be dangerous."

"Claire Marshall might be willing to press charges."

"For what? She was on his property."

"Maybe he'll get caught poaching."

"The boys from Wildlife and Fisheries have been after Daniel for years, but they've never caught him. And last I saw, he was putting his boat up. He's going out on the family shrimp boat. He'll be gone two, three weeks."

"Which is fine with you?"

"He'll be out of harm's way." Corlette reverted to his official voice. "Enough fun and games. The autopsy came in while I was at Daniel's. It's homicide. Palmer was suffocated."

"Not an overdose?" Yesterday, they'd found potentially lethal levels of drugs and alcohol, an ambiguous finding that left the question of homicide or accidental death unresolved.

"The doc said the whole thing didn't smell right. Death came too long before the fire. Plus he found fibers in the victim's mouth and nose. Consistent with passing out face down but, he thought, too many. He took another look and found a little broken bone in the victim's neck. Our killer held something soft over Palmer's face. Despite his intoxication, Palmer resisted. It's all there in black and white. We'll fax it to you."

"Nice job." Suffocation was a difficult diagnosis and often missed. "Anything else?"

"We'll send the fibers off to the state labs along with the least damaged portions of the sofa upholstery. It looks like the killer used a sofa pillow."

"It would have been handy." And it would provide no clue to the killer's identity.

"So, our victim was the cream of New Orleans society?" Corlette said. "The more I see of New Orleans, the happier I am to live down here. You're new in town aren't you?"

"I retired from the army the end of June and started here August first."

"What brought you to the New Orleans Police Department?"

"New Orleans seemed like a good place to re-enter the civilian world. The police department, because I'm a cop at heart." He'd worked both sides of the courtroom, prosecutor and defense attorney, but found neither as satisfying as investigative work.

"Me, I'm army too. I went in after high school and did my three years. They offered to send me to college if I re-upped, but I decided to go as a civilian. Another year of night school and I'll have my degree."

"Do you plan to stay in law enforcement?" Despite his flakey sense of humor, Corlette gave every indication of being a good investigator. He was smart and thorough.

"I'm thinking yes. That wasn't the original plan, but I'm enjoying myself. This afternoon was funnier than anything I've ever seen on TV. You had to be there. Daniel kept talking about spiders."

Mike couldn't match the deputy's jovial mood. A murder was most likely to be solved within the first forty-eight hours. Palmer was dead before the fire, which was Friday night at the latest. If Hatch set it, a real possibility, the fire was Wednesday, and the trail was cold before they knew a crime had been committed. He thanked Corlette for the update and signed off.

"What did Boy Wonder have to say?" Lieutenant Breton was leaning against the doorframe, a file folder in his hand.

"Come on in and close the door." Mike relayed the autopsy results.

"Oh shit," Breton groaned. "Wait until the press gets hold of this. I can see the headline, 'Civic leader murdered during drug orgy.'" He rubbed his face as if trying to erase the lines his job had put there. "Lethal levels of alcohol and downers, suffocated, and burned. Are we sure there wasn't a silver bullet? A stake through his heart?"

"They're faxing the autopsy. When we get it, I want you to call Palmer's physician to see if any prescriptions match the drugs found in his body. I'll check with Claire Marshall's doctor."

"She was out of it in Gilbert's office."

Mike nodded agreement. "Yesterday evening she popped a pill when she thought I wasn't looking." He'd seen her reflection in the window. "She was in Lafourche Parish today." He repeated the citizen's arrest story. Now that he had time to think about it, it really was funny.

Breton cracked up. "Corlette's poacher sounds like a real piece of work."

"At first I was thinking witness intimidation on her part," Mike said, "but she was unarmed." He raked his hair off his forehead. "Going down there was such a dumb thing to do, I'm wondering if she's not telling the truth." Corlette was sure she hadn't known Palmer's body was in the cabin. Last night, she'd been shocked by the arson finding. Or was she shocked that they'd figured it out?

"Try this scenario." Breton leaned forward, elbows on the desk. "She and Hatch are a team. While she's safely alibied in Michigan, he kills Palmer and torches the cabin. She drives down Saturday to make sure everything went as planned. That's what took her so long."

Mike had been expecting him to resurrect *cherchez la femme*. "We know she was there only because she initiated contact with Corlette. Why would she do that?"

"To explain her tire tracks. She was his fiancée. She knows we're going to check her out."

"Maybe, but where's Hatch? What happened to Palmer's Jeep? Lafourche Parish thinks it was booby-trapped." Mike wasn't comfortable with these two loose ends, which might be one big loose end.

"Did we ever find out who Hatch called?"

"A payphone down at the port. No help there." No help anywhere. He returned to his current priority, learning more about the victim. "What did Palmer's secretary have to say?"

"Jeanette Harlow," Breton rolled his eyes, "Her mother named her after the silent movie star. There is irony. The woman could talk paint off the wall. First I have to listen to Palmer's dentist bitching about kids breaking into his office looking for drugs—twice in one week, he says. Bobby Austin wants to talk about robberies at his branches out in the suburbs—like that has anything to do with us. Top it off, Jeanette Harlow wants to share every thought that has ever passed through her tiny brain."

"What did she think of Palmer?"

"He walked on water." Breton grimaced. "Her job was her life, she's worked for him for ten years and can't imagine ever working for anyone else. She's not going to say anything that might reflect badly on her sainted boss."

"Not intentionally, but she might say something useful. Talk to her again. Ask about the business, the people Palmer worked with. Someone had a motive for murder."

"Vernon stopped me in the hall. He thinks we should be looking harder at Claire Marshall."

"I'll talk to her again, but not tomorrow. It's Palmer's funeral." He pointed at Breton. "Wear your best suit; you're going. And don't say anything to anyone about the autopsy results. We're keeping them quiet until after the funeral."

"Is Vernon protecting the delicate sensibilities of our victim's friends?"

"He doesn't know yet," Mike said. "This is my decision. I'm in no hurry to let our killer know we've figured it out." Given the lack of leads, their best hope was that he or she would become overconfident and make a mistake.

"How about letting me get out of the building before you give Vernon the bad news?"

"Go now." Mike reached for the phone.

14

Claire spent Wednesday morning at her desk. She called the subs working on Frank's cottage and requested invoices for work to date plus written estimates of what it would cost to finish. Paul Gilbert would have to decide whether to sell the cottage as is, complete the restoration before putting it on the market, or do something in between. She wanted to give him options with dollar figures attached.

At ten-thirty, Brian Laurens came by to sign off on the plans for his house, really his great-great-grandfather's house. He was getting married in eight months, and Claire had promised him that, if they started now, the old family home would be restored to its original glory in time for him to carry his bride across the threshold. The thought brought a smile to her face.

This was her new favorite project. And it would be Authentic Restorations' biggest project to date. The Laurens house was as dilapidated as Frank's cottage but larger and a more complicated job.

After Brian left, she checked in with Jack, who was working on a porch addition in Lakeview, grabbed a fast food lunch, and drove over the Laurens house. She hammered an Authentic Restorations sign in the front yard, where the world—or at least the neighbors—could see it. They'd be happy to learn the house was going to be restored.

She began by measuring the perimeter of the structure and drew the shell. Then she walked through the interior, sketching the layout. Placing the rooms within the building was like fitting pieces into a puzzle. Once she had the overall arrangement, she measured each room. Transferring her sketch onto graph paper would have to wait. It was time to go home and dress for Frank's funeral. She'd thought about not going, but had decided to do what she would have done if there were no marriage rumors, attend the service and quietly pay her respects.

Most days Claire clipped her hair back from her face, applied moisturizer, and swiped a lipstick across her mouth. But this afternoon, appearance mattered. She applied concealer to the circles under her eyes, foundation and eyeliner but no mascara. If a flashback to Tom's funeral brought tears, mascara would run and leave her looking like a raccoon. Lipstick and a bit of blusher finished the job.

The careful attention to make-up made her feel like an actress preparing for the stage. It was an apt analogy. The newspapers and television were still describing her as Frank's fiancée. People would be looking at her.

Last night she'd rummaged through her closet, trying to find the right thing to wear. She hadn't regained all the weight she lost after Tom died, and most of her dress clothes were too big. She'd settled on a navy silk dress with a matching jacket long enough to hide the bagging around her hips. Its green and white ribbon trim would keep her from looking as if she was in mourning.

She put it on and checked her reflection in the mirror. Dreary. On an impulse, she rummaged through her jewelry box for the diamond and pearl earrings Tom had given her when they married. She'd had to stop wearing her wedding ring because it irritated her finger, but she could wear the earrings.

Because parking near the cathedral would probably be impossible, she took the streetcar down Saint Charles and walked the last few blocks. By the time she arrived, the sanctuary was half-full and filling rapidly. Frank's peers, the social and business elite of New Orleans, had come to pay their last respects. The people who had called and left messages on her phone would be here.

Paul Gilbert sat in the front pew by the center aisle. Jeanette huddled at the other end, her shoulders shaking with occasional sobs. Bobby Austin sat across the aisle, in the front pew with a woman, probably his wife. Lieutenant Breton slouched, alone, in the last pew on the right. Claire chose a seat two rows up on the left, knelt, and bowed her head to pray for Frank's eternal soul and for the strength to remain calm.

An usher stopped by her pew. "Excuse me, Ms. Marshall, would you like to join Mr. and Mrs. Austin?"

"No, thank you."

People sitting nearby overheard the usher's question. Several turned around, and then others noticed. Claire felt their curious eyes on her face. She ignored them and looked at the lovely rose window above the altar. Its intricate petal pattern glowed like an enormous multicolored flower. There must be a thousand pieces of glass in that one window—blues, reds, and greens. She touched the earrings Tom had given her. In an hour, it would be over.

A tall young woman, made taller by stiletto heels and hair piled on top of her head, hurried up the aisle. When she reached the first pew, Paul motioned for her to sit between him and Jeanette. She whispered something in his ear and settled back, staring straight ahead. Jeanette slid as far from the newcomer as possible, and the congregation's hum of conversation became a loud buzz.

Claire was relieved to have the spotlight on someone else, but she felt sorry for this young woman, who must be feeling a hundred eyes boring into her back. Her position in the first pew meant she was a close friend, or family. Could she be Annalisa?

Frank had described himself as alone in the world, but his obituary said he was survived by a nineteen-year-old daughter. Something dreadful must have happened to make him disown his only child, and now she'd come to his funeral. Claire's heart ached for the father and daughter who had never reconciled and now never would.

Bobby Austin walked back and sat beside her. He placed a consoling hand over hers. "Marie and I understand if you prefer to be alone, Claire, but please know that we share your grief."

"I'm very sorry Frank died, but we were no more than friends." Less than friends, really, but she wanted to be tactful. "The marriage rumors aren't true."

"But, Claire..." He looked bewildered.

She felt guilty. Bobby was a nice man, and that was his best friend's coffin in front of the altar. She tried to soften the impact of her denial. "Thank you for your kindness. And please extend my condolences to Annalisa."

"Annalisa's here?"

"Isn't that who just came in? Sitting beside Paul Gilbert?"

"No." Bobby started to say something more but stopped. "If you change your mind, Marie and I have a place for you." He gave her hand a parting squeeze and returned to his seat.

The acolytes came forward to light the candles, and the organist switched from gentle background to the stirring notes of the processional. The priest stepped forward, and gossip gave way to the funeral service.

I am the resurrection and the life, says the Lord; he that believes in me, though he were dead, yet shall he live; and whosoever lives and believes in me shall never die.

The eulogy reinforced this theme of loss and redemption. The priest opened his arms wide to address the congregation. "When God, in His wisdom, took Frank Palmer's family from him, Frank embraced a larger family, the troubled children of New Orleans." The cadence of his speech slowed as he recited a catalogue of Frank's good deeds, the years he'd worked with The Children's Home and his more recent work with a shelter for homeless veterans.

Listening, Claire grieved for a good man's life cut short. She was sorry, but she felt no personal loss. She watched dry-eyed as the pallbearers carried the casket out of the church. The choir sang of Christ's sacrifice and the promise of eternal life, the priest blessed the congregation, and the ordeal was over.

Her seat near the back put her in the first wave of mourners leaving the church. She stood for a moment at the top of the stone steps, blinking as her eyes became accustomed to the bright sunshine.

"Claire! Hey, Claire!"

She turned toward the voice, and a flashbulb exploded in her face. A man shoved a microphone in her face.

"Can you tell us…" he began.

"No, oh no." She turned around and fought her way back through the exiting crowd, seeking sanctuary in the cathedral.

"Let me help you, Ms. Marshall." It was the usher who had asked her about moving to the front pew.

He kept a firm hold on her arm as he cleared a path up the side aisle and guided her into a corridor beside the altar, down a flight of stairs and through a maze of empty hallways to a second flight of stairs that brought them back up to street level. He opened a door into a walled garden behind the cathedral and pointed to a gate. It would put her on Bayard Street.

She thanked him and hurried away, keeping her head down so that no one could see her face. On the far side of Jackson Square, she bought a soda from a street vendor and carried it to the small park atop the levee. There, she leaned against the fence and rolled the cold can against her flushed cheek. She was sweating, but from exertion not panic.

Below her, the Mississippi flowed dark with silt. An eddy swirled back around, carrying a milk carton and bits of wood destined to remain in New Orleans. Farther out, small pleasure boats zoomed around like so many water bugs, their random zigs and zags a skittering counterpoint to the purposeful tugs and heavily laden barges. Incongruous among the modern vessels, a red and white paddle wheeler carried a load of tourists up river. The jubilant cry of a Dixieland trumpet called to her from its upper deck.

"Play for Tom," she whispered, "and for Frank, and for all the people who die too young."

Tom never finished his residency, never became the doctor who was going to help poor children grow into healthy adults. The hospital could find another doctor, but she and Tom would never have the home and family they'd dreamed of. Their years together had been spent working toward a tomorrow that never came, and now, one year and three months after his death, she couldn't remember him.

The tears she had vowed not to shed wet her cheeks. The waves she counted on the river's surface were real ones, and the bubble hovered but never closed in. She stayed until fading light told her it was time to leave then walked back through the tourist heart of the French Quarter.

Bourbon Street's tawdry energy provided a welcome counter to the darkness that had enveloped her on the levee. Music blared from outside speakers, and open doorways allowed glimpses of shadowy interiors. Pleasure seekers crowded the sidewalks, laughing and jostling each other, while barkers made extravagant claims to entice customers. She bought fried shrimp in a paper funnel and ate as she strolled along, letting the sounds and smells flow over her, wiping her greasy fingers on the navy silk dress already ruined by sweat and tears.

The nightmares started that night. Claire was driving Felicia Miata, her beloved blue roadster, along an empty highway, a two-lane causeway that sliced through swamp forests at treetop height. The hot sun beat on her head, and heat waves shimmered up from the pavement. The trees thinned, and the causeway became a long bridge arched high over open water. An osprey flew slow circles before descending to its nest atop a channel marker.

She hadn't seen another vehicle in miles, but a prickle on the back of her neck made her glance in the rearview. A dark sedan was coming up fast. It closed the distance between them then tailgated. No one was coming in the other direction. Why didn't they pass? She waved it by.

The sedan pulled out, but instead of passing rode alongside, its dark bulk looming over her little Miata. She slowed and it slowed. She sped up and it sped up. She glanced over to see who was playing this dangerous game, but sedan's tinted windows hid its occupants.

The causeway climbed higher, and the sedan edged into her lane. It forced her onto the shoulder. Her tires chattered over the rumble strips. She hit the brakes again, but this time, her car didn't slow. She stepped on the accelerator. Nothing happened. Turning the steering wheel made no difference.

The big car pushed her up against the guardrail. Metal screeched, and sparks flew. The rail gave way.

She went off the bridge, out over the water, and hovered airborne for an agonizingly long time before plummeting into the water, deeper and deeper in an endless descent. Waterweeds coiled and twisted around Claire's arms and face. She couldn't release the seat belt. She couldn't move. She couldn't breathe.

Terrified and gasping for breath, Claire woke tangled in bed sheets, not weeds. There was no water, no seatbelt. It was all a panic attack wrapped in a nightmare. She lay exhausted, taking slow deep breaths to dispel the lingering sensations of the endless descent, the slimy tendrils wrapping themselves around her.

The clock radio read three-thirty. In six hours, she had another appointment with Captain Robinson.

15

Mike went in early Thursday, determined to get a head start on what was going to be a long day. Paperwork generated by his effort to raise the division's solve rate filled his in-box, and the Palmer case was demanding ever more attention. He began by scanning progress reports from half a dozen re-activated investigations, made notations for the lead investigators, and then fixed a pot of coffee, a reward for work accomplished.

Breton was due any minute. They had an eight-thirty with Vernon and were meeting half an hour ahead to get their ducks in a row before facing the Super who wanted an arrest yesterday. Vernon's favorite suspect, Claire Marshall, was coming in at nine-thirty.

Ms. Marshall had no criminal record, no previous brush with law enforcement, no points on her driver's license, and if she'd gotten any parking tickets, she'd paid them. For any other crime, that would have moved her way down the suspect list, but murder was different. People, who had never before broken the law, killed in the heat of the moment. Temporary insanity was a reality as well as a plea.

Mike had seen post-traumatic stress disorder in the military and thought he might be looking at it again. Claire Marshall spent a lot of time staring into the middle distance, looking at things only she could see. Corlette had noticed, too. She lived alone and appeared to have few emotional connections. She'd cut short her visit with her mother on what struck him as a weak pretext.

Monday night, he'd seen signs of anger much deeper than the redhead's temper Breton had mentioned. A psychotic incident could account for those lost hours Saturday morning; a flashback, for her strange reaction to his business card. For a moment, he'd thought she was going to faint.

PTSD occurs in response to a traumatic event. When Breton dug up her husband's obituary, Mike thought they'd found it. Dr. Thomas Marshall had died in a fire. Breton had been apologetic, said he should have remembered. It happened a year ago last summer and had been all over the papers. Brilliant young doctor runs into a burning house and throws two young children to safety, but he doesn't make it back out. The kids were home alone while their addict mother was turning tricks in exchange for drugs. It was one hell of a way to lose your husband.

Individuals suffering from PTSD could overreact to the point of violence when something reminded them of the initial trauma. Mike had noted the similarities between typical PTSD symptoms and Claire Marshall's behavior and was ready to believe that the marriage rumors, phony or not, pushed her over the edge. She returned Friday, drove down to the cabin to confront Palmer, lost control, and killed him. Faced with his body, she tried to make it look like he, too, died in a fire.

The pieces had been coming together: motive and opportunity. Much as he mistrusted coincidences, maybe the Jeep explosion was just that. But late yesterday afternoon, the arson analysis came in and blew his theory out of the water. The cabin burned on Wednesday, when Claire Marshall was in Michigan. If she was involved, she was part of a cold-blooded conspiracy.

Their only other suspect had been missing for a week. A second search of the ashes hadn't produced any hint of a second victim. It was anyone's guess if Hatch was alive and, if so, where.

"Are you ready to explain why we've made no progress?" Breton walked in the door asking questions. "More to the point, why are we treating Claire Marshall with kid gloves? You don't believe her getting lost story do you?"

"No, and we're not. She's due here at nine-thirty. Were you able to reach Palmer's physician?"

"He'd given Palmer a prescription for the sleeping pills, not the downers, but so what. You can buy that shit on any street corner."

"Claire Marshall's doctor prescribed both sedatives." It had taken the threat of a subpoena to get that information, and it could mean nothing. Breton was right about their wide availability. "How'd she behave at the funeral?"

"She saw me but pretended not to. Hurt my feelings when she didn't even say hello." He smirked and took the offered cup of coffee. "The only time she showed any emotion was on the way out. TV news ambushed her, and she didn't like it."

"Anything else?"

"Another woman, a real knockout, came in late and sat in the first pew next to Gilbert. I called him when I got back to the office. Turns out she's Palmer's long-term squeeze, name of Melissa Yates. He thinks we should talk to her, but he doesn't want her to know where we got her name. He says their relationship is already difficult." He wiggled his fingers, putting that last word in quotation marks.

"Did he say how to reach her?"

"She owns a boutique down in the Quarter. He practically drew me a map. Gilbert is throwing Melissa into our laps—or under the bus."

"Gilbert's slick, but he's also right. I want you to talk to her today. Tell her that Palmer was murdered and see how she reacts."

"Okay, but I'm thinking there's something between Gilbert and Claire Marshall," Breton said. "He helped her out Monday. Now he's pointing us at this other woman."

"I think you're fixated on her."

"Her husband dies in a fire. Little over a year later, a man who's planning to marry her is murdered and someone tries to make it look like he died in a fire."

"Someone could be trying to set her up."

"Vernon wants us to put more pressure on her. You don't want him thinking you're dragging your feet or, God help you, protecting her."

Mike appreciated the warning. He was also glad to see Breton finally showing some initiative, but he was withholding judgment on his scenario. He crumpled up his PTSD notes, threw them at the wastepaper basket and missed.

"Let's go." He retrieved the errant paper ball. "He's expecting us."

When Claire arrived at the police station, Captain Robinson wasn't in his office. The desk officer directed her to a waiting area. She was coming to a boil by the time he walked in, half an hour after their scheduled appointment.

"Sorry I'm late. A meeting ran longer than expected." He gestured toward the hallway. "Please. After you."

When they reached his office, he waited until she was seated before offering her coffee or water. His good manners did nothing to take the edge off her temper. She was tired, she didn't like being kept waiting, and she wasn't happy to be back in the principal's office.

"Thank you for coming in." He paused and then said, "Once again, I have to ask if you want a lawyer present."

"If I did, I would have come with one."

"You might want to reconsider." He pushed the hair back off his forehead. "I was trained as a lawyer, and I've worked as a defense attorney. Access to legal representation is guaranteed in our criminal justice system—and with good reason. Careless remarks can be misunderstood or misinterpreted. Circumstantial evidence can convict innocent people."

He sounded as if he'd recited this speech many times before, and he probably knew what he was talking about, but Claire didn't care. She wasn't interested in another civics lesson from another policeman. She was there because she really had no choice.

Paul had told her that if she refused to talk to the police, they could subpoena her and, if she still refused, jail her for contempt. However, she could refuse to answer specific questions on the grounds that she didn't want to incriminate herself. Captain Robinson had already told her that.

"I know what lawyers do," she said, "and I know that you're under pressure to make an arrest. Frank's death is all over the news."

"Ms. Marshall…"

Claire's nerves were rubbed raw. Neither the lecture she'd given herself on the drive here nor the extra half pill she'd taken to get herself through this interrogation could hold back her anger.

"I'd be a very convenient guilty party, wouldn't I? I'm not from here. I have no influential friends. No one will be embarrassed if I'm accused of burning down Frank's cabin or even of murdering him." As the words tumbled out, she realized their truth. She was a convenient scapegoat. If there were another interview—and there would be—she'd have a lawyer.

"Turn on your tape recorder and let's begin. I have a business to take care of." She folded her arms across her chest and glared at him.

"Let's start with your visit to in Lafourche Parish Tuesday. What were you doing there?"

Claire bit back the impulse to ask if he and Deputy Corlette ever talked to each other. Of course they did. That was how he knew she'd been there. And he also knew why, but she told him anyway. After exhausting the topic of her encounter with Daniel, he repeated his previous questions about Saturday morning, and she gave him the same answers. Then he asked a new question.

"We're looking for Ronald Hatch. Can you help us?"

"I barely know him and have no idea where he might be." She hoped that would end the interview, but Captain Robinson appeared to be in no hurry.

"A few minutes ago, you said no one would be embarrassed if you were accused of murdering Frank Palmer." He put his hands flat on the desk and leaned forward slightly. "I know the news is describing his death as suspicious, but no one has said he was murdered."

"Not in so many words." She concentrated on breathing slowly.

"Not at all, but you're correct. Frank Palmer was murdered. That information will become public at a press conference later today."

Claire had known it had to be murder, but hearing this policeman confirm her suspicions still shocked her.

"Homicide is a police matter," he continued. "If you recall anything that might help us unravel what happened down at Palmer's cabin, call me. Don't go charging off on your own like you did on Tuesday. What if you'd found the killer and not just some punk who poaches oysters?"

"Are we through?" She couldn't get out of there fast enough.

"Did you hear what I said about not interfering in our investigation?"

She nodded.

After another warning about the dangers of pursuing a murderer, he stood and started walking around his desk. She held up her hand to stop him.

"Don't bother, please. I can find my way out."

16

The watch had come from a boutique in the French Quarter, a long walk from police headquarters, but Claire was too rattled to drive. She fetched her sweater from the back seat, fed the parking meter, and set out. Her feet hit the sidewalk in a rhythm that sounded like chanting. Murdered, murdered, murdered.

Frank had been murdered.

Captain Robinson had said he didn't want to become convinced of her innocence when she was the next victim. He was just trying to scare her. Why would anyone want to kill her? Why did someone kill Frank? Absorbed in her thoughts, she walked past the shop and had to retrace her steps.

The sign read *Melissa's Got Time*. The display window held an array of jeweled timepieces resting on a painted backdrop that evoked Dali's surreal masterpiece of melting watches. A bell chimed when Claire walked in.

An attractive young woman held a tank top embellished with a sequined sundial against her chest and flirted with two middle-aged men, her only customers. With a start, Claire recognized the woman who'd sat in the front pew at Frank's funeral. Her arrival had caused a sensation, and Bobby Austin had hurried away when asked about her. Heat rose in Claire's cheeks as she realized why. The woman glanced her way.

"I'll be with you in just a minute." She spoke with a soft drawl, not the distinctive New Orleans accent that included a bit of Brooklyn.

"No rush." Claire walked past shelves holding cross-stitch pillows decorated with sayings about time and stopped beside a glass jewelry cabinet. The bracelets, pins, and necklaces inside ranged from trendy to antique and from expensive to very expensive. She'd been right about the watch's value, but everything else about the situation baffled her.

The men left, and the woman walked over. "Can I help you?"

"Please. My name is Claire Marshall."

"Hello, Claire." Her eyes widened in surprise then flicked up and down in a quick appraisal. "I'm Melissa Yates."

"Melissa. This is your shop?"

"That's right."

"I like your window display."

"Thank you."

"I saw you at Frank Palmer's funeral. I guess we both were friends with Frank."

"Friends?" Melissa's eyes narrowed. "The paper said you were getting married."

"That's not true." Claire answered more vehemently than she intended and quickly backpedaled. "I mean the story in the paper was inaccurate."

"I knew he wasn't going to marry you." Melissa folded her arms across her chest.

"I asked them to print a retraction."

"Frank and I have been together for ten years."

They stood, facing off like two gunfighters on the dusty streets of Laredo. If Frank weren't dead, Claire thought, this would be funny. But if he weren't dead, this wouldn't be happening.

"Please accept my condolences." Claire broke a silence that had lasted long enough to become awkward.

Melissa nodded, stone-faced.

"Before he died, Frank gave me a watch." She pulled the box from her pocketbook. "I was going to give it back, but now I can't, and so I'd like to return it to you. I'm going to donate the money to The Children's Home. In Frank's name."

"The Children's Home? You're serious?"

"I thought about giving it to Annalisa, but I don't know where she is or how to contact her. She didn't even come to his funeral." Claire waited to see if Melissa would say anything about Annalisa, but the woman had reverted to stony silence, so she plowed on. "I don't have a receipt, but your store's name is on the box."

Melissa opened the box, removed the watch and held it up to the light. "Frank paid four thousand. Retail is more like ten."

After a brief negotiation, they agreed Melissa that would try to sell the watch for a price of her choosing. When it sold or in three months, whichever came first, she'd give Claire four thousand dollars.

"If you want to give the money to The Children's Home, that's your business." Melissa' voice was as hard and flat as her eyes.

Claire searched for words to end this prickly encounter on a pleasant note. "Thank you for your help and for believing me about Frank."

"Who told them you were getting married in the first place?"

"I think Frank did, but I can't imagine why."

"Well," Melissa drew the word out to several syllables. "Neither can I." Another quick appraisal. "If he bought you those earrings, I can't help with them. They didn't come from here."

Claire put her hands to her ears. "My husband gave me these!"

"You're married?"

"I'm a widow. My husband was a wonderful man, a hero."

"Hey. No offense intended." Melissa held up her hands as if warding off an attack.

Claire realized she'd been yelling like a madwoman. "I'm sorry. I didn't mean to yell. I've been under a lot of stress. I'm really sorry."

"No problem, it's been a tough time for lots of people." Melissa walked over to the cash register.

Claire followed, being careful not to crowd the counter. "You knew Frank well. I didn't." She raised her palms in a gesture of helpless frustration. "This phony fiancée business... It's as if he was playing some kind of a game, but then he died. And now I'm trapped by some crazy chain of events that Frank set in motion. I just came from the police station."

"What were you doing there?" Melissa frowned.

Breton called in twenty minutes after he'd left the office. "Talk about killing two birds with one stone." He chortled. "Claire Marshall led me right to Melissa's boutique. Our victim's fiancée and his mistress are having a little *tête-à-tête*."

"Where are you now?" Mike said.

"On the sidewalk outside the shop."

Mike cursed under his breath. He'd wondered why Claire was in such a hurry to leave his office. Now he knew. He'd wanted to see how Melissa reacted when told that Palmer was murdered, but it looked as if Claire had beaten them to the punch. Maybe she was part of a conspiracy. He'd been fooled before.

"Melissa just slid something across the counter. Could be a key. Claire put it in her purse. Whoops. Here she comes."

"Don't let her see you."

"She's not looking anywhere but straight ahead. Our suspect is in a big hurry. Do you want me to stay with her?"

Mike weighed the options and went with discretion. "No. If she spots you, she'll know you saw them together. I'll meet you in front of the boutique in twenty minutes. What's the address?"

When they walked in, Melissa was alone in the shop. She looked up from the scarves she was folding.

"May I help you, gentlemen?"

Mike showed his badge. "We're looking into the circumstances surrounding the death of Frank Palmer and hope you can help us."

"I'll do anything to help the police." She sashayed to the door and flipped the sign to Closed.

Breton spoke out of the side of his mouth, "Showtime. Gilbert said she enjoyed flaunting her charms. I'm hoping for a lap dance."

Melissa returned and leaned against the counter, one hip outthrust and cleavage on display. "Now we won't be interrupted."

When told Palmer had been murdered, she neither expressed surprise nor admitted knowing anything that might shed light on a motive. She responded to questions about their relationship with a raised chin.

"As I'm sure you know, we were very close."

"When was the last time you saw last Mr. Palmer?" Mike said.

"He drove me to the airport Monday morning." She looked past them. "I was in Atlanta all week."

"When did you return to New Orleans?"

"Sunday afternoon."

"That's a long time in Atlanta." Breton said. "What were you doing there?"

"I went to the show at the Gift Mart, buying for the shop. I was supposed to come back Friday night, but I got sick and stayed 'til

Sunday. I didn't know anything had happened to Frank until I read it in the paper Monday morning."

"Can you document your travel?"

"I stayed at the Peachtree Plaza, and I flew Delta. I can prove it if I have to." She resumed folding the scarves.

"We're looking for Ronald Hatch."

"I'm looking for him myself. I have half a container sitting down at the port. Hatch and Jimbo usually pick up shipments for me."

Mike waited to see if she'd say more without being asked, and after folding another scarf, she did. "Jimbo's a big strong guy who has a truck. I don't know his last name or anything about him except he and Hatch are friends." She glanced at one of the myriad clocks on the wall. "I need to open back up. It's almost noon. People shop over their lunch break."

On the way back to headquarters, Mike and Breton discussed Melissa's behavior.

"Very cool for a woman who claims to be mourning her lover," Mike said. "She showed more concern over Hatch's disappearance."

"That's one tough cookie," Breton said. "And nothing we told her was a surprise."

"She had her alibi ready."

"I'll tell you. Seeing her with Claire Marshall made me think."

"They could almost be sisters," Mike finished the sentence. The thought had occurred to him the minute he walked into the shop. Palmer must have had a thing for tall slender redheads.

"Yeah. And wouldn't that be a kick in the head? But the resemblance is only physical, if you know what I mean. I'm thinking Ms. Marshall really isn't Palmer's type." Breton tapped his temple. "I can tell you what kind of a car a man drives by looking at his wife, and this guy drove a Jag. We're talking fast, sexy, and high maintenance."

"Can you tell what kind of car a woman drives by looking at her husband?" He wondered if Breton remembered that Claire Marshall drove a bright blue Miata, and if so, what the hell he thought that meant.

"Go ahead, make fun. But I'm right. A guy like Palmer wants a woman other men would give their left nut to have, not the girl next door. Have you seen a picture of his late wife?" He blew on his fingers as if he had touched a hot stove.

"A man can look for very different things in a wife and in a mistress."

"From your mouth to God's ear," Breton said. "But I don't think Palmer cared about home cooking."

Mike pulled the conversation back on track. "I'd like to know how long those two have known each other and how well. You saw them together. What's your impression?"

"Hard to say. It started out confrontational. They passed a jewelry box back and forth, and Marshall acted excited. Then everything calmed down, and they huddled like they were conspiring—or comparing notes." Breton snickered. "I think someone should take a good look at Melissa, and I'm happy to volunteer."

"You can start by checking with the airline and the hotel, but I'll be very surprised if her story doesn't hold up. The whole thing feels choreographed."

"How's that?"

"Both women in Palmer's life leave town shortly before he disappears. He drives them to the airport, separate trips. Then they do a little shuffle. The mistress scheduled to return on Friday waits until Sunday. The fiancée scheduled to return Sunday comes back on Friday. They shouldn't know each other, but they do."

"They could be in it together. Team Redhead. They find out about each other and decide to get rid of the cheating bastard. M-O-T-I-V-E." Breton sang the letters.

"Either or both of them could be working with Hatch," Mike said.

When they walked into the building, the desk sergeant handed Mike a package. The report from the state crime lab had come in.

"Maybe this will clarify a few things," he said to Breton. "Come on in my office. We'll find out together."

The cover memo said the analysis had been expedited at the request of the New Orleans Police Department. Some days, politics pays off.

Lafourche Parish was right. The Jeep had been booby-trapped. A small explosive device had detonated under the driver's seat. It set off the gasoline fumes in the car and that ignited the gas tank. In the analyst's opinion, if this had occurred while the car was on the highway, the bomb would have disabled the driver. The ensuing accident would have finished him off, if he weren't dead already, and they never would have found the bomb.

"That's two," Mike said.

"Are we still talking about redheads?" Breton leered.

"Two almost perfect crimes. Think about it. If Palmer hadn't resisted despite being drugged, his hyoid wouldn't have fractured—it was barely cracked—and we wouldn't know his death was a homicide. If some kid hadn't tried to steal the Jeep, we wouldn't know it had been booby-trapped. One more driver goes off the road, just another highway fatality. No one would have sent the vehicle to the state crime lab."

Breton scowled at the lab report. "I'll try to feel lucky."

"I don't care how clever our killer is, his luck is going to run out."

"What do you think? Two shots at Palmer?"

"Could be, but I'm leaning toward the Hatch and a partner scenario. The Jeep was booby-trapped because, once he'd torched the cabin, Hatch became expendable. And a liability."

"I can't see Melissa building a car bomb. Did you notice the fingernails? Imagine them on your back." Breton's leer returned. "Claire Marshall runs a small construction company. I bet she's handy with tools."

Mike had trouble imagining either woman building a car bomb, but maybe he was being old-fashioned. "If I'm right," he said, "Hatch better hope we find him before his partner does."

"If his partner hasn't found him already."

17

A peeling sign identified the two-story brick building as the Audubon View Apartments. Dark stains beneath dripping air conditioners said no one cared. The flat-roofed structure reminded Claire of an old motel alongside a highway made obsolete when the Interstate went through. Numbered doors opened directly onto a cement walkway that separated the building from the parking lot. At either end, a metal staircase led up to the narrow balcony that served as an outdoor hallway for the second floor.

Hatch lived in apartment 209, second floor near the back.

Claire pulled into a space labeled Visitors and scanned the half-empty lot. The spaces were numbered, and 209 was empty. She climbed the back stairs and inserted the key. Coming here which had sounded reasonable when Melissa suggested it now felt like a really dumb idea. The odds of finding a clue to Hatch's location had to be slim, but she might as well finish what she had started.

There was a mail slot in the door but nothing on the floor in front of it. Either someone else was picking up Hatch's mail or he was having it held at the post office. So much for that excuse.

She'd expected dirty clothes on the floor, a litter of empty beer cans, and overflowing ashtrays, but the apartment was tidy, almost Spartan. A single recliner facing the TV, one chair at the dinette table, and a single bed shoved against the wall testified to a solitary life. *Nothing wrong with that. I live alone, too.* An opening on the far wall led to a kitchenette. The two other doors, both closed, would be the closet and the bathroom.

The closet was two-thirds empty, which didn't prove anything. Hatch might not own many clothes. She glanced into the bathroom and moved on to the kitchen. The drawer by the phone held only old electric bills, phone bills with no long distance calls, and rent receipts—nothing to indicate where Hatch might be now.

Claire found the expected beer in the refrigerator, along with some soft drinks and condiments, but nothing else. Anything that might go bad—a partial loaf of bread, cold cuts, packages of butter and cheese—had been sealed in plastic bags and put in the freezer. Hatch had planned to leave. He intended to be gone for a while. Coming here had been not only foolish but also a waste of time.

On her way out, she stopped to read the framed document that hung above the bed. Private First Class Ronald D. Hatch had been honorably discharged from the US Army in December of 1978, fifteen years ago, and he still had his discharge papers on the wall. A military history of World War II and a copy of Soldier of Fortune magazine lay on the bedside table.

A layer of dust covered the table, but a clear strip beside the magazines showed they had recently been lifted up and put back in a slightly different place. She looked at the bed more closely and saw that the mattress lay slightly askew on the box spring. Someone had already been here, probably the police. What if they came back?

She retraced her steps, and used her sweater to erase her fingerprints from every surface she'd touched. She was wiping down the refrigerator when a pounding on the apartment door sent her heart into her throat.

"New Orleans Police. Open up."

She hurried to the door but didn't open it. "How do I know you're really the police?"

An identification badge appeared in the mail slot.

Claire unlocked the door and, for the second time in three days, found herself at gunpoint. This time there were two guns, one for each of the uniformed police officers standing on either side of the doorway. Instinctively, she raised her hands.

"That's right. Keep them up. Is anyone else in there?"

"Just me. What's this all about?"

"We'll ask the questions," the taller policeman said.

Once she'd demonstrated that she'd entered with a key and her story about checking the apartment for an absent friend was verified with a phone call to Melissa, the policemen holstered their guns. But they made no move to depart.

"I'd like the key back." Claire held out her hand. "And I'd like you to leave, so I can lock up and go."

"Please make yourself comfortable, Ms. Marshall. We're not quite through here."

She sat on the dinette chair, as far as she could get from the policemen, who stood by the open door. She tapped her foot, more from apprehension than impatience, afraid that she knew what they were waiting for. Her suspicions were confirmed several minutes later when a grim-faced Captain Robinson walked in.

He thanked the officers. "I'll take custody of Ms. Marshall."

She jumped to her feet. "Custody? For what? I haven't done anything wrong. I don't know why they called you."

"They called because they found you here. Custody because you're obstructing a police investigation." He stood in the doorway, filling it.

"I haven't obstructed anything."

"Earlier this morning, you denied any knowledge of Ronald Hatch. Now you're looking after his apartment."

"As I already explained, Melissa Yates is looking after the apartment. She asked me to stop by and check on things." It wasn't really a lie. Her coming here had been Melissa's idea.

"I work for a man who believes a stay in jail would encourage you to cooperate with our investigation. I'm beginning to agree with him."

"I've been cooperative. I've met with you three times in the last four days. I've told you everything I know about Frank Palmer. What more do you want?" She paced back and forth, becoming more irritated with each step, but also worried. Could he actually arrest her? For what?

"We can start with what you're doing here," he said. "The truth this time, not some story you and Ms. Yates cooked up."

She stopped pacing and glared at him. "Okay. I'm looking for Hatch. Now, can I go?"

"Did you expect to find Hatch here?"

"No, but—"

"Then what are you doing here?"

His tone was calm and his expression impassive, but she suspected he was angry. Well she was angry too, and she was sick and tired of his questions. She wanted to leave, but he was still blocking the doorway.

"I don't think I owe you an explanation."

"Ms. Marshall, you're on thin ice."

"I was looking for something that might tell where Hatch has gone. I didn't find it. Can I go now?"

"Not yet."

"Why not? I've broken absolutely no laws, yet those officers took the key. At gunpoint. They searched my pocketbook looking for a weapon. I have a screaming headache because I haven't eaten all day, thanks to you. I skipped breakfast, so I wouldn't be late for our meeting this morning. You were late, but that's okay, right? I'm missing lunch because your policemen made me wait for you to show up. I'm hungry and I want to leave."

"I'll buy you lunch. I haven't eaten either."

His offer surprised her, but then it reminded her of the saying about no such thing as a free lunch. There would be more questions. She exhaled loudly.

"I'll drive," he said.

"Okay, fine. Where's the key? I have to lock up." Let him drive. She might be talking a good game, but the shock of two policemen with their guns trained on her had left her feeling shaky.

He took her to a restaurant on Oak Street. When their food came, he let her eat in peace. Or else he was giving her time to think things over.

Claire finished the last of her sandwich and pushed her empty plate aside. "This has absolutely nothing to do with Frank's murder, but here's your explanation." She told him about the watch and how it led her to Melissa's boutique.

"Why are you looking for Hatch?"

Had he heard a single word she'd said? She considered suggesting that he record their conversation so that he didn't have to keep repeating his questions but thought better of it.

"I think Frank's cabin burned while I was in Michigan, and I'm looking for a someone who saw the fire. That's why I talked to Daniel. That's why I'm looking for Hatch." *And none of this is news to you.*

"How did you know Melissa had a key to Hatch's apartment?"

"I didn't. We were talking, the subject of Hatch came up, and she offered me the key. I took it. It was spur of the moment, not planned or thought through."

The look on Captain Robinson's face said he found that last painfully obvious. Claire wondered if Frank's mistress had set her up. She smoothed her napkin and placed it on top of her dirty plate.

"How did you know I was there?" she said.

"We're looking for Hatch, too. Remember?"

"You were watching his apartment?" *Of course they were. Melissa didn't have to set me up. I did it to myself.*

He answered her question with one of his own. "Did you think that you could find Hatch, and if you asked nicely, he'd tell you all about the fire?"

"I'm not that stupid."

"I hope not," he said. "What can you tell me about Ronald Hatch?"

"As I said before, nothing. Frank introduced us. Hatch grunted a hello. That was the full extent of our conversation and the only time we ever spoke." She lifted her shoulders and let them drop. "I thought he acted like a thug."

"Didn't you wonder why a successful businessman would employ a thug?"

"I did," she admitted, "and I asked. Frank said that Hatch provided companionship and protection." The word, protection, hung in the air, ensuring there would be more questions. She had regretted it the moment it left her mouth.

He gestured to the waiter, ordered a cup of coffee and asked if she wanted one. A busboy cleared their dishes, and the waiter returned with two coffees. When they were alone again, he said, "Did Palmer say why he needed protection or from whom?"

"No. It was a joke."

"Was that the end of the conversation?"

"Not quite." She had committed to full disclosure. "I said something flippant about getting a dog, something about a pit bull standing in for Hatch very nicely. Frank laughed and said he couldn't train a pit bull to drive a car. That was the end of the conversation."

"Why didn't you mention this before?"

Captain Robinson had mastered the art of interrogating someone while drinking coffee. He'd ask a question and then raise his cup to take a drink, watching her the whole time. She wondered if the man was ever off duty. Was he even human?

"I forgot about it," she said. "And maybe Hatch really isn't a thug." The relationship between Hatch and Frank had reminded her of a dog and his master, but learning more about Hatch had given her a different perspective. "He was in the Army. I think he saw himself as Frank's aide-de-camp. You know, General Palmer and Private Hatch."

"Hatch is an ex-convict."

"That's really none of my business." Claire winced. Even to her ears, the comment sounded prissy.

"Why has it taken you so long to mention that Palmer talked about needing protection?"

"I told you, I forgot. And I still think he was joking. Obviously, if someone murdered him, he really did need protection, but he was joking about it then." She added cream and sugar to the coffee she didn't want and took a sip. It tasted terrible. The waiter was hanging around, looking in the other direction but probably eavesdropping. "I have to get back to work."

"What did you plan to do if Hatch returned while you were in his apartment?"

Claire looked down at her hands. There was no answer to that question.

"Playing detective is both foolish and dangerous. I suggest you stay away from Hatch's apartment." He signaled the waiter for their bill. "I'll drop you at your car."

"Thank you, but I'd rather walk." She placed a twenty-dollar bill on the table. It was too much, but all she had. "For my lunch. Leave a good tip."

After a long look, he said, "Have a nice walk, Ms. Marshall. We'll be in touch. Meanwhile, don't leave New Orleans without notifying the police department."

By the time Claire reached the corner, the cool wind had raised goose bumps on her arms. Where had she left her sweater? A flutter of genuine panic hit as she remembered dropping it on the kitchen floor when the policeman banged on the door. If Hatch found it, he'd know someone had been in his apartment. As if Melissa won't tell him. Maybe not, she'd have to admit that she'd handed out his key. Claire walked faster.

The patrol car was still in the parking lot, although no longer blocking her car. If she went back inside Hatch's apartment, they'd stop her and demand an explanation, and she couldn't bear to talk to any more policemen—not today. It was a minor miracle she hadn't had a panic attack. It didn't look as if Hatch planned to return any time soon. She'd get her sweater tomorrow.

Captain Robinson had told her to stay away, but he couldn't forbid her to retrieve her sweater. Could he? She needed legal advice. The only lawyers she knew worked on real estate closings. Except Paul Gilbert. She hated to ask Frank's lawyer for more help, but it was him or the yellow pages.

18

Mike tossed his coat over the chair and fixed himself a fresh pot of coffee. The cup at the restaurant had tasted like battery acid. His was an improvement, although nothing like the brew Paul Gilbert served. If he left the police department, he could go into private practice, get a bunch of rich clients, and drink fine coffee. The hours would be better, too.

Heading up the homicide division was a full-time job, and now he was juggling those responsibilities with legwork on the Palmer case. Vernon had ordered him to keep a close eye on the situation, but that didn't require his personal participation—not any more. He should hand it off, assign someone else to work with Breton, but the case had gotten under his skin. He wanted this entirely too clever killer. And the detectives he trusted already had their plates full.

Breton knocked on his open door and walked in. "How was lunch with our favorite murder-arson suspect? Or is it arson-murder?"

"Word travels quickly." Very quickly. He'd left the restaurant thirty minutes ago.

"Did you find out what she was doing in Hatch's apartment? I hear she had a key."

"Looking for clues to Hatch's present location. You saw Melissa give her the key."

"So, our redheads are friends?" He waggled his eyebrows. "Bosom buddies so to speak?"

"Or, they met this morning." Mike let his tone convey skepticism. Melissa Yates didn't strike him as a woman who formed friendships quickly or trusted easily. "Claire went to Melissa's shop to return a pricey watch Palmer had given her."

"The day after they bury the guy, his fiancée cashes in an expensive gift, which he just happened to buy at his mistress's shop? I tell you, it gets me right here." Breton patted his chest in the vicinity of his heart. "Where's the key now?"

"Claire has it. I advised her to stay away from the apartment. We'll see if she listens. Her record's not good." He walked over to the windowsill. "How about some coffee?"

"No time. Vernon wants to meet with us. And that's the good news. The bad news is he mentioned your lunch date."

"She complained that we were making her miss meals, which was at least partly true. I offered to buy her lunch, hoping she'd loosen up and become a bit more cooperative."

"Candy's dandy, liquor's quicker. I don't know where lunch fits in." Breton cracked wise, as usual, but this time he added a caution. "You might want to rephrase your explanation. Before you arrived, there was a very public incident of an investigator getting cozy with an attractive suspect who turned out to be guilty as hell. The Vermin is still sensitive on the subject."

"Lunch was strictly business. She insisted upon paying for her meal." Hearing himself echo Claire's protest about a shared restaurant meal revived a question that had been nagging him. He sat back down. "There's a call I want to make first."

"Is it more important than not keeping your boss waiting when he's already pissed off."

"I want to talk to Palmer's travel agent." He picked up the phone.

"It's too late to leave town, podnuh."

Mike motioned Breton to be quiet. He identified himself and asked to speak to whoever had worked with Frank Palmer.

"That would be me, " the man who answered the phone said. "I handled all Mr. Palmer's reservations—business and personal."

"I'm interested in the honeymoon trip."

"Such a tragedy."

Mike listened impatiently while the agent expressed sorrow at Palmer's untimely death then asked when the reservations were made. The answer led to their first real break.

"I think it was just last Tuesday, but let me check my records. Yes, here it is. The very same day we made the reservations for Mr. Hatch's North Carolina vacation."

"Can you give me both itineraries? We've been looking for Mr. Hatch." He grabbed a pen and gave Breton a thumbs up.

"How'd you know?" Breton asked after Mike concluded the call.

"I didn't. I wanted to know if Palmer made the honeymoon reservations before or after Claire Marshall left town. The answer is immediately after. Your girlfriend Jeanette made that call. Palmer himself booked a roundtrip to Raleigh-Durham for Ronald Hatch, leaving early Thursday morning and returning tomorrow evening. Our friendly travel agent never watches the news or reads the paper. Too depressing, he says. He didn't know anyone was looking for Hatch."

"When Vernon hears this, he might forget about your lunch date."

Mike shook his head. It wasn't a date, but if he said so again, he'd be protesting too much. "One more call."

The airline said that Hatch had used the first half of the roundtrip ticket. Now, they were ready to talk to Vernon.

Melissa lifted her soda can and put it back down. She repeated the movement until she'd left a string of wet circles on the glass countertop. It looked like a giant pearl necklace. She went back and added an overlapping circle between each pearl. Now, it looked like a big chain. A crazy chain of events—that was the expression Claire had used.

When the cops called, she'd been tempted to say, What key? Who's Claire Marshall? It would have been funny but not worth being caught in a lie. The cops would wonder what else she was lying about—not that she knew enough to lie. Frank told her he was going to pull off the deal of a lifetime, but he never said what it was. It was going to be a surprise. Until something really screwed up the chain of events.

She wiped the glass clean and stared at her reflection. Blurry as it was, she could see the vertical lines etched between her brows. Twenty-four years old and she was getting frown lines. Frank hated it when age showed on her face.

She was thirteen when she caught his eye. She gave him her virginity on her fourteenth birthday; he gave her a real diamond bracelet like rich women and tennis stars wore. She'd considered herself a woman of the world, someone who knew what she wanted and how to get it.

Looking back from the perspective of twenty-four, she saw a more complicated reality and a higher price. When the other girls giggled about boys getting fresh, she'd remained silent, an initiate isolated by her sophistication. She left no girlfriends behind when she moved from The

Home, and she had none now.

Hatch was her only friend, and where the hell was he? He'd called her hotel Wednesday night, babbling about Frank's Jeep. She'd been cross-eyed after a long day at the Merchandise Mart and had blown him off. She'd spent the weekend cooped up in her hotel room, waiting for Frank's call that never came.

Frank was dead. Yesterday afternoon she stood in the cemetery and watched them slide his coffin into the tomb, but it still didn't seem real. The man who loved her was going to spend eternity lying next to the wife he despised—or whatever was left of her. Annie Lewis had been dead for five years. *Whatever was left of Frank.* Paul said the coffin had to be closed because his body was so badly burned.

Her phone rang. Paul Gilbert's lamebrain receptionist reminded her she had a four o'clock appointment with God's gift to the law.

"Of course, I remember. It's the high point of my day."

She locked the front door and adjusted her Back-in-a-Minute sign to five-thirty. Upstairs she prepared herself for a meeting with the son of a bitch who'd tried from the beginning to get Frank to dump her. All those years, she'd been terrified that he'd succeed. Now he never would, but she still hated him. Mr. Born on Third Base who'd be nothing without his family's money dared look down on people like her who had to make their own way. His snotty attitude infuriated her, but she knew how to make him squirm.

Melissa settled herself in the chair. As usual, Paul was hiding behind his big desk. She leaned forward, letting him see she wasn't wearing a bra. He looked away, pretending not to notice, so she straightened up and uncrossed and re-crossed her legs. Her stockings made a rustling sound as her legs slid against each other. She could hear it and so could he, but the game wasn't as much fun without Frank there to watch. She gazed at Paul through lowered lashes.

"You wanted to talk to me?"

"When we spoke the other day I was aware that Frank had made provisions for your future welfare."

"Frank always took good care of me." She switched legs again, and her skirt slid higher.

Paul kept his eyes on the papers he was fooling with. "Frank's insurance agent called to ask if I knew how to contact you. I mentioned this meeting and suggested he join us. I trust that's acceptable." He looked up and smiled at her.

"What does he want?" Anything that made Paul happy made her nervous.

"Why don't we let him explain?" He pushed a button on the intercom. "Suzanne, please send Mr. Reynolds in as soon as he arrives."

It turned out he was already there. The door opened and a gray-haired man wearing a gray suit walked in. Even his skin looked gray.

"Melissa dear, this is Don Reynolds, who was Frank's insurance agent. Don, this is Melissa Yates, who needs no further introduction."

"Nice to meet you." Melissa nodded to Don.

The gray man stared as if he'd never seen a woman before and said to call him Don. He dragged a chair up next to hers, pulled a folder out of his brief case and spoke to her chest.

"Shortly before his death, Frank modified a life insurance policy that I helped him set it up several years ago. It's what we call a key man policy. Its purpose was to protect FP Development in the case of Frank's death. The policy includes a double indemnity clause."

She turned away. Let the creep stare at her back.

"Don't bother with the details, Don," Paul interrupted. "Melissa only cares about what directly affects her. And Melissa, this does affect you."

The agent cleared his throat like he was going to make an important announcement. "You're going to be a rich woman, Melissa. Frank altered the terms of this policy to make you the beneficiary. As a result, you'll receive ten million dollars."

Paul's mouth was moving, but the roaring in her head drowned out his words. *Ten million dollars!* Frank never mentioned any life insurance. She ought to say something, but her mind wouldn't string words together. From the corner of her eye, she saw Don Reynolds reach over. She glared and he stopped, his hand fluttering above her legs. If he touched her, she'd knock his gray ass into next month.

She tugged her skirt down and tried to think. Had Frank decided to dump her, and this was the pay-off? Ten million dollars for ten years of her life? No. She only got the money if Frank was dead. He must have known his life was in danger—something to do with that big deal. This insurance policy was his way of looking after her in case things went wrong. Like they did. She cut to the chase.

"When do I get the money?"

Paul nodded toward the insurance agent, who cleared his throat again.

"Our usual procedure is to make the payment as soon as we receive the death certificate, but given the, um, circumstances we're also requiring an affidavit from the medical examiner. It's just a formality." He started putting papers back in his briefcase.

"What circumstances?" she said.

"The circumstances surrounding Frank's death," Paul said. "You have talked to the police haven't you, dear? No offense, but I think they'll be interested in your windfall." He smiled again.

It only took a moment before she understood. "This life insurance is going to make the cops think I killed Frank. That's what you're implying, isn't it?"

The son of a bitch had set her up, and he thought it was funny. That's why he couldn't stop smiling. When Paul Gilbert was involved, the lid stayed on, but even Paul couldn't make murder go away. Someone had to take the fall, and she'd been elected.

"I hope you don't find it presumptuous, but I've already considered your legal situation." Paul leaned back in his chair, Mr. Cool, Calm and Collected, now that she was in the hot seat.

"Are you offering to be my lawyer?" Before she finished the question, the snotty bastard was shaking his head.

"As the attorney for Frank's estate, I have a potential conflict of interest. And I believe your interests would be better served by an attorney who specializes in criminal defense." He handed her a business card. "Ben Patterson is apprised of the general situation. Whether or not you talk to him is, of course, your decision."

She grabbed the card and walked out, slamming the door behind her. Hard.

Paul chuckled. He had struggled to keep a straight face as the comedy unfolded. As usual, Melissa had dressed like a slut. He envisioned her going through her closet, asking herself what Barbie would wear if Ken died.

Don had played his role to perfection. Paul had known he would. When they were in prep school, Don had drilled a peephole into the girl's locker room. Whenever some pervert was arrested for looking up women's skirts in Wal-Mart, he thought of Don Reynolds. Watching the man gawk at Melissa's unfettered bosom had been truly amusing. Her obvious annoyance was lagniappe.

He opened the antique commode that concealed his liquor cabinet.

"I can offer you wine, or if you prefer, something stronger."

"Bourbon if you have it. No water." Don looked shaken. "Frank was murdered?"

"According to the police. It will be on the news this evening. I took the liberty of telling them about the insurance policy. You'll probably be hearing from a Captain Mike Robinson. He was most interested in the change of beneficiaries."

"Do you think Melissa had something to do with Frank's death?" Don gulped a twelve-year-old bourbon that deserved to be sipped.

"I don't know, but if she did, wouldn't it negate her right to the proceeds?" That Reynolds should consider this before authorizing payment went unsaid but, surely, not unheard.

"Should our legal department contact you?"

"Absolutely not. I'm Frank's executor, not Melissa's lawyer."

Paul would paint his naked body blue and beg for quarters on Bourbon Street before he took Melissa Yates as a client. Frank had directed him to look out for her interests when he was no longer in a position to do so. He'd meant after his marriage to Claire, but under the circumstances, Paul felt obliged to interpret the charge broadly. Ben Patterson was a top-notch criminal attorney, not quite as good as Felix Moreau, but Claire had asked first.

He took pity on Don who still wore a deer in the headlights look. "Stop by Suzanne's desk on your way out. She'll give you Melissa's contact information."

19

Felix Moreau, Claire's new lawyer, picked her up at her office Friday morning. He used the drive time to review his primary goal for their upcoming meeting, to find out what the police knew or thought they knew without telling them anything they didn't know or could misinterpret.

"Getting them to leave you alone is a secondary goal and one that might not be achievable, but I'll do my best."

Felix had insisted they talk to both Captain Robinson and Superintendent Vernon. If the head of homicide was conducting interviews, the case was top priority, which meant Vernon would be involved. Any meeting without him would be a waste of time.

Her lawyer's time was too expensive to waste. Yesterday afternoon's introductory session had cost four hundred dollars, and today would be another four hundred. The thousand-dollar retainer she'd paid was melting away. She couldn't afford to be a murder suspect for much longer.

"Remember," he said as they entered police headquarters, "do not, I repeat, do not answer any question until I've said they can ask it. That's why you're paying me."

"That won't make me look guilty?"

"Anything else will make you look foolish." He patted her shoulder. "Relax, you'll be fine."

When they walked into the conference room, Superintendent Vernon and Felix greeted each other with handshakes and smiles. They were on a first name basis, and that's how the meeting went, Henry and

Mike talking to Felix and Claire. Lieutenant Breton hadn't been invited.

Speaking only after Felix nodded his assent made Claire feel like a child sitting at the grown-up's table, but she was paying too much for his advice to disregard it. If Captain Robinson—she still had difficulty thinking of him as Mike—regretted telling her to hire a lawyer or was annoyed about her lawyer going over his head, he hid it well.

Under pressure from Felix, Henry Vernon acknowledged that, of course, Claire was free to travel as she pleased. If the police wanted to interview her again, Mike or someone working for him would contact Felix to arrange an interview. The meeting ended with a second round of friendly handshakes.

Claire left police headquarters convinced that Felix was worth every penny. "I'm so glad to have that behind me. Thank you," she said.

"I would not assume it's behind you. All we did was confirm that they don't have enough evidence to bring charges."

"Charges for what? They admitted that I didn't break any law by not reporting the cabin sooner. The fire was out. They practically admitted that everything happened while I was a thousand miles away from Frank or his cabin."

Felix didn't answer until they were in his car and underway. "I think the police either know or strongly suspect Hatch was involved in Frank's death. If you were conspiring with him, being in Michigan when the cabin burned doesn't mean much."

His words hit her like a slap across the face. He was right. That's why the police kept asking about Hatch. Going to his apartment had been unbelievably stupid.

"Don't look at me like that, Claire. I believe that you had nothing to do with either the fire or Frank's death."

"Were you and Frank friends?" When talking to the police, Felix had referred to Frank as Mr. Palmer but, when it was just the two of them, he said Frank.

"Not close, although certainly friends. In many ways, New Orleans is a small town."

She should have known. Paul, who was Frank's friend as well as his lawyer, had recommended Felix. Paul had called and made an appointment for her when Felix's secretary said his calendar was full until next month. These men all knew each other. She was the outsider, needing their help and dependent upon their goodwill. Had Frank told Felix they planned to marry?

"I'm afraid you'll be a suspect until the real criminal's found," Felix said. "If we need to, we'll hire our own investigator. It's an expensive option, and I don't think necessary at this point. For now, you should just sit tight."

Sit tight. That was easy for him to say. When he went to the bank, no sympathetic teller whispered that the police had been asking about his finances. His picture wasn't on the front page of the newspaper. No reporters lurked at the end of his driveway. He didn't wake up sweat-drenched and terrified at 2:00 a.m.

The nightmare had recurred last night. This morning, driving in broad daylight on city streets, she'd kept checking her rearview mirror, afraid she'd see the dark sedan. There was no point telling Felix any of this.

"Why on earth does anyone think I'd want to harm Frank?"

"Why doesn't really matter." He shrugged. "Human beings do all sorts of terrible things for the flimsiest of reasons. The police know that."

And so, apparently, did Felix. She was still learning.

He dropped her back at her office with a final warning. "Don't discuss anything with the police unless I'm present. I don't care how innocuous it might seem. And for God's sake, no more visits to Hatch's apartment."

"I left my sweater there."

"Buy yourself a new sweater. The police are looking for a connection between the two of you. Don't create one." Warning delivered, he drove away.

Claire changed into work clothes and drove over to the once and future Laurens family home. She found Jack supervising the removal of lowered ceilings on the second floor.

"How did it go?" he said.

"Well. Felix did a good job, and the police have backed off."

"They should have left you alone in the first place."

Claire appreciated Jack's loyalty, but she was all too aware that she had drawn attention to herself. Some of this was her fault.

"I'll be downstairs," she said.

She had already measured every inch of the bedraggled house and identified the original walls. Her next task was to discover what, if anything, remained of architectural features that had been covered up. This search for buried treasure was her favorite part of a restoration, but today she was distracted.

Slowly, she slid the stud finder along the wall, looking for the fireplace and mantel that she hoped lay behind the wallboard, and tried not to think about the police or Frank or Hatch. Through the open front door, she saw a police car cruise slowly past. It probably had nothing to do with her. Or maybe it did, if Felix was right. And he probably was. She moved the stud finder another four inches to the left and marked where it indicated the beginning of something solid. The mantel?

She put the stud finder down and picked up a utility knife to cut a peek hole in the wallboard. She pressed the knife against the wall, her hand slipped, and the blade caught her palm. It wasn't a deep cut, but it was bleeding. She wrapped a rag around her hand to staunch the flow. The first aid kit was in her truck. Her purse was there, too, and her pills. She hurried outside.

A tight bandage stopped the bleeding, but Claire still felt queasy. She lowered the windows and lay across the front seat, waiting for the pill to kick in and for the sick feeling to go away. Her new life, a haphazard reconstruction at best, was falling apart. The panic attacks were back unless she took extra meds, and then there were side effects. She'd cut herself because her concentration and coordination were off. What good were sleeping pills when sleep opened the door to nightmares? She wasn't thinking straight. Her attempts to find a witness to the fire had been a fool's game that only aroused suspicion.

Getting a lawyer had been smart. *Thank you, Captain Robinson.* Felix would help with the police and their interrogations, but he couldn't do anything about the reporters who waited at the end of her driveway with their cameras and microphones. He'd told her to be patient. Another scandal would push Frank's death off the front page.

When? Every day, some new event kept it there. Wednesday, it was the funeral. Yesterday, the police announced that Frank had been murdered. Jeanette had been on television every night, going on about the tragic romance and the honeymoon that never happened. She went to find Jack.

"I'm leaving." She showed him the cut on her hand. It was nothing serious, but the bandage made her clumsy, and she couldn't get anything done. "I'll see you tomorrow morning."

Jeanette opened the door before Claire rang the bell. "I'm so glad you called. I wasn't doing anything. Please come in. Let me give you a hug. You poor thing, how're you doing? Come in. Come in. Oh, Claire, it's so wonderful to see you. Don't mind me. I've been crying ever since I saw on the news last night that Frank was murdered. It was bad enough that he died, but murdered? I just can't believe it. Are you thirsty? Can I fix you a cola?"

The act of pouring sodas helped Jeanette regain her composure. When they sat down, she started talking about the honeymoon arrangements.

"I found a wonderful resort in Saint Barts. Frank said it was just what he was looking for. You had an ocean view from your private balcony, your own honeymoon Jacuzzi, everything. It was fantastic, right on the beach." The topic unleashed a new flood of tears. She blew her nose and added the dirty tissue to the growing pile on the floor. "They even had a stable so you could go riding. Frank said you liked horses."

The specificity of the honeymoon preparations erased Claire's last doubt. Frank must have planned to propose when he picked her up at the airport. He'd obviously expected her to say yes. The assumption astonished her. Was it arrogance? Had he confused her desire to do a good job on his cottage with something more personal? She couldn't remember doing or saying anything that could be misinterpreted that way.

"I was so happy for him," Jeanette said. "He'd been through so much, first Annie Lewis's accident and then Annalisa running away. The poor man was just torn up. Some people thought he became bitter, but I knew he was hiding his pain. And then, when he told me you all were getting married, he was happy, the man he used to be."

Listening to Jeanette burble, Claire realized that truth alone wouldn't dissuade her—not when Frank had told her otherwise. She listened with half an ear and cobbled together an explanation that might persuade Jeanette to see something closer to the truth.

"That honeymoon would have been quite a surprise," she said.

"Frank loved to surprise people." Jeanette smiled through her sniffling.

"I think he planned to surprise me—and not just the honeymoon. I promise you, Frank never proposed. He never even mentioned marriage." She saw Jeanette's incredulous expression and added, "Really, it was all a surprise." After several more references to surprises, Jeanette came on board.

"I bet he was going to ask you to go away with him for the weekend and then surprise you by proposing when you were in the airplane on your way to Saint Barts."

Claire smiled and nodded agreement, although she would never have gone away for a weekend with Frank Palmer.

Once Jeanette accepted the possibility that there was no engagement, Claire introduced the idea that there was no romance. Her first attempt elicited an outraged denial. She persisted, emphasizing her own shortcomings. She wasn't ready for a relationship with any man, not even Frank Palmer.

After several go-rounds, Jeanette finally, reluctantly, admitted that she'd never actually seen any show of affection. "But Frank said—"

"Frank was a charming man." *When it served his purpose.* "I think he was used to getting his way with women, and he was confident that I'd say yes. If he'd lived, who knows what might have happened."

The answer was nothing, but let Jeanette find comfort in the belief that her beloved boss died on the verge of a new love affair. There could be no harm in preserving that last bit of illusion.

Claire stayed another hour listening to rambling reminiscences and asking questions. She left with Jeanette's promise of no more interviews. In that sense, her visit was a success, but she'd also hoped to gain more insight into Frank's life and, perhaps, to find something that might have been a motive for his death. Neither had happened.

For all her talk, Frank's Girl Friday, as Jeanette liked to call herself, knew surprisingly little about his business. She said the company was experiencing cash flow problems because an important deal was interrupted, but she was fuzzy on the details. She thought Frank's murder had something to do with this mysterious business deal.

That theory struck Claire as farfetched. Botched deals lead to lawsuits, not murder. There was something very personal about murder.

Jeanette knew even less about Frank's private life. She had no idea why Annalisa ran away or where the girl was now. "It's no wonder she left. It was just awful. Annie Lewis's parents acted like it was Frank's fault. Whenever I think about how they treated him at his own wife's funeral, I could just spit."

Claire's questions about the accident brought only sobs and denials.

"I still can't talk about it," Jeanette said.

Did Frank bear some responsibility for his wife's death? That would explain the bad relationship with his in-laws and possibly the disappearance of the daughter whose existence he denied. Might it have a bearing on his murder five years later? Neither Melissa nor Paul Gilbert would confide any of Frank's secrets, and she didn't have the heart to ask Bobby Austin, but she knew how to find information in old newspapers.

20

Bad weather had aggravated the usual Friday night delays. Flight 583 from Atlanta to New Orleans and continuing on to Dallas was two hours overdue and counting. Mike and Breton were among a dozen or so people hanging around the gate. Most slouched in the rigid seats and stared sightlessly at the walls, the floor, the ceiling. Now and then, one of the more restless walked over to the window and peered out at the wet tarmac.

A cowboy napped, his ten-gallon hat tilted over his face and his blue jean clad legs stretched out so that people had to step over them. Mike noticed he was wearing brown oxfords, not boots. He pointed it out to Breton who muttered, urban cowboy.

A few seats away, a heavy-set man, wearing a black leather vest emblazoned with a grinning skull and *New Orleans Avengers*, pulled out a pack of cigarettes and lit one in blatant disregard of the large no smoking sign. He returned Mike's glance with a defiant sneer and turned to the heavily tattooed woman beside him.

"See those two guys? Five will get you ten they're cops." He jutted his chin at them and spoke loudly enough that several people turned to look. "Bet they're after someone on this flight. That's why the plane's late." His belligerent expression dared anyone to challenge his judgment.

No one did, although two people moved to the other side of the gate area. Breton mumbled something about telling the bigmouth where to put the cigarette. Mike told him not to bother. Several minutes later, the cowboy stood and ambled down the concourse. When time passed and he didn't return, Mike wondered if he'd found another flight to Dallas or wanted to avoid police.

Forty more minutes passed before a disembodied voice announced that flight 583 was in the area and would be on the ground within the next few minutes. People stood and stretched, finished their soft drinks and tossed the cups in the trash. They kept their distance when Mike and Breton positioned themselves on either side of the jetway door.

"Think he'll be on it?" Breton said.

"Someone's using his ticket."

Hatch exited in the middle of the pack. He looked scruffy in black jeans, a black t-shirt with the sleeves rolled up, and sunglasses. His arms and face were sunburned, and his nose had peeled raw in spots. Mike nudged Breton. "The man in black."

They fell in alongside their quarry. Breton whistled a few bars of "I Walk the Line", but Hatch didn't notice them until Mike spoke.

"Excuse me, Mr. Hatch. We're with the New Orleans Police Department, and we'd like to talk to you."

Hatch stopped and looked from one to the other. "We've got nothing to talk about."

"Let us be the judge of that," Mike said.

"Have a heart, man. I'm beat. It's been a shitty trip. The flight's delayed, and then we hit thunderstorms. Kid across the aisle puked all over the floor. And now you."

"It'll be a few minutes until your luggage comes up. We can talk while we wait."

"I tell you I'm clean." Hatch walked between them for several steps. "You want a crime? Look at how the airlines treat their paying passengers."

Breton clapped him on the back. "You can file a complaint down at headquarters, amigo."

They walked in silence to the baggage claim. Despite the late hour and relatively low lighting, Hatch kept his sunglasses on.

"You look like you've been at the beach." Mike said.

"I've been visiting my uncle, north of Wilmington. Last I heard it wasn't a crime to visit family."

"Why last week?"

"What the hell kind of question is that? Last week is when my boss gave me time off." Hatch warmed to the topic. "My boss is Frank Palmer. He's a big man in New Orleans, and he's got important friends. Frank's not going to be happy when he hears that cops are hassling one of his employees. Maybe you want to stop asking dumb questions and let me get my own luggage."

"Not yet." Mike saw his surprise reflected on Breton's face. What planet had Hatch been on that he didn't know Frank Palmer was dead?

"Oh yeah?" Hatch upped the ante. "Maybe I ought to call Frank right now."

"I'm afraid you can't do that." Breton said.

"The hell I can't. There's a pay phone over there, and I got a quarter."

"You can't do that, amigo, because Palmer is dead. That's why we want to talk to you."

Hatch took off his sunglasses, revealing bloodshot pale blue eyes. "What happened to Frank?" he croaked.

Mike wished Breton hadn't been so quick to spill the beans, but there was no going back. He settled into observation mode.

"Your boss's cabin burned down with him in it." Breton was enjoying himself.

Hatch's stunned disbelief turned into something close to amusement. "You expect me to believe that?"

"It was supposed to look like an accident, but we know better. Palmer was dead before the fire started. He was murdered. The fire was arson. Now, let's talk."

"You got to be joking."

"We're homicide. We don't think murder is funny."

Hatch opened and shut his mouth like a fish gasping for air. Apprehension replaced amusement, and his eyes darted toward the exit. Mike put a restraining hand on his arm.

"We're hoping you can help us with our investigation. Do you have any idea who might have killed Frank Palmer?"

Hatch buried his face in his hands.

"You were with him before he died. Did he appear to be nervous? Concerned about anything?"

At each question, Hatch shook his head from side to side, but he didn't look up.

"Do you know of any reason why anyone would want to kill him?" Mike persisted.

Frank Palmer's driver lifted his head. "I want a lawyer."

They weren't going to learn anything from Hatch, not tonight. Mike recited the Miranda warning and said, "You can call a lawyer as soon as we book you."

"No lawyer worth shit takes calls this hour of the night." Hatch put his bravado back on with his sunglasses. "You want to make me spend the night in jail? Big fucking deal. I've been there before."

Breton carried Hatch's suitcase as they walked to their car, one of a scattering of vehicles left in the pay-by-the-hour lot. They kept Hatch between them, blocking any possible escape with their bodies, prepared to tackle him if he made a run for it.

"What about my car?" Hatch said. "I leave it here another day, I got to pay another four-fifty."

"That's the least of your troubles." Breton opened the car door.

Hatch didn't speak again until they reached headquarters. "You're telling me that you found Frank's body in the cabin?"

"That's right," Mike said. "Do you want to talk about it?"

"I got nothing to say until I talk to my lawyer."

Mike signed the papers and handed Hatch over to the booking officer. "We're done for tonight," he told Breton. "See you tomorrow."

"It's gonna be tomorrow in twenty minutes. We've been on the job sixteen hours straight. Tomorrow's Saturday, and you want to be back here interrogating this clown?"

"If you wanted a nine to five job, why'd you become a cop?"

"I'm just saying that there's more to life. We have our man. Let him spend the weekend in a cell. We got seventy-two hours before he gets a hearing. Come on, Mike," Breton pleaded, "we can question him Monday morning."

"Ten tomorrow morning. Meet in my office at nine forty-five." Mike had little sympathy for Breton, who was going home. He was headed back to the office to call Corlette, a late call in more ways than one.

Corlette picked up, and Mike began with an apology. "Sorry to call so late."

"No problem. I'm wide awake, reading a chapter for my abnormal psych class. Seems everyone I know really is nuts. So, why aren't you in bed?"

"We just picked Hatch up at the airport. He's been visiting relatives in North Carolina for the past week."

"Someone spotted him in the airport?"

"We were waiting for him." This was the tough part. "We found out about the plane ticket yesterday afternoon but, frankly, we didn't bring you in on it because we weren't sure he'd be on the flight." Mike heard himself say "frankly" and cringed. Every cop knew that people prefaced a statement with frankly when they were about to shade the truth.

"You could have mentioned it when we talked this afternoon."

"You're right." He should have informed Lafourche Parish yesterday. He hadn't because Vernon ordered silence until they had Hatch in custody. Mike came from a military tradition that respected the hierarchy of command, but respect was a two-way street, and he'd had a bellyful of Vernon's micromanagement.

"So, what does Hatch have to say?"

"He claims he didn't know Palmer was dead, and I believe him."

"You do?"

Corlette sounded surprised, as well he might. The last time they discussed possible scenarios they'd agreed Hatch was the likely arsonist. The likeliest scenario said someone had hired Hatch to kill Palmer and torch the cabin and then tried to get rid of him with the booby-trapped Jeep. Finding Hatch alive had seemed like the best way to solve the case. Now they had him, it wasn't looking that way.

"When we picked him up, he threatened us with repercussions, starting with a phone call to Palmer. I don't think he was faking."

"Then what?"

"The news of Palmer's death knocked him for a loop, and he clammed up." Silence from the other end of the line, told Mike what Corlette was thinking. New Orleans had really screwed up. He admitted it and took responsibility for Breton's big mouth.

"I wish we hadn't dropped that bombshell so early in the conversation."

"I want to talk to Hatch."

"We booked him about twenty minutes ago. He's tucked in for the night. First thing tomorrow morning, he's calling a lawyer. We're planning to interview him at ten. I thought you'd want to sit in."

"Participate, not sit in, participate. It's our case. The crimes occurred in Lafourche Parish."

"We should have brought you in sooner." Mike offered another *mea culpa.* All in all, Corlette was taking the news better than he had a right to expect.

"I want a briefing before I talk to Hatch."

"Lieutenant Breton and I are meeting in my office at a quarter to ten. Show up before then and I'll tell you everything we know. Unfortunately, it won't take long."

"I'll be there at nine fifteen."

"Bring anything you have that might help." He told Corlette what he hadn't said to Breton. "I'm not confident we have enough to hold him."

21

Claire, who usually slept in Saturday mornings, was waiting at the door when the library opened. She went directly to the microfiche room, a familiar spot because old newspapers were a gold mine of information about historic houses. Today's quest was for more recent news. Jeanette had said five years ago, so Claire pulled the tapes for 1988.

The death of Annie Lewis Palmer made the first page of the March 16 metro section. Frank's wife had died instantly when her car struck a cement abutment on Claiborne Avenue. She'd been alone in the car, and no other vehicles were involved. Police said her car had been traveling at a high rate of speed. Claire knew that stretch of road. Narrow lanes divided by pillars supported the highway overhead. Frequent intersections and numerous stoplights precluded speeding unless the driver was very drunk or...

Did Frank's wife commit suicide?

Claire had thought about suicide. When panic attacks began making her life a misery, death seemed the only escape. One night she sat in Tom's old Toyota and imagined driving off a causeway or into something hard. She sat there for hours. Then she went inside and called her mother, who flew to New Orleans and took her to see Doctor Bennett. He prescribed the pills that blunted pain and blurred sharp edges. She told him about the panic attacks, and he added anti-anxiety meds.

Mother and daughter had returned to Michigan together. Her mother rented a house on the lake, and they spent hours walking the beach, sometimes talking but more often silent. Claire began walking alone, watching the waves and counting them, finding solace in their inevitability. She returned to New Orleans, grateful to the woman who'd given her life—not once but twice.

Annie Lewis Palmer's story had a different ending. Or maybe it was a different story. Claire scanned the next several days' papers but found no follow-up article. The obituary listed four surviving relatives; husband Frank, daughter Annalisa, and parents Mr. and Mrs. William Fulton of Whitfield, Alabama.

The Fultons would be the people Jeanette said were so hard on Frank. Nothing in the newspaper explained why, but if Annie Lewis Palmer had killed herself, her parents could easily blame Frank. They might think he'd driven her to it. Did this have any bearing on his murder? Would the Fultons talk to her? Even more basic, could she find them?

Long distance information had an A. Fulton and a Richard Fulton in Whitfield, but no William. Claire asked for both numbers and started with A. When a woman answered, she identified herself and said she was calling from New Orleans, trying to reach the Fulton family whose daughter had been married to Frank Palmer.

"I have nothing to say." Click.

By the time Claire had returned the tapes and walked back to her car, she'd talked herself into a road trip. If she could speak to Mrs. Fulton face-to-face and explain the circumstances, Frank's mother-in-law might be willing to talk about him. She found Whitfield, a little dot on her Alabama roadmap. It was just over the Mississippi line and Interstate most of the way.

Claire parked on the square in downtown Whitfield. She found a drugstore and asked the pharmacist if he knew Annette Fulton. Could he give her directions to the house?

The mailbox labeled Fulton was right where he said it would be. A black dog, taller than her Miata, raced down the lawn, barking furiously. The dog escorted her up the driveway and, when she parked, circled her car, still barking. No one came to the door to see what the fuss was about, and so Claire lowered her window an inch and tried to make friends.

"Hey there, big boy. How about letting me out of my car?"

The dog stopped barking and came closer. His tail wasn't wagging, but his hackles weren't up. He was reserving judgment.

"I bet you're a nice dog." She spoke softly and, being careful not make any move that might be interpreted as aggression, eased a flat hand out the window.

He sniffed her fingers.

"Are you hungry?"

She retracted her hand and slid it back out with the remnants of her fast food breakfast on her palm. A sniff, a tentative lick, and half a sausage biscuit disappeared. The dog licked his chops and looked up at her. Tan markings shaped like raised eyebrows gave him a quizzical expression. A graying muzzle said he wasn't young.

"If you chewed your food, it would last longer," she told him.

His tail made a long slow loop in the air.

She opened the door and when the dog didn't object, stepped out. He followed her up the walkway, sniffing her legs, and she assured him that the cat he smelled was back in New Orleans—nothing for him to worry about. They climbed the porch steps together, and he watched her ring the bell.

Chimes echoed inside the house, but no footsteps approached. Claire's shoulders sagged. She'd prepared herself for a hostile encounter but not for an empty house. She was debating whether to wait or go when the door creaked open. A gray-haired woman in a wheelchair glared at her.

"Are you the one who called this morning?"

"Yes, Ma'am, I'm—"

"As I told you and those other reporters, I have nothing to say. Please leave."

"I'm not a reporter. I'm hiding from reporters." Claire hoped the common enemy would gain sympathy.

Mrs. Fulton wasn't buying it. "Well then, you'd better find somewhere else to hide."

"Please. I'm only asking for a few minutes of your time."

"One second talking about Frank Palmer is asking too much." The old woman's voice trembled with emotion. "You get out of here before I call the sheriff."

There was no time for the careful words she'd rehearsed on the drive over, so Claire jumped to the end. "The police think I killed Frank."

Mrs. Fulton, who'd been rolling backwards, froze with her hand on the door. "His slimy lawyer said he died in a fire."

"Someone killed him and set his cabin on fire."

The old woman stared past her, silent, seeing what? Claire looked over her shoulder and saw only fields and fences, trees on a distant horizon. When she turned back, Mrs. Fulton was studying her with an unreadable expression.

"What do you want from me?"

"To learn more about Frank. If I can figure out why someone would want to kill him, I might be able to find someone else for the police to suspect." This lame explanation was the truth, and all she had. "I have to do something or I'll go crazy." More truth, although Mrs. Fulton wouldn't realize it was a literal rather than a figurative truth. The nightmare had invaded her days. She'd just driven two hours on an Interstate afraid to look in her rear view mirror.

"I can't help you. I've neither seen nor spoken to that man since my daughter's funeral." The old woman patted the dog. "I'm surprised Caesar let you out of your car."

"He can tell I like dogs."

"Strays would follow you home."

"Yes." Surprise made Claire smile despite her disappointment. "At least that's what I told my mother." She extended her hand, and the dog nuzzled it.

"That's what Annie Lewis used to tell me—Annalisa, too. Both of them were always bringing home strays. This oversized mongrel was Annalisa's dog. Weren't you, Caesar?"

The dog thumped his tail against the doorframe.

"You say Frank was murdered. I should feel satisfaction, but his death doesn't undo the damage he did to my family." Her eyes glittered with unshed tears.

The woman's distress shamed Claire. She knew Mrs. Fulton didn't want to talk to her, and she'd driven here anyway. She'd stirred up old sorrows, almost certainly memories of a daughter's suicide, and all for nothing. Mrs. Fulton hated Frank, but she was an old lady in a wheelchair who hadn't seen him in years.

"I'm sorry I bothered you. Please forgive me."

"None of what happened is your fault."

"I shouldn't have come. I'm leaving."

"I'll give you a glass of tea before you go. You look tired, and it's a long drive."

"Thank you, Mrs. Fulton. I'd like that." At least they'd part on a friendly note.

"If you're coming in, you might as well call me Annette. Everyone else does." She pointed toward the yard. "Caesar, you stay outside and try to act like a watchdog."

Claire followed Annette into a front room with very familiar furnishings. "My mother has the same sofa and chairs," she said. "Different upholstery, but the exact same furniture." For some reason this brought a lump to her throat. She swallowed hard.

"Where does your mother live?"

"In Michigan. The furniture's been in the family for ages."

"My great grandmother had ours shipped down from Grand Rapids."

Annette led her to the kitchen and took a pitcher of tea from the refrigerator. "We can sit in the sunroom. You'll have to carry your own glass. I'm quite used to making do, but this contraption takes one hand, and I can carry only one glass at a time."

The sunroom was an old porch that had been enclosed. Claire looked out at the rolling green fields.

"What a lovely view you have."

"Does your mother know that the police think you killed someone?"

"No." She sipped iced tea so sweet it made her teeth itch. "The police called and asked questions, but she has no idea how bad things are."

"I didn't know either, not until it was too late."

"I'm sorry. I didn't intend to upset you. I should have thought… I'm so sorry."

"When we were at the door, I felt my daughter's presence. Annie Lewis was there on the porch with you." Annette closed her eyes. "Every day I ask the Lord to help me understand His purpose for the sorrow that has marked my life." She spoke so softly that Claire strained to hear. "I believe He sent you to me. But I didn't help my own daughter, and I don't know how to help you."

"Please, don't let me make you sad. I'm sure you did everything you could. Let me pour you a fresh glass of tea. When you're settled, I'll leave."

"Fix us both another glass and tell me why the police suspect you. I pray I'll be shown a way to help."

Claire hesitated. She'd done enough damage. But Annette insisted, so she told her about wanting to confront Frank and finding the burned cabin. She didn't mention Tom. There was enough talk of loss without that. Nor did she mention her panic attack and taking too many pills. She simply said that she'd believed Frank was elsewhere and called from the beach to report the fire.

"You're very fortunate you didn't go there when he wanted you to."

"If I had, he might still be alive." It was an uncomfortable thought, but she had to face it.

Annette shook her head. "No. You'd be dead. Frank was up to no good, and whoever killed him wouldn't have spared you. If you don't see that, you're a very naïve young woman."

This possibility, something Claire had never considered, sent a shiver down her spine.

"Annie Lewis was naïve, too." Sorrow distorted Annette's face, and Claire thought she might start to cry, but she recovered and said, "It's almost one. Have you eaten lunch?"

Over pimento cheese sandwiches at the kitchen table, they talked about the farm, the weather, and the dog. When they finished, Claire cleared the table and Annette loaded the dishwasher. The routine reminded her of all the times she and her mother had shared this task.

As if reading her mind, Annette said, "Annie Lewis always helped me with the dishes. It was a good time to talk." She put the last plate in and said. "I want you to promise me that what's said in this room will go no further."

"I promise."

"All I know of Frank's life is his time with Annie Lewis. If God gives me the strength, I'll tell you about it." She rolled over to the hall bookcase and pulled out several photo albums, which she brought back to the kitchen table. "I have to start at the beginning."

Over the next hour, Annette walked her through old pictures. They followed Annie Lewis through childhood, grammar school, high school, and on to the University of Alabama. College brought the first mention of Frank Palmer.

"It was her senior year. Frank came to the LSU game with a friend who'd played ball for Alabama. Annie Lewis was a cheerleader. She caught his eye, and he found someone to introduce them. Frank was a good-looking devil, smart as a whip, and charming. He swept her off her feet. They married right after she graduated."

She picked up a slender album covered in white leather. Curling silver script on the cover read *Annie Lewis Fulton and Franklin Hugh*

Palmer II, June 21, 1972. Claire leaned forward, curious to see Frank as a young man, but someone had cut his face out of every picture.

"I did that the day after I buried my daughter." Annette explained without being asked. She moved on to the next album. "Frank worked for a construction company in New Orleans. Annalisa was born there." She showed Claire pictures of the newborn at home with her parents. Frank's face had been excised from these pictures also.

"After Annalisa was born, I went to stay for a couple weeks, just long enough to help Annie Lewis get settled with her new baby. It's the maternal grandmother's privilege and duty." Her smile was sad. "That's when I realized there was trouble in their marriage. Annie Lewis was always calling herself fat and ugly, messing with her hair and make-up." Annette's voice rose in outrage as she catalogued her daughter's growing insecurity, and then dropped to a whisper. "One day, she broke down and told me. As soon as she started getting big with Annalisa, Frank wanted nothing to do with her. He was either working late or out tomcatting."

Claire nodded. She'd met Melissa. There would have been others.

"He didn't want a divorce—no one did—and they came to an accommodation. Annie Lewis agreed to stay in the marriage so that Annalisa would have the advantages of being Frank Palmer's daughter. He was a failure as a human being, but he was a good provider."

Annette, who had been speaking rapidly as if reciting something learned by heart, closed her eyes. Her speech slowed, and each word carried a measure of pain. "It went on like that for years. I thought Annie Lewis had made a tolerable life for herself and her child, but the winter Annalisa turned thirteen…" She put her head in her hands and wept sobs so harsh that Claire felt them in her own throat.

"I'm sorry. I'm so sorry." Claire put her hand on Annette's arm. "Please, you don't have to go on."

"They'd come see us on holidays." Annette had stopped sobbing, but tears still streamed down her cheeks. "We didn't go there. Will had started to fail, and he couldn't travel. I didn't know. I didn't want to know."

She opened a folder that had been tucked into the last album, pulled out several manila envelopes and extracted a photograph from the newest looking one. "This is my granddaughter."

A longhaired young woman stood behind a shop counter, apparently unaware her picture was being taken. Her face showed resemblance to both Annie Lewis and Frank. Annette kept the photo, returned the envelopes to the folder and handed it to Claire.

"Davidson's reports will tell you how to find Annalisa. They found her, but she wouldn't talk to them. The letter from Annie Lewis says what I can't say. Read it and then destroy it." She stared into Claire's eyes as if probing her soul. "The other letter is for Annalisa. I want you to give it to her and make sure she reads it."

"I'll try." Claire wanted to help, but she couldn't promise to succeed where detectives had failed.

Annette grabbed her wrist. "You *will* talk to Annalisa. That's the reason the Good Lord led you to me." She loosened her grasp. "I'm an old woman with little time left. I want to make peace with my granddaughter before I die."

22

Mike finished the briefing. "I warned you. We don't have much."

"Hatch didn't know Palmer was dead?" Corlette said. "Are you sure?"

"As sure as I can be."

"So, what are we accusing him of?"

"Arson."

"You think a judge will issue a warrant?"

"Maybe. If we're lucky." They were supposed to get an arrest warrant within forty-eight hours. If they didn't get one within 72, Hatch could demand a hearing.

Mike and Corlette tossed ideas back and forth, searching for a scenario that encompassed Hatch torching the cabin but not knowing Palmer's body was inside. They still hadn't found one that really worked when Breton walked in. The Lieutenant looked more even disgruntled than usual.

"The Vermin has called a press conference for noon. We're talking to the judge at two. We better get a confession this morning." He acknowledged Corlette by explaining, "The Vermin, officially known as Assistant Superintendent Henry Vernon, is Mike's boss."

"If that's your idea of a joke." Mike didn't want to believe it.

"Check your messages. He wants both of us there."

"A press conference?" Corlette blew up. "So, your boss is going to stand up in front of the cameras and tell the world how New Orleans is solving our crimes for us?" Without waiting for an answer, he continued,

"I'm going to call Sheriff Taliaferro and tell him what's happened. Let's hope a reporter hasn't gotten there first."

"Use my phone," Mike pointed to it. "We'll be down the hall, second door on the left. When you finish, come get us and we'll walk over to the jail together."

A retreat to Breton's office would let Corlette talk to the Sheriff in privacy and give him a chance to tell Vernon they weren't ready to go before a judge.

The interview with Hatch began at ten fifteen. By ten twenty, Mike knew they weren't going to get a confession. Their suspect had hired Ben Patterson, one of the city's top criminal defense lawyers—and on a Saturday morning. Palmer might be dead, but Hatch still had friends in high places.

Under his lawyer's watchful eye, the man who, almost certainly, had torched Palmer's cabin insisted he never got there. He stopped at a Redi-mart on the way.

"I'm in the men's room when I hear this loud noise, and I run back outside to see what's going on. I see the Jeep's on fire. The next thing I remember, it's Thursday morning and I'm waking up in my own bed." Hatch was the picture of wide-eyed innocence. "I must have gone into shock."

Does anyone have any questions for my client?" Patterson said.

Mike gave the nod to Corlette, a courtesy and the least he could do.

"After the explosion, you called a pay phone at the port. So, who did you call?" The deputy's question came across as curious rather than accusatory.

Hatch looked upward, as if searching the ceiling for an answer. "I don't remember making any phone call."

"Has anyone told you that Jeep was booby-trapped? A kid died. When we find out who's responsible, they're facing a homicide charge."

Hatch threw a worried look at Patterson, who said, "Are you accusing Mr. Hatch of booby-trapping his own vehicle?"

Corlette nodded to the lawyer. "Good point." Then he turned to Hatch. "You were driving the Jeep. Looks to me like the car bomb had your name on it. So, who wants to kill you?"

Hatch paled and turned again to his lawyer. Patterson shook his head, signaling silence.

"Now if someone tried to kill me, I'd report it," Corlette said.

"Several witnesses saw you use the payphone. Who did you call?"

"My client already told you he doesn't remember making a phone call," Paterson spoke before Hatch could respond.

"Why didn't you call the New Orleans police when you woke up in your own bed the next morning?" Mike picked up the thread.

"I called Frank. It was his Jeep. I left a message on his mobile phone. There wasn't time to do anything else. I had a plane to catch."

"The whole week you were in North Carolina it never occurred to you to let your employer know his Jeep blew up?"

"I already left a message. And my uncle doesn't have long distance. It costs extra." Hatch looked particularly pleased with this answer.

Before anyone could formulate another question, Patterson announced that he and his client needed time to prepare for the hearing. They'd be happy to meet with the investigators later. The lawyer smiled and added, "After Mr. Hatch has been released."

Mike suspected Patterson would be proven correct. He'd tried to talk Vernon into postponing the hearing or, failing that, releasing Hatch and keeping him under surveillance, but the Super wouldn't listen. The press conference had already been scheduled. He wanted an arrest. Hatch had run once. No judge would let him out.

"The press conference is at two. I want you there," had been Vernon's only response.

The press conference was held in the second floor conference room. Mike, Corlette, and Breton sat on the dais, while Vernon read a statement to the assembled members of the media. The Super began by saying the New Orleans PD was working in partnership with the Lafourche Sheriff's Department. He introduced Corlette first, then Mike and Breton. It wasn't an apology to Lafourche Parish, but it was public respect. Whatever good it might have done went south with Vernon's next statement.

"We have a suspect in custody, and I expect to announce an arrest shortly."

"Did I miss something?" Corlette muttered to Mike, while several reporters pressed Vernon for a definition of shortly.

Corlette's question didn't call for an answer—they both knew Vernon was blowing smoke—but Mike offered an explanation. "He's convinced Claire Marshall and Hatch are behind Palmer's murder and thinks we can pressure him into a confession that will implicate her. He's overlooking the fact that every bit of evidence we have is circumstantial."

They went directly from the press conference to the bail hearing. Once again, Vernon assigned himself the lead role. He began with a nod to the Lafourche Sheriff's Department, which he credited with developing evidence. He put forth the identi-sketch and copies of witness statements, along with documents from the Department of Motor Vehicles showing the Jeep registered to a company owned by the late Frank Palmer.

Ben Patterson, who'd been staring out the window with a bored expression, asked to be heard in the interest of saving time. When the judge nodded assent, Patterson said he was happy to concede every point Superintendent Vernon had just made.

"The Jeep belonged to Mr. Palmer, who employed Mr. Hatch as a driver. Although Mr. Hatch has no direct knowledge of someone trying to steal the Jeep while he was inside the store, we accept the assertion that this occurred. No one is saying the Jeep didn't explode. We'll concede that before the police bring it up." The lawyer stepped closer to the bench and lowered his voice. "What I have not heard, and what my client vigorously denies, is that he broke any law or committed any crime. If the police have found evidence to the contrary, let them produce it. Otherwise, I'd like to go home. My son has a football game this afternoon."

Vernon cited the Jeep's tire tracks at the cabin as evidence that Hatch was lying. He was coming from, not going to, Palmer's cabin.

Patterson pointed out that it was the victim's Jeep. The tire tracks proved that Frank Palmer visited his own cabin, another fact his client did not contest.

The judge asked for any evidence specifically linking Hatch to the cabin fire. When Vernon came up empty-handed, the judge said he'd heard enough.

"Being a victim is not a crime. You can't arrest this man because his car exploded when someone tried to steal it. Not unless he was responsible for the explosion, and no one has suggested that was the case." He frowned at Vernon. "Does anyone have anything to add?"

Corlette stepped forward. "On behalf of the Lafourche Sheriff's Department, the law enforcement agency with jurisdiction over the crime scene, I request that Mr. Hatch be held in protective custody." He submitted a copy of the crime lab report and described the Jeep explosion as an attempt on the driver's life. His was a better argument than Vernon had mounted, but it didn't fly either. Hatch was going to be released unless someone came up with a better reason to keep him in jail.

After the hearing, they reconvened in Mike's office. A red-faced Vernon kicked off the post mortem with a rant against judges who cared more about protecting criminals than protecting the public. Without giving anyone else a chance to express their opinion, he walked out.

"The Vermin isn't happy," Breton said. "Neither am I. It's Saturday afternoon and I'm at work."

"We can stall releasing Hatch until Monday. That gives us the rest of today and tomorrow to strengthen our case. In other words, you're working tomorrow, too." Mike's tone dared Breton to protest.

"I still think Hatch is our arsonist," Corlette said. "The timing is right. Do you guys really believe he didn't know Palmer's body was in the cabin?"

"Maybe he's a good liar." Breton shrugged.

"He's not." Mike said. Hatch's performance during the hearing would have been funny if it weren't infuriating. Every answer began with a sideways look at his lawyer and ended with a smirk of relief. "We've been looking at Hatch as a partner. We're wrong. He's a puppet."

No one disagreed.

"Odds are the person pulling the strings is in New Orleans," Corlette said. "But if we find a witness who saw that Jeep anywhere between the Redi-Mart and the cabin, we've caught Hatch in a lie."

"Which might encourage him to talk." Mike finished the thought.

"I've put the word out, but I'm not expecting someone to step forward. Anyone hanging around there was probably supposed to be somewhere else. Daniel's the best bet. I'll find out when he's getting back."

"What about another poacher?"

Corlette shook his head. "That's Daniel's territory. It's possible one of our local Romeos was over there with someone else's woman." He grinned. "I'll ask the girls at the office. They always know who's doing who."

Breton rolled his eyes but, for a change, made no wisecracks.

"We'll talk to the victim's friends and business associates," Mike said, "looking for our puppet master."

On his way out the door, Corlette told them that his boss had been irate about the press conference. "He thinks you guys don't know the meaning of cooperate. I told him your boss is the problem, and I'm telling you, karma is a beautiful thing."

Mike knew what was coming. He'd been thinking about it himself.

"Vernon broke his arm patting himself on the back at that press conference," Corlette said. "What's he going to say when some reporter notices you guys had to release your suspect for lack of evidence? Your boss should be down on his knees thanking the Lord there weren't any cameras in that courtroom. Hatch's lawyer had him for lunch."

"Breakfast, lunch, and dinner." Breton's expression was glum.

23

Claire carried her breakfast and the folder that Annette Fulton had given her onto the porch. Late October had brought cooler weather but no real autumn. The deciduous trees were turning from green to rust to brown. When the leaves fell, they'd mold and rot. She missed the brilliant reds, oranges, and yellows of a northern fall.

She and Tom had never planned to settle in New Orleans; they'd already begun reading ads for New York apartments. But after he died, and despite friends and family telling her to come home to Centreville, she'd decided to stay. For some unfathomable reason, she felt at home here. At least she'd felt at home until Frank's death and the marriage rumors tried to make her someone she wasn't.

Dorian popped out the cat door and crouched at her feet, preparing for the jump to her lap. She tossed him a bit of toast to keep him on the floor and opened the folder. Last night, she'd been too tired and too emotionally exhausted to delve any further into Annie Lewis Palmer's life—her death, really. Nor did she want to now, but a promise was a promise.

She started with the manila envelopes from Davidson Investigative Services. Each report was barely two pages long, dry, and factual. Annalisa Palmer lived near Taos New Mexico in a commune called The Double Rainbow. She had attended the local high school and graduated two years ago. For the past three years, she'd worked for a small company called Dream Catchers, making and selling jewelry.

On her eighteenth birthday, Annalisa Palmer had changed her name to Phoenix, one word. Like the city in Arizona, the report said. Or, Claire thought, like the mythical bird that dies in flames and is reborn from its own ashes. That would be a compelling legend for a runaway girl carving out a new life.

Claire finished the detectives' reports and set them aside. Two envelopes remained. One, addressed to Annalisa Palmer at an RFD address in Taos, New Mexico was marked "return to sender" and hadn't been opened. This was the letter Annette wanted her to deliver. The other envelope, torn and crumpled, its address barely legible, contained the explanation for a tragedy that had devastated three generations of women.

Annette said this letter had been waiting at the post office when she and Will returned from their daughter's funeral. Will had wanted to turn right around and go back to New Orleans, but she had said to call first and let Annalisa know they were coming for her. It was too late. Their granddaughter had disappeared.

Claire held the envelope in unwilling fingers. Uneasiness about prying into the secrets of a dead woman warred with her promise to Annette. Fear that she already knew what was written, an explanation too awful to be true, increased her reluctance. She said a quick prayer that she be proven wrong and pulled out the letter.

Cramped, downward-sloping script covered both sides of a single sheet of paper. With tortured and rambling sentences, Annie Lewis Palmer begged forgiveness for a sin that wasn't hers. She asked her mother to rescue Annalisa, to step in and do what she, herself, wasn't strong enough to do. And then she said good-bye. Frank's wife had killed herself because she could neither stop nor live with the horror of a husband who abused their daughter.

Claire smoothed the paper, feeling the anguish behind the words. Here was a motive for murder. *Was it you, Annalisa? Did you wait your chance? Wait until you were an adult?* She returned the letter to its envelope, carried everything Annette had given her to her bedroom, and tucked it into the back of her sweater drawer. Then she called Melissa.

"Could we meet for Sunday brunch? I'll return Hatch's key."

"I just woke up," Melissa said. "What time is it?"

"No rush. I don't have anything else scheduled. Do you have a favorite café?"

Melissa was already there, sitting at a table in the sun. Claire sat down, and a waiter stepped from the shade of the awning. He sauntered over.

"Are you all ready to order?"

"The usual," Melissa said.

"What's the usual?" Claire asked.

"A chocolate croissant and a double cappuccino." The waiter said. "How about you, baby?"

"The same thing, please." She smiled at Melissa. "This is a treat. I usually have tea and toast for breakfast." Earlier this morning, she'd left that breakfast uneaten.

"I have tea and toast when I'm sick."

Claire ignored the dig. "I'm glad we were able to get together."

"Where's the key? Hatch is back, and I don't want him to know I gave it to you."

"Oh no! I left my sweater in his kitchen. He'll know I was there. Tell him it's yours. Please." She should have retrieved her sweater no matter what Felix said.

"He hasn't been home. The cops arrested him at the airport, and he's still in jail."

"Why did they arrest him?"

"Because he's an ex-con. Because they can." Anger made Melissa's voice harsh. "They have nothing on him. I got him a good lawyer, and the judge said to let him go. Yesterday. But everything's closed on the weekend, and the cops are using that as an excuse. He's stuck until tomorrow morning." Her anger ebbed as quickly as it had appeared, and now she only looked tired. "You have plenty of time to get your sweater."

The waiter reappeared with their order. Neither spoke until he'd left.

"I'll get it and return the key this afternoon," Claire said.

"Drop it off at the shop. I'm open one to five." Melissa tore off a piece of the croissant and put it into her mouth.

Claire looked for something that would reveal how this young woman, who'd made it clear she and Frank were lovers, was dealing with his sudden death. It must have left an empty space in her life. Did she remember his breath on her skin, how he held her? Or had she, too, lost all memory of love's touch?

"What do you want?" Melissa said.

"Excuse me?"

"You could've picked up your sweater and dropped off the key anytime. Instead you call this morning and want to meet. So, what do you really want? Frank is all we ever had in common, and he's dead."

She spooned more sugar into her cappuccino.

"The police think I had something to do with his death."

"They questioned you. They questioned me. They arrested Hatch the minute he walked off the airplane."

"They're still watching me. A squad car will drive by any minute now."

"Cops drive through here all the time. They drive past my shop. I don't get paranoid."

As if summoned by their conversation, a police car rounded the corner and moved slowly past the café.

"He looked right at us," Claire said.

"He's a man." Melissa broke off another piece of croissant and licked the chocolate filling. "Men look."

"I talked to Annette Fulton yesterday. She was Frank's mother-in-law."

"I know who she is. She hated Frank. Maybe she's the one who killed him."

"She's confined to a wheelchair."

"She could have hired a hit man." Melissa smiled as if the idea of a murderous Annette Fulton was funny.

"She asked me if I killed Frank."

"What did you tell her?"

"I said no. Do you think I killed Frank?"

"I don't think you're the type. But maybe no one's the type until they're pushed into a corner. Then, maybe everyone is." Melissa busied herself spooning up the sugar crystals, now melted into shiny dots on the froth of her cappuccino. "Annie Lewis was a lush. Did her mother tell you that?"

"No."

"Frank hushed it up, but she was driving drunk. That day like every other day. The old lady couldn't face the truth, so she blamed Frank, made a big point of snubbing him at the funeral. Then she got on her broom and flew back to Alabama."

Jeanette had said essentially the same thing, and she, too, blamed Annie Lewis' parents. All either woman ever heard was Frank's side of the story. They would have wanted to believe him.

"She told me about Annalisa," Claire said. "I guess you know she ran away?"

"Of course I know." Melissa's sneer said this was a stupid question.

"Do you know where she is? Did Frank know?"

"If I knew I wouldn't tell you. Annalisa wants to be left alone. And she's crazy, totally nuts." She shook her head. "I used to live in The Children's Home, and I've seen some screwed-up girls, but nothing like her. Maybe she's the psycho killer."

"Why do you call her crazy?" Claire held her breath, waiting for the answer.

"Why are you digging around in Frank's past? It doesn't matter anymore. He's dead." Melissa stopped playing with her cappuccino. "Someone killed Frank. If it wasn't you, and it wasn't me ..." She let the thought hang.

"Do you have any idea who?"

"Not a clue." Melissa pushed her cup aside and stood up. "I'm open until five. After that, slide the key under the door. Hatch gets out tomorrow morning, or this city is looking at a lawsuit."

24

Claire took a cab from the café to the zoo, entered through one gate, and minutes later, exited through another. If anyone had been following her, she'd lost them. With Hatch in jail, the police had no reason to continue watching his apartment, but she wasn't taking any chances there either. She walked past on the opposite side of the street, checking the parked cars. None were occupied. Reassured, she crossed at the next corner and backtracked.

A big black SUV sat in the parking space marked 209. Either the police had let Hatch drive his car home, or someone else had parked in his space, or... Claire hesitated. What if he was here? No, Melissa had been positive he was in jail until Monday morning, and she'd know.

A solid looking woman was sweeping leaves off the sidewalk, vigorously swinging her broom back and forth. A man, wearing a baseball cap and a windbreaker despite the balmy temperature, descended the back stairs and hurried away, taking a short cut behind the building. Claire made an innocuous comment about the nice day to the woman, who grunted and continued sweeping. She walked over to the back stairs, telling herself to act as if she had every right to be there.

Just in case Melissa was wrong about Hatch still being in jail, Claire rang the buzzer. No one came to the door. She inserted the key, slowly turned the knob, and opened the door a crack. The scent of cigarette smoke drifted out. The apartment hadn't smelled like smoke on Thursday.

Claire's eyes adjusted to the dim light, and she saw a man's arm dangling beside the recliner, inches away from a beer can that sat on the floor. Flickering light said the television was on, but there was no sound.

Opening the door had let in more light, but the arm didn't move. Hatch was home, but lucky for her, he'd fallen asleep watching TV.

Heart pounding, Claire stepped back, ready to close the door and sneak away. The rasp of broom-straw against cement ceased. She felt the woman watching and knew her only option was to brazen it out. She knocked on the open door.

"Hello, anyone home?" Her brain raced, looking for an excuse to be here. Picking up Melissa's sweater? Would he believe that?

Hatch made a noise somewhere between a snore and a gurgle, but his arm didn't move.

"Are you all right?" she called.

He gurgled again, louder this time, a terrible noise.

She hurried inside. "Hatch?"

He stared with glazed eyes. Bright red blood pulsed from holes in his chest, three circles spreading across the front of his shirt and merging to form one big bloodstain, pooling on the floor. So much blood, she could smell it. Fighting a gag reflex, she ran outside.

"Call an ambulance! Hurry!" she yelled to the woman below

She raced back inside, grabbed the pillow from the bed, and knelt next to the chair, pressing the pillow against Hatch's chest, trying to staunch the bleeding.

"Hang on, Hatch, please hang on. Help's on the way. They'll be here soon."

Any response was lost in the awful sounds of his struggle for breath.

Soap and water cleansed Claire's arms and hands, but dabbing at her clothes made little difference. "Do you have something I can put on?" she asked the police matron, who had accompanied her to the women's rest room. "My clothes are soaked with blood. The smell is making me sick."

"If you don't like the smell of blood, you shouldn't go around shooting people."

"I didn't shoot anyone. I tried to help a man who'd been shot. Please. The officers took my sweater. I'd like it back so I can at least take off my blouse."

"Captain Robinson is waiting to talk to you. Ask him about your sweater."

Claire remembered Felix's admonition about talking to the police.

"When can I call my lawyer?"

"Ask Captain Robinson."

There was nothing to do but wash her blouse in the sink. She rinsed it until the water ran clear, wrung it out as best she could and put it back on, soaking wet. She did the same with her slacks. The matron leaned against the wall and watched without commenting. She looked bored.

"I'm ready." Claire shivered in her wet clothes. She could still smell Hatch's blood.

Mike Robinson stood with his back to the door, looking out the window. The matron rapped her knuckles against the doorframe, and he turned around.

"Come in." Before she could ask about her sweater, he told the matron to fetch a blanket, "Quickly."

"Thank you," was all Claire could manage. She'd been fighting back tears ever since the police bundled her into a squad car, and this small kindness almost put her over the edge. He helped her wrap the blanket around her shoulders and held the chair while she sat down.

"How about coffee? Hot with lots of sugar. You've had a shock."

"No thank you. I'm okay, just cold and wet." If she ate or drank anything, she'd throw up. "I'd like to call my lawyer." She wanted to lay her head on the desk and go to sleep.

"Of course. But first I want to clarify that you're not under arrest."

"I'm not?" That's not what the uniformed officers had told her. Two of them had escorted her past a gawking crowd and put her in the back seat of a squad car. She'd seen scenes like that on TV when the police were arresting someone who'd held up a convenience store or murdered his wife. "They tested my hands for gunpowder residue."

"There's a witness, who is adamant that you couldn't possibly have shot Hatch. She mentioned a man who left just as you arrived."

Claire said a silent thank you to the cranky woman with the broom.

"She was watching you the whole time. Her story and the physical evidence support everything you told the responding officers."

"Did he make it?"

He raked his fingers through his hair. "Hatch died on the way to the hospital."

"I couldn't stop the bleeding. He was drowning in his own blood. I could hear it." She pulled the blanket tighter.

"You did all you could."

"When can I go home? And please sit down. You're making me nervous."

He leaned back against the desk so that he was no longer standing over her. "You're free to go, but I'd like to get your statement as soon as you're up to it. We're especially interested in the man leaving the premises. Did you see him?"

"Only from a distance."

"Can you describe him?"

"That other woman was closer. I want to go home and get clean."

"I'll have a squad car take you."

"Thank you."

"But I still need a formal statement."

"Can I call my lawyer?"

He slid the phone over to her.

Felix picked her up at the carriage house and drove her to police headquarters. Captain Robinson, Superintendent Vernon, Lieutenant Breton, and Deputy Corlette waited in a conference room. No one smiled when she and Felix walked in. She stopped in the doorway, not ready to face these policemen.

"You'll be fine," Felix murmured in her ear. He took her arm and guided her toward a chair. Then, he spoke to Superintendent Vernon. "You know the rules, Henry. My client will not be badgered. One person asks questions, not one person at a time, one person period."

Mike Robinson volunteered. He asked if she was comfortable and then began questioning her about the man who had been leaving the apartments.

"I told you already, I barely saw him. He was never close."

"Close your eyes, Claire," he suggested, "and picture him coming down the stairs. What do you see?"

She did as he suggested and was surprised by how well it worked. "He's a big man, tall with broad shoulders, not fat but maybe a little stocky. He's moving quickly down the back stairs. His hand is sliding along the banister. He might be limping a little. Yes, he's limping. I can't see his face, because he's looking down, and he has on a baseball cap and sunglasses, the wrap-around kind. He's wearing faded blue jeans, and a light tan windbreaker partly zipped. I can't really see the shirt underneath. Maybe a white tee shirt."

"What did he have on his feet?"

"I didn't notice them." She pictured him again. "I think regular shoes. Nothing that stood out."

"And when he gets to the bottom of the stairs?"

"He turns away from me, toward the back of the building. He goes around the corner, and he's gone. He seemed in a hurry, but nothing furtive, not like he'd just shot someone."

"About how old would you say he was?"

"I don't know. Not young but not old either. Middle-aged."

"You told the officers something about him looked familiar."

"I don't know why I said that." Too much had happened for her to recall feelings. "I'm sorry, but—"

"Don't apologize. You're doing very well. Do you have any other impressions of him?"

"I wondered why he was wearing a windbreaker. It was warm out."

After a series of questions about what she saw and did in Hatch's apartment, Mike asked if she'd like a break. She looked at Felix and he patted her hand reassuringly. So far he hadn't objected to any of Mike's questions.

"No thanks. I want to get this over with."

"Okay. Can you describe your trip from the café to Hatch's apartment?"

The change of subject took her by surprise. "I cut through the zoo."

"Why? You said you were in a hurry to get your sweater. The zoo was a side trip."

She buried her face in her hands.

"My client has been through enough," Felix said. "I'm taking her home."

"Before you leave, one more thing." Mike said that she was being put under protective surveillance and explained what that meant. He gave her his direct number and told her to call anytime something seemed out of line. "Whether it seems important or not, call. I'm concerned about your safety."

Felix held her arm as they walked back to the parking lot and helped her into the car. She waited until they were out of the parking lot then apologized.

"I'm sorry I didn't tell you about the zoo, Felix. I forgot." The horror of finding Hatch had erased everything else from her mind. "After

Melissa left the café, I took a cab to the zoo. I walked in one entrance and out another as quickly as I could without attracting attention."

He gave her a sideways glance.

"I thought the police might be following me, and I didn't want them to know I was going to Hatch's apartment. Mike Robinson told me not to go back there."

He pulled over and turned to face her. "So did I, Claire. And I can't help you if you don't take my advice. You and I both need to give this situation some serious consideration."

"I need your help, Felix. They said I wasn't a suspect, but that's not true, is it?"

"The police believe they're looking at a conspiracy that involved Hatch. Going back to his apartment makes you look like part of it, whether or not you fired the shots that killed him. If I were you," he continued, "I'd leave town before the police told me not to—this time, they can enforce it. And I wouldn't let anyone except my long-suffering lawyer know where I was going."

"You want me to run away?"

"I want you to go to a secure location. If you saw the killer, he saw you." He touched her arm. "Mike Robinson isn't the only person concerned about your safety."

25

Mike skimmed the weekend report: two homicides on Friday, two on Saturday, and one on Sunday. The bloodshed began Friday evening when a domestic dispute left the wife dead, stabbed multiple times with a large kitchen knife. Detectives were looking for the husband, who was thought to be hiding at the home of a relative.

Several hours later, a friendly poker game turned hostile. It ended with a gunshot. Responding officers found the remorseful killer standing over the victim, apologizing to his best friend and drinking buddy, who was beyond hearing anything.

Saturday night, gang violence claimed another victim, ambushed when he crossed the wrong street. Police had been nearby, not close enough to prevent the killing but close enough to apprehend the shooter.

An hour later, a convenience store clerk was killed during a robbery. The incident was captured by the store's security system, and detectives would be circulating the gunman's picture. He looked about fifteen. They'd probably find him at the local high school.

And then there was Hatch, the last victim, discovered about noon Sunday, when Claire Marshall went to his apartment, she said, to retrieve her sweater.

Barring unforeseen complications, the first four would be wrapped up quickly, one-day sensations on the local news that left barely a ripple in the lives of all but those directly involved. Media attention would stay focused on Hatch's death, which reflected badly on the police department and very badly on Assistant Superintendent Henry Vernon. He had ordered Hatch's release after Ben Patterson called him at home, furious that his client was still in jail after the judge said to let him go.

Vernon had acted on his own, and he'd failed to inform anyone working the case. If he had, Hatch would have been under surveillance and might still be alive. The man who held the key to solving Frank Palmer's murder walked out of jail at nine o'clock Sunday morning. Three hours later, he was dead.

Mike ran his fingers through his hair. Yesterday, when he told Corlette what had happened, the deputy had been incredulous, and rightly so. It would be interesting to see how Vernon handled the issue at the Monday morning staff meeting. The senior homicide staff usually met downstairs, but today they were meeting with the Super in his conference room. Mike glanced at the clock, in ten minutes. Time to go.

Breton was waiting for the elevator. "Did you see this morning's paper?" Without waiting for an answer, he said, "A reporter chased the ambulance to Hatch's apartment. There's a front page exclusive, complete with picture of Claire Marshall being escorted to a patrol car. It makes the connection to Palmer's murder and hints that she's a suspect in both deaths."

"Did they talk to anyone here?"

"Vernon, who said no one had been arrested for either homicide. Otherwise, no comment."

Mike remembered Corlette's remark about karma. He waited until they were alone in the elevator to ask, "Did they run any of Vernon's quotes from his press conference? You know, having a suspect in hand, being on the verge of an arrest."

"One sentence at the end of the article says Hatch had been held and released."

"Too bad."

Breton shook his head in disagreement. "Be grateful. I wouldn't mind seeing The Vermin covered in shit, but it won't happen. If things get hot, someone else will get burned. You don't want that to happen." The elevator doors opened, ending their conversation.

Vernon began the meeting by referring to the newspaper story, which he described as the work of a novice desperate for a by-line. He'd be talking to the press at nine-thirty to discuss the latest development in the Palmer case and clarify any misunderstandings. He blamed Hatch's death, described as the silencing of one criminal by another even more vicious, on a court system that was more concerned with the rights of criminals than with the well-being of society.

Mike, who had his own agenda for the meeting, listened without comment. Attacks on the judiciary might play well with the press, and with some policemen, but he'd sat in the judge's chair and, in his opinion, this judge had made the correct decision. The screw-up came later.

Vernon finished with the judiciary and turned his attention to the team that was keeping an eye on Claire Marshall. "A five-minute visit to the zoo, what the hell is that about? And you lost her?"

"Maybe she had to pee." Breton muttered behind his hand. He straightened up when the Super threw a dirty look his way.

"She's our prime suspect," Vernon said. "Perhaps you could keep track of her."

"I agree." Mike responded. "Top priority has to be protecting our witnesses." It was a jab that nobody could miss. "We'll be keeping a close eye on both Ms. Marshall and Irene Rukoski, who got a good look at the man leaving the apartments."

"Rukoski's the one says Marshall didn't do it?" The Super's dismissive tone reminded everyone that eyewitnesses were notoriously unreliable.

"Backed up by the missing weapon and the absence of gunpowder residue on her hands." Mike let it go at that. They'd argued about the case last night, and the rest of the division didn't need to hear a rerun.

Witness or no witness, gunpowder residue or no gunpowder residue, the only thing keeping Claire Marshall out of jail was the missing murder weapon. An intensive search of the scene had failed to turn it up, and she'd had no opportunity to dispose of a gun. A team from the Crime Scene Unit would be going over the walls with a metal detector today. Whether they found the gun or not, Vernon wanted her brought in for questioning. Real questioning, he said, as if they hadn't talked to her several times already.

"Have you identified this man yet, Mike?"

"Not yet. We'll be canvassing residents of the apartments this evening when people will be home from work, and we'll see if anyone claims him." No one would. Irene Rukoski said she'd never seen the man before, and Mike had the impression she didn't miss much.

"If he's our shooter, it's possible that Lieutenant Breton and I saw him Friday night at the airport." That realization had come to him in the middle of last night. The cowboy might have been waiting for Hatch. "The physical descriptions match. Both used a hat to hide their faces, and except for the hat, they dressed alike. The cowboy was wearing shoes, not boots. He left the gate area shortly after a loudmouth identified us as police."

"That's a stretch, Mike. This city is full of big guys wearing jeans, a windbreaker, and some kind of hat."

"I could be wrong," he agreed, "but if it was the same man, that would explain how the killer was able to act so quickly."

Vernon slapped the folder against the table, obviously annoyed by another reminder of his role in Hatch's fate. "You don't have much."

"We don't even have a motive." Mike suppressed a smile as the Super, who had argued against stepping up the pressure on Palmer's friends, fell into the trap. "Which is why we have to dig deeper into Palmer's life. We'll be searching his house. We have appointments to talk to his lawyer and his banker, the directors of two charities where he served on the board. If we don't get cooperation, we'll need subpoenas."

"Let's hope you don't need them," Vernon said, implicit admission that they might.

Mike moved on to the other cases, and those reviews went quickly. When the meeting adjourned, he left Breton to observe Vernon's press conference and returned to his office to check on the search warrant for Palmer's house and prepare subpoena requests for Gilbert, Austin, Melissa Yates, and Claire Marshall. Better to have one he didn't use than to need one he didn't have.

Forty minutes later, Breton stuck his head in the door. "You missed a show. The Vermin blasted the judge, and the press ate it up."

"I already heard about the lenient court system."

"You didn't hear the second stanza." Breton played an invisible violin. "We tried to hold Hatch in protective custody, but the victim, his lawyer, and the judge brushed aside our concern. The police can't protect someone who refuses to be protected. We can't work effectively without the support of the judiciary."

Mike didn't see the humor. A feud between the police brass and the judge might keep Vernon out of the soup in the short term, but long term, it wasn't good for anyone.

"What did he say about Claire Marshall?"

"That she found a mortally wounded man and tried to save his life." Breton grinned. "Seems her lawyer called and raised hell."

"He's doing his job." *And so was Hatch's lawyer when he called.* Mike changed the subject. "Corlette is waiting to hear from us. Shut the door, and I'll put him on speaker."

Their conversation began with a review of the steps New Orleans was taking to protect the two women who'd seen the likely shooter.

"That's locking the barn door," Corlette said. "Not that you shouldn't do it."

"What about your poacher? When does he get back?"

"Turns out he never went. His father heard about the fight with Sammy and told him to stay home. I talked to Daniel and to one of his cousins, told them what was going on. Daniel has enough family to field a small militia. They'll keep him safe."

"The family, not the sheriff's department?"

"If we tried, he'd disappear into the swamps. This is the better way."

"Anything else happening down there?"

"Nothing you'd care about."

Corlette hadn't located any other potential witnesses. If there was something else they wanted him to check out, he was ready, but it looked like the focus of the investigation had shifted to New Orleans. Mike agreed.

"We're talking to Palmer's lawyer in fifteen minutes," he said. "I'll keep you posted." He didn't have to tell Corlette how much he wanted this killer. Hell, even Breton had begun taking it personally.

Paul Gilbert greeted them warmly, offered his excellent coffee, and said that he was the executor for Frank's estate. He'd already begun an inventory of the house, and found nothing untoward, but it was all right with him if they wanted to conduct their own search.

Mike nodded a thank you. He hadn't asked permission, nor had he mentioned their search warrant. If this lawyer was as well connected as everyone said, he already knew.

"I want to cooperate with your investigation," Gilbert said.

That statement marked the end of his cooperation. He refused to discuss details of Palmer's estate on the grounds that the information was still incomplete. For the same reason, he couldn't speak about the financial status of FP Development. He'd hired a CPA to evaluate the firm, but the work hadn't been completed. In fact, they were meeting later today. He was unable to provide any information about Hatch.

"I barely knew the man." He frowned. "I saw the morning paper. Is Claire under arrest?"

"No. There should be a correction tomorrow."

"Ah. But the damage is done, isn't it?"

Mike heard the deserved rebuke. "Until we find the killer." He thanked Gilbert for his time and stood to signal an end to the meeting. "Lieutenant Breton or I will check back later this week." It was a promise. He intended to show up, subpoena in hand, and ask questions until he got answers.

Breton drove to their next stop, the First City Bank Building, while Mike checked his messages. Another of the weekend homicides had resulted in an arrest. He called the detective team working that case and told them to pick up the search warrant for Palmer's house.

"Palmer's lawyer says there's an appointment calendar in his desk. Take it. Other than that, all I can tell you is that you're looking for something off kilter, anything that suggests a motive for murder."

"Aren't those guys working the domestic dispute?" Breton had been listening.

"The husband turned himself in about an hour ago. He says the victim started it. He acted in self-defense."

"How many times did he stab her?"

"Too many, including multiple defensive cuts on her forearms and palms."

"Every case should be so easy." Breton pulled up in front of the bank and parked in a loading zone.

They were early, but the receptionist said Mr. Austin was expecting them. She led the way to a small but luxurious meeting room. Moments later, a haggard Bobby Austin walked in. He met Mike's gaze briefly when they shook hands and then looked away, moving his head as if his neck hurt. He did the same thing with Breton. The first time they talked he'd been solemn, obviously saddened by his friend's death. This morning, he was a wreck. What, Mike wondered, was behind the change. He thanked Austin for meeting with them.

"Whatever I can do to help," Austin said, without looking at him.

"We understand your bank counts FP Development Company among its clients. Is that a longstanding relationship?"

"We've financed Frank from the beginning." A momentary tightening of the banker's facial muscles suggested anger. "You're here to discuss financial matters?"

Mike nodded. It was the reason he'd given when he requested this meeting. Just as he'd told Gilbert that he wanted to discuss legal matters.

"I have to check with the bank's lawyer before we discuss anything in detail. Unfortunately, I've not had time to do so."

"Are you aware of financial problems?" Breton said.

"As I just said, I have to check with our lawyer before revealing specifics about the finances of a client firm." This time Austin made no attempt to hide his annoyance.

Mike tried a different tack. "Who would you suggest we talk to at FP Development?"

"Frank and I dealt directly with one another."

Gilbert was suave, Austin seethed, and neither volunteered anything about the victim. Mike wasn't surprised. Their completed subpoena requests sat on his desk. He'd submit them when he returned to the office. He moved to the next topic.

"You've probably heard that Ronald Hatch, who worked for Mr. Palmer, was murdered yesterday. We believe the two crimes are connected."

"I heard." Austin looked past him. "Hatch was a character. Frank found him amusing."

Several questions and non-answers later, Mike thanked Palmer's banker for taking the time to meet with them, and they left.

"Two interviews in under an hour," Breton said. "We might be ineffective, but we're damned efficient. Now what?"

"Hatch's apartment. I was there briefly the first time Claire Marshall visited, but that's all." When had that been? Last Thursday, just four days ago, enough time for Hatch to return, be arrested, released, and killed. The killer was efficient, too.

"You know, the whole thing with Austin was weird." Breton flipped on the blue lights and passed a line of cars waiting for the stoplight to turn.

"He didn't ask about Claire Marshall."

"True. Want to bet Gilbert called him the minute we walked out the door? Those two are tight."

"What do you know about Austin?"

"That's what's weird," Breton's brow puckered. "He's one of the good guys, a solid citizen, out there shaking hands, helping out where help's needed. I never would've picked him to stonewall."

"Or lie. I doubt Palmer was the only one who dealt with finances."

"I don't know. Jeanette said the same thing. Palmer ran the company out of his hip pocket."

"I thought you were going to follow up on that." When Breton didn't answer, he said, "Try Jeanette again. Ask who wrote the checks."

Breton's groan ended the conversation.

26

By the time Claire got to the office, Jack had been there and left. A note on her desk said he'd be at the Laurens house all day. Let him know if she was coming by.

"I'm sorry, Jack," she murmured. She should have called last night, told him about finding Hatch, the police, the whole mess.

She checked her phone messages. As requested, the supply house had put her order for kitchen appliances on hold. Paul still hadn't said whether or not he wanted them to finish work on Frank's cottage, which was where the appliances had been headed. The roofer wanted to discuss options for the Laurens house as well as an advance for supplies. Scott Cantrell had called to say they'd decided not to go ahead—no explanation.

Oh, no.

Scott and Lori owned a small Victorian in Uptown. Claire had been working with them for two months now, developing plans for updating the kitchen and adding a family room. They were waiting for their financing to come through before signing a contract. The bank must have turned them down. She reviewed the plans and called him back.

"Scott, This is Claire Marshall."

"Hi Claire." He sounded surprised, maybe a little wary.

"I'm sorry you're not ready to go ahead. You and Lori were so enthusiastic. I was too. If it's a financial issue, we could stage the work. I've gone over your plans and think we could divide the project into three distinct phases without increasing the overall cost. Would that make a difference?"

"It's not the money. It's just... I thought you were in jail," he blurted.

"Jail?"

"The paper this morning. There was an article, another murder. They said you'd been arrested."

"I haven't seen the paper, so I don't know what it says, but I can tell you what happened." She forced herself to remain calm. "I found someone who'd been shot. I certainly didn't shoot him. No-one thinks I shot anyone."

"I'm sorry, Claire. It's just too much. That business with Frank Palmer and now this. Lori doesn't feel comfortable."

"I'm sorry, too." More than sorry, she was furious, but the best she could do was leave the door open. "If you change your minds, I'd still like to work for you."

She hung up, counted to ten, and called Felix. "A client just cancelled a project we needed because the paper says I've been arrested or something. I haven't seen the article."

"I've already talked to Henry Vernon, who will be issuing a statement to the press this morning. He will say that you are not and never were under arrest, that you found Hatch after he had been shot and did your best to save his life. The officers were helping you to their car, not arresting you, and it is the sincere wish of the New Orleans Police Department that the local fish wrapper print a correction."

"Can I sue the paper?"

"If you lose business as a direct result, you can show damages. The more difficult task is proving negligence or intent. The article was carefully worded. My advice is to adopt a wait and see attitude. If things get worse, threaten a lawsuit and hope they settle out of court."

Sit tight. Wait and see. Felix's advice was good but hard to follow. "I'd like to throw a brick through their window."

"But you won't."

"Thank you for calling Superintendent Vernon."

"It was my pleasure, and there's no charge for this morning. If you throw that brick, I go on the clock."

Claire thanked him again and said good-bye, only partially reassured. What if this was just the first cancellation? What was going to happen to Authentic Restorations? She took a deep breath and visualized waves breaking on her office floor, washing up and receding, steady and reliable, one after the other, each one a breath. The bubble hadn't appeared. She wasn't going to panic, but she'd better tell Jack ASAP.

Rather than deliver bad news over the phone, Claire drove to the Laurens house. Jack was upstairs talking to a plumber about the most efficient way to re-plumb what had been two small bathrooms into one master bath. He looked up when she walked in.

"I knew you weren't in jail."

"Not funny, Jack. Scott Cantrell just canceled their project because Lori is uncomfortable working with an accused murderess."

Jack smacked his fist into his palm. "It all comes back to Palmer. I knew that guy was bad news. From the beginning. And remember how he was yelling at you. I should have punched him in the nose."

When Frank first contacted her, Jack had warned that the word among subcontractors was that FP Development, Frank's company, had slowed payments and was firing anyone who complained. Claire had trouble reconciling that portrayal with the charming man she'd met at The Children's Home, but she'd left the final decision to Jack, and he decided to go for it. Frank's cottage would be their biggest project to date, a step into a new league. There had been no problems, not even little ones, until the fuss about his fish camp. There'd been nothing but trouble since.

"Worse news than either of us dreamed," she said.

"We still have enough work to keep everyone busy. Right?"

"Unless Brian Laurens fires us. I should call him and make sure he knows I'm not in jail. I still don't know what's going to happen with Frank's cottage, but if we lose it and the Cantrell expansion, we'll just break even this year."

"Breaking even is better than I was doing on my own. You're doing a great job, and this crap will blow over."

"What crap?" The plumber had been following their conversation like a man watching a tennis match.

"On the bright side," Jack said, "not everyone reads the papers."

"I haven't seen it either," Claire said.

"There's one in my truck. Go read. I'll give you time to calm down and then we'll talk."

Ten minutes later, he joined her on the front steps. "I'm glad you're okay. When I saw that picture, I wanted to call, but I thought you might be asleep."

"I'm sorry, Jack." She was supposed to get the company on a sound financial footing, to bring in business, not scare away customers. "I should never have gone to that apartment."

"Don't beat yourself up."

She told him what had happened. "I have a lawyer. He says the police will ask the paper to print a correction. But nothing's going to erase that image from people's minds." A full-length picture of her, looking distraught and flanked by two policemen, accompanied the front-page story. "At least it's not in color. My clothes were covered in blood."

"What are you going to do?"

She shrugged. "Work on the foyer, as planned."

"That's not what I meant."

"Wait a week or so, give Scott and Lori time to reconsider, and then call back to see if they've changed their minds."

"I'm worried about you, not the business."

She pointed to a car parked across the street. "The man inside is a policeman. Someone follows me all day. At night, they'll drive by every fifteen minutes. It's called protective surveillance." That was how Mike Robinson described it. She suspected they had more than one reason for keeping track of her. Felix said it didn't matter why they were watching her, as long as they did.

"I'm here, too," Jack said. "And if you want to stay at our house tonight, we have an extra bed."

"Thank you, but I'm fine. The Clarkes' property is really secure." Jack's offer touched her. He and Mary Anne had six kids and no extra bed—someone would have to double up. "The best thing for me to do is get busy and stay busy."

She was going to uncover what she hoped was an intact fireplace. A sloppy installer had used ordinary nails to attach the new wallboard, which made removing it easier, and by mid-afternoon, the old fireplace was fully revealed. Except for the nail holes, which could be filled, the wooden mantel was in good shape. The marble surround was intact, and the old mirror unbroken although badly clouded.

The mirror gave her a good excuse to call Brian. She would ask about re-silvering. The cloudy look was romantic, but a mirror for that last check before you leave the house was a handy thing.

She should be happy about the fireplace, and she was, but... A policeman sat in his car out front. Every few minutes, Jack would find an excuse to walk through the front foyer where she was working. In the back room, three burly men were gutting what had been a kitchen. Here, she was safe; tonight, she'd be alone again. The secluded location of her carriage house, which she had considered such a plus, now made her feel vulnerable, especially with the Clarkes still in Europe.

Felix had advised her "as a friend" to get a gun if she insisted on staying in New Orleans. He'd offered to lend her one of his, and now she regretted saying no.

Last night, she'd fallen into an exhausted sleep, wakened from the nightmare about two, taken another sleeping pill and then wakened again at five, thinking she'd heard footsteps, a branch cracking. She'd barricaded herself in the bathroom with her mobile phone and not slept again until after sunup. Tonight, maybe she'd go to a hotel. First, though, she had to talk to Mike Robinson. She called his office for the third time that day. Once again, he was out.

27

Paul Gilbert was telling the truth when he said he lacked information about Frank's estate. FP Development represented the bulk of Frank's assets, but Ed Pelletier, the CPA hired to establish the company's value, had asked for more time to track down several missing documents. The evaluation of Frank's personal estate suffered from a similar lack of information.

Suzanne usually handled the inventory of a decedent's personal belongings, but sentiment had made Paul want to handle Frank's estate himself. Saturday afternoon, he'd gone to Frank's house. He'd walked down the long hall, half expecting to look up and see his friend standing at the door to his den, smiling a welcome and holding out a glass of fine bourbon, no ice. Instead, he was alone with his own intimations of mortality, feelings intensified by the absurd collection of hunting trophies that adorned the den walls.

In the top desk drawer, he'd found a Moroccan leather appointment calendar, his Christmas gift to Frank. Its final entry, the honeymoon itinerary, rekindled his sadness at a life cut short. Frank's personal checkbook listed a balance just over four thousand dollars. Paul had noted the account number, intending to transfer the funds into the estate account to cover the expenses that were already beginning to accrue, and began going through Frank's files.

Folders held everything from automobile insurance to utility bills to warranties on household appliances, all the paper records and receipts that burden modern life. He found the deeds to Frank's house and the cabin where he died, the closing statements for the ski lodge in Jackson Hole that Frank had recently sold, and the deed for the cottage he'd hired

Claire to renovate. He did not find any certificates of deposit, brokerage statements, bonds, or stock certificates. Nor did he come across a key to a safe deposit box.

He'd also failed to find anything supporting Andrew Walsh's contention that Frank had planned to give him a certified check for one million dollars during the Crescent City Club awards' banquet. Paul believed Andrew. This was the sort of grand gesture Frank loved. It also explained Andrew's frantic behavior when Frank didn't appear.

Andrew wanted the estate to treat the planned donation as an outstanding debt, and Paul had agreed. Doing so would allow The Home to receive their money promptly and reduce the taxable estate. Written confirmation is desirable when dealing with the IRS. Unfortunately, he'd found nothing about an intended contribution. Andrew didn't have documentation either.

Paul sighed. Frank hadn't expected to die in the prime of life, and his affairs weren't in good order. This morning, before the police arrived, he had asked Suzanne to call the local banks, starting with Bobby's, and ask if Frank had a box. So far, the search had been fruitless. He hope Ed Pelletier was having better luck. He'd know soon enough. They were meeting in Frank's office in just under an hour.

Ed was waiting for him in what had been Frank's office. They exchanged greetings, and he asked the CPA if he'd located the missing documents.

"Documents aren't the only thing missing." Ed pointed to a three-ring binder on the desk. "That's my report." His expression promised bad news.

Paul rested his hand on the binder and waited.

"As you know," Ed said, "I've been working with Sherry Leblanc, who is nominally the CFO of this corporation. Sherry has a certificate in bookkeeping from some school you never heard of. She takes care of payroll and makes the required tax deposits. Thank God for small favors. She wrote the checks Frank told her to write and signed the papers Frank told her to sign." Indignation brought color to his sallow cheeks. "I don't care what the corporate papers say. Sherry is a bookkeeper, not a CFO."

"Why is that an issue?" Paul found Ed's outrage puzzling. Everyone knew Frank was a one-man management team.

"Over the last two months, Frank Palmer looted FP Development. No one sounded the alarm, because no one knew what was going on— least of all Sherry. We're meeting here because I wanted you to talk to her, see her office, her records, see with your own eyes what she does and how little she knows."

"That's not necessary." He tapped the still unopened binder. "What's the bottom line?"

"FP Development's liabilities far exceed its assets." Ed swept his arms in a circle that encompassed the opulent office. "This is an illusion. The firm is gone. The only question is what goes with it. The most exposed creditor is First City Bank."

"How much money are we talking about?" Paul felt ill. First City Bank was Bobby Austin. Bobby's great-grandfather had started the bank. His grandfather and father had been presidents before him.

"My best estimate is twelve million, a two million maxed out line of credit plus another ten in construction loans. FP Development drew down the loans but paid subcontractors only enough to keep them on the job. The majority of the money simply disappeared."

"Money doesn't disappear. People hide it."

"Frank hid it. He told his staff that he was working on an important deal and needed the funds for leverage. No one in this office knows anything about the deal—certainly not Sherry. I doubt she knows what leverage is."

"Perhaps Bobby Austin knows." Even as he spoke, Paul realized that wasn't the case. Bobby might have let his good friend slide on occasional details, but he never would have countenanced irregularities on this scale.

"He doesn't. I asked him." Ed's outrage, which had been palpable as he detailed the financial sins, faded into sadness. "Bobby made those loans based on a handshake. He should have required written verification that FP Development controlled the assets put up as collateral. He didn't, and it doesn't. The bank should have checked to ensure work was actually being done and the subs were being paid. None of that happened. You know what that means."

Paul nodded, of course he did, but Ed told him anyway.

"The bank is big enough to absorb the loss, but Bobby failed to exercise proper fiduciary responsibility. He has no choice but to resign. Sherry is in more serious trouble. She signed false financial statements. She never read them, and if she had, I doubt she would have noticed the discrepancies. It doesn't matter. Neither irresponsibility nor incompetence excuses her. She committed fraud."

Paul held up his hand. "Bankruptcy isn't my field. I'll have to bring in a specialist. Meanwhile, I'm relying on your discretion."

"I'm sorry, Paul, but there's more. As I'm sure you know, there should have been a wall between Frank's personal finances and the finances of FP Development Company. There was none and, as far as I can tell, never has been. You can expect FP Development's creditors to file suit against Frank's personal estate."

"I'm counting on your discretion," Paul repeated. He pushed the binder back to Ed. "Please check again with Bobby before you finalize your report. I'll look for it next week."

He picked up his brief case and walked out. He didn't speak to Jeanette who sat at her desk in the outer office, staring at him with big cow eyes. She'd learn the truth soon enough, and so would the police. Mike Robinson, who was no one's fool, was already looking into Frank's finances. He'd be back with more questions, possibly a subpoena.

If Ed was correct—and there was no reason to believe otherwise—Bobby Austin, one of the finest men in New Orleans, would leave his job in disgrace, his family's wealth diminished. Sherry, a thoroughly inoffensive woman, faced a possible prison term. Jeanette, Rose Taylor and, of course, The Children's Home all had expectations based upon Frank's assurances. It would be his unhappy task to explain that Frank's will was meaningless. The money was simply not there. Only Melissa would benefit from Frank's death—ten million dollars that should go to the company's creditors.

When Don Reynolds called to discuss the policy, Paul had damned whatever whim made Frank change beneficiaries and asked if it was ironclad. He'd been disappointed when Don said yes, but he hadn't realized how much it mattered. Ten million, added to the value of Frank's real property, would be enough to clean up the mess at FP Development.

Paul returned to his office and called Henry Vernon. He explained that he wanted to cooperate with the investigation of Frank's finances but neither he nor Bobby Austin would be able to answer questions with any certainty until next week when the CPA finished his audit of FP Development. He also suggested the police take a close look at Melissa Yates. Frank's ex-mistress and the beneficiary of his life insurance had also been close to Hatch. Had they considered the possibility that she conspired with Hatch to kill Frank and then disposed of her accomplice?

Melissa's guilt, if proven, would be a godsend. It would make her an ineligible beneficiary. The ten million would revert to FP Development, which owned the policy, and the debts could be paid. Bobby would quietly resign. There was no escaping that, but it could be handled discreetly There would be rumors—there were always rumors—but there would be no scandal.

28

Mike walked around the big SUV. "I've ordered a thorough going over."

"His car? What do you expect to find?" Breton said.

"I don't know, but I want to be sure we don't miss anything. Hatch was an anomaly in Palmer's life, and I want to know why a successful businessman had anything to do with him. Have you seen his record?"

Breton shook his head.

Of course not. That would require effort. "Hatch was an ex-con, a drug user who did time for breaking into a hospital pharmacy. He went to prison because he was already on probation for breaking into a drug store. You met him. He was a punk. But Palmer hired him as a driver slash bodyguard. He invited him to go fishing."

"You still think he torched the cabin?"

"That's why he's dead." He led the way up the back staircase, took down the crime scene tape and unlocked the door. Hatch's apartment had been dusted for fingerprints, and powdery residue covered every hard surface. Breton ran a finger across the dining table, leaving a diagonal line from one corner to the other.

"They find anything?"

"The victim's prints in the kitchen, bath and closet, Claire Marshall's in the kitchen, and nothing in the main room," he told Breton who apparently hadn't taken the time to read the crime scene report either. "It had been wiped clean."

"Our killer wasn't in any hurry."

Mike nodded. No one who lived in the apartment building knew anything about the man in the windbreaker. He was their shooter, and he'd felt secure enough to do a thorough housekeeping before leaving. If Claire Marshall had arrived five minutes earlier, she would have walked in on him.

Breton apparently had the same thought. "Lucky for her she stopped at the zoo. Or maybe that's why. She was running ahead of schedule."

"She was making sure no one followed her. I'd told her to stay away from here." He walked around the room. "It's hard to get a sense of the man who lived here. This could be a motel room."

Breton scuffed a dark stain in the rug. "One that rents by the hour."

"It doesn't look like Hatch had many visitors."

"Outside of Claire Marshall and whoever killed him. You really think it was the cowboy?"

"It's a strong possibility." Mike flipped through Hatch's reading matter, military and survivalist publications but nothing hard-core. "Palmer and Hatch," he said. "Employer and employee, murder victims, why?"

"Hatch drove Palmer around. He'd know a lot about his boss's business. Maybe he saw more than was healthy." Breton patted his ample stomach. "I'm getting hungry."

"We have time to pick up a sandwich. Then I want to stop by Palmer's house to see if our guys have found anything."

Mike recognized the unmarked car parked at the curb. The team was still here. Rose Taylor opened the door, looking even older and more fragile. She wore a faded sweater and baggy slacks. Anything would be baggy on this woman. She couldn't weigh ninety pounds.

"There should be a team of officers here," Mike said, "with a search warrant."

"They showed up about an hour ago. I called Mr. Gilbert and he said to let them in. They're back in Mr. Frank's office. You want anything, I'll be in the kitchen. Mr. Gilbert told me I could have the food."

The team was finishing up in Palmer's office. They'd found the appointment calendar Gilbert had mentioned and the victim's checkbook but nothing else notable. Mike recognized the contents of a bottom desk drawer as photography paper plus the materials for making slides. Palmer must have been an amateur photographer. He went to ask Rose if there was a darkroom in the house. She was in the pantry, stacking canned goods into cardboard boxes.

"Mr. Frank did his photography in the big bathroom," she said. "I never go in there except once a week to clean. He told me not to fool with that stuff." Her demeanor said she didn't think they should either.

"We'll be careful," he promised.

Cabinets in the master bathroom held photography equipment and chemicals along with metal file boxes for negatives. Breton picked up random strips of film and held them to the light. "Our victim liked taking pictures of big houses, big fish, and big boats—no people. Maybe there's something here, but it'll take days to look through all of these."

"Tell the team to bring them back to headquarters. We're going to the homeless shelter."

"Remind me, why?"

"Palmer was on their board of directors. Let's go."

The New Life Center occupied a converted industrial building on the airport side of town. A knot of unkempt men loitered around the entrance. Wary eyes followed Mike and Breton as they walked toward the front door.

One of the men stepped forward. "Can I help you?" His hostile tone belied the polite question.

"We're looking for Rick Russo," Mike said. "He's expecting us."

One of the other men turned and yelled. "Hey Rick. The cops are here. They say you're expecting them."

A short man with dark facial hair and a ponytail hurried out. "Sorry. I lost track of time."

In his faded jeans and worn shirt, Rick Russo looked only slightly more respectable than his clients. He led the way to a small office and as soon as they sat down said, "You're here to discuss Frank Palmer. His death is a real loss to the community."

"The police department has made finding his killer a top priority," Mike said.

Rick looked him in the eye. "I wish you considered our clients worthy of such concern."

"Is there a specific problem?"

"One of our men went missing a few days before Frank died. I reported it right away, but your people weren't interested. He hadn't been gone long enough. Another man's been missing a couple months now. You aren't looking for him either. He's been gone too long. I feel like Goldilocks when I talk to the police. This trail's too hot. This trail's too cold. When will a trail be just right?" He gestured toward the window. "Those men out there are veterans. They risked their lives to protect our freedom, and now they struggle at the margins of society. Some are disabled from wounds received while fighting for our country. Others are addicted to painkillers."

Rick's voice faded into the background, and Mike heard again the raucous sounds of nighttime Saigon, the dull thump of mortars in the distance. He saw the glazed eyes of soldiers who'd found forgetfulness in narcotics. Some had been able to leave the habit in Viet Nam. Others weren't so lucky.

"I was an MP in Saigon at the end of the war," he said. "I've seen what you're talking about, and I respect what you're doing."

Mollified by this unexpected support, Rick asked what he could do to help them. It turned out the answer was nothing. Palmer's involvement with the Center was recent, and the director had no insights to offer.

"I liked him. I appreciated all he did for us, but I never felt as if I knew him on a personal level. He'd only been working with us a couple months."

"I thought he was on your board." Breton said.

"He was. We put him there right away. We're a relatively new organization, and Frank was a gift. He brought connections, resources and brains. We were lucky to have him. His death is a blow, a big one."

Mike thanked Rick for his time, gave him a card and the standard call me if you think of anything speech. He promised to get in touch when there was time to talk about improving relations.

Back in the car, Breton warned, "You just volunteered for a thankless task. The Mayor thinks our job is to keep Rick's guys from bothering the tourists. He wishes they'd all disappear."

Their next appointment, The Children's Home, was across town. Breton navigated the rush hour traffic, while Mike checked with the office. His messages included three "call me's" from Claire Marshall, no topic specified. She was probably upset about the newspaper article, and he didn't blame her, but he wasn't anxious to bear the brunt of her outrage.

Paul Gilbert wanted him to know that Melissa Yates had been, to his knowledge, closer to Hatch than anyone else. She had a troubled past and was an alumna of The Children's Home. Superintendent Vernon wanted to talk to him.

Mike returned Vernon's call and got bad news. The Super wanted to see if the search of Palmer's house produced anything before he approved the other subpoena requests.

"Welcome to The New Orleans Children's Home, and please call me Andrew." Shorthaired and clean-shaven, with wireless glasses perched halfway down his nose, Andrew Walsh provided a sharp contrast to Rick Russo. "Would you like a tour? We can talk while I show you around."

He slid easily into the role of guide. The facility was newer than it looked. The antebellum plantation was actually a reproduction constructed in the nineteen twenties for a wealthy man who'd romanticized the Confederacy. His heirs had given it to the state, which tried to make it a tourist destination. When that didn't work, the state turned it into an orphanage. It was now a home for troubled teenagers.

Mike looked at the white-pillared mansion, which was imposing but not that big. "Where do the children live?"

"Ah, that's an amusing story. The original owner had a dozen, quote unquote, slave cabins built on the grounds. Those cabins have been renovated into residences. Each one houses a counselor and up to six young people. As you can imagine, the provenance of the buildings inspires numerous jokes."

The tour skirted the pseudo slave cabins. Walsh explained that it was policy to disturb the residents as little as possible. "They're here for help, not to be gawked at. Even family members aren't allowed in the residential area." He lowered his voice. "Given your line of work, I'm sure you know that family is often part of the problem."

"This is quite a layout," Breton said, "and it looks familiar."

"An occasional movie or commercial is shot on the grounds. We're always looking for ways to raise money."

"Nah. I got it," Breton said. "We just came from Frank Palmer's house. I was looking through a stack of negatives, some were pictures of this place."

Walsh's reaction to this innocuous comment was a startled double take.

"You didn't know he was a photographer?" Mike said.

"I d-d-didn't remember," Walsh said. "You have to excuse me, Gentlemen. It's been a difficult time with Frank's death, and..." Without finishing the sentence, he led them back to the main building and a room with comfortable leather chairs arranged around a wooden table.

The chairs showed some wear, as did the oriental rugs scattered on the floor, but the overall effect was warm and hospitable. Walsh apologized for the worn furnishings, citing a perpetually strained budget, and then segued into the expected speech lionizing Frank Palmer. He, like Rick Russo, bemoaned the loss of a major patron, but unlike Rick Russo, Andrew Walsh said he knew Frank Palmer well. The murdered man had supported The Home for at least a decade and had been on their board for most of that time.

"Frank died on the eve of a million-dollar contribution. We expect to receive the funds from the estate, but it breaks my heart that he won't be here to see the difference his generosity makes."

The speech was smooth, but Walsh responded to follow-up questions not only with praise for Palmer's charity and compassion, but also with nervous tics. He straightened his tie, adjusted his cuffs and squirmed in his seat.

Mike wondered about the source of his discomfort. He remembered Gilbert's message and poked a possible sore spot. "Are you familiar with a woman named Melissa Yates?"

"The name doesn't ring a bell."

Maybe not, but something was making sweat bead on his upper lip. "It's probably been a few years."

"If she was one of our residents, there are confidentiality requirements. Unsealing any record requires special action of the court because minors are involved."

Walsh was literally wringing his hands. Mike wished Gilbert had said more. He didn't know enough to be specific. He waited to see if Walsh would give him a hint, but the man remained silent, so he moved on. When the topic shifted to Hatch, Walsh's relief was palpable.

"I've seen him driving Frank, of course, but we've never spoken. I don't know anything about him."

Mike stood up. "Thank you for your cooperation." He spoke without a trace of the irony he felt. "If we have any more questions, Lieutenant Breton or I will call you."

They walked back to their car in silence.

"That guy's hiding something." Breton pulled into the rush hour traffic.

"He's not the only one," Mike said. "Have you noticed? The closer someone was to Palmer, the less they have to say. There's something about our victim that his friends don't want us to discover."

"We've been banging our heads against brick walls all day. Stone walls," Breton corrected himself.

"Drop me off at headquarters and go home. It's going to be a long week." A stack of paperwork, more unsolved cases, waited on his desk, he had a five-thirty meeting with Vernon, and he was going to add Andrew Walsh's name to the list for subpoenas. The idea of an adult volunteer taking up with one of The Children's Home residents struck him as wrong on several dimensions.

Mike hadn't been at his desk long when his phone rang. Cursing interruptions, he picked up. It was Claire Marshall, and she wanted to talk to him about Frank Palmer.

"You have my full attention." For five minutes. They owed her that much, but he had work to do.

"Not on the phone, please, in person."

"I'm about to go into a meeting with Superintendent Vernon. How about tomorrow morning?"

"This is important."

Her tone was both incredulous and outraged, and Mike saw her point. He'd insisted upon talking to her when she wanted to be left alone. Now that she wanted to talk to him, he was putting her off.

"I'll finish here about seven, then I'm going to Salerno's for dinner. If you'd like, we can talk there. That's the best I can do."

"Salerno's is fine. How do I get there?"

Mike had surprised himself with the invitation, and he was surprised that she accepted. When word got back to Vernon—a sure thing—he'd regret it. He gave her directions.

"I'll see you at seven thirty." She hung up.

29

Captain Robinson—Claire still had trouble thinking of him as Mike—had said the restaurant was just off the highway and easy to find. Easy for who? If he'd told her it was a left exit, she'd forgotten, and if there was a sign, she hadn't seen it. She cruised past in the far right lane, unable to cross over in the heavy traffic, and took the next exit. She meant to double back around, but there was no re-entry to the highway, and the surface street was one way in the wrong direction.

Several turns and one dead end later, she pulled over and waved to the car that had been behind her the entire discombobulated trip. It pulled alongside.

"I'm trying to find Salerno's Restaurant," she said. "If you know the way, I could follow you for a change."

"Can't do that, Ms. Marshall," the policeman said with a grin. "But I can tell you how to get there. It's not far."

His directions led her to a nondescript strip mall sandwiched between an area of old warehouses and the elevated highway. Neon signs with missing letters flickered behind steel grating. They identified the stores as a mini-mart, a combination washateria/game room, and a check cashing service. An unkempt man slouched out of the mini-mart, a six-pack in each hand, and gave her the once over. The policeman honked and gestured for her to keep going.

She drove around to the back, and there it was. A big red, green, and white sign painted on the side of an old warehouse read Salerno's Ristorante. The windowless brick building didn't look promising, but cars filled the lot, and the variety of vehicles—she parked between a Mercedes roadster and a beat-up Dodge truck—indicated a diverse clientele. She picked her way across the potholed parking lot and opened the door onto a different world.

Amber globes, hung from heavy ceiling girders, bounced warm light off stuccoed walls. Ceiling fans turned lazy circles, fast enough to keep the air moving but slow enough to be unobtrusive. To the right of the door, a wooden bar with a brass rail and red leather stools beckoned the weary. Claire was glad she'd showered and changed into good slacks and a silk blouse. She gave her name to the maître d.

"The gentleman has been waiting for you." He led her to a booth.

"Hi Mike. Sorry I'm late." She slid in the other side.

"I gave up on you a few minutes ago and put in my order." He pushed his hair back off his forehead, a sign of frustration she recognized from previous encounters.

"I missed the exit and got all turned around." She smiled. "If it weren't for the policeman following me, I'd still be lost. Being a murder suspect has its benefits."

He neither returned her smile nor denied that she was still a suspect. He'd said protective surveillance, and she'd believed him. Fool. She was still a suspect and he was still a policeman.

"I recommend the grilled shrimp special," he said. "It's messy but delicious."

"No thanks. I'm not hungry, but you go ahead. I'll talk while you eat."

"I'm not going to attempt a serious conversation while you watch me peel hot shrimp. Nor am I going to let my dinner get cold while you explain what's on your mind. We can reschedule this meeting."

"What I have to say is important," she protested.

"So important that you're half an hour late." He unfolded his napkin and put it in his lap.

"I told you. I got lost."

"I have a nine o'clock appointment tomorrow morning. It should take less than an hour. I'm available to meet with you before or after. When would be convenient?"

"Now is convenient. I've gone to a lot of trouble to get here. The least you can do is listen to me." She leaned closer and lowered her voice. No one in a neighboring booth should hear what she was about to say.

"I've learned some things about Frank Palmer."

"I appreciate—"

"Please." She raised her hand, flat palm toward him. "Listen to me."

He met her gaze, and she said, "Frank was an evil man, a sexual predator with a taste for young girls. You've talked to Melissa Yates."

He nodded.

"She was his mistress for more than ten years. And how old is she now? Twenty-four! I asked her. He seduced her when she was fourteen. All those years at The Children's Home, Frank sponsored programs for adolescent girls. Think about that." She had and the thought made her sick.

Mike's expression said he took her accusation seriously. She didn't have to mention Annalisa.

"There's something else," she said. "I think Frank's business was having financial problems. Remember, I got involved in this whole mess when his check bounced. The other day Jeanette asked if I knew what happened to the money for some mysterious deal. I don't know what she was talking about, but Frank might have been doing business with the wrong people. You should look into that.

"You keep asking me questions when you should be talking to people who really knew him. Like Melissa and Bobby Austin and Paul Gilbert. That's how you're going to find out who killed Frank. And Hatch. And that boy who died when Frank's Jeep blew-up."

She stood abruptly, almost colliding with a waiter, and strode to the door. She had to get out of there. She'd made it through without losing her composure, but she wasn't good for much longer.

Garlic butter congealed on shrimp growing cold while Mike watched bubbles drift up to the surface of his beer. Watching bubbles reminded him of Claire's explanation for her behavior after discovering the burned cabin. She went to the beach because she liked to watch the waves. His bubbles and her waves—at least you knew what direction they'd take. Claire was unpredictable. She cried and popped pills when he told her the fire was arson. Then yesterday, she found a dying man and handled the situation better than many a rookie cop.

Who is she?

He'd replayed the tape of her interview with Corlette, searching for clues to her mental state. He'd interviewed her several times, including the infamous lunch date. But the woman who'd just left was someone he'd never seen before. The hazy stares into the middle distance had given way to a level gaze. Instead of evading questions, she demanded his attention. Eyes intent and jaw set, her outrage was tangible and, given what she'd told him, understandable. Had he just met the real Claire Marshall?

Vernon hadn't abandoned his theory that Claire conspired with Hatch to kill Palmer, and for the first time, Mike could see a scenario that made sense. He remembered her outburst about having neither friends nor influence in New Orleans. Put that up against a well-connected and influential pedophile, and you had a motive for murder. She, and others, could have seen killing Palmer as the only way to prevent future molestations. The cowboy could be the man in the windbreaker, could be the father of a girl Palmer had seduced. Claire could be his partner. Hell, there could be a dozen more people involved.

Mike pushed his dinner aside and declined the waiter's offer of another beer. Breton was supposed to be looking into Palmer's finances, but tonight was the first time he'd heard about missing money. The possibility of financial irregularities cast new light on Bobby Austin's barely suppressed anger and his refusal to discuss FP Development's finances. The banker couldn't stonewall forever, and neither could Gilbert. He'd put in to subpoena them both, but the paperwork sat on Vernon's desk. Working this case under the Super's watchful eye was like walking through a swamp in lead boots.

Hatch was probably their arsonist, but he'd been a foot soldier in someone else's army. The police department, in the person of Superintendent Henry Vernon, had really screwed up by failing to protect him. If they screwed up again, they could lose another witness, perhaps another foot soldier in the shadowy conspiracy, perhaps Claire. That thought killed what was left of Mike's appetite. He signaled the waiter to bring his check.

Salerno's was off the beaten path. He should have cut her a little slack about being late. His patience had worn thin after a heated discussion with Vernon, which was hardly her fault. Or maybe it was. She could have been more forthcoming sooner. With what she'd just told him, he might have been able to convince Vernon to move the subpoenas. And what about her timing? Why had she chosen to tell him now? Did she realize she'd given him a motive that could be hers?

Whatever was going on, Mike saw no reason to believe it was over. Rather than go home and pace the floor, he drove back to the office and checked with the surveillance car.

"Yes sir, Ms. Marshall just returned home."

"What took her so long?"

"She stopped for take-out. "

"Oh." She'd been hungry after all.

"I followed her to the edge of the property and waited on the street until the gate closed."

"Then what?"

"I watched her headlights go down the driveway and at that point, shifted into overnight mode. I'll drive past at fifteen-minute intervals."

"Can you see if there are any lights on in her house?"

"Not really, sir, not from the road."

He knew that. Why did he ask? "Call me if anything changes."

"Yes, sir."

He dialed her home number and got the answering machine. This time, she didn't pick up when he began speaking. He asked her to call him.

The scene in Salerno's had knocked something loose. A thought lurked at the edge of his consciousness, blurry and incomplete but important. Rereading the files might bring it into focus. He pulled them out and started at the beginning.

Despite the lack of cooperation from Palmer's associates, the interviews hadn't been a complete waste of time. Gilbert's efforts to direct suspicion toward Melissa Yates suggested a hidden agenda. Austin had simmered, and Walsh had sweated. Only Rick Russo, with his tirade about police indifference, had felt genuine. No, not just Rick. Claire Marshall was telling the truth—at least the truth as she saw it—but he couldn't shake the conviction that she was also holding back. Why? And what?

He dialed her number again. Again, no one answered. He contacted the surveillance officer and told him to go knock on her door.

30

Seventeen dollars of secondhand clothing transformed the ordinary Joe seen leaving Hatch's apartment into a tourist from the Midwest. No more jeans and t-shirt—tonight he wore dark gray slacks and a navy golf shirt, a straw boater instead of a baseball cap. The forty-five in his shoulder holster was as unobtrusive under a madras sports coat as it had been under the windbreaker.

Although loafers without socks would have been the best complement to this costume, he stuck with his brown oxfords. He'd overcome his reservations about wearing another person's clothing, but the thought of putting his bare feet into someone else's shoes made his skin crawl.

He could easily have purchased everything new, but the lightly worn garments contributed to the authenticity of his disguise. Clothes make the man. Or unmake him. The cowboy disappeared when his ten-gallon hat went into a dumpster. With a baseball cap, he became just another blue-collar worker. As for tonight's costume, he didn't know anyone who'd be caught dead in this plaid sports coat.

The killer chuckled at his own wit.

He took the Saint Charles streetcar to Washington, got off along with several other tourists, and followed them toward The Commander's Palace. At the cemetery, he crossed the street and doubled back around. His usual gait was a purposeful stride, but tonight he strolled through the evening dusk, limping a little because his right knee was acting up. He carried a shopping bag from a souvenir store in the Quarter and a walking map of historic New Orleans that he'd picked up in a hotel lobby.

He knew exactly where he was and where he was going, but he amused himself by pausing under a streetlight to study the map. Then he tucked it back in his pocket and kept walking. When he reached the Clarke mansion, he stopped and stared as if he'd never seen it before. Only the outdoor lights were on. The family must still be in Europe, a convenient but not necessary circumstance. Half a block of lushly planted grounds separated the big house from Claire's rental.

An article in today's paper implied that she was suspected of the murders he'd committed. What a cosmic joke. Claire had neither the strength of character nor the courage, the daring, it took to kill. Her role was victim—not exactly as first imagined, but still, a perfect victim.

He'd had a bad moment when he saw her at Hatch's apartment, standing between him and Hatch's car. He still had the keys, but only a fool would go back there or drive that car now. Claire shouldn't have been there. Because she was, he had two problems, no car and a witness who might someday realize who she'd seen. His solution addressed both.

The police were watching Claire openly, the fools. They'd made it easy for him to learn their schedule, figure out when she'd be vulnerable, and calculate how much time he'd have. He glanced around to be sure no one was there to see him and slipped through the servant's entrance, unlocked because he'd disabled the latch earlier today. Once he was inside, the tall hedge sheltered him from prying eyes.

He exchanged the conspicuous madras jacket for the hooded navy sweatshirt that had been in his shopping bag. The jacket and straw boater went in the shopping bag, which he tossed into a trashcan. Pick-up was Tuesday morning, another happy coincidence. By the time anyone realized Claire was gone, the trash would be gone too. Even if it weren't, the contents of the shopping bag would reveal only his jacket size.

He kept to the shadows at the edge of the driveway in case Claire was out on her porch. As he drew closer, he saw his caution had been unnecessary. The carriage house was dark, and her car wasn't there. It didn't matter; he could wait.

A big orange cat that had been lying on the porch step leapt to its feet, hissing at his approach. He pegged a magnolia cone at it, and the cat retreated through a flap in the door. He bounced another cone off the door to keep the animal inside, where it couldn't possibly alert Claire, then found a sheltered spot between a tall shrub and the porch.

Time doesn't fly when you're standing in the bushes keeping most of your weight on your good leg, but his patience paid off. After what seemed much longer than the thirty-five minutes his watch recorded, two cars rounded the corner and stopped. Metal creaked as the big gate opened. The low headlights of Claire's Miata came toward him, and the other car moved on down the street. He had fifteen minutes.

She parked no more than ten feet from him, climbed out, and began stretching a protective cover over the car. Her concentration on the mundane task infuriated him. He imagined her neck in his hands, the terror on her face, and the snap when he squeezed. Throttling her would be most satisfying, but he knew better than to give in to anger—no matter how justified. Tonight, he needed her alive. Then, after she'd served her purpose... Didn't some philosopher say revenge was a dish better enjoyed cold?

He drew his gun and smoothed his face into an amiable expression. His plan required her cooperation, so he had to convince her that he'd let her go once she'd helped him escape. She would believe the lie because she'd want it to be true.

Claire put her take-out on the swing and rummaged in her purse for her front door key. Something rustled behind her. Startled, she spun around. A man stepped out of the shrubbery. He no longer wore the windbreaker or the baseball cap, but she recognized him. She'd almost recognized him at Hatch's apartment, but her brain had refused to believe her eyes. She inhaled sharply, drawing breath for a scream.

"Quiet," he said.

She saw the gun and heard the click as he released the safety. She remembered the blood pulsing bright red from holes in Hatch's chest. He'd shot Hatch, and he'd shoot her too. No one would hear. The Clarkes weren't home, and the police car had gone. She looked the killer in the eye.

"Hello, Frank." Her voice belonged to someone else.

"Hello, Claire." He smiled. "Really, I expected more of a reaction. Aren't you surprised to see me?"

"Of course. I thought you were dead."

"The reports of my death were greatly exaggerated." He kept the gun trained on her.

"There was a body in your cabin." The police would be back. If she could just keep him talking...

"Ah, Lou. He was nobody. He won't be missed."

"The police think it was you."

"I went to a lot of trouble to convince them it was me. The police are no problem. You on the other hand." He shook his head in mock sorrow. "Nothing but trouble. Coming back early, going to Hatch's apartment. Why you did that, I can't imagine. It's not as if you two were friends."

Claire tightened her grip on her pocketbook. If she could get close enough, she could swing it and knock the gun out of his hand. She could run and hide until the police came back. She knew her way around the garden. Frank didn't.

Her mouth was dry. Would she be able to scream? Would the policeman in his car hear her? She kept her eyes focused Frank's face and concentrated on breathing slowly, staying calm.

"I apologize for the inconvenience, but I need one small favor." He smiled again, as if they were having a normal conversation.

"What kind of favor?"

He held out his hand. "Give me your purse."

She gave it to him as slowly as she dared. At least five minutes had passed since she drove through the driveway gate. Ten more …

"I need a driver, and Hatch is no longer available." He glanced at his watch. "Take the cover off your car. The police will return in ten minutes. I want to be gone before then."

"The police?" She pretended not to know what he was talking about.

"Do you think I'm stupid, that I don't know they're watching you?" He grabbed her arm and dragged her down the porch steps. "If you keep stalling, we'll have to wait until they go past. Waiting annoys me. You don't want to do that." He shoved her toward the car.

Claire removed the cover with shaking hands. She dropped it on the ground and waited for Frank's next order.

"Give me the remote control for the driveway gate."

She unclipped it from the driver's seat visor and handed it to him.

"Now, get into the driver's seat, and slide the passenger seat forward." Frank climbed in and wedged himself into the space behind the seats. He held gun barrel behind her right ear and handed her the keys.

"Start the car and put the top up."

She complied, while time crawled.

"Alright, let's go. And Claire, rest assured that I'll pull this trigger the minute you don't do exactly what I tell you to do. I can see you, and I can see where we're going."

"If you shoot me while I'm driving, we're both in trouble."

"You're right. We need each other. Unfortunately, we can't trust each other. I'm the one with the gun, and you're the one who has to take things on faith." He aimed the remote at the gate. It swung open. "Turn right and wait while I close the gate. We don't want anything to alarm your protectors when they return." He looked at his watch. "In four minutes."

"Where are we going?"

"To my fish camp."

Claire drove as slowly as she dared, but cars passed without anyone giving them a second glance. Look at me, she wanted to scream. Help me. At a red light on Saint Charles, a police car pulled up next to them. She turned toward it and felt the gun barrel hard against her neck.

"Don't do anything stupid."

The light turned green, and they continued in silence. She took the ramp onto the highway and merged into traffic. She should have hit something down on Saint Charles. Now it was too late. Crashing at highway speed could kill them both, and she didn't want to die.

"Take the next exit," Frank said. "There's a shopping center on the right. Pull in and drive to the far end of the parking lot."

Claire's knees wobbled as she downshifted to make the turn. Tears stung her eyes, but she wouldn't cower or plead for her life. She'd seen enough of Frank to know that begging would earn contempt, not mercy. She drove to the far side of the lot, certain he planned to shoot her, throw her body into the weeds, and take the car.

"Stop here. Now reach over and open the passenger door. All the way."

Following orders, she opened the door wide enough that it stayed open. Her left hand rested on her door handle. Could she sneak her door open and roll out? Roll out to where? She was surrounded by empty asphalt.

"Give me the car keys." Frank moved the gun.

Claire tensed as the barrel brushed the base of her skull. Her hand shook so badly she could barely pull the keys from the ignition. She clenched them in her fist, the end of the key sticking out, but he was behind her and out of reach.

"Don't even think about it." The hand without the gun grabbed her wrist and squeezed until she released the key. "Now pick it up and hand it to me. Gently."

She gave him the car key.

"Relax, Claire. All I want is a ride. You'll be fine as long as you do what you're told."

He climbed out, all the while keeping the gun trained on her. She almost wept with relief when he pushed the passenger seat as far back as possible and climbed back in. He massaged his right knee, and she remembered that he had lingering problems from an old football injury. This sign of weakness gave her hope. She spoke to see if she still could.

"I'm not sure I can find the way in the dark."

"Don't worry. I'll direct you." Again, he smiled as if nothing was wrong. "In another hour or so, I'll be on the boat, and you'll be on your way home. By the time you get to a phone and alert the police, which is what I fully expect you to do, I'll be long gone."

"I'd like to believe you, but I keep thinking about Hatch."

"Please Claire, let's not be hypocritical. As I recall, you compared him unfavorably to a pit bull." He chuckled. "Don't worry about what happened to Hatch. He was a danger to me. You're not."

He was lying.

31

Mike heard Breton's voice and walked down the hall to see why, after all the complaints about working late, he'd come back in. The Lieutenant was on the phone. He looked up when Mike rapped on the doorframe.

"Sherry, do you mind if I put you on speakerphone? My boss just walked in. I know he'll have some questions for you."

"I'll do anything I can to help you find the murderer." Her voice trembled.

"Let me bring him up to speed. Mike, I'm talking to Sherry Leblanc, who is the CFO for FP Development Company. Sherry, would you repeat what you just told me."

"Millions and millions of dollars are missing. We don't know exactly how much."

"When did you learn money was missing?" Mike said. Claire had mentioned possible financial problems. This sounded more serious—certainly the scale was beyond anything he'd imagined.

"Last week when Ed started going over the books, he noticed." A sob broke through Sherry's self-control.

"Ed Pelletier is a CPA working for Gilbert." Breton interrupted her. "Okay, go ahead, Sherry."

"He kept asking me where the money went. I told him Mr. Palmer was putting an important deal together and needed funds for leverage, but Ed says the money's missing."

"Did Ed mention embezzlement?" Mike said.

"Oh, no. Mr. Palmer moved the money, but then he died, and now no one knows where it is." Sherry moaned. "I think someone killed him and stole the money."

Breton mouthed the word motive.

"Who else knew about this important deal?"

"Jeanette thought Claire knew, but she said no."

"Does Bobby Austin know about the missing money?"

"I think so. Ed says it was mostly the bank's money." Her voice broke. "Ed and Mr. Gilbert were here when I was at lunch, and Jeanette says they were talking about it. Ed yells all the time, but no one's ever seen Mr. Gilbert angry. Jeanette said he walked out with this terrible expression on his face and didn't even speak to her."

"Who else knows?" Mike said. Pieces of the puzzle were beginning to fall into place.

"I only told Jeanette. She's my best friend, and she recommended me for this job. We didn't really believe Ed until today when she saw how upset Mr. Gilbert was. Now we're scared." The last word ended on a rising note of panic. She agreed to come to headquarters at ten the next morning and make a statement.

Breton switched off the speakerphone. "Sherry writes the checks. Nice call, Mike."

"I thought you'd left for the day."

"The wife went out with the girls, so I decided to make a few more calls. Nothing better to do." He shrugged. "The missing millions give us a motive. Bobby Austin and Gilbert are the ones who called Lafourche Parish and insisted they search what was left of the cabin. I'm thinking Austin knew what they were going to find."

It wouldn't be the first time a murderer stepped forward to discover his victim's body, but Mike saw a different picture. "Don't forget the ten million in life insurance, very recently made payable to Melissa Yates."

"They could be in it together. Hell, maybe Melissa and Austin have fallen in love. Or, failing that, in lust." Breton took it to another level. "Austin, Melissa and Claire Marshall would make a fine threesome, a redhead sandwich with a banker in the middle." He sniggered. "Austin looked tired this morning."

"I spoke to Claire about an hour ago. She's finally talking about Palmer, and it's all negative. She says he's a sexual predator with a taste for young girls."

"You believe her?"

"I reviewed the case notes, looking for corroboration, and found it at The Children's Home. Remember how nervous Walsh was when we talked to him? How he fell apart when you mentioned Palmer's photography hobby?"

"Yeah?"

"Pedophiles often take pictures of their victims—you know that. What if Palmer had taken pornographic pictures of adolescent girls, residents of The Home, and Walsh found out? That million-dollar donation could have been blackmail." Pictures and money, this was the thought that had been tickling the edge of his consciousness.

"Palmer and girls from The Children's Home." Breton whistled. "You better have the pictures before you lob that grenade onto the table."

"Claire said Melissa's been his mistress for ten years. She's twenty four."

"Are you sure? She looks more like thirty."

"She's twenty-four, and according to Gilbert, she used to live at The Home. I think we can find other girls, establish a pattern of behavior."

"Say we can, what's the point? Palmer's dead. But if Claire Marshall believes he abused young girls, there's another motive. She's going to marry the guy, and then she learns about his nasty habits." Breton rubbed his face. "First we can't find a motive. Now we're at two and counting. Palmer must have been a real charmer."

"A real charmer who checked out in time to avoid making a million dollar donation that smells like blackmail. Millions more are missing from his company, and he's the one who moved the funds. His mistress is the brand new beneficiary of a ten-million dollar insurance policy." Mike ticked off the millions. "All in all, it was a convenient and profitable death for Frank Palmer—and Melissa Yates."

"Gilbert has been pointing us at her. It's a good bet he knows more than he's letting on." Breton paused. He narrowed his eyes. "Hey, wait a minute. Are you going where I think you're going?"

"Palmer, the cowboy, and the shooter—all middle aged white men about six feet tall, a little stocky."

"Them and a thousand other guys."

"A thousand other guys who don't hide behind their hats, who weren't at the airport, weren't at Hatch's apartment, and don't have sex with fourteen-year-olds," Mike said, gaining certainty as he spoke. "Start with Palmer as the killer, and things start making sense. We've agreed Hatch likely torched the cabin on orders from someone else. Right? Who did Hatch work for?" It was obvious now, but the fact in front of your nose can be the hardest to see.

"You're serious, aren't you?"

"Remember Hatch's reaction when you told him Palmer's body was in the cabin? At first, he thought it was funny."

Breton nodded. "Yeah."

"Hatch knew that Palmer was alive after the cabin burned. He didn't know what the hell was going on, but as long as we couldn't pin anything on him, he was keeping his mouth shut. I'm going to call Corlette. Lafourche Parish identified the body."

"It's almost ten."

"I have his home number. My office in five minutes. "

Mike put Corlette on speakerphone, brought him up to date, and laid out the reasons behind his growing suspicion that Frank Palmer had staged his own murder.

"If Palmer's alive," Corlette said, "someone else is dead. We found a man's body in that cabin."

"Brilliant, Boy Wonder." Breton muttered under his breath.

"And," the deputy continued, "if Palmer is alive, he's one ruthless bastard. So, where's Claire Marshall? He would have recognized her at Hatch's apartment. He has to be afraid she'll realize who she saw."

"We think she's at home," Mike said.

"You think? Aren't you watching her?"

"She rents a carriage house on the grounds of a large estate. It's a secure property, surrounded by a tall fence. An officer followed her to the edge of the property and he's been driving past every fifteen minutes. He says she's there, but no one answers the phone."

"So, that doesn't bother you?" Corlette said.

"I told him to knock on her door. I'm waiting to hear back. Can you find someone awake in your medical examiner's office?"

"I can wake them up, but the ID was confirmed by the dental records you provided."

"I'll talk to the dentist, but let's start with your ME." Mike sent Breton to find the dentist's home number and told Corlette he'd stay in touch.

The patrol officer reported in. "I was able to access the property through an unlocked pedestrian entrance," he said. "Her car's gone, no lights in the house, and no response when I knocked on the door. She left, and I missed it." He paused for breath. "She could've been giving me the slip. She knows the schedule, and it looks like she left in a big hurry. Her take-out is sitting on the porch unopened. Her car cover's lying on the ground. But that gate, the way I got in, the lock was broken."

"Don't touch anything," Mike said. "Lieutenant Breton is on his way. Meet him at the pedestrian gate."

"I'm on my way," Breton had just walked back into the room. "Where am I going?"

"Claire Marshall's residence. An officer is waiting for you there. She and her car are gone. Look for signs she was abducted when she returned home this evening."

"Shit."

"I'm putting out an APB."

As Mike described Claire and her vehicle, it hit him that he cared. Not only because it was his job to protect the public. Not only because he wanted to get this much too clever killer off the streets. He cared what happened to Claire Marshall.

Lots of people are vulnerable under a tough façade. She was tough behind a vulnerable façade, and he liked her for it. He wondered if he was jumping the gun because he'd lost his professional detachment, weighed the alternatives, and decided it was no contest. If he was wrong, he'd have egg on his face. If she'd been abducted, they'd already wasted too much time.

Ten minutes later, an officer called in to report seeing a woman driving a bright blue Miata on Saint Charles. "This was a good forty-five or fifty minutes ago. She appeared to be alone in the car, but the top was up and I couldn't really see. I'm sure about the red hair. She was heading toward the Quarter. Or the highway."

Mike called Corlette and brought him up to speed. "I'm operating on a hunch," he warned. "This could be a wild goose chase." He wanted that to be true, but his gut told him otherwise. "Breton's on his way to her residence. We'll see what he finds. What about your medical examiner?"

"He's positive about the match. He was ready to sign the affidavit for the insurance company, but Palmer's executor asked him to hold off for a week. That's the only thing seems out of line to me."

"Paul Gilbert, one of the men who met you at the cabin, is the executor. Did he give any reason for requesting the delay?"

"Nothing the medical examiner could remember. I asked him to check his notes and give you a call. Send us your APB. I'll be at the office in ten minutes."

Mike fixed a fresh pot of coffee and looked out the window at the brick wall that was his only view. Claire stared out this window whenever he interviewed her. He wondered what she saw on those bricks. What had she known that she didn't tell him? What was Gilbert up to? The phone rang and he grabbed it.

"Robinson here."

Breton described a trampled area in the shrubbery next to the front porch and two sets of footprints between the porch and the driveway. The larger footprints came from the shrubbery where it appeared a large heavy person had spent some time; the smaller ones were only in the driveway and on the porch. His interpretation was ambivalent.

"Looks like a man waited in the bushes. He confronted her when she came home, and they left in her car. There's no indication of a scuffle. She might have gone willingly. But there's a porch swing that would have been a more comfortable place to wait."

"Treat the area like a crime scene. I'll update the APB with a warning about a possible abduction and let Lafourche Parish know where we are."

Corlette was waiting for the call. "If Claire Marshall drives into Lafourche Parish, I'll hear about it," he said. "So, let's proceed with your worst-case scenario. The murderer, possibly Palmer, has her. Why? And where's he taking her?"

"He must need her. I wish I knew why." There was a beep on the line and Mike said. "I have a call waiting."

"I'm going to check on Daniel. This number will ring through to the two-way in my car."

His call was the Lafourche Parish medical examiner who said there was no question about the identification.

"It was a piece of cake, but the executor said to hold off on the affidavit because there are 'outstanding issues that require clarification,' whatever that means. And now you want to talk to me. What's going on?"

"I apologize for bothering you at home."

"No problem. I was just watching TV. You know, it's really too bad the guy dies right before his wedding."

"Uh huh." Mike said. He'd been so sure.

"It's a tough world," the medical examiner continued. "Anyway it was him. Recent x-rays plus lots of fillings, every one of them brand new, made my job easy."

"All new fillings? On a middle-aged man?"

"He was getting himself in shape for his bride. Men and women both do that." The medical examiner chuckled. "Didn't your Daddy tell you to check a woman's teeth before you marry her?"

No, but his father had told him to trust his instincts. He thanked the medical examiner for his cooperation and called Palmer's dentist.

Dr. Menendez answered the phone in the wary manner of a man who doesn't expect good news from a late night call. He became affable when Mike identified himself.

"Captain Robinson, thank you for calling. I didn't expect such a high-ranking officer to be dealing with my little issue, but I really appreciate it."

"Excuse me, sir?" What was Menendez talking about?

"As I told Lieutenant Breton, my insurance company won't reimburse any damages not documented in a police report. I reported the break-ins but didn't mention any damage. I've since learned it will cost twenty-five hundred dollars to repair the floor, which was scratched when the file drawers fell on it. The building manager says he has to refinish the whole room."

Now he remembered. Breton had mentioned the dentist complaining about kids breaking into his office. "When did the break-ins occur?" Mike asked.

"Two days in a row three or four weeks ago. Isn't that in the report?"

"I haven't seen the report," Mike said. The timing was right. Why in hell hadn't they seen the connection before this?

"Then why are you calling?" Menendez said.

"I'm investigating the death of Frank Palmer. You were his dentist?" Asking the necessary questions without raising Menendez's suspicions would be difficult if not impossible.

"Yes. I was," came the cautious response.

"Did Mr. Palmer recently have a large amount of dental work done?"

"Nothing out of the ordinary. A replacement filling or two."

"Frank Palmer did not have all his fillings replaced very recently?"

"No. The one with all the work was the guy Frank brought in, I forget his name, one of Rick Russo's veterans." A pause. "Wait a minute. What's this about?"

"It's just procedure." Mike threw up a smokescreen. "Will you be available tomorrow? We'll need to see the damage. Then, we'll revise the report and give you a copy for your insurance company."

They set an appointment for tomorrow at ten. A detective would stop by Menendez's office, ostensibly to look at the floor. While there, he'd ask the dentist to check Frank Palmer's file to be sure everything was in order. It would not be. The body in the burned cabin was Rick Russo's veteran, the one who went missing a few days before "Palmer's body" was discovered.

Frank Palmer, the great philanthropist, had taken a homeless veteran to his personal dentist and paid for treatment that included x-rays. Hatch, who had a previous career as a burglar, broke into Menendez's office and removed two sets of dental records. Everything Palmer needed to switch the x-rays had been in his desk drawer. The second break-in returned the altered records to the files. If Hatch had talked, he would have blown the scheme sky high.

Mike called Corlette. "Palmer's alive. He conned us all."

"I was about to call you. One of our patrols saw a man and a woman in a blue Miata half an hour ago. Before the APB. The woman was driving. He's pretty sure she had red hair, but the top was up. "

"Do you think he's going for his boat?"

"I don't think he can get it out of there before daylight. More likely he's headed for a runway and a small plane or another boat waiting down at the Gulf."

"I want to cover all the options," Mike said. Anyone with the money Palmer had stolen would have no trouble making travel arrangements.

"I'm on the road. I'll call back to the office, have them notify the Coast Guard and Civil Aviation. I'll send deputies over to Palmer's boat, but those dirt roads are slow going in the dark."

32

On the highway, they'd been one car in fast-moving stream of vehicles. Now they were alone on a narrow country road. Neither situation offered an opportunity to escape. Claire wiped her sweaty palms on her slacks, one at a time, hoping Frank didn't notice this sign of nervousness.

"You were going to kill me, weren't you?" she said. "Fixing up your cabin was a just ploy to get me there. They would have found two bodies in the ashes. People would have thought it was you and Melissa."

She was almost ten years older than Melissa, but about the same height and weight—both were redheads. Her body would have been badly burned. Just like Lou's, whoever he was.

Lou and I. Two nobodies.

"Hasn't anyone ever told you excessive cleverness is not attractive in a woman?" Frank sat with his arms crossed, the gun in his right hand inches from her ribs.

"Is Melissa waiting at your boat?"

"Not that it's any of your business, but no. When you didn't cooperate, I went to plan B, which doesn't include her."

"Then why am I here?"

"Because you went to Hatch's apartment."

"I didn't recognize you."

"I let you go to Michigan. You were safe, but you had to come back early. You had to tell everyone we weren't getting married." He jabbed the gun into her ribs. "Do you think you're too good for me, Claire?"

"Why did you tell people we were getting married?"

"You were part of the illusion, my reason to live." His mood shifted and once again they were having an amiable conversation. "With just one body in the cabin, there was the risk my death would be ruled a suicide. But does a man who's about to marry to the girl of his dreams kill himself? Of course not." His voice dripped sarcasm.

"Why did you care?" They'd left the pavement behind; seeing another car was unlikely.

"Cowards commit suicide. I'm not a coward."

Claire remembered Annie Lewis and didn't trust herself to respond.

"There was another, more practical, concern. Melissa gets a good-bye gift from my life insurance. The policy won't pay for a suicide."

"Does she know you're still alive?"

"Pay attention to your driving," he warned. "You want to make it safely to my boat."

She nodded as if she believed that safety lay ahead of her, and leaned forward, peering through the windshield, carefully steering around the potholes and ridges. Frank's gun poked her ribs every time she hit a bump.

"I still don't understand how you fooled the police." She had to keep him distracted while she looked for a reason to get out of the car. Otherwise, she had no chance. He could shoot faster than she could climb out.

"Careful planning," he bragged. "A month ago, I took Lou to my dentist and paid to fix his rotten teeth. Then I paid Hatch to switch our x-rays. He was a burglar before he became a chauffeur, and it's like riding a bike. You never really forget how." Frank laughed at his own joke.

"When the big day came, I drove Lou down in my car and made sure he died happy. Hatch came later. He dropped me at the Biloxi Airport and drove back to switch cars and burn the cabin. My cabin, my car, a body with teeth that matched my dental records... I'm a dead man." He snickered. "It's a shame I had to miss my own funeral. Was it well attended?"

"Why do you want people to think you're dead?" They were on top of the old levee; she was running out of time.

"I told Hatch to drive straight back to New Orleans, no stops where someone might see him." He slapped the dashboard. "He should have been on the highway when the Jeep blew. An accident, and that would have been the end of it. I'm dead. The man who knows better is dead. Case closed."

"Are you sure Hatch didn't tell the police the whole story? He was in jail for a couple days. They questioned him."

"He didn't know the whole story." Frank pointed to the marked trees. "Don't miss the turn."

They'd left New Orleans under cloudy skies, but now the clouds were breaking up and a bright moon emerging. She stopped at the edge of the clearing. Moonlight illuminated the skeleton of his cabin and turned the ash-covered ground white, ghostlike.

"I could get a flat tire driving through the debris," she said. "Can we park here and walk to the dock?"

"Keep going. I don't feel like walking, and you've already caused me too much trouble."

"Me?" She was indignant. "I was nothing but a pawn."

"You *are* nothing but a pawn, the least important piece on the board."

Had only nine days passed since she found the burned cabin? Had she really cried because she thought that Frank Palmer, this monster, was dead?

They passed through the clearing and continued on the track leading to the dock. As they approached the water, the ground became muddier, and water filled the low spots. Claire steered into a puddle and, when she felt her tires lose traction, pressed the accelerator. The wheels spun, digging holes in the muck.

"We're stuck."

"I've been waiting for you to try something," he said. Their eyes met and she realized Frank was enjoying himself, playing with her while confident that he controlled the outcome. Any pretense that he'd let her go had ended.

"Why don't you just shoot me and get it over with?"

"Because I don't want to." He opened the door and eased out of the car. "Get out and start walking. I'm right behind you."

They continued single file down the muddy path. If she tried to run, he'd shoot her before she'd gone three steps. They passed through the last scattering of trees before the water's edge. She stumbled on the step to the dock, and he yanked her to her feet.

"Keep moving."

She pressed her hand against her chest and drew a ragged breath. "I'm having a panic attack," she gasped, "I can't breathe. I can hardly walk." If he thought she was falling apart and unable to resist, he might let his guard down. Just for a moment. That's all she needed.

"You want something to be scared of?" He waved his gun toward a root sticking out of the water. "See that moccasin, over there on that cypress knee?"

The coiled snake was the same dark gray as the gun in Frank's hand.

"Predators come out at night," he said. "There's an old bull gator hangs out here. I don't see him, but you can be sure he's watching us. If you stick your toe in the water, he'll know it. He's big enough to take your leg in one bite."

Claire searched the water for the half-submerged log that was really an alligator, for ripples that could really be snakes. Moonlight shimmering on the black surface obscured whatever lay below. If a big alligator got hold of her, he'd roll her until she drowned. It would be horrible but over quickly and better than whatever Frank had planned.

"Get on the boat." Frank shoved her forward.

She went with the push and kept going, across the dock into the water. Arms wrapped around knees held tight to her chest, she sank to the bottom then crawled along until she could hold her breath no longer. She pushed off for the surface, and her head hit the bottom of the boat. She felt her way to an edge and, being careful not to make a splash, straightened up.

She was at the back of the boat, wedged between the propellers. Frank couldn't see her, but this shelter was only temporary. Metal blades pressed against her shoulders. She'd be cut to ribbons when he turned the engines on.

A thump told her Frank had jumped onto the boat. His footsteps thudded along the outside railing, he moved to the other side, and a glow appeared in the water. He was shining a spotlight under the dock. She swam to the far side of the boat and looked for refuge.

A bulkhead lined this side of the channel. It and the floating dock were both a good two feet above the water's surface. Climbing onto either would attract Frank's attention. Her only hope lay in the marshes on the other side, tall grass where she could hide. She'd have to swim across the channel. Thirty or forty feet—she could do that underwater.

A splash that could have been an alligator entering the water made her heart stop. She looked in the direction of the sound but saw only ripples.

Go, now!

She took a deep breath, dropped beneath the surface. Staying deep, reaching her arms, and scissoring her legs until her lungs burned and her muscles screamed for oxygen, she swam for the other side. She kicked upward, broke the surface, and was horrified by the distance that remained. The current was running against her.

A gunshot cracked, and furious thrashing roiled the water. She dropped back down. Strength born of terror propelled her forward until the bottom began rising up to meet her. This had to be the shallows on the other side. She clawed at the mud, pulling herself along, afraid to kick for fear that her foot would break the surface and reveal her location. Her fingers touched the first hummocks.

She tucked her legs under her body, sprang into the shelter of the marsh grass, and lay on the ground, gasping for breath. Somewhere close, an alligator bellowed. Its guttural growl had obscured the sound of her exit, but if it pursued her, even on land, she was doomed. Another gunshot and the growling stopped, leaving a silence so absolute that she could hear her heart beating. The insects and frogs resumed their songs. In the distance, a nutria screamed.

"Claire, you better listen. I just saved your life. That gator was after you. I got him, but his blood's going to draw others. They'll tear you apart. Show yourself, and I'll pick you up."

Cautiously, she inched farther away from the water's edge. Swarming mosquitoes formed black swatches on her exposed flesh. She slathered mud on her arms, her face and neck, ankles and feet. The mosquitoes found vulnerable spots around her eyes and mouth, in her ears and nose. They were driving her crazy.

Two more gunshots punched holes in the swamp sounds. A bullet hit the ground near her leg and sent shards of oyster shell into her thigh. She bit her lip to keep from crying out. The mosquitoes dispersed for a moment, but her blood drew them back, and a black cloud descended on her wound. When she batted them away, they attacked her hands. She wanted to scream.

She crawled deeper into the marsh. The tall grass sheltered her, but it also prevented her from seeing more than a couple feet in any direction. Half-buried oyster shells shredded her slacks and scraped the skin from her hands and knees. Sharp blades of grass sliced her arms. Each cut drew blood that sent the mosquitoes into a fresh frenzy.

A bright light moved toward her. Frank had a spotlight. Claire crawled faster, moving away from the light as quickly as she could. Her right hand slid forward onto nothing. She lost her balance and fell forward, somersaulting down a bank into waist deep water. She had landed in one of the salt-water creeks that ran through the marsh. The light swung in the direction of her splash. She huddled against the creek bank until the light moved on.

Half-swimming half-walking against the current and staying as low as possible, Claire followed the winding stream until it curved around a bend and spread into wide shallows. Moonlight glittered on an expanse of open water, a lake too large to swim across. It offered neither haven nor help.

Claire let the incoming tide carry her back around the bend. The little creek was safer than the open lake, less likely to harbor alligators that would be attracted by the wound on her leg. If she knelt on the bottom, the water came to her neck. Tenting her blouse over her head sheltered her face from the mosquitoes. She could hide here until Frank gave up and left. When daylight came, she could look for a way back to her car that didn't involve swimming across that channel.

When Claire was a little girl, she'd made deals with God, promising to be good if He would just talk her mother into letting her stay up late to watch a favorite television show or help her pass the math test. Things like that. She hadn't asked for favors in years, and after Tom died, she'd stopped believing that God cared what happened to her. Tonight, kneeling in the creek, she prayed for her life.

As if he'd intercepted her prayers, Frank called, "Are you listening, Claire? The next sound you hear will be me pulling wires out of your car."

She heard the sound of metal on metal and then a splash.

"That was your distributor cap," he said. "You're going nowhere."

Frank cursed his impatience. He'd seen movement in the water and fired too quickly. Instead of hitting Claire, he'd taken out the alligator that was going for her. He must have hit the beast right in the brain. It was a tough shot at a tiny target, and if he weren't furious, he'd appreciate the irony. He wanted her dead, and the gator would have done the job for him. Now, she was unfinished business. He couldn't leave her here alive—not even with her car disabled. There was an off chance someone would find her while she could still talk, and she knew too much.

The forty-five that had kept Claire obedient and killed the gator wasn't accurate at distance, but he had other options. No one went unarmed in the Gulf; too many smugglers were looking for a new boat. His armory included an AK-47 that would slice through marsh grass like a hot knife through butter and cut Claire in half. The thought tempted, but sound travels across water, and volleys from a machine gun would raise a big red flag. He selected a shotgun, more than enough firepower to take care of an unarmed woman. Claire Marshall had screwed up his careful plans for the last time.

Frank had devised his exit strategy after that sniveling hypocrite Andrew Walsh accused him of molesting girls from The Home. Molesting, what a laugh. Those girls were ready, willing and able. Their pretending to be reluctant made it more fun for everyone. Andrew had demanded he stay away from the girls and asked for a million dollar donation. He called it an act of contrition. Anyone else would call it blackmail.

Paying had never been an option, because Andrew's noble justifications were bullshit. There'd be another demand and then another. Some of the money would stick to his fingers.

Frank had considered arranging a fatal accident for Andrew, but the bloodsucker had thought of that too. He'd warned that certain pictures would surface if anything happened to him. More pictures. Frank shook his head—his photography hobby was his Achilles heel.

He feigned remorse, said it had never happened before and would never happen again. He told Andrew that he needed ninety days to get the money together, knowing he could do it in sixty. Promising to make the donation at the awards ceremony had been a stroke of genius. One of his few regrets was not being there to see Andrew's face when he realized his meal ticket had expired.

Frank was ready to move on. He'd had enough of crooked inspectors and lazy subcontractors, of Bobby's bank demanding money back, with interest, while he did all the real work. He was tired of the same people saying the same things at the same parties, and he was getting tired of Melissa. Still, he resented the attempted blackmail that had catalyzed his discontent. The slate wouldn't be clean until Andrew Walsh suffered his fatal accident, but it could wait. Tonight was Claire's turn.

He set a bow anchor to hold the boat in the middle of the channel, a position that allowed a clear view across the marsh to the lake. He imposed a mental grid on the tall grass and began a methodical search with a high-powered marine flashlight.

When he found Claire, he'd give her one more chance to return. If she refused, he'd shoot her and leave her body for the gators. He'd rather take her on board, have a little fun before tossing her to the sharks, but he didn't have time to go into the marsh after her, and she wasn't worth missing his connection.

33

Daniel slouched in the booth, one of several lining the back room of Ray's Café. He studied his cards and contemplated the stupidity, or perhaps the brilliance, of bluffing with a pair of fives. He, Ray, and Vinnie were into their third hour of penny ante poker. Thanks to a series of crappy hands, he was down six dollars. He'd not decided whether to bet or fold when the sound of an engine brought everyone to attention. Ray killed the light. Vinnie picked up his shotgun. Outside, a car door slammed.

"Hey Daniel, it's Jason Corlette. Your Mom said I'd find you here." The deputy was out front and hollering loud enough to wake the dead.

"Shit. He's going to get me killed," Daniel hissed.

"I need a hand, Daniel. Are you inside?"

Ray was halfway to the door when Jason kicked it in.

"Aw, man, you didn't have to bust in. I was coming."

"Sorry, Ray. If anything's broken, the Sheriff's Department will send someone over to fix it. Is Daniel here?"

"He's in the back. Him, me, and Vinnie, we've been playing cards." Ray flipped on the lights. "It sounded like you did real damage."

"Vinnie, Daniel, how're you doing?" Jason acted like he'd been invited.

Vinnie said hello, but Daniel wasn't going to pretend everything was okay. A man who hadn't done anything wrong ought to be left in peace. Jason pulled a chair up to the end of the booth and made small talk with Vinnie until Ray came back from examining the door.

"I'm going to need a new lock."

"Tomorrow, no problem." Jason said. "Tonight I'm here about that cabin fire." He looked straight at Daniel. "From day one, we knew it was arson. Tonight, we figured out that Palmer was the killer, not the victim."

"What a kicker." Daniel hooted. "I knew he was an asshole."

Jason didn't crack a smile. "So far, Palmer's responsible for three deaths," he said. "One of them was your cousin Jimmy. Claire Marshall could become number four. He's kidnapped her."

"Why are you telling us?" Vinnie said.

"I'm looking for help. Palmer could be taking her to his boat. We have cars on the way, but it's slow going. I'm looking for someone to motor me over there. How about it, Daniel?"

"No way, José."

"What the matter Danny? Are you yellow?" Ray said.

"I ain't yellow, but I don't go looking for trouble. This is not my business." He glared at Jason, who was supposed to protect people and had just told the world where he was hiding. If Palmer was anywhere around, he'd heard.

"What happened to Jimmy is family business, and you're part of the family." Ray said. "Why do you think Vinnie and I are watching over your sorry ass?" He spit on the floor.

"Hold on." Jason put his hand on Ray's shoulder. "Give the man a break. Me, I'm not looking to confront Palmer, and I'm not yellow."

"How come you want to go over there?" Daniel appreciated the good words, but he wasn't going to get sucked in.

"All I want is to see if anyone's there. We scope it out and radio the guys in the cars what to expect."

Daniel picked his cards back up and studied them. They were playing seven-card stud, and barring a miracle, a pair of fives with nine high was another losing hand. He folded everyone's cards back into the deck.

"Whose deal?" he said.

Vinnie finished his beer and tossed the bottle in the trash. "I'll take you, Jason," he said. "I can find Palmer's cabin."

"I appreciate the offer, Vinnie, but I'm not sure you're the man for the job. I need someone who can get in close and stay out of sight."

Daniel felt everyone looking at him. He spread the cards on the table and mixed them around. His hand was still swollen from hitting

Sammy, and it hurt to shuffle.

"Maybe I'm not your first choice, Jason, but I'm what you've got." Vinnie stood up and walked over to Jason and Ray. "Danny, you couldn't find your dick in the dark if you used both hands."

"His boat's out of the water," Ray said. "I got a key to the lift."

"Hey, no one's taking my boat anywhere," Daniel jumped to his feet. "Jason, you gonna let them steal my boat?"

"I'm commandeering your boat."

"You can't do that."

"This says I can." Jason pointed to his badge.

Daniel looked from Jason to Vinnie to Ray. He couldn't believe his own cousins were ganging up against him and stealing his boat. Vinnie didn't know his way around. He'd run aground, bend the propeller blades, and muck up the engine.

"All I want to do is look," Jason said. "That's all. You with me, Daniel?"

"Forget him," Ray said, "He's yellow."

Daniel realized that his boat was going with him or without him. And with Vinnie at the helm, it might not come back. He slid out of the booth. "You heard what the man said. He needs someone who can find his way, which ain't either of you."

With all four of them pitching in, putting the boat in the water went quickly. Vinnie pulled off the tarps, Daniel reseated the motor, and Ray unlocked the pump so Jason could fill the gas can. Jason sat up front, and Daniel started the engine.

"I can get us there in ten-fifteen minutes," he said as he pushed off from the dock. "But Palmer's not stuck 'til daylight. All he needs is four feet of water at the mouth. Rest of his channel's plenty deep, and tide's coming in. Another thirty or forty minutes, he can find his way out."

"He's that good a sailor?"

"He doesn't have to be. He's got a depth finder, sonar, you name it. His control panel looks like a fucking rocket ship."

Jason gave him a funny look.

"All I did was look around. I didn't take nothing. Palmer swamped me once, and I wondered how come he could go so fast."

"So, tell me what he's got."

"It's a twenty-six footer with a deep vee-hull and twin 250 Yamis." He saw Jason look at the single motor mounted on their stern, the big four-oh written on its side. It didn't take a genius to know that forty horsepower versus five hundred was no contest. Palmer would blow them out of the water.

"The Coast Guard can chase Palmer," Jason said. "I'm worried about Claire Marshall. If he can leave in thirty minutes, they'll be gone before our cars get there."

"You said we're just going to take a look around." He hadn't signed up for any rescue mission. "If that's not the plan, count me out."

"The plan is to see if he's there." Jason pointed to the sky where the clouds were scattering. "Full moon. So, if Palmer is there, he'll see us coming."

"Not unless he has x-ray vision." Daniel didn't want to brag, but no one saw him if he didn't want them to. "What he'll do is hear us."

"Yeah, but he doesn't know we're on to him."

"Ignorance ain't going to make him deaf."

"Say we get close, turn off the motor and pole in?"

"He'll hear us coming, and he won't hear us leaving. He'll know we're there. He might be hearing us already."

"Slow down a minute. Let's think this through."

Daniel held the boat steady in the water. If they turned around now, it was good with him.

"What if we come in fast," Jason said, "making lots of noise, and then when we get close, start slowing it down, real gradual, so he'll think we're moving away."

"No one's dumb enough to fall for that." Except perhaps this deputy sheriff who was supposed to be smart but obviously didn't know shit about boats.

"Palmer doesn't spend a lot of time on the water, and I noticed your engine's quieter than most."

"It's a four stroke."

"So what can we do to fool him? Come on, Daniel, help me out."

Daniel thought about it. Jason was right about Palmer not being a waterman. He could be conned. "We could do what you said plus we use wet bags to muffle the engine."

"So, I'll get them wet." Jason pulled several burlap bags out from under the deck.

Daniel would never admit it, but now they were underway and making plans, he liked being part of it. He felt kind of bad about the way he'd treated Claire Marshall, and he'd never liked Palmer. He waited until Jason had the bags back in the boat then opened the throttle wide.

The sound of a motor cut through the drone of insects and frogs. Claire returned to the mouth of the creek, hardly daring to hope, but there it was. A black dot sped across the water's silver surface, heading straight toward her. It drew closer, and she saw that it was a small open boat. The sound of the motor faded, as if the boat was moving away, but it still appeared to be approaching. Was the moonlight playing tricks on her eyes?

The boat slowed, its motor died, and a man climbed onto the front. He used a long pole to pull the boat through the water. A second man sat in the back, paddling. They reached the marsh and disappeared into a tidal creek. Could she attract their attention without alerting Frank? She swam a little way out into the lake and waited, treading water, for them to reappear.

"Hey Claire," Frank called. "You hear that boat? Smugglers come up this bayou, bringing drugs in from Mexico. Those guys play rough. You don't want them to find you."

The small boat emerged just short of the channel that led down to Frank's dock. They must have heard him. She stared, willing them to stay quiet, stay hidden. Whoever they were, they couldn't be more dangerous than Frank Palmer.

"Last chance, Claire. I'm not going to hang around all night. Let me know where you are and I'll toss you a life jacket. Tide's coming in, you're going to need it." Frank's words were conciliatory, but his voice vibrated with fury.

She raised one arm out of the water and waved to the men in the boat. One of them lifted something to his eyes. Binoculars? She waved again, and he waved back. She placed her index finger across her lips.

Please be quiet. Don't let him hear you.

If that boat came to her, Frank would see it. He wouldn't hesitate to shoot them. But she could go to them, swimming underwater when she crossed the channel. Once again, she'd be swimming against the tide. She studied the ripples on the water's surface, gauging the speed of the current. A dark form moved even faster. A long head and a sinuous ridge showed above the water. As she watched, another alligator swam into view. Both headed down the channel toward Frank's dock.

Blood from the alligator he'd shot could be attracting them, or maybe it was their feeding ground. Why they were there didn't matter.

Swimming across their path would be suicidal. The man with the pole beckoned. She shook her head and pointed to the alligators.

Daniel had already seen them. "Gators," he whispered, "big ones. We got to get her out of that water."

"Can we reach her without Palmer seeing us?"

The answer was no, but they couldn't leave her there. "He'll see us, but if we're fast, by the time he's cast off, we'll be where he can't follow."

"Ready when you are." Jason picked up the pole. "I'll haul her in with this."

"Make sure she grabs it on the first try. If that don't happen, we'll be out there backing and turning like a sitting duck."

Daniel switched the motor on and sped across the channel. As Claire swam toward them, an alligator veered toward her. Daniel maneuvered into its path. Jason swung the pole and smacked its snout. The gator turned, and a blow from its massive tail rocked their boat. A bright light blazed out the mouth of the channel. Powerful engines roared into life. Palmer had been ready to go.

"Get her," Daniel yelled. "I've got the gator." He grabbed the wet burlap bags, now steaming hot, off the engine and threw them at the animal's head. One fell across its eyes. The gator bellowed and dove.

Jason leaned over the side and extended the pole to Claire. She grabbed it, and he pulled as fast and hard as he could. As soon as she was within reach, he lifted her out of the water.

"Got her," he said. "Let's go."

"Get down." Daniel opened the throttle and raced toward the mouth of the creek. Palmer's boat was out of the channel and turning around. In twenty seconds, he'd be bearing down on them.

"He's got a gun," Claire said. She crouched against the side of the boat.

Jason unholstered his revolver and followed her example. Daniel hunkered down beside the motor, steering blind. They bounced through the shallows and into the mouth of the creek. Behind them, Palmer's boat ground against the bottom. His engines screamed as he reversed into deeper water. Palmer couldn't follow, but he knew where they were. They weren't out of trouble yet.

Once they rounded the first bend, Daniel cut off the motor and swung it up out of the water. Their momentum and the incoming tide carried them deeper into the marsh, at times through water so shallow that shells on the bottom reflected white in the moonlight. He lay on the prow deck, using an oar to keep them off the sandbars and away from the sides. They weren't making any noise, and the tall grass hid them, but Palmer wasn't giving up. He patrolled back and forth in the lake, and his spotlight raked the marsh.

At one point, they were close enough to see him holding the wheel in one hand and a machine gun in the other. Daniel pulled up tight against the near bank. Jason kept his gun trained on Palmer but, to Daniel's relief, didn't use it. Disabling Palmer with the first shot would be tricky at this distance, and one shot was all Jason would get before that machine gun came into play.

They reached the inlet that separated the marsh from the swamp forest. Keeping his voice low, Daniel explained the situation. For twenty feet, they'd be in the open. They'd cross the next time Palmer turned his boat around, when he should be looking where he was going, not scanning the marsh for them.

He handed Jason an oar. "I'll be up front with the pole. Soon as he starts to turn, I'll say go. You paddle as hard as you can."

Claire picked up the other oar. "I know how to paddle, and I'm stronger than I look."

They took up their positions and waited.

"Now." Daniel dug the pole into the bottom and pulled with all his might. He steered as they paddled across the open water and into a dark sanctuary. The thick tree canopy blocked the moon's light, and hanging vines formed walls on either side of the channel. He grabbed a cypress knee and pulled the boat through an invisible opening. Vines surrounded them. Roots and branches arched overhead. Someone six feet away and looking right at them wouldn't see them.

He'd spent time here in broad daylight with Wildlife and Fisheries patrolling nearby, and they never had a clue. Palmer's boat was still out there, but they'd made it. He collapsed, scared stiff now that the chase was over, closed his eyes, and thanked Saint Andrew.

"Nice job." Jason pulled out his radio. "If I turn this thing on, will he hear me?"

"Not you talking quiet, but he might hear static from that thing." He pointed at the radio.

"I'll keep it in broadcast mode." Jason turned it on and spoke softly into the handset. He explained the situation and handed the radio to Claire. "They need directions to the dock."

She described the orange painted trees marking the turn off the levee road. "Keep coming past the burned cabin, but don't run into my car. It's stuck in the mud about fifty feet short of the dock." She handed the radio back to Jason.

"We're keeping a low profile," he said. "You do the opposite. Soon as you get on top of that old levee, switch on your lights and sirens like the Fourth of July. The sooner Palmer knows you're coming, the better."

Daniel, who had been listening, warned, "He'll run."

"I'm counting on it." Jason grinned. "Like I said, the Coast Guard can chase him."

"You really weren't looking to take him on, were you?"

"Hell, no." The rest of Jason's response was lost in the WHOOP WHOOP WHOOP of sirens, the sweetest song Daniel had heard in a long time.

34

Claire woke to the murmur of strange voices. She opened her eyes, didn't recognize the room, and sat up, alarmed. Her suitcase lay on the floor. A blanket stamped "Property of the Lafourche Parish Sheriff's Department" hung over the chair. It all came back—Frank, the swamp, the alligators, being rescued. She was in one of the big downtown hotels, a safe place where Frank couldn't find her. The police had brought her here last night. The voices must belong to other guests, talking in the hall.

Her heart stopped pounding, and she became aware of pain. Muscles ached, knees throbbed, her arms and face both itched and hurt, but the worst was her left thigh. She threw off the covers and took inventory.

She was bumpy and swollen with mosquito bites so numerous they looked like a rash. Scratches crisscrossed her arms, and scrapes covered her knees, but nothing looked serious except her left thigh. Infection had already set in. Swollen skin surrounded an oozing cluster of cuts. She poked gingerly and felt fragments of shell embedded in her flesh.

Last night's trip to New Orleans was a blur. She'd huddled in the back seat, wrapped in a blanket. Lieutenant Breton drove. He had joked about her keeping him up past his bedtime, but most of the time Mike Robinson had talked to her. They wanted to take her to a hospital, but she'd refused, so they stopped at her house to pick up clothes and feed Dorian then brought her here.

A house detective had met them at a downstairs entrance and promised to keep an eye on her room. She'd taken a shower and fallen into bed. For the first time since Frank's funeral, she hadn't awakened in the throes of a nightmare. Had she been too tired or too frightened? Should she laugh or cry?

The bedside clock read 7:23. That thigh needed attention, but Dr. Bennett's office didn't open until nine. She limped to the bathroom, and turned on the shower. At first the hot water stung, then it soothed.

Mike Robinson called while she was eating her room service breakfast.

"How are you this morning?" he said.

"Has the Coast Guard caught Frank?"

"They found his boat. It burned about fifteen miles out in the Gulf. There were no survivors."

"Did they find his body?"

"They hadn't when I spoke to them, but he's presumed dead."

"He's been presumed dead before." And that time there was a body. Frank was out there somewhere. Fear heightened her senses. The voices in the hall took on an ominous undertone, and she tightened her grip on the receiver.

"I understand how you feel, Claire, but the Coast Guard is certain no one survived. We can talk more about it when you come in."

"After the doctor. I have an appointment at ten-thirty."

It was closer to eleven when Dr. Bennett walked into the examining room and asked what in the world had happened to her. He listened to her story then shook his head.

"Frank Palmer," he said. "Just when you think you've heard it all." He looked at her thigh. "Nasty. The police should have taken you to an emergency room."

"I wouldn't go. My husband was a doctor. Remember? I know how triage works. I'd have been the last person seen."

"I'll clean it out and stitch it up, but we're a little late. It's infected, and you're going to have a scar." He gave her a shot to deaden the pain then removed several pieces of oyster shell from her leg.

"I'm putting you on a broad spectrum antibiotic." He pointed to the red swelling that surrounded the wound. "Keep a close eye on that. If it gets worse, call me. If you see red streaks coming off it, you need immediate medical attention. If I'm not available, go to an emergency room."

She opened her mouth to protest, and he said, "Show them the streaks, and they'll see you right away. Trust me. Over-the-counter medications should take care of everything else. Tylenol for pain—that leg is going to hurt. Get yourself some Benadryl lotion for those mosquito bites."

"I look like I have chickenpox."

"The swelling will go down in a day or so. Keep up the Tylenol as needed but no more than the dosage on the label. I don't want to add a heavy-duty painkiller to the sedatives you're already taking." He handed her the prescription. "How are you doing with those panic attacks?"

She told him about the nightmare that disrupted her sleep and intruded upon her waking hours until she wasn't sure what was real. She confessed to taking extra pills.

"You've been taking the Xanax longer than I like," he said. "Let's get you back to the prescribed dosage, and then I'll switch you to a different anti-anxiety medication."

"I don't want to depend on pills."

"I don't want you to. Start by cutting out the extras. Next week, we'll talk about further reductions. Are you still seeing a therapist?"

"No, but I'm still trying to figure out what triggers my attacks. It has to do with the circumstances of my husband's death, but beyond that... I don't know." She spread her hands, palms up. Maybe the hidden fear would abate without ever being identified. "What if I just stop the meds?"

He shook his head. "It doesn't work that way. Your body becomes accustomed to the drugs. You have to be weaned off slowly or you'll suffer withdrawal symptoms, which I promise you, are both more unpleasant and more dangerous than any panic attack. If you haven't taken a pill this morning, take one now." His final prescription was immediate bed rest and taking it very easy for several days.

"The police want me to come in and give a statement."

He handed her his telephone. "Tell them you'll be available tomorrow at the earliest. If anyone objects, I'll talk to them."

Claire flipped through a magazine while she waited for her prescription to be filled. Dr. Bennett wanted her to rest, but she wasn't tired. It was lunchtime, but she wasn't hungry. She ought to call her mother and Felix, tell them what had happened, but she'd already been through it with Dr. Bennett, and she didn't have the strength to go through it all again. Not yet. She could go back to the hotel and check out, but she wasn't sure she was ready to spend the night alone in the carriage house.

Taking a long walk was her usual response to this kind of mood, but this morning, every step made her thigh throb. She decided to go home, check on Dorian, change her clothes, and see how she felt about being there.

Her taxi was a block away from the Clarke's mansion when she heard the THWAP-THWAP-THWAP of a helicopter.

"Something's happened up ahead," the driver said. "The road's blocked. Can I drop you at the corner?"

She looked where he pointed. Blue lights flashed. A policeman stood in the middle of the road and waved his arms at a TV news truck trying to turn in the Clarke's driveway. Another news truck had parked across the street. A group of people loitered on the sidewalk. Some carried cameras.

"No. Take a right and keep going. I've changed my mind." She pretended to look for something on the floor until they'd turned the corner. When she straightened up, the driver was eyeing her in his rearview.

"You some kind of celebrity?" he said.

"Not me. I'm just an innocent bystander."

"You sure you're not the victim? Looking at you, I thought maybe you'd been in a wreck."

She was an innocent bystander who almost became a victim. Thinking about it made her mad. Mad was better than scared. Anger gave her energy to keep moving, and she had things to do—arrange to retrieve her car, make sure work was proceeding on the Laurens house. She gave the driver the address of her office.

35

Mike was waiting by the front desk. When he caught sight of her, he smiled a hello and said, "Thank you for coming in, Claire. I'm sure there are places you'd rather be."

"Like home. I stayed at the hotel again last night, but I'm going home today." She tried not to limp as they walked down the hall to his office.

"Superintendent Vernon wants to be there when you give your statement, and Deputy Corlette is on his way." He held her usual chair for her, pulled his chair around the desk and sat down facing her.

"How are you?"

"All things considered, I'm fine." She'd be even better when this meeting was over.

"The Police Department failed to protect you. I don't know if you're going to get an official apology, but please consider this mine. It will be a long time before I forgive myself for letting you leave the restaurant alone."

"How could you have known? Besides you did figure it out. I don't know what would have happened if Jason and Daniel hadn't come after me."

"Did I hear my name?" Jason Corlette strolled into the office. "Morning, Claire, Mike. How's everybody."

"I've been apologizing," Mike said.

"Which is not necessary," Claire said. She turned to Jason. "But I owe you a thank you. You saved my life."

"It was a team effort. Mike sounded the alarm. And don't forget Daniel. I'd have been lost without him, literally."

"From day one, Jason believed you were an innocent bystander," Mike said.

That's what she'd called herself yesterday afternoon, but she'd been thinking it over, and this morning, she wasn't so sure the label fit. She had been more than a bystander and not totally innocent. "Some of what happened was my fault."

"No, it wasn't." Mike jumped on her words. "What happened in no way reflects on you."

"Frank saw me as insignificant. He called me a pawn." Frank was a predator, and predators select the weak, the wounded, and the isolated as their victims. The woman she'd become after Tom's death was all of those things.

"Don't let Palmer define you," Mike said. "Criminals are egotists. To them, everyone else is insignificant. That's what allows them to kill."

"Give yourself credit," Jason said. "You escaped from Palmer. You made your way through the marsh at night. That took real courage."

"What if he escaped too?" She was afraid the police underestimated Frank.

"I was skeptical, at first," Mike said, "but we've received additional details from the Coast Guard. Three boats saw the fire and raced to the rescue. They were there in minutes, but by the time they arrived, Palmer's boat was engulfed in flames. The dinghy was still attached. They searched the water and found no one. The boat burned to the waterline and sank."

"They still haven't found a body, have they?"

"After twenty-four hours, they stop looking," Jason grimaced. "Sharks. No one's going to find anything."

"He could have arranged for another boat to meet him. Frank always had a plan B." On a rational level, Claire could be convinced that Frank was dead. On an emotional level, she needed reassurance.

"Someone would've seen that boat," Mike leaned forward as if getting closer would give his words more weight. "Every question you're asking me, I asked the Coast Guard. They're adamant. No one survived."

Lieutenant Breton stopped by the door to say Superintendent Vernon waited for them in the third floor conference room. For a moment, Claire wished Felix were there. He'd offered, but Mike had told her she didn't need a lawyer unless she wanted one.

As they walked to the elevator, Mike took her arm. "Don't worry," he said. "You'll be fine."

The meeting was easier than Claire had anticipated. A typist and a tape recorder captured her words as she described the events of Monday night. Although she hadn't taken any extra meds, the new regimen, she was able to talk about what happened without reliving the terror. When Jason described finding her in the marsh, he made her sound like a heroine instead of the frightened woman she'd been.

Afterwards, Mike escorted her to the front door. "Before you go," he said, "I want to ask if there's anything we can do to help you get your life back to normal. The Department offers counseling."

"No, thank you." She'd been there, done that.

He persisted. "Victims of violent crimes frequently blame themselves. It's perfectly normal, but it's self-destructive. Counseling addresses this."

"I. Don't. Need. Counseling." She spoke more sharply than she'd intended.

"Please don't be offended, but I think you should consider it."

"Thank you, but no. This is between me and me." As she walked down the steps, she felt his gaze on her back, but she didn't turn around. At the corner, she hailed a taxi.

A uniformed officer stood at the end of the driveway and kept the reporters away as her taxi drove through the gates. *Thank you, Mike.* She walked in her front door and collapsed on the sofa. Dorian jumped up immediately, no playing hard to get this morning. She stroked his soft fur and let his purring soothe her. She was going to be fine; she could cope, one day at a time.

The answering machine light was flashing. She checked to be sure she hadn't missed anything important. The first two messages were reporters wanting interviews. She erased them but listened to the third.

"Are you okay? I heard the news. It can't be true. It just can't be. Frank would never do anything to hurt you. I remember what you told me. I know you didn't love him, but he said he loved you, and I believed him." Jeanette's words dissolved in sobs that continued until a beep ended the message.

The next message was a continuation. "It's me again. Time ran out before I finished. I feel so bad if anything I did was wrong. I would never... But Claire, I just don't believe... Frank would never... I only did… I'm so upset…" The sobs resumed. "I'll call back when I can talk."

Her third message was brief. A more composed Jeanette said, "Please, call me," and left her home phone number.

Poor Jeanette. She'd worked for Frank for years. Her life revolved around her job and her identity as Frank's Girl Friday. She had no other life, no real life.

No real life, that phrase summed up the thoughts that had been whirling around in her head all morning. Since Tom died, she'd had no real life, nothing outside her job. Her only non-work relationship was with her mother, who wouldn't let herself be pushed away. She'd cut herself off from the rest of the world.

I made myself Frank's perfect victim.

If she'd met him at his cabin, his plan would have worked. No one would have missed her until long after her badly burned body had been identified as Melissa Yates. She and Lou would be dead and buried in mislabeled graves. Frank and Melissa would be leading new lives. Maybe Melissa would have objected, probably not.

"You'd miss me wouldn't you, Dorian?" She scratched behind his ears, and he purred.

People would have missed her, too. Eventually. If she didn't show up for work, Jack would wonder where she was, but he knew that she had bad days, and he respected her privacy. He'd wait a few days before calling, a few more before realizing that she had disappeared. If she didn't call for a couple weeks, her mother would worry. If she didn't pay her rent on the first of the month, her landlord would stop by.

She'd escaped. Others had not.

Frank was responsible for three deaths—no, four—he drove his wife to suicide. He'd abused who knew how many young girls, including his own daughter. Melissa, seduced at fourteen, was also a victim, whether or not she knew about Frank's plan.

Mike meant well, but she didn't want counseling. Months of counseling after Tom died hadn't uncovered the fear behind her panic attacks. And this was different. This time, she needed to fight back. She couldn't undo the damage Frank had done or change history, but she could comfort Jeanette. She could return her call, listen as a sympathetic friend, and reassure Frank's girl Friday that no blame fell on her. Talking to Annalisa would be more difficult, but she'd deliver Annette Fulton's letter or die trying.

That night, her mother called. "I can't stop thinking about you and what you've been through. It would do you good to get away. Come home, Claire. Let me pamper you."

"I'd love to, Mom, but not this weekend. What if I came for Thanksgiving? It's only a month away."

"Thanksgiving is a terrible time to travel." There was a long pause. "Are you hurt and not telling me?"

"No. I'm going to New Mexico, flying there Saturday morning." She explained why.

"You shouldn't be running around trying to solve someone else's problems," her mother said. "You need to take care of yourself. Rest, give yourself time to recover."

"I am recovering, and I'm getting plenty of rest. Promise. I'll call when I get back, and we can plan a visit then."

Claire didn't fully understand herself, so she couldn't explain why extending a hand to Frank's other victims was important. It just was. Part of it went back to her mother, the woman who was always there for her. Annalisa hadn't been that lucky, and neither had Annie Lewis. The lucky ones owed the others a hand.

36

Once again, Claire glanced over her shoulder. Nothing had changed. No snake coiled around the potted plant in the corner, no alligator slithered across the carpet, and none of the people waiting in line to rent a car looked anything like Frank Palmer. Anyone watching her was simply impatient. She'd given her driver's license and credit card to the agent several minutes ago, but he continued to frown and peck away at his keyboard.

"I have a car reserved," she said.

He nodded.

She checked one more time to be sure Annette's letter was in her purse. She'd also brought the front section of Wednesday's Times Picayune with its stories about her kidnapping and rescue. The newspaper might come in handy when she found Annalisa. The agent finally looked up.

"I see you're from New Orleans," he said. "Where are you going?"

His curiosity heightened Claire's unease. "I don't plan to leave New Mexico."

"No problem going to another state. Just don't cross into Mexico." His frown returned. "Those border towns are nowhere you want to be, but that's not why I asked. You reserved a subcompact."

"I did." It was the cheapest option and plenty big enough for her and one suitcase.

"If you're hanging around Albuquerque or going down into the desert, you'll be fine. But most people who fly in from the East are driving up to Santa Fe and Taos. We're talking seven thousand feet above sea level, uphill all the way."

"Yes?"

"Your subcompact won't go forty up those hills. You'll drive everyone behind you nuts. And heaven help you if you need to accelerate quickly. You need a bigger car."

"How much would a bigger car cost?"

"Where're you headed?"

She leaned across the counter and whispered, "Taos."

The agent gave her a funny look, and she straightened up, feeling like an idiot. There was nothing to worry about. Frank was either dead or he'd escaped, but he wasn't in the Albuquerque Airport.

"I can let you have a Ford Taurus for another six dollars a day. It should be twenty, but I'll upgrade you at cost because I don't want to rent you an unsafe car." He resumed typing, all the while muttering to himself about the irresponsible idiots taking reservations.

The agent lived here, she didn't, so Claire heeded his advice. She picked up one of the maps stacked on the counter and studied it while he revised the paperwork.

"What's the road like?"

"The road's good. Just take it easy on the curves until you get used to the front-wheel drive. It says here that you're returning by 10:00 a.m. on Wednesday November 3. Is that correct?"

An hour and a half later, Claire parked the Taurus and went looking for a place to eat lunch in Santa Fe, a city she'd long wanted to visit. She walked around a large plaza, admiring the adobe architecture and lingering on the shady side where vendors sold crafts from blankets spread on the sidewalk. She selected a silver bracelet for her mother and remembered that Annalisa sold jewelry. Buying something might be a good way to approach the girl. Maybe her mother would get two bracelets.

The vendor recommended a place where the locals ate lunch, a small café several blocks from the square. Claire sat at a table on a patio shaded by a vine-covered trellis and took the waiter's advice about what he promised were the best chiles rellenos in New Mexico but decided against the state's finest margarita. So far it had been an easy drive, uphill all the way as promised, but on a wide and straight highway. According to her map, the road between Santa Fe and Taos was two lanes with lots of curves.

She was traveling into the mountains, not to a border town, but that term had stuck in her head. Nowhere to be, the rental agent said, and he was right. She'd been living in her own border town since Tom died. Fifteen months spent going through the motions on the edge of normal existence, alive but not really living. That was no way to honor Tom, and it was going to change. In a perverse way, she owed Frank Palmer a thank you.

On her way out, she flipped through the brochures stacked on a table by the door. One featured the art galleries and outdoor sculpture gardens of Canyon Road. Another described the Georgia O'Keefe Museum. A local church had a miraculous spiral staircase, built without external support. Legend said Saint Joseph was the carpenter. She took a brochure to show Jack. If she had time, she'd spend at least one night here on the way back and see that staircase for herself.

North of Santa Fe, the road narrowed and the countryside changed. On her right, tan and gray, ochre and burnt sienna colored vast hillsides dotted with shrubs the gray-green color of slate. Wire cages, twice the height of her car and filled with rock, lined the roadside. Heavy mesh blanketed the slopes, restraining huge boulders poised to plummet downward. The subtle hues and huge scale created a landscape as exotic as the moon.

On her left, the ground fell off abruptly. Far below, a stream burbled bright blue around more rocks. Claire imagined enormous boulders crashing down the hillside and landing in the water with an earthshaking splash. A sixteen-wheeler, barreling downhill, rocked her car as it passed. She tightened her grip on the steering wheel and thanked the rental car agent for questioning her choice of vehicle.

Going north, she was next to the cliff. The drive back would be more daunting. Only a narrow shoulder and an intermittent guardrail separated the southbound lanes from that long drop down. White crosses beside the road marked where someone had gone over.

Claire pulled off to use the facilities at a national recreation area. A browse through the displays revealed that she'd driving beside the Rio Grande. It didn't look very grand, barely a river, but then it was a long way down.

Back on the highway, she resumed her climb until one last hairpin curve swooped up to a broad expanse of flat land ringed by an arc of distant mountains. Roadside buildings became more frequent, traffic increased, and a sign welcomed her to Taos. The architecture here was like Santa Fe, only more so. Low adobe buildings seemed to grow from the earth. One of them was the Mesquite Inn.

Claire's room was ready and nicer than she'd expected, spacious with two queen beds and a small sitting area. The windows offered a view of distant mountains turning lavender in the fading light. The desert would cool off quickly once the sun went down.

She wasn't hungry for dinner, not after the late lunch, so she decided to locate the store where Annalisa worked. According to the detective's report, Dream Catchers was on the first floor of an enclosed mall at the west end of the plaza. She put on a warm sweater and headed out, stopping at the reception desk to ask directions to the plaza.

"Turn left at the corner and walk fifty feet," the receptionist said. "You can't miss it. Taos is not a big place."

"Thank you."

"It's usually a busy place, but we're in a lull right now. The summer tourists have gone home, and the skiers don't show up until Christmas."

Claire ignored the unspoken question about what brought her to Taos in the off-season. "I'm going to walk around a bit, maybe get a bite to eat." Several minutes later, armed with three recommendations for dinner, she set out to explore the plaza.

She still hadn't decided how to approach Annalisa. Pretending to be a customer and then revealing her real reason for being there would be too devious. If she just introduced herself and handed over the letter, that would be too abrupt. One of Davidson's detectives had tried a direct approach and been thrown out of the shop. Annette Fulton had told her that she'd know what to do. Claire wished she had that much faith.

Claire had no trouble finding the mall or the shop where Annalisa worked. Dream Catchers was still open but empty of customers or salesclerks. Claire stepped inside to look around, a chime sounded, and the person she'd traveled a thousand miles to see walked in from the back.

"Hello. Can I help you?" Annalisa's smile was pleasant and impersonal. The nametag pinned to her blouse said Phoenix.

"Yes." Claire told the simple truth. "I've come to see you."

"Why?" Annalisa said. A furrow appeared between her brows. "Do I know you from somewhere?"

"No. My name is Claire Marshall. Your grandmother sent me."

"My family is here." She folded her arms across her chest, and the furrow became a full-fledged scowl.

"You have a grandmother in Alabama."

"What do you want?"

"I just want to talk to you."

"We've talked. You've earned your money. Now you can leave." The young woman closed her eyes and opened them again as if hoping that would make Claire vanish.

"No one's paying me." Just the opposite. This trip with its the last minute airfare was costing plenty. "I'm trying to help your grandmother because she helped me." *And because I need to.* "I'm sure Paul Gilbert has told you that your father's dead."

"Frank Palmer is not my father, and he's not dead." She spoke without emotion but with complete certainty.

"Frank faked his death two weeks ago, but a lot's happened since then." Claire pulled the newspaper out of her pocketbook. "Here. It's a complicated story. The easiest thing would be if you just read this."

Annalisa glanced down at the headlines. "Fine. I'll read this. Later. But he's not dead."

"Can we meet tomorrow? After you've had time to read the newspaper and think it over? I'm staying at The Mesquite Inn."

"I'll call you if I want to talk to you." It was a curt dismissal.

"Good night. See you tomorrow." Silently berating herself for being so clumsy, Claire left the shop.

The sun had gone down while she was in the mall. On the western horizon, the mountains shadowed deep purple, while gold rays streaked upward, passing through orange to scarlet, then violet. It was the most spectacular sunset Claire had ever seen, and she'd forgotten to bring a camera. Not forgotten, it had never occurred to her. This wasn't a pleasure trip, and she was making a mess of it.

37

The margarita Claire drank before dinner had gone to her head. Or perhaps it was the altitude, or the travel that had left her fatigued, or all three. Regardless, she didn't dare take a sleeping pill until the tequila wore off.

No, I will not take another sleeping pill, period.

Fine, stay up all night and be a wreck tomorrow.

I will not depend on pills.

The telephone interrupted her argument with herself. "This is the front desk. I'm sorry to bother you at this hour but there's a young woman here who wants to talk to you. I told her it was too late to disturb you, but she insists."

"Can I speak to her?"

A brief rustling was followed by a whispered, "It's Phoenix. I have to talk to you."

"I'll be right down."

"No, he might see us. I'll come up. Please. What's your room number? Tell the desk clerk it's okay."

Phoenix slipped into the room, pushed the door shut, and engaged both locks. "You have to get out of here," she whispered. "If he finds you, he'll kill you."

"Who will kill me?" Claire knew the answer. Melissa had said Frank's daughter was deeply disturbed, and it looked as if she was right. Considering what had happened, how could Annalisa be anything else?

She probably saw her father as an all-powerful monster who couldn't be destroyed.

"Don't play games. You know who I'm talking about."

"I understand how you feel. I've been looking over my shoulder all day, but it's only nerves. Frank is dead. His boat burned and sank miles out in the Gulf. There were witnesses. People on nearby boats went to the rescue. The Coast Guard said it would be unusual to find a body. There are sharks…" Claire offered all the reassurances Mike and Jason had given her.

"There was no body because he's not dead."

Nothing she could say was going to convince Annalisa that her father was dead, and maybe he wasn't. Claire had her own doubts. "If he is still alive," she said, "he's living under a new name in some foreign country where he's stashed lots of money. He bragged to me about the millions he'd stolen."

"He's right here in Taos, possibly at this hotel. He might have seen you already." Annalisa eyed the walls as if she expected Frank to crash through from an adjoining room. "After I read that newspaper, I tried to call, but the desk wouldn't put me through because it was too late. I drove back to town as fast as I could. Please, you have to leave. You're here because of me, and I don't want your blood on my hands."

"Thank you, but—"

"Listen to me." Annalisa grabbed her shoulders. "He showed up last month, told me he was leaving the country. He promised he'd never bother me again, but first, he wanted the pictures." Her mouth turned down in disgust. "He photographed himself with girls. He'd make me look at them. Do you understand what I'm saying?"

"Yes." Claire wanted to hug Annalisa, but she didn't dare.

"Before I left New Orleans, I hid some pictures in a safe place. He's in them, and if anything bad happens to me, a friend knows where to find them. She'll give them to the New Orleans police."

"You don't need the pictures anymore. Either Frank died Monday night, or else he's somewhere like Thailand."

"He came into the shop yesterday morning. I didn't recognize him until he spoke to me. He was dressed like a cowboy, wearing a hat and sunglasses. He needed a shave."

During her few hours in Taos, Claire had seen a dozen men dressed like cowboys, wearing a hat and sunglasses, and needing a shave. She hadn't paid attention to any of them, but if one had been Frank Palmer, he would have recognized her. She sat down on the bed.

"You're starting to believe me, aren't you?" Annalisa said. "I can see you getting scared. Now, will you leave?"

"You're right, I'm scared. But I came here to give you a letter."

Annette Fulton had given her the letter, and she'd given Annette a promise. Now Annette waited, alone with the dog that used to belong to this young woman, praying for a word that would say she was forgiven. Claire took the envelope out of her pocketbook. "It's from your grandmother. She asked me to be sure you read it."

"I don't need to read it. I know what it says." Annalisa brushed the letter aside. "She's been asking me to come back ever since she found out where I was living."

"You're all she has left, you and Caesar. Do you remember Caesar? He lives with her now. He's a nice dog, but he's getting old. So is your grandmother."

"You should never have come here." Annalisa paced, head down and face invisible behind a curtain of hair.

"That's what I thought when I went to see your grandmother. I felt guilty because my visit upset her. I should have left her alone. But then she helped me, and I promised to help her. I can't just give up and leave because I'm scared."

Heavy footsteps approached in the hall. They stopped talking and stared at the door until the sound died away.

"I don't want your blood on my hands," Annalisa repeated.

"You warned me. It's all on me now." Claire stood up, prepared to escort her visitor to the door. "I'm not leaving until you read the letter. I'll see you tomorrow morning."

Annalisa closed her eyes then opened them as she had done in the store.

"I'm still here."

Annalisa expelled an exasperated breath. "If I read the letter right now, will you leave?"

"You read the letter, and I'll leave tomorrow morning, not tonight. It's late, I'm tired, and I don't have anywhere to go." Her return flight wasn't until Wednesday, but she could spend the time in Santa Fe. Or she could change her flight.

"Early tomorrow morning. Like sunrise." Annalisa picked up the envelope.

"Deal." Claire walked over to the window to give Annalisa some privacy. She put her hand on the drapery pull.

"Get away from the window! Keep the drapes closed!"

She jumped back in surprise. "You really are nervous."

"You should be too. You know what he's capable of. This letter isn't worth getting killed."

"I'll leave first thing in the morning."

"And I'll read the letter." Annalisa leaned against the wall and opened the envelope. When she finished reading, she looked up, her face twisted with anger. "If you expect me to be moved by this, you're mistaken." She crumpled the paper and threw it in the wastebasket. "Did you know that my mother killed herself?"

"Yes. I'm sorry."

"My grandmother's sorry too, and she ought to be. Mom told her that Frank was a bad man and we needed to leave him. But Grandma said a woman's first duty was to be a good wife to her husband. She refused to help us."

Claire nodded. Annette Fulton had said that she'd failed her daughter.

"Of course, Mom didn't tell her the whole story. It was too ugly, and my mother tried to avoid ugly. When life got ugly, she escaped by getting drunk. When drinking wasn't enough, she made her escape permanent." Annalisa walked around the room as she spoke, picking things up and putting them down—the pen and pad by the telephone, a magazine about Taos, the remote control for the television. "I was barely fourteen years old, and she abandoned me. To him."

"I don't think that's what she intended."

Annalisa stood, hands on hips as if challenging the world. "It's what she did," she said. "But there's no point in being mad at a dead person, is there? It's a waste of emotion, bad karma and all that."

Claire wanted to answer, but a paralyzing dread silenced her. Her breathing grew shallower and shallower until each inhalation was a frantic gasp for air. The bubble tightened around her. Fear filled her throat, choking her. Annalisa's voice faded into silence, leaving nothing but the suffocating bubble, the stench of burned plastic, and darkness.

Claire opened her eyes, Annalisa was bent over her, wiping her face and neck with a cold washcloth. "I'm okay," she said. "That was just a panic attack. It looks worse than it is."

"I didn't know if you'd just fainted or if you were having a heart attack or what. If you hadn't come to so fast, I would have called for help." She shuddered. "Frank might have seen us."

"Usually I can keep it under control, but tonight, I lost it. I really am okay now. Don't worry. My doctor promises me that no one ever died from a panic attack." *It just feels like you're dying.* "I have pills if I need them." Exhaustion rolled over her in waves. She was so tired. Every word took effort, but she had to reach this young woman.

Annalisa laid the damp cloth across her forehead. "I can see why you'd have panic attacks after what you just went through. I was in pretty bad shape after mom died."

"It has nothing to do with that." This was the worst panic attack she had experienced, and for the first time, she knew precisely what had triggered it. "You mentioned being angry with someone who has died. My husband died a little over a year ago."

"Did he kill himself, too?"

"He didn't intend to. He ran into a burning house to rescue two little children. He threw them to safety, but he didn't get out."

"I'm sorry."

"I am too. I loved him very much." Then she said out loud what she had never before admitted, not even to herself. "But I'm also angry. He didn't choose to die, but he chose to risk dying. Running into that house was heroic, and it was reckless." The children's own mother had been afraid to go back inside. She'd stayed on the sidewalk, and she was still alive. "In his own way, he abandoned me, and I was furious with him and with the world."

Tom's death had left her without a reason to live. From freshman year in high school until the day he died, everything in both their lives had revolved around his dream of becoming a pediatrician. She'd switched her college major from architecture to accounting because accountants can always find work, and she'd be supporting both of them during his residency and internships. It had paid off.

She worked in the university accounting office while he was at Johns Hopkins. When they moved to New Orleans for his residency at Tulane, she'd taken the actuarial job at the insurance company. She hated the hours spent staring at a computer, but the money was good, and they needed money because Tom had decided to specialize in childhood cancers, which meant another two years of study. Everything she did was for him, and then he died.

"I understand," Annalisa said. "At Mom's funeral, everyone was pitying me, whispering and shaking their heads. I almost exploded every time someone looked at me. I wanted to scream curses and spit in their faces." She was back to walking around the room picking up loose objects.

"I felt the same way." There'd always been anger mixed in her grief, and she had panic attacks because she was afraid, and deeply ashamed, of that anger. Condolences made her cry, and those had been tears of rage as well as tears of sorrow.

"Then you should understand why I didn't want to read the letter, why I don't want to see my grandmother, why I'm never going back."

"I also understand that we both have to—forgive isn't the right word, but it's close. We each have to move on, find our own path through the ashes."

"Move past being abandoned by my own mother because she was too weak to face the truth? She married that man. What happened wasn't my fault, but she punished me." Annalisa walked over to the door. "I read the letter. You leave in the morning."

Annalisa's anger was directed more at the mother who abandoned her than the father who abused her. Annie Lewis had blamed herself as well. It struck Claire as an incredible injustice.

"There's another letter you should read. It's the last letter your mother wrote to your grandmother." She had tucked the letter into her dresser drawer, unsure what she was going to do with it but unable to throw it away.

"Where is it? That's what I'm supposed to ask, isn't it?" Annalisa leaned against the door, her hand on the knob, her posture more resigned than hostile.

"It's back in New Orleans, but I remember every word. Your mother told your grandmother the whole truth. She asked her to save you, and then she said good-bye. By the time your grandmother got the letter, it was too late. You were gone."

"You want me to read my mother's suicide note?"

"I want you to know that your mother loved you very much and that she didn't intend to abandon you."

38

Claire glanced over at the other bed, at the tangle of blonde hair on the pillow. She no longer thought of this young woman as Annalisa or Frank's daughter or even Annette's granddaughter. Certainly not as the troubled teenager Melissa Yates had described. Her name was Phoenix, and she was living proof that a person could build a new life for herself. Like her namesake, she had risen from the ashes.

Nothing could erase the past, but its burdens could be eased. Claire believed that once the police caught up with Frank, Phoenix would feel a weight lift. She dared hope that she would soon contact her grandmother. The letter had been retrieved from the wastebasket.

She dressed and packed as quietly as possible. If Phoenix said Frank was in Taos, he was. She had promised to leave, and she would. She left a brief good-bye note with her phone number in New Orleans and tiptoed out of the room. When the elevator door opened, she scanned the lobby before stepping out.

"Happy Halloween." The same woman was working at the reception desk. This morning, she sported a multi-colored fright wig and a nametag that said *Bad Hair Day*.

"Happy Halloween to you too." Claire paid the bill but didn't check out. "I ended up having company last night. She'll be leaving later this morning."

The parking lot attendant wore his version of a Playboy bunny costume with an enormous overstuffed bra and a nametag that said *Bad Hare Day*. In spite of everything, Claire had to laugh. Someday, when she was absolutely sure Frank was in jail or dead, she'd come back to

Taos, but for now, she wanted to be miles away. She hoped with all her heart that Phoenix was right about the hidden pictures guaranteeing her own safety. They had for five years.

Claire drove as fast as she dared, any thought of lingering in New Mexico gone. If she couldn't get to New Orleans today, she'd fly to Dallas or Atlanta and spend the night at an airport motel. She'd taken her morning pill but still felt edgy, a rational emotion if Frank Palmer was in Taos. She made herself check the rearview. A red dot on the road behind her disappeared when she went around a curve. The next time she looked, it wasn't there. She was alone with her thoughts.

Talking to Phoenix had been emotionally exhausting and cathartic at the same time. They shared the sad knowledge that loss is irrevocable. There's no going back and no do-over. They both knew the emotional confusion of being angry at what had been done to you and heartbroken by what you had lost. They had talked about moving beyond anger and guilt, while acknowledging that some wounds are so deep they heal slowly and maybe never completely. A scar may never disappear, but it can fade.

Last night, she'd learned that what she feared most was her own buried anger. That knowledge opened the door to resolution. Her starting point was to accept the inevitably of what had happened and take responsibility for her choices. She had every right to be angry, but the person who was Tom Marshall couldn't stand by while those children were in jeopardy. He couldn't wait until the fire department arrived, and that was why she had loved him.

She'd been dazzled by his conviction, even as a teenager, that he could make a difference in the world. No one made her hitch her wagon to Tom's star. It was her choice. If it was a mistake, it was her mistake. She'd been too young to know better and too stubborn to listen to her parents when they suggested she date other people and explore things that interested her.

She had no life after Tom died because she'd had no life of her own before. Everything she had done was in support of his dreams. Because she'd had none of her own. That didn't mean she couldn't live a full life now. It might take a while, and there'd be bad days, but she was on her way. Next week, when she and Dr. Bennett discussed cutting back the meds, she could tell him that she'd discovered the cause of her panic attacks.

I am going to be okay. And so is Phoenix. Frank did his worst, but we're both going to be okay.

The road twisted steeply downward, and she lightened her pressure on the accelerator. An oncoming car went by, only the second car she'd seen since leaving Taos. She glanced in her rearview and saw the red dot, bigger now and coming closer. For a scary moment, it reminded her of the car in her nightmare, but she shook it off. She wasn't driving across Louisiana swamps in her little Miata. She was driving through the high desert of New Mexico in a rented Taurus and, no doubt, driving more slowly than the locals.

She passed the national recreation area, closed this early on a Sunday morning. By the time she reached Santa Fe, something would be open. She'd call Mike Robinson, tell him what Phoenix said, and see how he responded.

Last night, she'd been ready to ask him to contact the Taos police, but Phoenix had been adamantly opposed. She'd left her past in New Orleans, and she wanted it to stay there. Claire had acquiesced. She'd wait and inform the New Orleans police. But now, in the cool light of morning, she realized that Mike might not find her story credible. She hadn't actually seen Frank; Phoenix had convinced her. Could she convince the New Orleans police?

The road resumed its twisting descent. Behind her, the red dot had become an SUV. Again, Claire felt a shiver, which she dismissed. The SUV was closing the gap because she was barely going the speed limit. She wasn't comfortable going any faster—not in an unfamiliar car on an unfamiliar and winding road.

The SUV had caught up to her and was tailgating. Claire looked for a wide spot where she could pull over and let it by. The SUV tapped her bumper. Jolted, she looked in the rearview. The driver was wearing a cowboy hat and sunglasses. He needed a shave. He stuck his left hand out the window and pointed his index finger at her like a child pretending to shoot a gun.

Frank Palmer had followed her from Taos, and he'd picked this spot to make his move. On her right, an intermittent low guardrail separated the highway from a sheer drop to the rock-strewn river. Across the road, the hillside rose nearly vertical, its rugged surface covered with wire mesh. Cages and big rocks lined the road. Frank had chosen well.

She pressed the accelerator to the floor. Her car leapt ahead, sliding out of her lane on the curves. She gripped the steering wheel white-knuckle tight and prayed there'd be no oncoming vehicles. Her sedan, lower to the ground and more nimble than Frank's big SUV, was faster around the curves, and she increased the distance between them. Then they came to a long straight stretch, and he had the advantage.

He caught up and pulled into the other lane as if he intended to pass her. Then, like the dark sedan in her nightmare, Frank rode alongside. His SUV pinned her in her lane. He moved closer and she edged over. Any farther and her right wheels would be on the shoulder. If her car went over the cliff, she was dead.

She eased her right hand onto the gearshift and her left foot onto the brake pedal, all the while watching Frank from the corner of her eye. When he turned the steering wheel toward her, she threw the Taurus into neutral and hit the brakes.

He slid across in front of her, but his back bumper caught the edge of her front grill. Desperate to stay on the road, she wrenched her steering wheel to the left and slammed into the SUV. The two vehicles spun round and round, like manic dancers, before breaking apart.

Momentum carried her across the oncoming lane onto the far shoulder. The Taurus screeched along the wire mesh cages, metal on metal sending sparks into the air. A huge rock loomed dead ahead. She tried to steer back onto the highway, but her tires couldn't gain traction on the uneven ground. She braced herself for the impact. The world exploded. Her car rocked and shuddered to a stop.

Claire opened her eyes. The windshield was intact, but the hood had crumpled like an accordion. Hissing steam billowed upwards. She moved her arms and legs and felt her face. Everything worked; nothing was bleeding.

The driver's side of the car had jammed against the rock, and the passenger door was smashed in. She twisted around to see if either back door might open, and pain pierced her chest. Hand pressed against her ribs, she unfastened the seat belt and, wincing with each movement, crawled into the back seat. The passenger side door opened.

Where's Frank? Why didn't I take Felix's gun?

Cautiously, she climbed out of the car and crouched behind a rock. There was no red SUV, nothing but rocks and empty road. Her eyes followed the path marked by scraped mesh back to where she'd left the pavement. Skid marks on the other side led to a break in the guardrail. She crossed the highway and looked over the edge.

Yellow flames rose like a torch from the blue river. At their center was the red SUV, impaled on a large rock. No one could have survived that crash. Could they? This was a real accident, not something Frank had planned.

Claire scanned the water for a rhythmic splash or a bobbing head, any sign of a person. She searched the banks for any movement that might be Frank pulling himself to safety. She sat down to watch.

The Steelers had a bye, so Mike watched the Saints game. The home team eked out a win over Phoenix and, according to the post-game wrap-up, could be on their way to the Super Bowl. New Orleans would go nuts if that happened. When the phone rang, he expected it to be Corlette calling to gloat over the Saints' victory. The deputy didn't have much use for the city of New Orleans, but he was a big fan of their football team. Instead, it was the desk sergeant.

"Some sheriff in New Mexico wants to talk to you, Sir. I told him you were off this weekend, but he asked me to contact you. He'd appreciate a little help with a serious matter. The surviving participant referred them to you."

Mike didn't know anyone in New Mexico, and none of the homicide files on his desk had a New Mexico connection. But twenty plus years in the military had embedded a sense of duty that wouldn't let him ignore the sheriff's request.

"What's his number?"

Sheriff Oscar Flores thanked Mike for getting back so quickly. He explained that the Taos Sheriff's Department and the New Mexico Highway Patrol were trying to sort out a fatal accident, possibly vehicular homicide. One driver, a man, was dead. It appeared he had been alone in a vehicle that went off a cliff into the Rio Grande. The emergency room doctor was refusing to let them question the second driver, who was injured and suffering from shock. They were reasonably sure she'd also been alone in her car.

"She told the officer on the scene that her name was Claire Marshall, and that matches her driver's license and credit cards."

"How badly injured?" Mike interrupted. What the hell was Claire doing in New Mexico?

"Broken ribs, scratches and bruises, but no serious injuries, which is amazing when you look at the car. But..."

"But what?"

"When the Highway Patrol arrived, she was sitting on the edge of the cliff like she was in a trance. The officer approached her as a potential suicide and pulled her back. She tells him she's fine, just, quote, making sure he's really dead this time, unquote." Flores sighed audibly. "The doctor is keeping her in the hospital under observation, which is okay with me. I can use the time to sort things out.

"From the looks of the skid marks, they were playing high-stakes bumper cars. Which might account for her attitude. The only coherent information she gave the officer was your name. She said you'd explain everything."

"Have you identified the other driver?" *Could Claire have believed it was Palmer?*

"We're working on it."

The sheriff described their so-far fruitless efforts. The other car was a rental. The company had faxed over a copy of the rental form filled out by a man who gave his name as Lewis Franklin and contact information in Atlanta, Georgia. A deputy called the phone number Mr. Franklin provided, looking for a next of kin. The woman who answered swore she'd never heard of any Lewis Franklin and thought New Mexico was a foreign country. A call to the Atlanta Police revealed that the address Franklin used didn't exist. By that point, no one was surprised when the Georgia DMV said the driver's license was a phony.

Mike hadn't been one hundred percent convinced Frank Palmer was dead. The mystery man's fake name, a combination of the maybe not-so-dead man's first name and his wife's maiden name, said he wasn't.

"You still with me, Captain?" Sheriff Flores said.

"I'm here, and I'm trying to sort it out myself."

"Any insights would be appreciated."

"Claire Marshall: white female, early thirties, five-eight, slender, green eyes, shoulder-length auburn hair."

"Sounds right, but she's not the question mark."

"A man named Frank Palmer has a history of faking his own death. He supposedly died several days ago—a boat fire out in the Gulf—but no one recovered his body."

"We have a body looking for a name."

"White male, mid-forties, six feet, two hundred pounds, brown hair, brown eyes."

"The body was badly burned, but the size is right and the rest matches the description on the phony driver's license."

"*Déjà vu* all over again."

"What's that?"

"If Claire says Palmer was trying to kill her, believe it. He's tried before. Give me your fax number. It's a long story."

He went into the office to fax Palmer's dental records, the real ones this time, plus a copy of his most recent memo to Vernon. Then he called Jason Corlette and brought him into the picture.

"What were they doing in New Mexico? What else did the Sheriff say about her condition? Did you get the name of the hospital?"

"Jason, I've told you everything I know. I'm waiting to hear back from Flores. If I could think of something else to do, I'd be doing it."

"Have you told that jackass boss of yours?"

"He's my next call."

39

Claire had been home almost a week, but this afternoon was her first visit to a work site. She parked in front of the Laurens house and slowly pulled herself out of her car. Even taped, her ribs hurt when she moved from sitting to standing.

Jack was in the kitchen talking to a building inspector. "Aren't you supposed to be taking it easy?"

"Sitting around gets boring." She nodded hello to the inspector. "How's it going?"

"I'm doing your structural."

"I've already sworn by everything holy that we only removed new additions. We aren't touching any supporting walls, nothing structural," Jack said. "But he wants to see for himself."

"Show us both." She smiled at her partner. "I want to see how my favorite project's coming along."

After the inspector left, Jack fetched a couple Cokes from a cooler in his truck. They sat on the staircase that curved up from the foyer.

"It looks really good," Claire said. "I can already see Brian carrying his bride over the threshold."

"But not up these stairs." Jack laughed. "She's a big girl, and I counted twenty-six steps. These are sixteen foot ceilings." The foyer walls were scarred ten feet up where the lowered ceiling had been. Four feet higher, ornate woodworking girdled the room. Claire pointed to it.

"This molding's intact, but I noticed chunks missing in the living and dining rooms where new walls had been attached."

"I've already ordered the millwork. I'm way ahead of you."

"As usual. And you're already worried about what we're going to do when this project's finished. Right?"

"Have you talked to the lawyer about Palmer's cottage?"

"I have and we're through. The estate doesn't have the money to finish up. They're going to sell it as is." Paul Gilbert had told her to submit invoices covering any work for which they hadn't been paid and to do it quickly so that they could be registered as liens against the property. That way Authentic Restorations would receive what they were owed when it sold. Implicit in his explanation was the statement that not everyone would fare as well.

"There's always a chance the new owner will want us to finish."

Claire reached over and patted his hand. "No thank you. We'll be fine without it." She'd said the same thing to Paul when he offered to buy the cottage from the estate and have her firm finish the work. It had been a generous offer and a strange conversation. It seemed that Paul, like her, was trying to mitigate some of the damage Frank had done.

"We've got another two months of work here, three weeks on that Lakeview addition. After that?" Jack shrugged.

"We're fine," she repeated. "Scott Cantrell called me at home. He and Lori have their financing, and they're ready to go. I'm talking to three more potential clients next week."

The notoriety stemming from her unwitting role in Frank's crimes appeared to be good publicity for her business. Or maybe these people just wanted to meet her so they could tell their friends they had talked to the woman who killed Frank Palmer.

"You're shivering, and it's not cold. Are you sure you're okay?"

"A goose walked over my grave. That's all. I'm more than okay, but I can't stay much longer. Remember Mike Robinson, the policeman who kept questioning me? He's taking me out to dinner. It's his apology."

Jack shook his head. "Flowers are an apology, Claire. If he's taking you out to dinner, it's a date."

"Then I really better head home and clean myself up. I haven't been on a date since college." And all those dates were with Tom. She hadn't been on a first date since high school. She held out her hand, and Jack helped her to her feet.

It was a date and it wasn't. When Mike picked her up at her house, he asked if she'd like to give Salerno's another chance. Claire, who'd spent half her childhood on horseback, suspected it was his version of putting her back on the horse that had thrown her. She hit the issue head on.

"Salerno's sounds good. Last time I was there, I thought how nice it would be to come just for dinner, no unpleasant business to discuss."

When they walked into the restaurant, the maître 'd greeted Mike like an old friend. He showed them to the booth where Mike had been waiting for her when she told him about Frank. Claire slid in, wincing when the movement jarred her ribs.

"Sure you're okay being back here?" he said.

"I'm fine. It's my ribs. Three of them are broken. The doctor says there's not much they can do but tape them and tell me not to laugh or cough for the next month."

"Sheriff Flores told me no one who saw the car you'd been driving could believe you walked away from the accident."

"It wasn't an accident, Mike."

"You really don't want to be coddled, do you?"

"Nope." She smiled. "But I do want to be fed, and I saw the shrimp special up on the blackboard."

While they were waiting for their meals to arrive she asked him if they'd been able to track down any of the money that Frank stole.

"Not yet, but we will."

"I hate what's happened to Bobby Austin. He seemed like a nice person."

"Whether or not we find the money, I'm afraid he's out of a job."

"An article in the paper said that Andrew Walsh had resigned as Director of The Children's Home. It didn't mention any connection to Frank, but..."

"You might be surprised at the connection. Walsh was blackmailing Palmer, at least attempting to. We think that's why Palmer decided to fake his own death."

"Wow. Andrew seemed so mild-mannered. I never would have guessed." Frank had bragged about his cleverness, but he'd ignored her questions about why he wanted to start a new life.

"We wouldn't have either if you hadn't told us Palmer was a pedophile. It was the missing piece, Claire. Once we had that, the rest of it fell into place." He paused. "How long had you known?"

Claire recognized the real question, and it was one she'd been asking herself. Should she have told him sooner? What if she'd called him

Sunday morning as soon as she read Annie Lewis's letter? Or she could have read the letter Saturday night and called then. Would Hatch still be alive? Would Frank be in jail instead of dead? Those were questions without answers, so she answered the one he had asked.

"I found out Sunday morning." It was the truth and unless she explained further, he'd assume she found out during her coffee with Melissa. "I told you Monday."

Mike studied her thoughtfully over the rim of his beer mug. She marveled at how difficult it was to be completely honest. He must suspect that she was once again telling him part of the truth. Maybe one day, she could tell him the whole story.

"I wish I'd told you Sunday, before Frank killed Hatch."

"Don't beat yourself up on that count. It wouldn't have made any difference. I didn't know he'd been released."

"Thank you."

He nodded. "You're welcome."

"What about Melissa?"

"We have no evidence that implicates her, and you told us Palmer planned to leave her behind."

"That's what he told me."

"As far as she's concerned, Palmer's plan came to fruition. He died an accidental death while the insurance policy was in force. Melissa gets ten million dollars to start her new life."

"Poetic justice," Claire said. "I hope she has a good life."

"She seems resilient."

"She'd have to be." Maybe Melissa had known about Frank's scheme, maybe not. She'd still been a fourteen-year-old girl living in an orphanage when he seduced her. Melissa was another victim and, like her, determined to be a survivor. Claire wished her well.

The waiter placed two steaming bowls of shrimp on the table and asked if they wanted anything they didn't have.

"I think we're all set," Mike said.

Claire picked up her fork. *"Bon appétit."*

If you enjoyed reading A Perfect Victim, please consider leaving a review. If you would like to read more about Claire, turn the page for the first chapter of the next Claire Marshall novel, Secrets, Lies & Homicide.

Patricia Dusenbury

SECRETS, LIES & HOMICIDE

CHAPTER 1

January 11, 1994

This house? Really? Claire double-checked the address. Seven-twelve Terpsichore, this was it. She studied the façade. Screening the front gallery had been a mistake, but it would be an easy fix. Remove the screens, restore the columns, and *voilà*, a fine-looking house. Fine-looking, yes, but still modest and still in a neighborhood that was far from exclusive.

Why does a wealthy celebrity want to restore this house? She climbed out of her car and went to take a closer look.

Several of the windows were old glass, wavy in the sunlight. Nice. The siding was the original cypress and in decent condition. Nice again, but still nothing special. She walked around back.

The front yard had been shabby but sunny and lively with birdsong. The back was a jungle. Weeds by the house gave way to a thicket of scraggly azaleas and towering camellias. Vines climbed a long dead pine. A faded path led through the overgrown shrubs toward the far corner and a barely visible outbuilding. She followed the path to the edge of a small clearing.

Later, when the secrets had been uncovered and the lies stripped away, Claire would remember how this derelict little building demanded her attention. She would wonder if she'd heard the dead man's call for justice—or revenge. She'd regret the damage caused by events she set in motion. But on first sight, she felt only curiosity.

The outbuilding was the size and shape of a double garage but elevated on piers and boarded up. Weathered two-by-sixes crisscrossed the door, and warped plywood covered the windows. Black mold, so thick she could smell it, streaked cinderblock walls once painted white. More black covered the far corner. Perhaps there'd been a fire.

Claire stepped closer and saw the spiders, dozens of them, each one as big as a child's hand. They waited in webs hung from the rotten eaves. Gray tatters of old web glued dead leaves to the walls. People had abandoned this building long ago; the spiders owned it now. Something moved behind her. She whirled around, a scream rising in her throat.

"Hey, I'm sorry. I didn't mean to scare you." He held out his hand. "Tony Burke."

"Claire Marshall." She cursed her startled reaction and the blush warming her cheeks. "I was early, so I took the opportunity to look around. I hope you don't mind."

"You found my dad's studio. He was an artist."

"This was your parent's house?"

"And mine, until I moved to Italy."

She should have guessed. She knew he'd grown up in New Orleans. She remembered a name, a local artist who'd died years ago. The timing was right. "Was Jim Burke your father?"

"You've heard of him." Pleasure warmed Tony's voice.

"I'm a big fan of New Orleans' art as well as her architecture." Claire looked at the dilapidated building with new eyes. "Are you planning to restore his studio?"

"No." For a moment, Tony stood with his hands in his pockets, staring at the studio, his expression unreadable. "Let's go look at my house."

"Lead the way." She stepped back to let him pass, but he took her arm, and they walked side by side on the narrow path.

"How'd you get involved in the construction business?" he asked. Everyone asked.

"I like fixing up old houses. Jack Giordano and I met when his company did some work for me. He's a wonderful craftsman, he was looking for a partner, and I wanted a new career."

It was her standard answer and, as far as it went, true. That she had foundered lost and alone after her husband died, that she'd quit her well-paying job with the insurance company and invested not just her money but also herself in Jack's little construction company, that she lay awake wondering if she'd done the right thing, if the business would make it, if she would make it—none of that was Tony Burke's business. She looked up and caught him studying her.

"Are you and Jack partners outside the office?"

"No." She laughed. "Jack is a happily-married man with a charming wife and five kids who call me Aunt Claire."

They climbed the front steps, Tony unlocked the front door, and they walked into a too-small foyer. The living room was visible through a wide arch on the left. He opened a door to the right.

"I don't know what this room is supposed to be, off by itself."

She pressed her hands against the doorframe. "There was an archway here, like on the other side. A double parlor extended across the front of the house, and a wide center hall ran all the way back."

"How do you know?"

"That's how these houses were built." She pointed to the back of the foyer. "This wall was added, probably to create a space for a half bath." She had his full attention, so she backed off a bit. "If there's no half bath, there's a closet."

"Half bath. You had it right the first time." He shut the door. "On your left is the living room, previously known as the other half of the front parlor." He grinned. "I'm a quick study."

As he walked her through the rest of the house, Tony explained that he'd returned to New Orleans, intending to move into his boyhood home, but one look and he'd gone to a hotel. "The next day, I found a furnished apartment."

Their tour ended in the kitchen, a cavern with dark wood cabinets and a water-stained acoustic tile ceiling. His gesture encompassed it all. "Half kitchen, half dungeon. I'd forgotten how ugly this house is."

"Your house isn't ugly. It's just a bad renovation. This kitchen would be fine if you got rid of that back stoop, let in some light, and put the ceiling back to its original height."

"If we do that, I won't hit my head on the chandelier." He pointed to the yellowed globe hanging from the ceiling.

Claire heard the "we." Things were going well. "We might get rid of that chandelier," she said. "Your house has good bones, Tony. I think you'll be pleasantly surprised by the difference a few changes can make."

"I'm already pleasantly surprised. I was expecting a woman, but not a beautiful redhead. Can you turn this dump into something special?"

"If you give me free access, I can have rough plans by the end of the week. Then, you can judge for yourself." She wasn't beautiful, but she'd be very happy to get this job.

"Four o'clock Friday. Here." He handed her a key. "Bring your plans and a contract. I'm in a hurry."

"I'll start this afternoon." She zipped his house key into her purse, and they walked outside together.

He nodded toward her car. "Is that yours?"

"Her name is Felicia, Felicia Miata." Claire loved her bright blue roadster. When she was feeling down, a ride in Felicia could brighten her mood.

"His name is Igor." Tony pointed toward the gleaming black Ferrari parked behind Felicia.

Jack was at the big table, pouring over a set of blueprints. She gave him a big smile and a thumbs up. "The Burke project looks like a go. We're meeting again Friday afternoon. Tony wants plans and a contract."

"In three days?"

"I volunteered. This is a real opportunity for us. Think about it. People are always interested in how celebrities live. We could do a before and after spread in the Sunday paper. Tony would have to agree, of course, but why wouldn't he?"

"Sloooow down," Jack raised his hand like a traffic cop. "You're counting your chickens when you might not even have eggs."

"What?"

"You wouldn't be the first woman to learn the hard way that Tony Burke didn't exactly say what she thought she'd heard."

"Jack, this is business. I'm not ..." She saw his grin and stopped.

"Gotcha," he said. She shook her head and he continued. "I'm just giving you a hard time. If we get the job, that's great."

"Did you know that Jim Burke was his father?"

"Never heard of Jim Burke."

"He was an artist, a pretty good one, who died in an automobile accident back during Hurricane Camille. And his son becomes a racecar driver? Those little cars that go two hundred miles an hour, right? That is an interesting career choice."

"Word is he's faster off the track than on."

"Tony flirts, but he's not pushy. I like him. He's funny. I bet he's smart."

"You're smart too, and I wasn't kidding about his reputation. Didn't you read those articles I left on your desk?"

"Supermarket tabloids aren't the world's most reliable source of information."

"Yeah, but every one says essentially the same thing. Where there's smoke..."

"You know, I thought a race car driver would be small, like a jockey, but Tony's tall with broad-shoulders. I bet he's strong. And pictures don't capture his charisma. There's this energy field around him." Claire's sigh turned into laughter at Jack's alarmed expression. "Gotcha back. That's one for me." She licked her finger and painted a vertical line in the air.

"Okay, but I'm right about him."

"Tony's a good-looking man. So are lots of other guys. I don't understand the fuss."

"Other guys don't hang out on the Riviera drinking champagne with movie stars. What is Tony Burke doing with that house? I bet the neighbors are falling out of their windows."

"He grew up there."

"That doesn't mean he still belongs there."

"I like him. I like his house. I hope we get the job."

"We could use the work."

Friday afternoon, Claire walked Tony through her proposal, marking the suggested changes on a diagram of his house. He approved everything she'd roughed out, so she moved on to price, a crucial topic. Before she came on board, Jack's company had teetered on the verge of bankruptcy. He tended to price projects too low, and he'd misjudged a big project. She'd bailed him out, and the money side was her responsibility now.

"I usually spend more time with a client before we get to the contract stage," she said. "But we've been on a fast track, and there are expenses I can't estimate. For example, you can spend $15,000 on kitchen cabinets or you can spend $50,000. Appliance costs are all over the board. I don't know what your budget is." She'd called his office twice and left messages, which he'd either not gotten or ignored. "Given that, the only contract I can offer today is cost-plus, which protects us but leaves you a lot of uncertainty."

"I understand how cost plus works, sweetheart, and if you'll hand me that pen you're waving around, I'll sign on the dotted line."

"You don't want your lawyer to look it over first?"

"My lawyer wouldn't approve, but I've checked your references, and

I'm ready to go." He winked. "Unless you want to run it by your manager."

She gave him a blank look.

"Sorry, Claire, a bit of car salesman humor. You know I bought a BMW dealership?"

She nodded. Jack had told her.

"I've been spending too much time with the sales force." He took the pen from her hand and signed his name with a flourish. "When can you start?"

"As soon as we get the permits. I'll start the application process Tuesday. Monday, the city is closed for the Martin Luther King holiday."

"This calls for a toast." He disappeared into the kitchen and returned with a wine bottle and two stemmed glasses. "Prosecco. I developed a taste for it in Italy." He opened and poured the wine with an expertise that suggested long practice.

She raised her glass. "To your house."

"To our project." He touched the rim of his glass to hers. "I've been too busy to return your calls, but that's going to change. I intend to be involved. I can give you pictures showing how I want the kitchen to look. Then we'll talk budget."

"Pictures would be great." She took a sip of the bubbly wine. "What about old photos? Do you have any that would show what the house looked like when you were a child?"

"It looked like this only in better shape. Come on, Claire, the house is over a hundred years old, and I'm thirty-four."

"Which leaves a few years unaccounted for," she agreed. "Does your mother still live in New Orleans?"

"She lives about an hour north, outside Greensburg on a farm she's turned into a refuge for abused horses." His lip curled. "Geneviève Burke, savior of the Tennessee Walking Horse."

"I'd like to talk to her about the house. If she agrees, I could drive up there."

"You don't have to. She fell off one of her precious horses last week, dislocated her shoulder, and broke her hip. She's staying in town for rehab."

Tony's attitude suggested a poor relationship with his mother, which was none of her business unless... "Does she still have an interest in the house?"

"Neither financial nor otherwise. She gave it to me as a wedding present, and I kept it in the divorce. I'm your only client." He lifted the wine bottle. "Another glass?"

"Thank you but no. My workday isn't over yet. Where can I reach your mother?"

"I'm already sorry I mentioned her."

"You didn't. I asked, and I'm eager to talk to her."

"Why?"

"Your house was renovated back in the fifties. If your mother was responsible, she might remember details about what was there before or, better yet, have pictures. How can I reach her?"

"I don't see her being helpful, but who knows." He shrugged. "She's at Sunny Gardens, a new assisted living place over on Claiborne."

"Assisted living. Is the move permanent?"

"No. They have a few apartments for people with short-term needs. The doctors expect a complete recovery."

"That has to be good news."

He drained his wine glass before speaking. "From everything I've seen and heard, you're a nice person. Geneviève is not. When you meet her, she'll be charming. She'll ask about you, your family and where you come from, play a couple rounds of who-do-you-know."

"Lots of people do that." Most of the people she'd met in New Orleans did.

"Lots of people are looking for a context to help them feel comfortable with you. My dear mother is looking for your weakness. She has an instinct for the jugular and enjoys what she calls stirring things up, which translates into causing pain for other people."

Tony's warning struck Claire as melodramatic. She wondered if he was letting her know that he was aware of her history. Last fall, she'd been falsely accused of murder. She'd caused a man's death. It had been self-defense, but some people would never see her as totally innocent. Had the story reached his ears in Italy?

"I'll be discreet." She stood up to leave. "Thank you for the wine."

"I'll see you out." He took her arm. "Be careful where you step. This place is a mess."

"Tony, I'm used to walking around construction sites."

"Yeah, but this afternoon you've been drinking." She looked up, ready to protest, and saw his teasing grin.

Before she drove away, Tony delivered one more word of caution. "Don't forget her name is *Zhon*–vee–ev, the French pronunciation. If you call her Jen-ah-*veeve*, she'll come out from behind her walker and kick you across the room." He pantomimed drop kicking a football.

"*Zhon*-vee-ev." Claire enunciated each syllable.

"And she insists upon calling me Layton. She knows I prefer Tony, but she doesn't care."

"I'll call her next week."

ABOUT THE AUTHOR

As a child, Patricia Dusenbury read under the covers when her parents thought she was asleep. (She still reads into the wee hours but now uses a Kindle.) Despite sleep deprivation, she managed to get through college and a career as an economic analyst/strategic planner. Now retired, she hopes to atone for all those dry reports by writing stories that people read for pleasure.

A Perfect Victim, Patricia's first book, won the 2015 EPIC (Electronic Publishing Industry Coalition) award for best mystery. The sequel, Secrets, Lies & Homicide, was a finalist in the EPIC competition and a top ten mystery in the Preditors and Editors Readers Poll. A House of Her Own, the third and final Claire Marshall novel was nominated for a Rhone Award. Her work in progress, the first book in a new series, is a Claymore Award Finalist.

Patricia lives in a little apartment on a very steep street in San Francisco. When she isn't writing, she's hanging out with the grandkids or exploring the fabulous city that is her new home.

www.ingramcontent.com/pod-product-compliance
Lightning Source LLC
Chambersburg PA
CBHW031309170626
46807CB00001B/343